M000169485

WALK AWAY WEST

A JOURNEY OF CORNELIA ROSE NOVEL

J.F. COLLEN

WALK AWAY WEST
Journey of Cornelia Rose – Book 2
Copyright © 2020 by J.F. Collen

All rights reserved. No part of this book may be used or reproduced in any manner whatsoever, without written permission, except in the case of brief quotations embedded in articles and reviews. For more information, please contact publisher at Publisher@EvolvedPub.com.

FIRST EDITION SOFTCOVER
ISBN: 1622536371
ISBN-13: 978-1-62253-637-5

Editor: Kimberly Goebel
Cover Artist: Kabir Shah
Interior Designer: Lane Diamond

EVOLVED PUBLISHING™
www.EvolvedPub.com
Evolved Publishing LLC
Butler, Wisconsin, USA

Walk Away West is a work of fiction. All names, characters, places, and incidents are the product of the author's imagination, or are used fictitiously. Any resemblance to actual events or persons, living or dead, is entirely coincidental. Additionally, the dialogue in this book accurately reflects life speech in the 1850s. The language and terminology used by the characters has been only moderately censored and does not reflect the opinions, sensibilities, or culture of the author or publisher.

Printed in Book Antiqua font.

BOOKS BY J.F. COLLEN

JOURNEY OF CORNELIA ROSE

Book 1: *Flirtation on the Hudson*
Book 2: *Walk Away West*
Book 3: *Pioneer Passage*
Book 4: *The Path of Saints and Sinners*

DEDICATION

To my band of hardy travelers,
thank you for your love and support.
May we continue to grow in number.

TABLE OF CONTENTS

BACK-OF-THE-BOOK EXTRAS
Acknowledgements
About the Author
What's Next?
More from Evolved Publishing

PART ONE

CHAPTER 1
When We Get Behind Closed Doors

Sing Sing, New York, February 1852

"Ouch!" Startled by a loud thud, Cornelia Rose pricked her finger on her needle. *Tarnation that smarts,* she thought, tossing her darning egg, with the stocking still dangling over it, onto her table and putting her finger in her mouth. *What urgent matter shatters the blissful quiet of this late morning?*

Bang, bang, bang!

Mercy! It sounds like a foot hitting the door. Nellie sprang to the entry hall and opened the heavy front door. The posterior of a workman greeted her. Bent over a large object, the man backed his way into the newly created opening, tracking snow and mud from his dirty work boots onto her rug.

"Mercy! What in the world...?" asked Nellie, forced to step aside, and flatten herself against the wall, as the man, followed by a large piece of furniture, and a second red-faced man with bulging biceps, passed in front of her.

"*Es machts nichts,* it doesn't matter." Her mother's authoritative voice floated over the velvet upholstery, and the two men who carried it, to Nellie's ear squashed against the wardrobe's door.

"I have purchased this settee designed by the acclaimed Prussian furniture maker, Julius Dessoir...." Mrs. Gertrude Entwhistle's stout figure filled the doorway at the tail end of the men holding the sofa. "It complements the carved rosewood armchairs you inherited from your Aunt Elizabeth Dowling. Consider it my little gift to the newlyweds."

"Another gift among so many?" Nellie extended her arm to hug her mother, but the woman charged through the alcove so briskly the gesture became a mere pat on her shoulder.

Nellie followed her into their formal room. "I do so adore the carved birds and flowers that adorn the sofa's lavish Louis XIV's form," she gushed. "What a stylish parlor you have helped me fashion around our extravagant marble fireplace." Nellie forced herself to ignore the trail of dirty footprints and admire the intricately wrought figures in the curved rosewood back and arms of the sofa.

"Now you simply *must* purchase the sideboard and étagère to complete the suite," proclaimed her mother, arms crossed, scanning the bare walls of the parlor.

One of the workmen leaned, adjusted the carpet under the couch and straightened, a groan escaping his lips.

"Mr. McNamara," cried Nellie. "What ails you?"

"Jist me back," he said in his thick Irish brogue, a smile lighting up his broad, wrinkled face. "'Tis a occupational hazard, 'tis."

"I have just the thing! Tarry a moment, please." Nellie ran to the larder, shouting, "Midwife Rafferty and I have perfected the recipe for a poultice curing muscle strain: mustard seed stirred into rye and boiling water." She was back in a whirl of petticoats and handed him a neatly wrapped white parcel.

"You must dip this entire packet, bound as it is in the linen, in boiling water, just until it is warmed through. Apply it to the aggravated area," Nellie prescribed.

Mr. McNamara took it with his thanks. "I know'd from t' moment I saw ye, a wee colleen, hanging around t' diggin' o' t' Croton Aqueduct, way back in '42: yer were a Lady and there warn't no flies on ye. Sure n' begora, I could tell ye had t' markings. Ye must be the apple o' yer proud fadder's eye. Right capable ye are."

Nellie blushed and gave a little curtsey. "Give my best regards to your wife, and that whole brood of McNamaras you call your children. I fondly recall, I was there, assisting Midwife Rafferty, when the last one of them was born."

"Mebbe not the last," laughed Mr. McNamara.

Nellie's blush deepened at his implication. *Quite the droll rogue!* The men turned to leave, wiping their feet on the doormat on their way *out*.

Nellie laughed out loud.

Her husband, Obadiah, appeared in the open doorway, glanced at the retreating deliverymen, wiped his feet, and approached the parlor. He greeted both women with a perfunctory kiss and fixed his look on the sofa, his aspect betraying disapproval.

"To whom do we owe the debt of gratitude for this marvelous piece of furniture?" he asked, forcing a smile on his face.

"I decided you simply must have a Dessoir settee to create the appropriate ambiance in your parlor," proclaimed Mrs. Entwhistle.

Obadiah took her hand and bowed over it. "My gratitude is yours. We will be the most fashionable newlyweds in town. A luxurious sofa in our humble abode will cause the entire dwelling to aspire to further greatness."

Mrs. Entwhistle looked confused, but Nellie laughed.

"*Mutter*, you must acclimate yourself to Mr. Wright's sense of humor. There are few men in Sing Sing, nay few men in the whole metropolis of New York, as witty as my new husband."

Now it was her mother's turn to look disapproving.

Obadiah quickly tried to make amends. "You and Mr. Entwhistle have graced us with truly a most generous gift. We shall cherish every moment spent reposing on such a fine piece of furniture."

Obadiah coughed. "I have but a short time for my noon repast...." He bowed and turned toward the hallway. "If you will pardon my hasty retreat to the kitchen?"

"Tarnation!" said Nellie, picking up her voluminous skirts and scurrying past her mother into the kitchen.

"Be mindful of your vocabulary, Cornelia. Have you still not broken yourself of that vile habit? 'Tis a word most unsuitable for the lexicon of a woman of your upbringing...."

Nellie gave her mother a quick but enthusiastic hug and a warm kiss on her way past.

Mrs. Entwhistle called, "I will see you anon at Mass on Sunday. Do not neglect the sauerkraut for our family dinner—cooking it is your responsibility this week. We anticipate twenty-two, not counting Agnes' new little one, of course. Be sure to simmer it until the cabbage is soft and succulent—not crunchy! The last time our menu included your sauerkraut, it was a bit too *al dente* for my liking.

"And mind, do not forget we depart for the theater *promptly* at noon on Saturday next. Good day to you both!"

In the kitchen, already ladling oxtail soup, Nellie risked further disapproval from her mother by shouting, "Fret not, *Mutter*, I shall comply with your detailed instructions. *Toot-a-loo!*"

"Cornelia, do not corrupt the French expression *á tout á l'heure*, or I shall *not* desire to see you at a later time. *Gott im Himmel*, God in

Heaven...." Mrs. Entwhistle's retreating voice found its way back to Nellie's kitchen.

Nellie shrugged and took her seat at their small kitchen table, chattering away as she and her husband enjoyed their noontime dinner.

Suddenly, Obadiah pushed back his chair and declared, "I will not have our treasury frittered away on a matching suite of parlor furniture made by anyone, Julius Dessoir notwithstanding." He paused at Cornelia's thunderstruck look.

"Come, come, my dear bride, do not look so deluded. I am merely cognizant of conserving funds for our newly booked and ticketed honeymoon." Obadiah's face lit up with a huge grin.

Nellie shouted and leapt into his arms, bumping into the table, sloshing soup everywhere. Her surprise and joy erupted in fervent kisses.

"Come, come," said Obadiah again, but this time with an entirely different tone in his voice. He disentangled himself from her arms. Nellie opened her mouth to protest, but Obadiah laughed. "I simply defer to the more practical side of my nature." He tapped his head. "If you carry on in this passionate manner, my subject of communication shall be wiped clean from my mind, and replaced by a subject of an entirely different nature!"

Nellie blushed bright crimson, but Obadiah did not notice, for he had taken her by the hand and led her to their newly acquired couch.

"We depart Thursday next," he began.

"But what of your obligations to Judge Urmay?" Nellie interrupted.

"I have arranged for a sabbatical of two weeks' time," Obadiah rubbed his hands together with satisfaction. "To begin, I have booked tickets on the Hudson Day Line for a luxurious and leisurely cruise up your beloved Hudson River, to the flourishing capital of our fair state, Albany. At this destination...."

"How long do we stay?" interrupted Nellie again.

Obadiah laughed, and playfully clamped his hand over her mouth. "You are teasing us both with your constant interruptions. *May* it please the court, I continue?" he looked at her with mock severity. "I promise I will quickly sketch our agenda and then permit you free rein to pepper me with all the inquiries you can contrive. Interrogate me to your heart's content. Here, look at the dossier I have prepared; you can see it is quite specific."

Nellie examined the paper covered with Obadiah's fine penmanship as he pointed out each delightful detail.

"People's Line day cruise up the Hudson River, on the *New World.*" Obadiah moved his finger to the next line.

"Two nights stay at Albany's finest: The Mansion House Hotel, *en suite* breakfast, dinner, and dancing." He tapped the next line.

"Item three—sight-seeing in historic Albany—including a tour of the Orange Improvements. At six o'clock on the nose, we set sail, returning south on the most well-appointed and opulent of the Hudson Night Line Ships the *Daniel Drew.* This is the crown jewel of shipbuilder Thomas Collyer. Anticipate if you will, dining in the finest of restaurants, dancing the evening away to the music of a superlative band, retreating for a moonlit view of the Adirondacks, only to retire in the grandest suite money can buy, as we steam toward New York City."

Nellie pressed her lips against Obadiah's cheek in delight.

"How is it that our fare is a mere fifty cents for our northward journey, and we travel up the river on the People's Line and return on the Hudson Night Line, you may ask? Why the now infamous Supreme Court case decided by our scholarly and constitutionally discerning Mr. Justice John Marshall enabled this convenience. Brilliantly argued by the great orator Daniel Webster himself, on behalf of Mr. Gibbons, and of course Mr. Cornelius Vanderbilt, *Gibbons versus Ogden* holds that New York State had no authority to grant a monopoly of shipping rights to Mr. Ogden. Transport, and verily navigation itself, on the mighty Hudson River is interstate commerce, regulated solely by Congress. Therefore, my dear Lady, the free market reigns. The price of our ticket has been reduced, due to the fierce competition for passengers, and we are free to buy one-way tickets without fear of pecuniary penalty."

Nellie, bursting with pride over this display of her husband's acumen and knowledge, exclaimed, "Your facility with the law is as impressive as your perspicacity! For this, my husband, I commend you with a single, laudatory kiss." Nellie kissed Obadiah on the cheek and jumped up to curtsey low in front of him.

At his surprised look, she burst out laughing and sat down on his lap. A flurry of excited kisses followed, Nellie sprinkling them all over his face, and finishing with a nibble on his ear.

"I warned you," growled Obadiah, kissing her fully and passionately on the mouth.

Nellie giggled, kissing him back.

A second later, the precious itinerary thrown carelessly on the floor, Obadiah swept her into his arms and carried her to their bedroom.

"Mercy! What of the agenda?" whispered Nellie into his neck with a laugh.

Obadiah, laughing, responded by licking her ear and slowly sliding his tongue down her neck. He whispered, "My humble apologies, Madam. Howsoever, I have just become aware of a situation that takes precedence over any and all outstanding agendas. Protocol simply requires it be elevated to the top of the list."

Unwilling to resist the delightful shivers running down her spine at his touch, and the fire flaming in her soul, Nellie reclined on the bed and turned her full attention to the passion welling within her.

CHAPTER 2
No Ordinary Love

Sing Sing, New York, March 1852

Nellie removed her boiled wool cloak and tossed it on the Dessoir sofa. *Thank the Lord I took my heaviest cape.*

"The wind whipped up the Hudson River, thrilling me with white-capped waves, chilling me to the bone." The joyful lilt of Nellie's voice bounced off the ornate stone of their grand fireplace as Obadiah, kneeling in front, worked to ignite the kindling. "It is quite fortuitous that my brother Patrick, captain extraordinaire, commanded the helm, for surely our craft would have tossed and turned in the wind all the more with a lesser sailor steering."

"A most chilling temperature for this time in March, I do concur," responded Obadiah in a chipper tone, as he bent to his task. "Most unusual that we shall require a fire for our evening repast."

"Mayhap it is due to the dearth of heat in the house, empty for two nights while we luxuriated at the Astor House and hobnobbed among the elite at the theater. Most gay socialites are we," said Nellie. *Mercy, I am weary! But what an excellent adventure we just concluded.*

"The next time we overnight in The City in March, we shall stay at the Saint Nicholas," Obadiah said, routing in the kindling by the fireplace for a large log. "I read an advertisement in this morning's paper touting that fashionable establishment's central heating. The inventive system's pipes force warm air from a central boiler into every guest room."

Nellie smiled her agreement. "Although," she said, with a coy expression on her face and moony, love-filled eyes. "There is no warmer or cozier feeling than two people under an eiderdown in a chilly room watching the last embers of a fire dwindle."

Obadiah laughed, with a low, masculine sound that made Nellie's knees wobble. He turned to her and winked. "Come to think of it, you are correct, our passion generates a fair amount of its own heat."

Nellie blushed, the knee wobble turning into a toe tingle. Giggling, she changed the subject. "It tickles me when I contemplate our last night's evening entertainment. The Niblo Opera House! How grand." Nellie waltzed over to her husband and practically sang her effusive praise. "My handsome Mr. Wright hosts a sumptuous meal, at an intimate table for two, in the fine dining refreshment hall of the Niblo Saloon. After a most tasty and satisfying repast, I am treated to the theater's finest entertainment."

Parading around the room, Nellie paused and lowered her voice to a whisper for better dramatic effect. "Is this fine lady seen at an Italian opera? No. Mayhap an evening of song with famous singer Jenny Lind, or perhaps the more conventional tones of the Hutchinson Family Singers? No. Only the highest society has the sophistication and taste required to appreciate the entertainment we viewed: A *vaudeville* act!" Nellie laughed out loud, and plopped down on the couch in a most unsophisticated, vaudevillian manner.

"Shhhhh!" Nellie picked her head up off the couch, put her finger to her lips and leaned forward to again whisper. "Do not tell *Mutter* the grand Niblo Opera proffered a vaudeville act instead of an Italian Opera!" She sank back down, the merry melody of her laugh overlaying the crackling of the now roaring fire. "We were party to a vaudeville act, in all its bawdy grandeur." She shook her head. "*Mutter* will deem it a most inappropriate form of evening entertainment."

Obadiah rose and in one long step, pulled her up from the couch and folded her into his arms. "I must make one fact certain in your mind." He drew his eyebrows together and assumed a very serious expression.

"Whatever troubles you?" questioned Nellie, pulling back from his embrace.

"Comedy and humor are *never* inappropriate!" He threw back his head and laughed. His arms tightened around her. "Cornelia Rose, life is full of joy and mirth with you, my fair Lady." He kissed her with such ardor Nellie felt the now familiar tingles and thrills running from her lips to her nether regions. Obadiah looked her in the eyes. "Wherever in the world we are, I find my refuge in you," he said, tucking her stray hair behind her ear and sliding his fingers tantalizingly down her neck.

"We are right here...." Nellie smiled back up at him. "...in our cozy new home."

Obadiah leaned in, planted a kiss on her nose, scooped her into his arms, and carried her into their bedroom.

"What of the fire?" whispered Nellie. "All your hard work for naught."

"Later," Obadiah whispered in her ear. "We shall return to its dying embers. The fire, having done its duty, will have warmed the room, making the perfect venue for you to appear, wearing naught but your green velvet robe...."

❧

"I could wear my gingham dress," offered Nellie. Her sisters, Anastasia and Agnes, her friend Augusta, and even her mother shrieked in alarm.

"Gingham is *never* appropriate on a honeymoon tour, neither day, nor especially, night," counseled Augusta, her fashionable friend.

"Especially in June," seconded Anastasia, with a frown. The ladies sat in Nellie's parlor, working on their embroidery.

Cornelia's mother voiced her opinion. "You simply must have the dressmaker concoct two new dresses for your honeymoon trip. You'll need a more fashionable day dress for travel. I cannot abide the thought of my daughter traveling on the People's Line dressed in gingham, much less the thought of being observed in a theater box in The City in a reworked gown.

"Furthermore, for the ship's evening of dining and dancing, as well as for the dancing at Coney Island House, you must have new apparel, wrought in silk," Mrs. Entwhistle decreed.

"Pshaw, such extravagance. New silk is far too costly. I must learn the art of husbandry, commencing immediately. I can make do with re-trimming my organdy," Nellie stated.

"Tsk, tsk, these are not the standards I raised you to uphold. Your sister's husband has managed to keep her finely and stylishly dressed, in spite of the strain on the pocketbook engendered by their new baby." Mrs. Entwhistle's speech strayed from direct to hurtful.

"*Mutter!*" exclaimed both Agnes and Anastasia.

Agnes said, "My husband, Mr. Long, has been employed by the United States Army as a civil engineer. Mr. Wright should aspire to such a skilled profession."

Leave it to Agnes' acid tongue to worsen the affront!

Anastasia attempted to salvage Nellie's feelings. "My fiancé, Professor Searle, is an exceptional scholar. He has long been established at West Point, where we shall be standard bearers of polite society for the young minds we help shape. You must not hold Nellie to this same standard."

Further insult? Nellie sat stock still, in the middle of her well-appointed but small sitting room, spirit crushed. *This poor defense has cut even more deeply than Mutter's original slight.* Through tightened lips she said, "My husband is currently a prodigious provider, with boundless expectations for his future potential. Furthermore, I *shall* be stylishly dressed, in my organdy russet gown, with reworked sleeves. And I shall thank you all to say no more about it."

Nellie glared at them defiantly. Mrs. Entwhistle leaned over and gave Nellie a hug. "I meant no disrespect to Mr. Wright. I am merely trying to ensure your attire reflects our family's criteria for proper apparel. When I was young, I permitted *meines Mutter* to assist me in presenting myself to the world in a well-tailored manner, and I do wish you would permit me the same pleasure."

Her three companions nodded and exclaimed in agreement.

Nellie softened. "Goodness, of course," said Nellie, hugging her back. "I would welcome your aid."

Her mother beamed.

"But there must be no further barbed insults, or I shall simply wear my organdy with its old sleeves!"

All the ladies laughed.

"Do not deceive yourselves that a solitary moment of laughter provides a facile and full resolution," said Nellie, glaring at her sisters.

"Prithee forgive me, Nellie," said Anastasia, wringing her hands. "I do get quite flustered when *Mutter* makes an imperious command. I lack the facility with our language you possess! I must confess I often blurt words I do not quite mean in the heat of a moment, only to find they are quite un-retractable."

Nellie laughed at this sister's display of remorse. She jumped out of her rocking chair, embraced Anastasia, and stared at Agnes.

Agnes just sniffed, and bent over her mending. "You must concede I remain exceptionally well dressed, in spite of having only recently ended my confinement."

"*Ach du Liebe,*" said Nellie. "Your baby is over two months old."

"You will soon see how difficult it is," said Agnes, wagging a finger at her. Nellie let the subject drop, knowing full well Agnes had deliberately diverted the conversation to avoid apologizing for her dig at Nellie's husband.

Her friend Augusta spoke up. "Tsk, tsk. A re-worked dress? Of organdy? It must be silk! Organdy may suffice for the theater, but at the Coney Island House resort, you will need an appropriate silk evening dress for dinner and dancing."

Mrs. Entwhistle agreed, "Donning organdy reveals a lack of comprehension of convenances."

A thundercloud rose on Nellie's face. She opened her mouth, but before she could speak, all three of her companions and her mother offered her their own silk dresses. Nellie looked confused.

"Cornelia," said Agnes. "Do not be prideful. Augusta has had her honeymoon, wearing fine gowns specially made for the purpose, gifts of her relatives and friends. I have several silk gowns from my trousseau I shall not wear now that I am a mother. Anastasia is working on her hope chest as we speak; yet her wedding date is not yet set. Allow us to share our bounty and rework these treasures for you. We happily extend the kindnesses performed for us."

"Do not be so wasteful!" Augusta appealed to Nellie's practical side. "But for you, these fine silks could languish in a dark wardrobe awaiting an occasion which may never present itself."

"The moths shall be the only ones to enjoy them," seconded Anastasia.

Nellie's hand, plying a needle, arrested its path.

She sighed and looked out the window, contemplating the Hudson River while she automatically resumed stitching the hem of her new sleeve. Her small, but well-built, house on lower Broadway in Sing Sing offered her a different perspective from her childhood view out her garret window in the Entwhistle's large house on Main Street. From her sitting room, her panorama swept past the trees on Colonel McAlph's estate to the Upper Dock, across Miss Van Wyck's more modest home, all the way to the side of the massive, architecturally intricate Brandreth factory building.

But she almost never dwelt on the landscape. Her gaze was, more often than not, drawn to the river. Today, the storm that helped push her brother's sloop on their return from The City still gusted, churning the river into choppy little waves. *White caps atop brown muddy waters; not the most alluring look of this vista,* she giggled. *But 'tis far cozier than the frozen palate of icy blues and greys visible just over a fortnight ago. Further, the gay colors of the many ships' brunt of flags brighten the dreariness of the day and the pre-spring landscape. Is there a more picturesque view in all the world? The retreating late afternoon sun warms a golden swath across the breadth of the river, and emblazons its beauty in my heart,* she mused as she blinked in its bright, shimmering light.

"Tarnation! Again?" She pricked her finger and searched in her sewing basket again for her missing silver thimble. It was stuck inside a knot of thread. She slipped it on. *Eureka! Even if I do close the barn door after the horse has left its stable,* she thought. *My silver thimble shall protect me from the tiny clouds in a life full of silver linings.*

What a marvel to be Mrs. Obadiah Wright, honeymooning with my sweetest of hearts, in the bosom of my hometown surrounded and supported by my loving family. Life is grand! Just as I always dreamed, working together for our common good by day... passionate kissing and wedded bliss at night. She finished her thought with a blush, a tingle of desire rising from her toes, even though, with his varying schedule, Obadiah might not be home for several hours.

Wedded bliss. She sighed again, and bent over her stitching, adjusting the new gas light sconce near her chair, to better see the tiny stitches in the final rays of the pale March sunlight.

The front door opened, introducing a gust of wind. In two steps, Obadiah was at her side, scooping her into his arms, burying his head in her neck, whispering, "My longing for your sweet lips edged me to despair!"

Nellie giggled, trying to keep her needle from jabbing him in the ear. "Do tell! You tasted them at luncheon."

"Too long ago," said Obadiah. Nellie let her stitching drop as he carried her to the fancy sofa and covered her lips with kisses.

CHAPTER 3
Sailing

Hudson River, New York, June 1852

The day dawned grand and glorious.

It seemed the whole town assembled to send them off on their honeymoon. When the *New World* docked, Nellie had both family and friends embrace her, wishing her a bon voyage, and congratulating Obadiah again on their marriage. *'Tis our wedding day revisited.* Some dear friends and relatives even folded bills into her hand saying 'for a souvenir' or 'enjoy a luncheon at a riverside café'.

The three long blasts sounded, warning that the steamer would set sail in ten minutes.

"All ashore that's going ashore," called the First Mate. Straggling passengers intending to disembark now scrambled to the gangway, juggling luggage and parcels.

In a whirl of suitcases and confetti streamers, the happy couple boarded the gangplank and waved their way on board.

VOOT! VOOT! VOOT! Three short blasts foretold their impending departure. The crew onboard retracted the gangplank as dockhands on the pier cast off the lines. Nellie and Obadiah watched from the main deck rail as their waving family and friends grew smaller and smaller.

The ship swung north. They steamed ahead, easily overtaking some smaller boats. The nautical reds, blues, and yellows of the small crafts' flags waved cheerfully as they passed, and some captains even dipped their colors or the burgee in a quick salute.

"West Point, Newburg, Poughkeepsie, Kingston Point, Catskill, Hudson and Albany! We shall visit every picturesque pier and village lining the shore on the river route. The stops shall be a quick tour down memory lane—revisiting my many childhood trips up and down this watercourse," said Nellie. Wearing a big smile, she leaned over the rail and felt the water's spray kiss her face.

"We shall *not* disembark at West Point," growled Obadiah.

Nellie turned a pleasant pink at the remembrance of her various courtships and forays to the Military Academy. *Especially the perambulations on Flirtation Walk. Mercy! My band of beaus: Otis, Magruder, Baker. Heavens! The cadre of cadets! Now my sisters' unions with two more cadets, Searle and Long add to my memories of this place, strung together like little pearls of bliss over my heart.* Nellie sighed, the picture of happiness.

Lawrence Simmons Baker, that incorrigible Southern romantic, she reminisced. *Merciful heavens, 'tis good to know the corps of them now dull someone else's conversation.*

Nellie ran down the gangway to her favorite perch at the bow of the ship. All her life she had chosen to ride at this spot. The allure of the mighty river gripped her. She raised her head, feeling the wind and the spray, riding the rise and the fall of the bow, becoming one with the journey. Her husband, after attending to their luggage, dutifully took a place at her side, smiling indulgently.

Nellie appreciated anew the familiar beauty of the mountains, forests, and towns that rose on either side of the ship as they made their way north. *So familiar, so dear, this precious landscape. Yet, each time I observe this panorama, I discover something new. I shall cherish this scenery my entire life; how ever could one tire of it?*

The clattering of a train suddenly broke the rhythmic *swish, swish* of the tide swirling beneath them and the soft hissing of the steam engine. Nellie started, eyes straining to see the ship's competitor for travelers. *There's the culprit – rattling and clanking through the hills on the west side of the river, despoiling the natural beauty and calm of the scenery around me.* The noisy locomotive belched a steady, ugly black cloud as it labored and pulled its load through the Hudson Highlands. *If this be 'progress' we are far better served by suffering less convenience.*

The steamer turned into the first half of the S-curve of the river, signaling Nellie that West Point wharf was just around the next river bend. As the ship churned toward the landing point, Nellie felt a surge of excitement. The noise from ship's lines thrown by the sailors, then caught and made fast, clanked in Nellie's ears as she gazed at the all too familiar landing and spied the beautiful woodland path dubbed Flirtation Walk.

Suddenly, a crimson tide of embarrassment flooded her as she recalled Obadiah's remark about West Point.

She saw the antics of her younger self and her behavior through Obadiah's eyes. *'Tis mortification in the extreme, to relive my selfish and saucy behavior through the lens of my current principled standards and maturity. Mercy, the sheer number of my courtships deepens my humiliation. Shameless! I shall strive to forever subdue my former outlandish behavior and henceforth only comport myself with the greatest, and gravest, dignity.*

She touched Obadiah on the arm, determined to put her young, selfish past behind her. "Perhaps now is the moment to make a foray below deck and peruse the amenities of the ship," she said.

Obadiah smiled at her, reading her acquiescence to his desires on her face. They retraced their steps along the gangway and walked through the hatch.

"First, we must register with the purser," said Obadiah, patting her hand as she glided through the passageway into a large room.

Nellie examined her surroundings, delighting in the architectural details of the luxurious quarterdeck, which sported a grand staircase to the main deck, a baggage room, and the purser's office. *I have perused many a ships' hull, yet none so pleasing as this truly well-appointed interior.* They chatted with other passengers and confirmed that their luggage was safely aboard — their day-case in their stateroom and the rest in the baggage room.

As soon as they cast off from the West Point quay, Nellie returned to the bow on the main deck. *The incoming tide shall speed our journey north. No matter how dignified, elegant, and restrained I become, my sensibilities revel in the sensation of a spritz of spray on a sail up the river.*

It was only after enjoying the fresh air of a still-salty breeze from the brackish water, and the wooded greenery of the shoreline through several more stops that she noticed her stomach rumbling. After a twenty-minute stretch walking the pier at Newburgh, Nellie's stomach insisted she find the dining room for their midday meal.

They entered the interior of the large ship once again through the hatch to the quarterdeck. Nellie ascended the grand staircase, remembering her best posture and most dignified bearing, to the boiler deck while Obadiah retrieved something from their luggage in the hold.

Nellie caught her breath at the sight of the main saloon on the boiler deck. "This most indubitably earns the moniker 'floating palace'!" she exclaimed. The steamer's recent renovation produced spectacular results; the main saloon now occupied not one deck, but two.

"Mercy, regard those majestic Gothic columns," Nellie instructed as Obadiah again appeared at her side. "They buttress quite the architectural design. Moreover, the two-level grandeur of this main seating area affords both tiers of private day parlors a view of its splendor."

"Truly imposing," agreed Obadiah. "In addition, the engineering is quite clever. The columns encase the masts of the ship, running from the bottom of the hull though the superstructure. The construction is a feat of modern ingenuity as well as a thing of architectural beauty."

Nellie located their private parlor on the lower level, noticing it was the balcony's width larger than the ones above. "Mercy, Obadiah, such extravagance from the gentleman who deigned not expend money on a matching Dessoir étagère to compliment our settee," she teased. "I fail to comprehend the rationale for this expenditure. The ship's parlor provides only fleeting comfort, whereas the Julius Dessoir étagère would grace our home forevermore. Moreover, I am quite sure, in such an elegant ship, reposing in the main saloon should be quite satisfactory."

"Cornelia, we shall sail approximately twelve hours on this leg of our journey." Obadiah drew her into their private day parlor. He slid his hand from her elbow to her shoulder and then slowly walked his fingers along her bare skin up to her neck. The fingers left a trail of electric tingles that shot into her heart. She blushed. Obadiah leaned his lips closer and whispered, "This voyage is our honeymoon. There is a certain amount of affection I wish to express to you, which society dictates shall not be displayed in public...."

Nellie barely registered the meaning of his words; she was so heady from the sensation of his seductive whispering in her ear. Obadiah kissed her and she grasped the necessity of a private parlor.

Afterwards, as she inspected all the amenities of the room, Obadiah said, "Come, I have reserved us a table at the window for luncheon in the upper saloon."

Right in the middle of enjoying her fine dish of mutton, Obadiah leaned across the table and picked up her hand. Surprised, she put down her fork and met his gaze.

"Cornelia Rose, my sweetest of hearts, I present you with just a small token of my love and esteem." He smiled at her, opened his other hand and revealed a small blue box.

"Mercy, Obadiah! As if this trip was not pampering enough. Honestly, you shall spoil me yet," laughed Nellie. She took the box and lifted the lid. A beautiful mother-of-pearl inlaid pendant on a necklace of gold gleamed at her. She looked at Obadiah, speechless, with tears in her eyes.

"The finest charm the renowned jewelry store of Tiffany, Young & Ellis offers," he said, taking the box, and pulling out the necklace. She leaned forward, and he wrapped it around her neck. It hung just above the beautiful silver brooch of intertwined flowers he had given her last Christmas. She fingered the charm in wonder as he grinned at her. "Your silver brooch shall no longer be lonely!" he teased.

A quartet of musicians strummed their instruments in the far corner of the elegant room. The music filled the saloon. Nellie, smile beaming, feet tapping, thought her joy would overflow and spill from her eyes.

Their voyage was filled with strolls on the promenade deck as singing quartets and wandering musicians provided a musical backdrop for their sightseeing from the ship's rail.

Almost before she was ready, the steamboat nudged the dock in Albany. In a flurry of activity, passengers scampered to and fro, assembling their baggage and hand luggage, readying to disembark. The sailors threw the ship's lines to the deckhands, who held firm, and tied them fast to the shore-side chocks.

The crew extended the gangplank. It nosed out and landed ashore with a *bang* as the engines cut and the steamboat heaved up and down in the water it had made choppy.

"Last stop, all ashore," sang out the First Mate and the passengers scurried toward the gangways.

It was a far greater scramble to assemble luggage than Nellie anticipated. She was relieved when all of their cases were collected and entrusted to a bellman from their hotel.

"Come," said Obadiah, extending his elbow to Nellie. "'Tis far too fine an evening to take a carriage the short distance to our historic Mansion House Hotel."

"I would enjoy a moment to adjust my gait back to the unnerving stillness of *terra firma*," agreed Nellie.

Obadiah nodded. "If you don't mind a slight uphill incline, 'tis just a short walk to the center of town."

Nellie gazed around, up and down the streets, orienting herself. "I located the State House, finely situated on the brow of the hill. It seems to afford a fine destiny for an evening's perambulation. Howsoever, I do confess, after being spoiled by the majestic and imposing architecture of buildings in New York City, my first glimpse of the capitol reveals a building of some extent, but no grandeur."

Obadiah smiled and squeezed her hand. "My experience of the lack of stateliness of the state building forces me to agree with your astute observation. Howsoever, let us stroll down the streets of our eminent state's brilliant capital and appreciate the proffered amenities.

"Lest you think I expect you share my tremulous excitement at the thought of walking the same paths as our most luminous statesmen, Benjamin Franklin, Alexander Hamilton, Aaron Burr, and John Jay, just to name a few, our sightseeing lens shall consider far more breadth than merely the political realm."

Mr. Wright's extensive list of statesmen alone belies that statement. Nellie giggled to herself, but she smiled her thanks.

"I do hope I can infect you with a modicum of the thrill I feel, as a man qualifying to stand before the bar and practice law, upon walking these hallowed streets." Obadiah's excitement was palpable. "Through the city of Albany, one of the oldest cities in our nation, we shall encounter the very origins of our law. Its 1686 charter confers it seniority to even New York City. Ambulating here, I step with reverence. In these august streets 'I tread in the footsteps of illustrious men in receiving from the people the sacred trust confided to my illustrious predecessors.'"

"My word, you quote the inaugural address of our Eighth President and fellow New Yorker, Martin Van Buren. Brilliantly done!" exclaimed Nellie.

"Cornelia, how is that speech known to you?" asked Obadiah, eyebrows raised in astonishment.

"A harsh and demanding teacher at Sing Sing's Mount Pleasant Military Academy tasked my brother Jerome with reciting that great oration. While he struggled for weeks committing it to memory, laboring in my presence, I inadvertently took it to heart along with him," she answered, looking up into his eyes.

"My learned beauty," he whispered into her neck, kissing it gently.

Nellie blushed and tingled. *How truly seductive: to be admired and appreciated for both my God-given comeliness, and my knowledge.*

Obadiah cleared his throat and stepped back a half step. "Somehow in your presence I lose my sense of public decorum." He paused, visibly trying to remember what they had been discussing.

"Hopping horsefeathers... yes. Let us not forget another native son—our sitting President, Mr. Millard Fillmore. His footsteps I shall follow exactly, as I fulfill my last requirements to join other New York attorneys at the bar."

With a demure tone to her voice, Nellie replied, "May I be as worthy an aide in the completion of your studies as Abigail Powers Fillmore was to her law-learning husband. What great heights she helped that 'farm boy' attain!"

Obadiah grinned.

The grin encouraged Nellie to continue. "I would be remiss if I did not apprise you: you have already walked the same streets as President Fillmore. Are you acquainted with the intelligence that, at the age of fourteen, Mr. Fillmore's father apprenticed him to Benjamin Hungerford, a cloth maker and miller in Sing Sing's neighboring town of Sparta? Many a Sing Sing resident swears that, unhappy with his lot there, the future Mr. President frequented the cemetery where you and I picnicked last year. Rather than applying himself to making cloth, Mr. Fillmore lounged in that calm bucolic setting, reading and learning far more than he did at his apprenticeship."

Nellie interrupted herself with a merry laugh. "Although, Doctor Brandreth, first citizen of Sing Sing and our current New York State Senator, swears President Fillmore actually spent his free time across the road from the cemetery at Jug Tavern." Nellie covered her mouth with her gloved hand and her laugh changed to a giggle.

"You are a veritable font of knowledge, my love." Obadiah squeezed her hand.

He stopped walking and turned Nellie around to face himself. "On a more serious note, my list of statesmen and luminaries promenading these streets also includes my own father, Silas Wright, Jr. Fourteenth Governor of our fair state, United States Senator, state comptroller, Congressman, nominee for the vice-presidency of James K. Polk.... By the sword, his list of accomplishments stretches almost endlessly." Obadiah bowed his head and paused for a breath. "A herculean legacy for a son to emulate. Howsoever, his most important one, revered father, may someday soon be attainable."

Nellie blushed furiously at the innuendo.

"Cornelia Rose, I am your husband." Laughed Obadiah. "No need for maidenly modesty with me!"

Nellie smiled, still blushing, and decided to side-step the subject. She slipped her small, gloved hand into his, and squeezed it tight. "What a fitting tribute you offer him, my loving husband. A fine son, bringing joy and honor to his father."

Obadiah pinched his nose, coughed and straightened. "Now, I remind you, I do not intend to limit our purview of the capital to exploration of its political hot bed roots. I shall allow that passion of yours for history to percolate through our sightseeing. We shall explore the historic Dutch district, view the sights of the Old City, and discover buildings harking back several centuries to the time the town was named Beverwyck or even before, to its birth, begotten from Fort Orange."

Nellie clapped quietly, eyes shining. "Politics, history, entertainment; it does make a girl's head spin fast and furious, like a spinster working a spinning jenny!"

"But no spinster shall *you* be for the prevailing occupation surrounding and predominating all of these daily events shall be our tender and amorous romance." Obadiah smiled down upon her. At that moment, Nellie's foot caught a crack in the cobblestone, and she lurched into Obadiah's chest. "Exactly, my love," he said into her hair. "Never stray any farther from my arms."

CHAPTER 4
I'm in Heaven When You Smile

Coney Island, New York, June 1852

The rays of the early morning sun over the eastern shore lit her familiar hometown shoreline with a rosy glow.

"Just breathtaking," Nellie said to Obadiah. They both waved as they sailed past their home docks of Sing Sing. Nellie heard the familiar blast of her father's tugboat, the *Gertrude,* sound a muffled greeting.

"Goodness, could that whistle be intentional? I wonder if my brothers Patrick or Jerome, or even Papa, saw our ship? They have surely seen our itinerary and realize we are due to steam by at this exact moment!" exclaimed Nellie.

"That dedication to their kinfolk's well-being is the very warmth, the very essence of familial love," agreed Obadiah. Nellie slipped her hand into Obadiah's and he squeezed it. She smiled, basking in the glow of her family's love. *Thank you, Lord, for this blessing,* she prayed.

"The thought never occurred to me before, but I wonder if, with all the ships my father and his company built, *Mutter* took umbrage that the only one he named after her was a work barge?" she asked Obadiah.

He raised his eyebrow and said, "I'll be a cocked hat if your mother didn't crow like a rooster with pride at that honor. Yessir, I'd wager if your mother were truly vexed, she would rumble like thunder until the church bells rang out the news."

Nellie giggled in appreciation of his wordplay. "A beautifully aired double entendre. I so value your adroit tongue! To proffer a sentence where both the literal meaning of 'church bells' and the figurative — gossiping women — make sense to the ear. How droll." She squeezed his arm, charmed by his cleverness.

They strolled in happy harmony for a moment, and then she changed the subject. "After dancing the night away, and luxuriating in our stateroom during its waning hours...." She counted the indulgences on her gloved fingers. "...This glorious morning, punctuated by the call of the tugboat is the *pièce de résistance* to this adventure," Nellie said, leaning her head on his arm.

"The day is only beginning, my Rose," said Obadiah leaning his lips into her hair and kissing it. "Many new adventures await."

Nellie smiled in anticipation.

"Duck!" shouted Obadiah. Nellie bobbed her head down, shrinking into her shoulders, waiting for a blow.

Obadiah laughed.

Nellie looked up, and her laughter joined his. To her relief, Obadiah just teased. High above her head, the iron cast lining of one of the great arches of the Croton Aqueduct Bridge sailed over them. They were almost in Manhattan.

"I am still rather inordinately proud of this aqueduct, lo these many years later," said Nellie, looking up at the arches of the great bridge as the boat steamed under one with a larger span, specifically engineered for easy passage of the largest steamships. "Furthermore, I am grateful to be sailing *under* the conduit, rather than *through* it as did those six men on the *Croton Maid*, testing the original flow of the reservoir's water."

Obadiah beamed at her. "Once again, your command of a subject is inspiring. I expect to be dazzled with your further knowledge of this engineering feat later, during our land journey across Manhattan Island. I planned our agenda to include a visit to one of your favorite spots: the Murray Hill Reservoir and Distributing Tank."

Nellie, forgetting her resolve to maintain a restrained and dignified manner in public, threw her arms around her husband and squealed, "The wonder and joy of this adventure never ceases!" The passengers around them smiled, and exchanged knowing glances.

A short coach ride from the Hudson River Line's 22nd Street pier brought them to the extension of Fifth Avenue in Murray Hill. Nellie bolted out of the carriage and ran to the entrance of the distributing reservoir. The Egyptian Revival style façade encasing the retaining wall contained a stairwell.

Her pace mounting the stairs was so brisk she fairly burst onto the promenade on top of the wall. "I marvel that Papa had a hand in constructing this reservoir, from overseeing the physical labor to participation in design of the whole system. New York City's water was polluted with the fetid matter of its own sewage systems in the 1840s. The fires and cholera of the 1830s were linked to an inadequate supply of fresh water. This innovative clean water system has fairly eradicated cholera." Nellie smiled at Obadiah, who listened with interest.

"Since the aqueduct's completion, The City expanded exponentially. Yet the Croton Aqueduct has kept pace. Through its inventive masonry-enclosed structure, its gravity feed system sends fresh potable water forty-one miles from the Croton River into the heart of New York City, around the clock."

Nellie continued her narrative, twirling her parasol as they strolled along. "Papa was particularly proud of the novel mixing of hydraulic lime and mortar, creating a material that, once it sets, is impervious to water. That material lines the aqueduct tunnel and forms the walls upon which we now stand." Nellie shook her head. "My wonder at this edifice continues. We are perched upon the hollow walls of the reservoir's structure. On top of the world, privileged to view The City laid out before us."

The pair stopped on the south side of the promenade to observe the busy downtown view. The neighborhoods below teamed with activity.

"Civilization at its finest." Nellie smiled as she gazed down on the familiar scene.

Strolling arm in arm, they stopped frequently to observe various details of the activity occurring below them. When they reached the west side, the view of a construction site surprised Nellie.

"What new wonder sprouts before us?" asked Nellie.

"A marvelous exhibit is to open in The City," informed Obadiah. "I read of it in the morning paper."

"Do advise of the details," requested Nellie. "I overlooked that story."

Obadiah smiled. "I do believe you were rather absorbed in the theater review section." Nellie blushed.

"'Tis not meant as a chastisement; I acquiesce to your well-established passions," Obadiah said. "Perhaps you recall the hullabaloo and acclaim of the Crystal Palace in London in 1851?"

"My word, yes! The exhibits at the Crystal Palace spawned many a stimulating conversation with my male kinfolk. My brothers waxed just as eloquently as my father on the industrial wonders displayed at that exposition," Nellie replied.

"This new building we see growing in front of us shall house the United States' first Exhibition of the Industries of All Nations. It is modeled on London's Crystal Palace, but the builders here will employ superior materials; glass and iron formulated with the many innovations and advancements that have improved construction since the building in Hyde Park. Your beloved reservoir promenade provides many a curious onlooker a bird's-eye view of the project's progress... which, I am sad to say, is woefully behind schedule."

"Mercy," said Nellie. "It certainly shall be magnificent. Look at the enormity of the structure. Observe the stacks of iron bars and many sheets of glass yet to be incorporated. The edifice will be massive—truly a grand palace."

"Now that we have sufficiently stretched our limbs and enjoyed the visible splendors of our vast metropolis," Obadiah said, taking her by the arm and leading her to the stairs for their descent back to the street. "Let us make our way to the Twelfth Avenue street car. We have just sufficient time for a leisurely rail ride to the Coney Island ship."

In anticipation of the next leg of their journey, Nellie sighed with joy for what must have been the hundredth time this trip. *Reunited with my first love — the seaside. Merciful heavens! I can still picture my first glimpse of the Coney Island House, though I was a mere five-year-old tot. How utterly I enjoyed every minute of our family's summer holiday!* She clasped her hands in delight. *We cap our most remarkable honeymoon excursion with a stay at the seashore. Lord, I thank thee for a beautiful, bountiful, and positively bewitching life. I am truly blessed.*

Nellie could not summon the words to communicate her joy to Obadiah. *My cup simply spilleth over... especially on this bumpy railcar drawn by horses.* She giggled to herself.

The rails ran through a busy market, and more than once the car ground to a halt, narrowly missing pedestrians. Urchins crowded the car at an intersection, begging. Hawking peddlers swarmed too, pestering the passengers to purchase newspapers and flavored shaved ice. The constant stop and start of the car began to tax her energy. Rather than complain, she asked, "Have you verified the departure time of the ferry?"

"'Tis no longer a ferry trip to a stagecoach," said Obadiah. "Transportation has much improved since your childhood visits to this island."

"As I can see from this fine railroad," Nellie said with a wry smile, as the horses halted yet again. One of the old workhorses pulling the railcar noisily relieved itself in the middle of the tracks, sending a group of pedestrians scattering.

They both laughed, high spirits revived.

"In truth, though, notwithstanding this trolley, the laboriousness of our journey is much improved. We bypass the old ferry, and instead catch a nifty little side-wheeled steamer, departing from one of Manhattan's fine docks on the East River, and landing on a short pier jutting out into Gravesend Bay. The boat trip, much faster than the half-day ferry and bumpy stagecoach route, costs only fifty cents and requires a mere two-hour sail down the bay." He winked at his bride as he spoke.

"From there a short carriage ride transports us over the Shell Toll Road you remember from your childhood. We shall arrive in time for tea." Obadiah patted her hand.

Nellie smiled, but still looked at him expectantly.

"But of course. In answer to your question—yes. I verified the timetable in today's *New-York Tribune*," confirmed Obadiah.

"The joy of our honeymoon trip increases exponentially as we leap from one experience of a lifetime to another," whispered Nellie. They boarded the steamboat and she rushed to her favorite spot. Soon she felt the water's spray and the wild wind kiss her face. Obadiah bent down and added his kisses to her upturned cheeks.

"To Coney Island," she said, turning her face to the sun.

The voice of her mother nagged at her inner ear, '*Cornelia Rose, you shall ruin your complexion. Retreat from the sun, and take your seat like a proper lady.*' Nellie opened her eyes and looked toward the benches under the protective overhang. She gave a vehement shake of her head. *I am a married woman now; I may carry on as I please.*

Eventually, she deferred to the propriety and fashion of the times and settled on a sun-sheltered bench. From there, she watched her treasured sprays of salt water and a colony of seagulls scattering before their path. The shipyards of Brooklyn passed behind them as they rounded the tip of Long Island, hugging the shoreline just close enough to view the changing landscape. The terrain grew more rural and the smell of the salt air trumped the fading, less enticing, city smells.

"The name Coney Island is a corruption of the Dutch, *Conye Eylant*," Nellie said into Obadiah's ear, her voice competing with the loud wind. "*Conye* is Dutch for rabbit. They grazed livestock on all the sandbar islands, not just this one which has become a seaside destination."

"I do so love you whispering 'sweet nothings' into my ear." Obadiah laughed and pulled her closer. "Just think of me as your buffer against stormy seas."

Nellie drew in a deep breath and held it. *The salt air, direct from the sea!* She pulled the curtains open wide and stuck her head out on the balcony. *Not filtered up the Hudson Valley, but straight from the ocean itself. What a luxury. A suite overlooking the wildness of the sea from the grandest Coney Island resort, for three decadent nights!*

"Ready for a stroll along the seaside promenade?" asked Obadiah.

Nellie was ready almost before he completed the question.

"Our poet laureate, Walt Whitman, rhapsodized over these grand vistas," said Nellie, as the wind swept them across the path by the sea, along with some sand and the salt spray. "He enticed other notable literary figures from the Knickerbocker school to visit here—my acquaintance, the renowned writer and editor, William Cullen Bryant, not to mention my arch nemesis, the humbug Washington Irving."

Obadiah threw back his head and laughed. "It never ceases to amuse me, your peeve with Washington Irving. He enshrined your beloved Hudson Valley in fame, verily steeped it in legend, yet you never miss an opportunity to excoriate him."

"Steeped it in stolen legends! He is merely a skillful plagiarizer and adapter of other countries' folklore, why if I...."

Obadiah stopped her speech with a kiss. "This is why I dared not mention his name during our rapturous journey along that fabled river. Fret not now, we can delve into the latest salt rubbed into the wound of your grudge at another time. Do not let his former appearance here cloud your enjoyment of the breathtaking serenity that surrounds us. Think instead of the famous politicians who have viewed this very seascape: Henry Clay, John Calhoun, the esteemed orator and statesman, Daniel Webster."

Nellie laughed. "I shall take our repartee one step further; from the sublime Mr. Webster to the ridiculous—P.T. Barnum!"

"Or...." Obadiah grinned. "...from the sublime back to the humbug!" He grabbed Nellie, bestowed a passionate kiss, and then turned her around in his arms and nestled his chin into the side of her neck. Together they faced the sea.

She stood there, sunlight in her eyes, breathing in the marvelous sea air, gazing at the turbulent ocean, happy and content to her core. She sighed.

"What troubles you, my love?" Obadiah whispered into her neck. His breath, so warm it melted her, sent enough chills down her spine to make the whipping wind jealous.

Nellie wheeled around in his arms, to make sure he heard her heartfelt words of love. "Why not a thing! Not a scintilla of the least little thing. I am blissfully content. Happy as a clam." Obadiah's response was another long, lingering kiss.

"Mayhap not a clam," Nellie said, after another blissful moment in his arms. "A clam cannot enjoy the view, *and* look forward to the evening's entertainment of dining and dancing in the tented beer garden."

They shared an intimate laugh and another long passionate kiss.

CHAPTER 5
Seems like Old Times

Sing Sing, New York, July 1852

"I shan't permit myself the luxury of dallying any longer. We depart for the concert and other festivities at West Point in a mere hour's time. I must undertake the last-minute preparations for our journey," said Nellie, edging away from Obadiah as he reclined at table after their noon meal.

"How many times must you change your gown in less than a day's stay?" teased Obadiah.

"The capricious nature of the summer weather is the root of my agitated state. I shall need a full complement of options, for my garb depends upon the chill of the night air, the absence or presence of brilliant sun or drenching rain... and *bien sur*, of course, the attire of the other ladies. Mercy, my lilac muslin with the tucker of Dresden lace might just be the ticket! Or perhaps my organza with the leg o' mutton sleeves...." Nellie flew out of the room.

The sail to West Point on her father's steamship, the *Leprechaun*, seemed to last just one exhilarating minute to Nellie. At her usual perch on the main deck, she was delighted to encounter both Horace Greeley *and* William Cullen Bryant.

"We journey to the same destination," said Nellie with delight. These prominent gentlemen also enthused over the summer entertainment at The United States Military Academy. Obadiah promptly engrossed Greeley, editor of *The Tribune* and prominent political analyst, in a discussion of local government. Nellie took it upon herself to renew her acquaintance with Mr. Bryant. *After all, we were properly introduced during my debutante season.* She reveled in the opportunity to discuss contemporary literary works with Bryant, the preeminent romantic poet and current editor of *The Post*.

"Here we are at World's End," announced Nellie to the group.

Obadiah raised his eyebrows. Nellie giggled. "I promulgate the nautical term for this length of the Hudson. As it winds through this deep valley, the river churns roughly in these shadows of the granite Highland Mountains. To a less experienced ship captain than my brother, or on a less yar vessel, this passage can be 'world ending'."

"As long as the phrase does not refer to any sentiment you've entertained when visiting the Academy," Obadiah mumbled under his breath.

"My sentiments assume the aspect of a homecoming," said Zetus Searle, her sister Anastasia's fiancé, as they disembarked on the quay. "For soon, my love, 'twill be our home again."

"Attendance at this Academy was time spent in purgatory. I have nary a fond recollection of this place," drawled Armistead Long, Agnes' husband. Agnes glared at him. "True enough, this place graced me with my first encounter of my true love." Agnes raised an eyebrow at this hasty addition to his thought, but did not say anything. Shifting his feet uneasily, Armistead continued, "Verily, I suppose when I look back upon it I *do* feel twinges of nostalgia."

Agnes sniffed and said, "Mayhap now that I have born you a son and fulfilled my duty to carry on *your* name, my importance in your life has diminished."

"Never, my love," protested Armistead. "Blazes, short-sweetenin', your wellbeing is the very reason I agreed to leave baby Cuthbert at home. I propose I shall dazzle you with a of bit of romance and rekindle that fiery spirit of yours."

Agnes looked aghast at the impropriety of this conversation within the earshot of her entire family and strode ahead. Armistead hurried after her.

The group smiled sympathetically and walked up the path from the river to the West Point Hotel, following a cart containing their suitcases. Zetus grabbed Obadiah by the elbow, drawing him close. "What are your impressions of the place, old boy?"

Nellie sensed Obadiah's discomfort at the direct question; she saw his barely perceptible grimace, and slight squirm. "I deduce Obadiah is conducting a recognizance of the locale and harmonizing his impressions with the intelligence he has already gleaned from our conversations," Nellie answered for him.

Nellie could see that her quick reply had the desired effect; it gave Obadiah time to formulate his answer. He cleared his throat and said, "The scenery, now clad in the verdure of summer, certainly transcends all I have ever seen on this extensive scale."

Nellie drew herself up in mock horror. "You find it more beautiful than our own Sing Sing grand vistas? On behalf of my native land, I take umbrage!"

Everyone laughed.

"What strikes me is the *combination* of landscape beauty," Obadiah continued. "Taken separately, I will concede, one can conjure a higher mountain, a mightier river, a more contoured rock, a more verdant meadow, a leafier forest. The charm lies in the harmony of detail that produces a symbiotic beauty of the highest order."

""'Tis not a lip or cheek we beauty call... but the joint force and full result of all'," quoted Nellie.

The entourage laughed. They soon arrived at the reception desk at the hotel. A pleasant scramble ensued while they sorted their room assignments and luggage.

The evening's events melted together like flavored ices on a hot July day, one blending into the next, sweetened with music, conversation, laughter, and dancing.

During the band concert, Obadiah squeezed Nellie's hand, and whispered, "I do confess, the performance is brilliant, the scenery exceptional. This pageantry provides me with a glimmer into the allure of the place. But I still shake my head in disbelief at the excessive amount of time spent in your flirtations."

Nellie hung her head, feeling chastised. At that moment Augusta tapped her shoulder and remarked behind her fan, "I see the grand Drum Major still sports the same resplendent uniform, delighting the eye with its precise fit." Nellie's mouth popped open at Augusta's shameless ogling. *Mercy, she is a married woman, and a mother to boot!* She sighed. *Who am I to judge? I must cast my own girlish delights from my thoughts, lest any slight regression cloud this fine excursion.*

The merry group concluded the night's events with the Midnight Serenade boat ride. Several rowboats, manned by white-gloved cadets, followed a boat carrying a ten-piece orchestra. Musicians serenaded the boats as the cadets rowed south, down the Hudson. The crafts drifted back upriver to the strains of Mozart and Strauss. Nellie sat, one glove in her lap, hand trailing in the water at the side of the boat, talking and laughing with the cadet rowers and her sisters.

The boats glided around the base of Storm King Mountain and floated back toward the lower wharf; the grand finale, Weber's *Hunter's Chorus* floating in the air along with them.

"All my favorite things wrapped in one package," Nellie said. "My dearest family, transcendent music, and the majesty of the Hudson." Her sisters and their beaus agreed. Nellie smiled at Obadiah.

He frowned back at her.

Nellie's stomach dropped. *Mr. Wright frowns? What strange discordancy!*

One of the cadets caught her wet hand in his big white glove and distracted her from her thoughts.

"I was honored to row for you, Ma'am." The cadet smiled at her. "Your lively conversation and exceptional wit propelled this boat ride into an outstanding evening."

Nellie blushed, smiled, and said, "'Twas truly magical. Thank you for a lovely night."

As the group meandered up the path from the dock toward the West Point Hotel, Anastasia asked, "Which of your ships takes us home tomorrow, Papa?"

James Entwhistle gave a sheepish look, running his hand over his hair. "I thought we'd spy on t' competition and ride that famous racer t' *Henry Clay*," he replied in his thick Irish brogue. "Collyer boasts his ship can run as fast as twenty-five miles an hour, and I want to verify t' deceit of that braggart's exaggeration."

"Aye," said Patrick. "We run a tight ship at Entwhistle Enterprises. 'Twill be interesting to assess the state of our main shipbuilding competitor."

"More pertinent, of course, to your inquiry, are the details of our return," said the ever-practical Mrs. Entwhistle to her daughters, who nodded their heads. "In the morning, we shall attend Mass in Buttermilk Falls, breakfast at Cozzens' Hotel, and then board the *Henry Clay* from the Cozzens' Landing early in the afternoon."

"Land sakes! The Meteorological Table, posted in *The Eagle*, Poughkeepsie's newspaper, on Saturday last, predicted tomorrow's weather to be upwards *of eighty-five degrees*. Whilst we shall have the river's breeze to aid our personal temperature regulation, I do believe our lightest lawn or even cotton dresses shall be the order of the day," said Agnes.

As they walked up the path through the starry night, Cornelia extended her hand to catch Obadiah's, but he snatched his hand away.

Tarnation! What could be the cause of such ill humor?

She was not enlightened until she lay down in their hotel bed, and felt him beside her, rigid as a board.

"Mercy, Mr. Wright, what ails you?" she asked.

"As my wife, you should already be well cognizant of the source of my displeasure," he replied, staring straight at the ceiling, keeping his arms at his sides so she could not nestle into them.

Nellie shook her head, reviewing the evening of laughter. She could not think of a thing that had gone awry. "Please, tell me what troubles you. I perceive no malady in this merry evening of song and dance partaken and enjoyed with our cherished family."

But Obadiah did not reply; he lay there, unmoving.

Nellie lay her head on his arm. "Well, then, good night my sweet. I love thee truly." She closed her eyes.

Obadiah moved with a sudden jerk, startling her from her drowsy state.

"Have you no thought of the welfare of your husband? Have you no time, when trifling diversions present themselves, to address *my* wellbeing?"

Nellie bolted upright, heart racing. Frightened out of her contented demeanor, she felt her stomach twist into a knot. *What have I done?*

"Demeaning yourself in flirtation with every man in a uniform! Why would you think it acceptable to dance with other partners? Trailing your naked hand in the water, and then giving that ungloved hand to a cadet?"

Nellie opened her mouth to reply but Obadiah rushed on. "Why did you not sit next to me, *only*, on the serenade boat, rather than invite Nathan and Augusta to squeeze in beside us? Am I not companion enough for you? It is your wifely duty to attend to me, ensure I am comfortable and happy in all situations. Must I prod you to *attentiveness* — to thought and courtesy for my needs and desires?"

"Were you not enjoying the evening?" asked Nellie.

"The evening elapsed pleasantly enough. But I noticed you gave me naught but a passing glance as you amused yourself with music and conversation."

"Did you not amuse yourself with the same pursuits? Were you not sharing in the general camaraderie and frivolity of the evening?" Nellie put her finger in her mouth and bit her nail, a habit she thought her mother had successfully exorcised from her, and leaned closer toward him, her eyes anxiously scanning his face.

Obadiah kept his eyes cold and impassive and focused on the ceiling. "As I said, I found these diversions agreeable, but that in no way diminishes the fact that you did nothing to please me the entire evening. You never addressed me directly—you only included me as one of the general crowd. You did not keep your hand on my arm and you danced with other partners."

"Were you not pleased I was enjoying myself?" asked Nellie.

"Cornelia, you enjoyed yourself at my expense. I shall not suffer myself to be so ill used." In an angry, violent movement that rattled the whole bed, he turned over on his side.

Shaking and distraught, Nellie breathed hard and clenched her hands. She bit another of her nails.

She turned potential responses over and over in her head, formulating and reformulating a reply, trying to balance her expectations with his. Suddenly, she noticed Obadiah was breathing regularly and evenly. *Mercy! Is he fast asleep?*

Nellie crossed her arms over her chest and lay back down, staring at the ceiling. "I am sorry I was inattentive," she said quietly.

Obadiah flipped to his other side and opened one eye. "It is high time you apologized for your actions," he said.

A moment later, he was back asleep, while she turned and cried softly into her pillow.

CHAPTER 6
In the Air Tonight

Hudson River, New York, July 1852

The steamer chopped through the waves with amazing velocity. *Mercy! How fast do we travel?* Nellie wondered. "If this doesn't cap the climax! 'Tis quite a stimulating voyage — whizzing through the waves with the speed of Poseidon's chariot, the thrill enhanced by a veritable roster of famous people and dignitaries onboard emitting invigorating conversation."

"Aye," said her father, James Entwhistle. "I've already gone toe-to-toe with that old rascal of a rival o' mine, Thomas Collyer. An' I've pulled yarn with the Honorable Steven Allen, the former mayor of New York City... but a veritable roster of dignitaries? I didn't ken any other renowned figures on board."

"*Au contraire,*" said Nellie, "I have conducted a tête-à-tête with Mr. Andrew Jackson Downing, the editor of *The Horticulturalist* and renowned landscape designer of Knickerbocker movement fame. Tarnation! If I had my druthers, I would have perused the passenger list earlier to ascertain our fellow travelers' celebrity. I surely would have paid a more assiduous devotion to fashion and worn my lace trimmed lawn dress instead of this old cotton skirt and shirtwaist!" She fingered her skirt self-consciously.

"Nonsense," said Augusta. "You look ravishing." Nellie felt somewhat reassured, but then she looked at Augusta's daringly exposed décolletage framed by the beribboned bodice of her *haute couture* lavender dress and her doubts rushed back. *Augusta is the mother of a little girl, yet still looks the quintessence of flirtatious fashion.*

"Cornelia, it is unbecoming to fish for compliments. I will say this — you are the embodiment of matronly fashion, even if your skirt is last fall's couture," said Agnes, with one eyebrow raised.

Nellie bristled at the catty insult. *Is Agnes' sole function in life to irritate me? Matronly? Surely not! Agnes' figure is far more matronly than mine. Tarnation! Augusta is in fact a matron — yet her fashionable attire remains as daring as ever.*

"Your shirtwaist creates a charming effect upon your figure, and further, it is far easier to don on such a hot, humid July day as this," said Augusta.

Moreover, 'tis far easier to remove in anticipation of a cooling bath, or even a blissful swim in the Hudson. Goodness, would that I were a child permitted the joy of a swim in the river on this hot day. Aloud she said, "At least current fashion has blessed us with the new hoop underskirt — far cooler in this weather than petticoats."

"I thank the Lord for the cool southerly breeze," said Anastasia. Then her face assumed a devilish expression. "May it whip under our hoop skirts as effectively as it has whipped the river into a choppy rough!"

"*Ach du Liebe*, Anastasia, must you evoke such churlish images?" Mrs. Entwhistle tsk-tsked.

"I remain firm in my gratitude to the Lord that fashion sense has replaced six petticoats with a single, airy hoop skirt," said Nellie, with a wink at Anastasia, adding fuel to the fire.

Mrs. Gertrude Entwhistle grimaced and changed the subject. "I took the liberty of scheduling us for the early seating of dinner, as the temperature will continue to rise all afternoon. The enjoyment of this fine dining shall elude us entirely in warmer, even more stifling air. *Ach du Liebe,* I now anticipate a complete lack of *any* appetite at all."

"I never met a dish that could 'na tempt me, come hell or high water," James Entwhistle said with his usual joviality.

"Papa!" exclaimed Agnes, as Nellie and Anastasia chuckled.

Obadiah joined their group, clustered on the forward part of the hurricane deck, overlooking the bow.

Nellie changed the subject. "Mr. Wright, I so hoped you would join us."

Obadiah frowned in response. Nellie could see his foul humor from the night before still lingered. She rushed to make conversation. "I just concluded a stimulating exchange with Mr. Downing, the States' premiere land design engineer. He has been to Sparta Cemetery, that wonderfully bucolic spot on top of the hill that sports the tombstone with the *Vulture's* cannonball hole, and lauds what he calls the outdoor landscaping. The components of the spot quite conform to his artistic sensibilities. My conjecture is that cemetery has played a part in Mr. Downing's fame and recent coups. As you know, our New York native son and current President, Mr. Milliard Fillmore, spent some time apprenticing in Sparta... local folklore claiming this time was spent in that very cemetery. I believe love of that spot led our President to commission Mr. Downing, who is famous for engineering similar layouts. At the President's behest, Mr. Downing created a detailed plan for the landscape of the grounds between the White House and the Capitol in Washington D.C. Downing's design shall extend from those buildings all the way to the new Smithsonian Institution. My word, such a prestigious project, of national importance.

"Mr. Wright, I did so want you to make his acquaintance," Nellie continued. "Where had you secreted yourself?"

For the first time in almost twenty-four hours, Obadiah gave a genuine smile. "I engaged in a conversational escapade of my own. That renowned 'Philadelphia lawyer' who actually hails from Philadelphia, Mr. J. J. Speed, Esquire, also sails with us. A scintillating debate raged, assessing the merits of the United States Supreme Court case *Genesee Chief v. Fitzhugh*. We now await the decision of Chief Justice Taney, who opines on the question of the scope of federal jurisdiction and admiralty law over fresh water navigation in the Great Lakes."

"A relevant inquiry as we jaunt through the section of the Hudson River more proximate to the freshwater of its northern tributaries," said Nellie. Obadiah smiled in return but his eyes remained cold. *More's the pity; his smile does not necessarily indicate a change of heart or humor, just a satisfaction with his own conversation....* Nellie sighed. "Turning my thoughts from stimulating conversation, I submit my boundless gratitude that this navigation transpires on a quintessentially beautiful summer day."

"One could not conjure a more picture-perfect summer's day," agreed Augusta.

"Land sakes, I vacillate between regret that my darling baby boy is home missing this spectacular day, and relief that he will be spared this oppressive heat," said Agnes.

"I fear your statement encapsulates the universal plight of mothers," said Gertrude Entwhistle, with a sympathetic smile.

"I shall make a renewed attempt to enjoy the blissful peace away from his fussing and engross myself in the spectacular scenery. Howsoever, it is difficult to fixate on any specific aspect along the shore. We travel at such a rapid pace!" complained Agnes.

"I barely discern the beauty of the mansions and estates before we have left them in our wake," agreed Anastasia.

Suddenly, hot embers shot from the smokestacks towering directly above their heads and showered upon them. All the passengers on the hurricane deck exclaimed in alarm. Another burst of coals spat down, scorching shoulders, singeing hair, and burning holes in the awnings that sheltered passengers from the blazing sun.

"He's running her too hard," exclaimed Mr. Entwhistle. He folded his newspaper into a scoop and whisked the burning embers off the deck, tossing them overboard. "The boiler is overtaxed, and generating too much steam! 'Twill surely ignite a fire."

They heard the pilot's bell clanging furiously.

"T' pilot's calling for *more* steam! Rascal! The cheek of t' man," said Mr. Entwhistle, running his hand over his hair, ending in a head scratch. He turned and engaged in a heated conversation about the ship's capabilities with a gentleman standing next to him.

Tiny hot meteors of burning coal continued to spurt sporadically from the smokestack. "Mercy, little hot peas falling from the sky," said Anastasia, in an attempt at levity.

"'Tis a worrisome situation," fretted Agnes.

"There's no danger," said the ship's clerk, James Jessup, overhearing her remark. Jessup continued to placate exclaiming passengers as he passed through the deck on his way to the pilot's house.

"Certainly not for you," Agnes muttered. "But what about the passengers who cannot swim?"

Mr. Entwhistle rejoined their conversation group. "I've just gleaned from fellow passengers, wots been aboard since Albany, that t' *Henry Clay's* been racing with t' *Armenia*. Damn fool captain cut t' *Armenia* off, back at Kingston Landing. Thankfully, t' *Armenia* crew had t' good sense to fall back. Some passengers claim t' *Clay* deliberately blocked her from t' landing, giving her a whack on her fender. Mercifully, t' *Armenia* blew off steam after t' *Henry Clay* went nose to nose with her."

"*Gott im Himmel!* God in heaven, if the *Armenia* blew off steam back in Kingston, whom in heaven's name are we racing? I see nary another steamboat in sight," said Mrs. Entwhistle.

"Our legislatures should outlaw passenger steamboat racing," declared Cornelia. "Needlessly placing women and children in such peril!"

"All to satisfy t' ego of t' captain or t' shipbuilder," Mr. Entwhistle shook his head and rubbed his neck in dismay.

The dinner bell rang for the first seating and the Entwhistle party went below to the dining room. On the whole, far more liquid was consumed than food, for the heat successfully suppressed their appetites. Only James Entwhistle, true to his word, ate with his usual gusto.

After dinner, their party went their separate ways. The men climbed to the promenade deck to further explore the ship and discuss her workings, while the women went below to the ladies' parlor.

Nellie hated being indoors. After a few minutes of polite conversation, she was itching to go back to the bow. She excused herself from the ladies and nosed her way back to the promenade deck just in time to hear her father's loud, angry exclamation.

"We'll disembark at t' next stop. I'll not be a party to this egotistical race for glory," said Mr. Entwhistle. He turned away from the seaman and saw her. "Nellie, me love, go advise t' women to gather their belongings. We disembark at our next landing."

Nellie ran to the ladies' saloon to alert her family as she was told. She left the women gathering their things and returned to the promenade deck to disembark.

But the ladies never surfaced, for the ship never stopped. It blew right by the Annsville Wharf in Peekskill, full steam ahead, engines straining.

"By all the Saints in heaven, I'll be an organ grinder's monkey!" exclaimed Mr. Entwhistle. "We are *building up* our head of steam!"

"By all appearances, we are racing still!" shouted Patrick, scanning the water beyond their ship's wake for evidence of the *Armenia*.

"The whole ship shudders and the smokestack is throwing off enough heat to give the fires of hell a run for their money," said Zetus.

"T' planks o' this ship seem anxious to move from their places. None o' our ships shake, groan, and creak so, like tortured souls in t' fires o' eternal damnation," said James Entwhistle.

"We make sure to run 'em so they won't shake," confirmed Nellie's brother Jerome. "We won't stoop to racing 'em."

He reached out and caught the elbow of a man hurrying by. James took one look at the man Jerome waylaid and demanded, "Look 'ere, Collyer, this is an outrageous business! I've watched ye scurry to t' pilothouse and back on a dozen occasions, and I've only just boarded at Cozzens' Landing. I don't know what game yer playing, but I don't rightly appreciate ye preventing me from disembarking at me stop. What's t' meaning o' this?"

"James! Jest a little competition between two of the best built ships anywhere," boasted Collyer, poking James in his well-padded ribs. "Jenkins over there...." Collier pulled Entwhistle over to the rail and pointed up the river at the ship following about a mile behind them. "...owner and captain of my shipyard's *Armenia*, attempts to prove the merits of his finely crafted vessel. But this here little filly, the *Henry Clay*, has earned quite the reputation for her speed. Welcome to the show— we're giving the passengers what they paid for."

"T' speed is excessive Collyer. All the passengers are protesting the showers of hot coals ye be tossing on their heads, and remonstrating for a safer passage. Ye must tell Captain Tallman if he doesn't slow her down, she'll combust! And then, by gum, his eighth interest in t' ship will be an eighth o' nothing," said Nellie's father.

"Tallman is indisposed today. Sure, he is onboard, but I am calling the shots, acting captain for the day. What do the passengers know? Are they expert seamen? No. They must mind their own beeswax. Are they skilled engineers? No...."

"For t' love o' Saint Michael, I *am!*" interrupted James. "And I say it is time to put a stop to this folly. Look here man, ye've beat t' *Armenia* handily. We've been full throttle, full steam ahead, since Cozzens' Landing. We are almost to Yonkers' wharf and t' *Armenia*'s no longer in sight. The race is won. Time to let off the steam. I'm gonna speak to pilot Edward Hubbard meself and put an end to this Tom Foolery."

"I'm with you, Mr. Entwhistle," said Obadiah. Armistead, Patrick, Jerome, Zetus, and several other men standing within earshot shouted 'Aye'. That was support enough for James. He waved his hand in a 'come on' motion and the men stormed up the quarterdeck to the pilot's room, with Thomas Collyer marching behind them.

Nellie looked at the shore as they whizzed by. *Our daring speed increases. Tarnation! Papa is up in arms... something is dangerously awry....*

She hurried back to the ladies' parlor to advise her family.

"Now! Mama, I want walk. Now." Augusta's little girl, Perpetua, pestered her mother as Nellie walked toward the seated ladies.

Before Nellie reached the group, the girl darted across the parlor and Nellie scurried after her.

"FIRE!" yelled someone from the deck directly above them.

"Fire?" all the ladies shouted in alarm.

"Remain where you are," said a steward, in a calm voice. He walked through the cabin saying, "I assure you, there is no danger. These fires are easily extinguished."

Nellie suddenly smelled burning wood. "No!" she shouted. She caught Perpetua and ran back to her family. "We must go to the bow. 'Tis the safest part of the ship."

"But the officers are telling us it is safe *here*. We must remain sheltered here," said Agnes.

"Zetus just relayed that the barkeeper told the men in the bar to go aft!" cried Anastasia, walking toward them.

Nellie said, "The bow is usually the safest point in a ship. Seems a strange instruction to 'go aft'."

Mrs. Entwhistle said, "We must listen to the crew. They'll not steer us astray."

Nellie scrunched her face in a look of doubt. She tried to reason with her mother. "How well apprised of the situation is the barkeeper? What can he glean from his post behind the bar? Does he know the full extent of threat to our safety?"

All the women stared at her. Nellie made up her mind. "I, for one, am not so trusting of this racing crew. You heard Papa. *He* believed this speed was not prudent. I resolve we immediately venture forward and seek his counsel and aid," Nellie declared.

"*Gott im Himmel,*" said her mother. "God in heaven, I shall stay here with the ladies. I will instill and maintain calm in this cabin and await further information."

"I shall stay with *Mutter*," said Agnes, resuming her crewelwork.

Nellie's face took on its stubborn expression. She clamped her mouth shut, picked up her handbag, turned on her heel, and strode out of the lounge toward the bow. Anastasia followed her.

Augusta and her daughter followed on Anastasia's heels.

Smoke, already billowing out of the interior of the midsection of the ship, made it difficult to walk along the outside gangway. Suddenly Nellie gagged, overpowered by the acrid smell. *Is that tar or wood resin?* she wondered, trying to remain calm and practical as she picked up Augusta's daughter to hasten their progress. Anastasia clutched Nellie's elbow, coughing and sputtering as they passed through the smoke to the bow of the ship.

Nellie picked up her skirt with her free hand and covered her mouth with it, screening her breathing. She felt Augusta's fingers slip from her arm. Smoke bit at her face, choked her breathing and stung her eyes. Tears streamed down her face.

Nellie's elbow brushed against the wall as Perpetua squirmed in her arms. The intense heat emanating from the wall singed her sleeve. Nellie surmised the smokestack and fire lay directly behind it. After what seemed like an eternity, but in reality, was only a minute, they burst out of the smoke onto the main deck. Behind them they could see flames leaping into the sky and hear fire crackle.

"Unless they follow us immediately, *Mutter* and Agnes shall never penetrate that fire," screamed Anastasia.

To Nellie's immense relief, Obadiah and Patrick stood at the bow. "Where are the other men?" Nellie asked, as Anastasia shouted, "Where is Zetus?"

Obadiah grabbed Nellie and crushed her in a big bear hug, disregarding Perpetua stuck in between them. "Zetus and your father joined the bucket brigade. The firemen work feverishly to extinguish the flames."

Anastasia burst into tears.

"Where is Augusta?" asked Nellie.

"With your mother and Agnes?" asked Obadiah.

"No! She was walking right behind us," said Nellie. She shaded her eyes under her hat and looked around. She could not see Augusta in the black smoke billowing from the passageway. Her eye caught a figure on the ladder climbing from the hurricane deck to the pilot's house. To her amazement she saw it was her father, high above them, shouting at the pilot as he climbed.

Suddenly, the bow of the ship rose in the air. Nellie felt her feet rising up as she desperately clutched the frightened Perpetua.

The entire dense crowd, gathered on the forward main deck, gulped an audible intake of breath. In that breathless silence, the ship lurched upwards and then suddenly all forward motion stopped.

Screaming, some passengers fell to the deck.

The abrupt stop sent travelers pitching forward. Nellie dropped to her knees and prevented herself from falling on top of Augusta's little girl.

There was no sound but the crackle of the fire and the hiss of steam. A few men jumped to their feet, climbed up to the rail and looked down.

"The Captain's run us aground," shouted Patrick. "Abandon Ship!"

CHAPTER 7
Help!

Yonkers, New York, July 1852

Nellie jumped to her feet and in one horrified glance saw the ship's bow rammed into the shoreline, arrested inches before the railway tracks. Patrick grabbed the rope ladder and pulled people forward, assisting them up over the railing and down to safety. People on the hurricane deck above jumped, dangled from ropes, or scrambled down the bulwarks to reach their deck. Not even pausing to catch their breath, many ran across the planks and leapt over the railing to the shore.

Nellie, still carrying Perpetua, clambered up the bollard and swung the child over the guardrail. Obadiah appeared out of the crowd and steadied her. "Let me jump first. When I shout, throw Perpetua to me. I will catch her, and then you."

"I shall drop Perpetua, but then should I not search for the others?" Nellie asked, looking over her shoulder where a crewmember was busy throwing luggage overboard.

"Your father will find them."

"Papa! Is he alright? I saw him hanging on the ladder to the pilothouse just before we struck land," cried Nellie.

"Right as rain," said Zetus, suddenly standing next to her. "I saw your father on the hurricane deck already helping people down to the promenade deck."

Anastasia leapt into his arms and covered him in kisses.

Obadiah said, "I'll leave the onboard rescues to your father and Jerome's capable hands. I shall attempt search and rescue from the sea—that wall of fire raging from the midsection makes passage aft to fore impossible."

"Mayhap I can assist people below deck, on this side of the smokestack and boiler room, and conduct them to the bow," said Zetus.

"Obadiah, you take the ladies ashore and see what can be done from there."

"That was my plan," said Obadiah stiffly.

"Of course," said Nellie.

Obadiah jumped over the railing. In a flash, he landed on all fours in the dirt and quickly regained his feet, holding out his arms to catch Augusta's little girl. Nellie looked down, suddenly apprehensive. She hesitated. She drew in her breath, and leaned as far over the rail as she could, speaking soothingly to the bewildered Perpetua.

Augusta stumbled to the front of the bow from the smoke-filled gangway just as Nellie aimed and dropped her little godchild. Augusta saw Nellie drop Perpetua and covered her eyes, biting back a scream.

The girl landed safely, right in Obadiah's arms.

"Praise the Lord," Nellie shouted.

Augusta rushed to the bollard. She looked down and saw her baby safe in Obadiah's arms. Without a word to Nellie, she climbed over the rail and jumped.

Augusta scrambled to her feet on the dirty terrain, and grabbed Perpetua, crying, and covering her little girl in kisses. The smoke from the fire mushroomed, encompassing the shoreline and shrouding them from Nellie's vision.

The wind blew and Nellie spied Obadiah peering through the greyed atmosphere, scanning the boat rail to find her. She heard him shout, "Ready? Cornelia? Ready?"

Nellie jumped. Obadiah caught her, easing her impact so she alighted on her feet. She stood, blinking smoke from her eyes, in shock.

Several at a time, passengers leapt over the side of the ship and dropped out of the black gloom on to the ground around them. Obadiah assisted as many as he could, sometimes catching a child or a lady, breaking their fall, other times helping people right themselves. Augusta crooned to her crying little girl, rocking her in her arms as they backed out of the line of fire. The flames and smoke gathered strength, darkening more of the shoreline.

"The bucket brigade is making no visible progress," exclaimed Obadiah.

"I left *Mutter* and Agnes in the ladies' cabin! We must go back to rescue them," shouted Nellie.

"You stay here!" commanded Obadiah. "You attend to the womenfolk. I shall swim to the aft of the ship with Armistead and Nathaniel."

"The impossibility of that plan is self-evident—neither man can swim!" shouted Nellie, her hands on her hips in indignation. "Unless you can procure a boat...."

Obadiah turned and ran toward the water.

Out of the smoke-darkened beach Anastasia appeared, limping.

"Thank the Lord!" cried Cornelia, grabbing her in a hug. "You are safe!"

"I tried to help Zetus, but my skirts kept catching fire, and my foot fell through a burning deck board. Zetus forced me to jump to safety whilst he continued down the smoke-filled gangway." Anastasia's face was grimy with tears and soot, but she was not crying.

"Where are *Mutter* and Agnes?" they both asked each other.

"I left them in the ladies' parlor," they both answered, simultaneously.

"I followed Zetus—in my agitation I determined I must render assistance in this misadventure," said Anastasia.

"I could never abide riding in the ladies' saloon! And now it seems it is a dangerous place, even if we *were* sitting at the window," said Nellie, dropping her bag on the sandy dirt. "Help Augusta with Perpetua and find somewhere comfortable to perch. I shall locate *Mutter* and Agnes."

"Shouldn't you leave that dangerous task to the men?" asked Anastasia, watching in horror as Nellie unfastened her skirt and loosened her hoop beneath it.

"Thank goodness I wore my new hoop and don't have to remove six petticoats," grunted Nellie. In one smooth move, she yanked both her garments and, stepping out of their folds, discarded them on the sandy shore. Augusta and Anastasia gasped, in spite of circumstances, shocked at seeing Nellie in her shirtwaist and drawers.

"I must go. Neither Nathaniel nor Armistead can swim!" Nellie ripped the buttons off her boots in her haste to remove them.

"Nellie don't," cried Augusta.

Nellie waded into the water. Within three steps, the waves rose to her waist. Women and children jumped off the side rails of the boat and splashed into the choppy surf. The smoke expanded its pall, engulfing the view as far as the eye could see, fanned by the wind that continued to whip the river and exacerbate the surf. Fire, bellowing out of the midsection of the boat, inched its way along, both forward and aft, devouring everything in its path. Chunks of wood spit out of the ship and became missiles, randomly striking both those struggling to escape the fire and those brave enough to help.

Passengers fortunate enough to be forward on the steamship jumped, and some landed in shallow water. Rescuers assisted anyone languishing in the water to shore. Men, standing in water chest high, pushed boards to passengers who floundered in the deeper water.

The distance to the stern of the boat was not great, but the water was deep and choppy. The shoreline dropped precipitously, so very few who jumped could keep their heads above the dangerously rough surf. Plumes of black smoke obliterated the sun, making it dark and difficult to see. Flying ash and burning wood shot in deadly projectiles into the water. Loose deck chairs and stray baggage randomly helped keep passengers afloat, or perversely knocked unconscious those struggling to survive.

Utter chaos reigned.

Nellie could see faces surrounded by wet, waterlogged clothes, and dangerous debris in the choppy water. Right in front of her, a woman struggled to keep her head above the water.

Suddenly, she disappeared.

Nellie stepped further into the river and the shore fell away from her feet. Treading water, she reached out and grabbed the woman by the hair. In her desperation, the woman clawed at her, causing Nellie to lose her buoyancy. The desperate clutch of the woman pulled Nellie under. Nellie held her breath and dragged the woman, walking her feet along the river bottom until she gained firm footing close enough to shore to stick her nose out of the water. Gasping for breath, she tugged the heavy bundle a few more steps until she could stand with her head above the water. Still struggling to fill her own lungs with air, she pulled the woman's head up out of the water and dragged her toward shore.

A rescuer standing in knee-deep water spotted her, lifted the woman from Nellie's grasp, and carried her to shore.

Nellie turned back into the water to see a woman and child jump from the midsection of the ship. As she waded back in, the pair disappeared underwater. Nellie raced toward them. The woman resurfaced for an instant and then was gone, her heavy skirts pulling them back under water. Nellie, treading water furiously, helped push the lady up from the water into a small skiff.

But where was the child?

In a daze of distress, part of her brain recognized the arms and face of Armistead, pulling the woman into the boat. *But where is the child?* She repeated to herself. She ducked back down and felt around. Her arm hit something hard, sending pain rocketing all the way up her shoulder. She surfaced, grabbed a breath of air, and went under again, forcing herself to open her eyes. The murky, debris filled water made it impossible to see.

Alleluia, here he is!

She swam over and pushed the child up, head above the water, in the direction of the rescue boat. In seconds, Armistead reached into the water and lifted the little boy into the boat.

Praise the Lord, the sparse boy clothing saved him from drowning. If the child had been a girl, her dress would have dragged her below, to her doom.

She rubbed her eyes, once again treading water. *Obadiah and the men had somehow commandeered a small boat.... Armistead's massive arms are the true prescription for saving these women encased in heavy, water soaked material.*

Nellie turned back toward the ship, trying to locate the windows of the ladies' parlor. She forced herself to concentrate, to disregard the intimidating flames exploding from the hurricane deck, and only look at rail level for windows. She dodged a deck chair floating in the water and forced herself to ignore the hysterical screams and shouts all around her. *I must locate Mutter and Agnes before it is too late.*

One, two, three, Nellie counted windows from the bow. *They were seated in the parlor around the sixth window, only two from the end of the saloon.* As her legs grew tired from this unaccustomed exercise, her theory finally proved correct. She recognized her mother's distinct profile and called to her through the open window.

"We were told to go aft!" her mother shouted. "But we cannot climb the stairs, the smoke billowing down is too overpowering."

"*Mutter,*" shouted Nellie. "Take off your skirt and jump through that window. You too, Agnes!"

"Indecent," said Mrs. Entwhistle.

"You are a strong swimmer, but your dress is too heavy. It is the only way to survive. Women are struggling in the water all around me!" said Nellie, treading water to save her life. A passing cushion hit her in the back of her head. *Thank you, Lord, that was not timber!* She grabbed it, glad for the temporary respite from trying to keep afloat.

"I'll wait for the small boats," said Agnes. "The crew shall rescue us."

"There are not enough boats! There is no lifeline! There are so many people—but no directions." Nellie gasped. *Mercy, they* argue *with me?* Panicking at the thought of running out of time and breath, she shouted, "The fire is getting closer to the parlor."

As if to illustrate Nellie's point, a large burning pole flew down into the water right near her and her heart skipped a beat. "There is *no time.*"

Mrs. Entwhistle, calm and collected, even in the face of impending disaster, took darning scissors from her handbag and in seconds, cut off her skirt. Agnes sat in protest, arms folded stubbornly across her chest. Suddenly, she shrieked and pointed. Nellie could not see from her position in the water, but Agnes recognized her friend Harriett Kinsley. The poor girl struggled and bobbed in the water. As Agnes watched, the heavy, soaked material of the woman's skirt enveloped Harriet's head and her face disappeared under a wave of water.

Without another word, Agnes ripped open all her buttons, pulled off her dress, stepped out of her hoop skirt. Clad only in her bloomers, she climbed through the window and jumped into the river.

The current beat at Nellie and tossed her further out into the river, but she managed to push floating wood to two passengers struggling to keep their heads above the water.

Mrs. Entwhistle stuffed herself through the ladies' cabin window. She grabbed ahold of the guardrail. A flame burst out of the window behind her, backlighting her figure as she awkwardly pulled herself up on the rail. At last she climbed over it and splashed into the water. Nellie swam to her, dodging more debris.

But Gertrude Entwhistle needed no help. She followed Agnes, swimming to shore with sure, strong strokes.

As Nellie swam beside them, someone grabbed her legs, pulling her under. She turned to try to free her legs. A woman frantically clutched at her, trying to save herself. Nellie was able to seize the woman by the shoulder, put her arm under her neck and swim forward. *When I played 'fireman's carry' in the water with Jerome and Patrick at Crawbuckie Beach I never dreamt I would be called upon to use this skill in an existent emergency..*

She kicked on. Fatigue hampered her forward progress; the woman she towed felt heavier and heavier. *Keep swimming! Full steam ahead! Ach, that is the causation of this disaster in the first place. Tarnation! One ruminates on the most bizarre thoughts during a disaster.*

When they stumbled up the shore at the water's edge, Anastasia spotted them and ran over. She still clutched Nellie's skirt, which she tried to wrap around Nellie. Nellie fought it off. Mrs. Entwhistle, shivering and dripping, took the garment, found the two seams, and ripped it carefully in half. She and Agnes wrapped themselves in it.

Nellie turned back to the water and looked at the disaster. Thick columns of smoke billowed from all openings in the ship now, making the sky darker still. An even thicker column rose from the smokestack. Together the columns poured into the sky, making it one black, roiling cloud. The fire, roaring and consuming all the hot wood in its path, edged closer and closer to the people still trapped on the stern deck of the ship. The scene in the water was no better. Faces of people and pieces of debris loomed into vision and then disappeared. It was impossible to know how many were submerged in the water. Men still pushed boards out to people struggling for their lives. Several boats circled the stern. Men shouted and gestured for women and children to jump but bizarrely, petrified passengers remained on the aft deck, watching the fire come ever closer.

A few more passengers straggled out of the water near Nellie and her family. A man carrying a young girl dumped her on the sand and ran back into the water.

"Is she alive?" asked Agnes, coming closer to see if she could help.

Nellie stepped back into the river and hesitated.

"Cornelia, go no further!" her mother shouted, running to her, not stopping at the river's edge, not noticing she immersed her feet in the water. Gertrude Entwhistle grabbed Nellie by the arm. "*Ach du Liebe*, let the men shoulder this burden—they are imbued by the Almighty to bear this toil."

Cornelia opened her mouth to protest, but was too exhausted to reply.

"You'll catch your death of a cold," her mother scolded and folded her in her arms. "Look, look! The *Armenia* has arrived and dropped a small boat."

Around the edge of the menacing cloud of smoke and the frightening red flames, she could just make out the bow of the *Armenia*. "Thank heavens!" Nellie cried, sobbing in a combination of relief and exhaustion. "The ship's crew shall throw a line and all those people in the aft can be saved!"

Her mother led her out of the water and said, "The *Armenia* crew shall send small boats with skilled seamen. Joining the volunteers working from shore, they will soon wrest the remaining passengers from the fire and secure them in boats. You are a lady—you have already given aid above and beyond your station."

"Nonsense," said Nellie. "We can at least join the men on the shore and in waist deep waters pushing boards out to those who are still struggling."

Anastasia shouted, "Have you taken leave of your senses? Augusta and I shall perform that task. You must render first aid. Look at the multitude of injured crawling out of the river! Many passengers, while safely delivered upon shore, still teeter on death's doorstep."

Nellie shook her head. *Am I 'off my chump'? Mercy! My first thought should have been to apply my dearly gained healing skills. Passengers fortunate enough to attain dry land might still sustain severe wounds. I must prevent the injured from degenerating into fatalities.*

A woman washed up at Nellie's feet. *Mercy, ask and ye shall receive.* Nellie choked back a sob at the horrific sight. She dragged the poor sodden creature to higher ground, laid her flat on her back, turned her head to the side and pressed on her abdomen. The lady vomited bilious saltwater. Nellie checked the pulse on the woman's neck, and put her head down to hear her breathing. *No sound!* Nellie put her mouth over the woman's and forced air into it. The poor soul responded by upchucking more water. Nellie tried again. Even in the smoke filled, darkened light, Nellie could see the woman's lips turning blue. She pinched the woman's nose and blew in another breath. The woman coughed and sputtered, but began to breathe.

Alleluia! She straightened and felt someone grab her elbow.

"Have you seen my son?" asked a distraught man.

Anastasia immediately recognized him. "Professor Bailey! No, I am sorry I have not." Both Nellie and Anastasia looked around the water's edge. There were wet, injured, bodies everywhere.

The man wandered away, dazed and distraught, muttering, "They pulled me through the flames to the wharf. I tried to hang onto my children, but someone grabbed me around the neck to save herself. She pulled me under. It was black as the night, I could not see my kin...."

Before she could think of a way to help Professor Bailey, a rescuer dumped an unconscious man on the other side of her. He had a burned arm and lacerations on his head. She turned his face to the side and pumped his abdomen. Water spewed from his mouth, but she could see he was breathing. He opened his eyes and groaned. *Mercifully, I never go anywhere without my salves!* Her eyes searched to locate her dropped bag, but Agnes already stood at her side, handing it to her.

Nellie grabbed the salve and told her mother to start ripping her discarded skirt into strips for bandages. Before she finished a hasty bandage for the man, Anastasia dumped a soaking wet little girl into her lap. Dazed and confused, the girl stared with unseeing eyes, blood smeared across her face from a gash on her forehead. Anastasia relieved Nellie's hands of the man's bandage and Nellie sprang to compress the little girls' wound to stop the bleeding. Anastasia finished tying the man's wound and helped him to drier ground while Nellie unleashed her full arsenal of ministrations.

The ladies applied themselves to give whatever assistance they could.

Anastasia worked at Nellie's side as Nellie triaged whomever the rescuers brought to shore. She pumped lungs clear of water, staunched bleeding, and applied salve for burn relief.

More than once, however, her assistance was to no avail.

As Nellie treated passenger after passenger, the chaos in the river continued.

Agnes assumed the grim job of dragging the victims who could not be resuscitated to the side, and arranging them in a dignified manner, so they could be identified.

Tears slipping down their cheeks, the sisters worked side by side, doing all they could to save the poor souls' lives, or at least their dignity.

CHAPTER 8
The Long Day Is Over

Sing Sing, New York, July 1852

At first the group just huddled in stupefied silence at the bow of an Entwhistle Enterprise ferryboat dispatched to pick up survivors. The heat of the day had dried all their clothes. Nevertheless, Nellie could not stop shivering.

"At long last the nightmare is over," offered Anastasia, holding Zetus's hand with both of her own.

Mrs. Entwhistle, eyes on the seagulls following their boat, tears silently streaming down her face, whispered, "Can we be certain that it is truly ended?"

"I would have preferred to take the cars north," said Augusta in a low voice to her husband Nathaniel. Nathaniel sat stock still, gripping his daughter, looking at her with shocked eyes as the little girl lay sleeping in his arms.

Nellie overheard. "Who is to say locomotives are any safer? They depend upon steam engines too. Papa's boats comply with all safety regulations. Entwhistle captains run their steamship engines only at the capacity for which they are certified. They blow off their heads of steam at all landings, precisely as the law requires. Most importantly, they do not tie down the safety valve of the boiler in order to over-stoke the engines," she declared.

"Hopping horse feathers, Cornelia, prudence plays no part in your allegations," said Obadiah. "Blazes! Have you any realization of the insinuations of your speech?"

Nellie looked at him in surprise and said, "I am fully cognizant of the implication of my words. This disaster springs from clear wrongdoing!"

"Aye, 'tis no time for reticence o' speech," said Mr. Entwhistle. "Cornelia's words rightly cast blame."

"I saw nary an officer throw a line or dispatch a small boat," stated Patrick, his eyes grim and his jaw set. "I only thank the good Lord above we are all safe and my wife and my little ones remain securely at home."

Agnes burst into tears and Armistead patted her shoulder with a clumsy hand. She said, "Thanks be to God Cuthbert stayed home, or he might have met the same terror and harm as many of the children onboard."

Nathaniel choked on a sob and clutched the sleeping Perpetua closer to his chest. Augusta leaned on his shoulder, tears streaming down her face.

Thank you, Lord, for sparing us all, Nellie prayed.

Obadiah said in a low voice, "Do not misunderstand me. I agree — this tragedy was a foreseeable result of reckless behavior and folly. But slanderous speech foments turbulence. Let us leave the assessment of blame to the capable hands of the authorities. I am certain the Yonkers' coroner will find foul play. As soon as he arrived on the scene, Coroner William Lawrence formed an Inquest jury, selected jurors and began to hear testimony."

Anastasia spoke. "I noticed men questioning male survivors. Jurors were selected with remarkable alacrity."

Agnes shouted, "As we worked furiously to ensure more would be saved, others thought it more important to gather evidence to exculpate the ship owners?"

"Yes," said Obadiah, shaking his head in bemusement. "Word of the disaster spread quickly, as the smoke was visible to all the Hudson River towns."

"Once my lungs were taxed to the breaking point, and could no longer withstand the inhalation of more smoke, I jumped ashore, the disaster still unfolding behind me," said Jerome, his voice low and dazed. "I noted people streaming to the site. Good Samaritans and kinfolk arrived, ready to help find and rescue their loved ones."

Patrick nodded his head in agreement. "The smoke signaled the disaster to all the river traffic as well. I saw the *James Madison* and the *Advance* stop and send small boats long before the *Armenia* arrived."

"Moreover, the ship ground to a halt veritably *on* the railroad tracks causing every inbound and outbound locomotive to stop and all onboard offer help," said Nathaniel.

"And identify the dead," said Armistead, grimness grating his voice.

Mr. Entwhistle shook his head, his hand traveling over his hair coming to rest on his neck. His brogue even thicker in his consternation, he said, "In truth, trains performed t' noble service o' carrying both t' injured and t' dead to T' City as well as to destinations north."

Mrs. Entwhistle sighed. "We each did what we could to save our fellow passengers." The rest of the ladies wept and nodded.

Agnes said, "Mercifully, the disaster has ended."

"Would that we could be certain," cried Nellie. "With the turbulence of the water, debris from the ship littered far and wide, and the black smoke of the fire obscuring visibility, who's to say an accurate accounting of passengers occurred?"

"The Yonkers' coroner," said Obadiah.

"Rightly so," said Nellie. "But I do recall the boat was uncommonly crowded."

"Yes," agreed Mrs. Entwhistle. "There were no seats to be had in the ladies' parlor. *Ach!*" Fresh tears streamed down her face. "All those poor souls."

"Passengers on the promenade deck were squeezed like herrings. Goodness, I noticed the moment we boarded how overfilled the accommodations. I recall we climbed to the hurricane deck and secured the last grouping of chairs, vacant only due to lack of overhang or any type of shading," Anastasia corroborated.

"Is there a passenger list enumerating every person on board?" asked Mrs. Entwhistle, turning to her husband. "Has anyone accounted for all the innocent lives on the ill-fated voyage?"

Mr. Entwhistle sighed. "Who's to say how many people were aboard? 'Tis t' responsibility of the clerk to complete the ship roster, but as Jessup was acting captain for the day, due to Captain Tallman's illness, he brooked no opportunity. Moreover, I doubt any one of those ticket sellers would have taken t' time to record t' particulars of those buying passage. They were just out to sell as many tickets as possible and earn their commissions." He shook his head and scratched his neck. "By t' shamrocks of St. Patrick, here's one more omission exacerbating this tragedy. T' responsibilities of the Coroner are only just beginning."

"Yea, but it's well begun. As I said, I saw his jury of twelve men commence the inquiry," said Obadiah. "Eyewitnesses gave testimony even while the disaster continued to worsen."

Jerome, his eyes full of tears, said in a low voice, "The jurors could not have appreciated just how many people were trapped aft, waiting for help as instructed, or left floundering in the water. If they had, they'd have realized they were 'eyewitnesses' too. From stem to stern, the water surrounding the boat was littered with men, women, children and debris." He passed his hand over his eyes. "I did what I could. I cut a settee from a cabin chaise and sent women and children overboard on the windward side of the boat, hoping they would cling on and be saved. I just don't know how many actually survived...."

"Each of us strove to assist the victims with utmost courage," said Patrick. He looked down at the deck planks, shaking his head. His words caused fresh visions of the horrors they just witnessed to swim before their eyes. "Death by fire and water. Lord, have mercy on us!"

"I thank the Lord he saw fit to save us all. But for the grace of God we would be burned or drowned. I pray thanksgiving that we were chosen instead as the Lord's instruments, rendering aid to our fellow travelers," said Mrs. Entwhistle.

Agnes put her still wet handkerchief to her face and burst into fresh tears. "Women and infants stranded on the aft deck or in the ladies' cabin perished in multitudes. They could not swim. Those who tried, drowned but...." Now even the men were openly crying. "...I am sure some, who may still be trapped onboard or who have yet to wash up on shore, were burned to death."

Armistead put his arm around his wife. "I wished not to burden you with what we were helpless to prevent and could only witness, as we pulled oar on our small craft and endeavored to assist those flailing in the sea. A horror show, a nightmare, unfolded before our eyes."

"Amen," said Zetus, engulfing the sobbing Anastasia in his strong arms.

Mr. Entwhistle shook his head, sorrowful tears spilling from his eyes. Obadiah kept his eyes down. Mr. Entwhistle clamped one hand on Obadiah's shoulder and the other on Zetus' broad muscular one. "'Tis no shame in letting t' keening begin."

Obadiah shrugged off the hand, pinched his nose, and shook his head. He cleared his throat. "We must reserve final opinion on the culpability of the ship's owner and crew until we can ascertain all the facts. I have volunteered my legal services to the fact-finding Inquest and to the prosecution of criminal charges," Obadiah offered to the sobbing crowd.

"Little that will do to restore the lost, innocent, lives," sobbed Agnes.

"Or aid the gravely injured who might still succumb to death from their wounds," said Anastasia, picturing the victims she had assisted Nellie in doctoring.

Obadiah gave a snort of anger.

Nellie laid a reassuring hand on his arm. "We all suffer distress beyond rational thought at the tragedy we have witnessed first-hand," she said. "We mutually ache from the painful awareness that further efforts, now, shall spare none of the victims. Agnes, the legal proceeding shall assess culpability. Moreover, the Inquest could spawn new legislation banning all racing on the Hudson River.

"If only it were permissible for the ladies to give sworn statements at the judicial proceedings. I would willingly subject myself to that torment for the privilege of aiding this investigation. Would that women had citizens' rights and could effectuate a change in the law," stated Nellie.

"Cornelia, such pie-in-the-sky thinking. That day shall never come," said Obadiah.

One more sorrow to heap on this calamitous day.

Suddenly Anastasia giggled. All eyes turned to her in disbelief. "What a ragtag bunch we ladies are," she said. Nellie looked at the women. Her mother, Agnes and she were still only half-dressed with men's waistcoats or the other woman's shawls covering their bloomers.

"*Mutter*, I dare say you have not been this scantily clad on a summer day since you were a wee tyke," Anastasia's giggle turned into a laugh which suddenly became hysterical laughter. Everyone looked on in unsmiling sympathy as Zetus gathered her in his arms and pulled her head to his chest, stroking her head to calm her.

"More breach of etiquette," sobbed Anastasia into his shoulder.

The next morning brought no relief from their post-traumatic stress. The entire Entwhistle clan gathered for breakfast at their parent's mansion on Main Street. As the women helped prepare the meal, they commiserated about their lack of sleep. Just as the ham and toast were ready, the kitchen door opened and Augusta and Nathaniel appeared.

"I see this is a gathering of the survivors," said Nathaniel.

"We have brought some of the morning papers," said Augusta, giving her husband a silencing look.

Every newspaper in The City and the Hudson Valley contained news of the tragedy. Everyone reached for the papers at the same time.

The visitors read headlines and extracts aloud: "'Terrible Catastrophe'."

"'Dreadful Calamity on the Hudson River'."

"'Terrible Steamboat Calamity'."

"'Forty-seven bodies recovered'," read Armistead.

"'Reckless disregard for life and limb'...."

"'Unknown how many still unaccounted for'...."

"'Race for Life and Death'...."

"'Meeting of the Passengers at the Astor House'," read Nellie, picking up the *Tribune,* which landed at their kitchen door every morning and had already been read by her father and her husband. "I shall attend!"

"Read further, Cornelia," said Obadiah.

Nellie read, "'The male sufferers who escaped from the *Henry Clay,* which was burned this afternoon on the North River, are requested to meet at the Astor House, on Thursday, (this day) at eleven o'clock, A.M. It is hoped that none will fail to attend this meeting punctually.'" Nellie dropped her arms with the paper, not noticing the newspaper's ink left a smudge on her morning robe. "The 'male sufferers'?" she exclaimed.

Obadiah frowned at her. "You have tarnished your gown. Attend to it."

Nellie did not move.

Anastasia reported, "'Coroner Lawrence continues his Inquest at the scene of the disaster. The bodies still lay at water's edge waiting to be identified'."

Agnes burst into tears. Everyone looked at her. "'In the midst of the debris-littered beach lies a tiny girl, dressed in pink lace lying on a plank, the only clue to her identity is the initials 'J.B.M.H.' embroidered on her dress'." She looked up, sobbing. "*The Tribune* has the temerity to write 'a more angelic picture we never beheld'."

The men left the table immediately; some with toast still in hand, to steam to The City to attend the meeting at the Astor House.

As he checked his pocket watch on the way out the door, Obadiah summoned Nellie to the foyer. She looked questioningly at him. He caught her in his embrace and hugged her fiercely. "Cornelia Rose, I cannot repeat oft enough the words I whispered in our bed last night. I rejoice that we were spared personal disaster. 'Come what sorrow can, It cannot countervail the exchange of joy, that one short minute gives me in her sight'," he said.

Nellie looked at him with shining eyes.

Obadiah grinned. "When words of love elude me, I rely upon my depth of knowledge of Shakespeare."

"Obadiah, my truest love. My heart sings with joy at your attentions," said Nellie. She kissed him passionately.

"As reluctant as I am to extricate myself from your embrace," he said, slowly pulling his arms away. "Duty calls. I must make haste. I have the skills and knowledge to help right this wrong, and use them I must."

"You are my valiant knight in shining armor," said Nellie.

At day's end, there was still little good news.

The men at the Astor House took a vote and agreed that many irregularities contributed to the disaster. They formed a committee and issued a formal List of Resolutions which included "...4. To adopt such measures... as to bring the offenders to punishment."

"'Resolutions' shall hardly ease the grief and horror that linger in my heart," sobbed Agnes.

Armistead gathered her in his arms. "I do have one consoling note, my dearest. Professor Bailey attended the meeting and told me, 'An angel of mercy arranged my drowned wife and daughter so they looked as if in living repose, cherubic, peaceful smiles upon their faces, as if they were already reaping the joys of eternal life'." Armistead reported the man's words verbatim, with a tender smile for his wife.

Agnes brightened and dabbed her eyes with her handkerchief. "Mercifully, I had some help," she said. "For it was a grim task indeed. A Miss Jeannette McAdams, a resident of Yonkers, walked down to the shore and gave any aid she could."

Nellie wiped her own eyes and said, "Mayhap our small consolation is in the many acts of mercy performed for the distressed."

CHAPTER 9
My Blue Heaven

Sing Sing, New York, October 1852

Tarnation! I neglected the milk and it curdled! How shall I ever make pudding for Obadiah's supper?

Nellie scurried outside to the chicken coop looking for eggs, an illogical panic mounting. *I must conjure something tasty for Obadiah's evening meal. Mr. Wright returns from his clerkship in just two short hours. I must have his supper ready, for tonight my knight in shining armor once again rejoins the prosecution team for the Henry Clay disaster. Now that the Inquest culminated in an indictment for manslaughter, Mr. Wright's agitation and workload increases whilst he aids in assembling evidence. His evening nutrition must strengthen and fortify his endeavors.*

Not a single egg.

Those inferior hens! What causes their malfunction?

Tears sprang to her eyes before she could stop them. Lately every little thing made her weepy. She shook her head, swiped at a straggling clump of hair, and scolded herself. *How could I be so irresponsible and neglect supervision of my dairy provisions? Obadiah shall be justifiably furious at my waste of his hard-earned money. My inadequate judgment is deplorable – over-purchasing necessities and now, through careless husbandry, abandoning them to rot. Would that we had a cow!*

She foraged in the garden, in search of vegetables to compensate for the loss of pudding. *My garden flounders pitifully! Must I now squander his income on store-bought vegetables? Why have I failed so miserably in tending my crop?* She was so distraught that even her fine view of the Hudson did nothing to cheer her. The river's shimmering, glass-silvery color, licked by a touch of orange from the last vestiges of the sun, was usually a sight she cherished.

She found some withered plants where her green beans grew. *I do not recall picking the last of the crop. Mayhap that pesky cottontail hopped in, and gobbled them!* The two remaining pumpkins were not yet ripe. Nellie dropped to the ground and sobbed. *Focus on the task,* she scolded herself again. *These theatrics border on the absurd. There must be some recipe in my cooking repertoire that requires only the ingredients remaining on hand.*

She gathered herself together and marched back to the kitchen. But once she stormed through the door, she felt winded and lost her new resolve. Nellie flopped down in a chair and put her head on the table.

Suddenly, the door opened and Mrs. Entwhistle appeared. "Just making my rounds, Cornelia my love, checking on my newly wedded daughter, ensuring *alles ist im ordnung,* everything is in order," she announced. She took one look at Nellie and her face softened.

"Cornelia Rose, what plagues you? You must cease this unduly taxing fixation with the disaster of the *Henry Clay.*"

Nellie looked at her mother, startled. A picture of the little girl with the gash on her head, bleeding profusely, flashed before her eyes. A fresh sob caught in her throat.

"Or is it a new hardship that precipitated your state of distraction?" Mrs. Entwhistle stopped in mid-motion, hand poised on her half-removed hat, and scrutinized her daughter with concern.

"Alas, *Mutter,* I have spoilt the milk through my careless husbandry. I do not know how I shall conjure a single dish for my husband's supper," Nellie confessed. "My husband's *pro bono* assistance with the investigation into the *Henry Clay* disaster, interviewing survivors, finding experts on steamboat engineering, in addition to his usual endeavors on behalf of Judge Urmy and the local Sing Sing judicial system, have overtaxed him to the point of agitation. Inadequate nourishment betrays lack of wifely capabilities and reneges my midwifery oath to preserve health." She looked down at her hands and burst into tears again. "Furthermore, I have exhausted my supply of lye for the washing."

"*Ach du Liebe,* nonsense, my child. It is always darkest before the dawn. You must throw all your laundry into your old cart and avail yourself of my copper kettles. We shall invent a 'washing bee'. All the womenfolk will help."

Nellie brightened visibly at the thought of her mother's sparkling clean laundry room. Eight huge kettledrums gleamed in a row for various stages of washing, like a platoon of polished soldiers. The first seven handled everything from cottons to calico; the special eighth drum, reserved for the finest silk fabrics, stood aloof from the rest like a rich socialite at a commoner's tea party. The room was ringed with four sinks, one kept exclusively for bluing and bleaching white fabric. The next room sported gas heated pipes to warm the clothes until they dried. *Mercy, what a contrast to my one tub and solitary washboard!*

"'Twould be laundry heaven *Mutter!*" exclaimed Nellie, but burst into a fresh shower of tears. *How shall deluxe conditions for washing fix my spoilt supper?*

"*Ach*, now, let us apply ourselves to the more immediate difficulty and see what we can fashion for an acceptable repast." Mrs. Entwhistle pulled a freshly ironed apron from Nellie's cupboard, tied it briskly around her matronly waist, and tossed her shawl and hat on the plain wooden chair next to the small table.

"What is in your larder?" Gertrude Entwhistle asked, but before Nellie could tell her she was already poking around the corner. "Where are your vegetables? What herbs do you have growing in your garden? *Wunderbar*, wonderful, some fine potatoes." She pulled four potatoes out of the basket in the pantry, turned and bustled over to Nellie.

"I shall confide a well-known secret of seasoned, frugal cooks: mashed potatoes actually taste better when prepared with curdled milk."

Nellie looked skeptical. "Truly, *Mutter?*" she asked. But she dried her tears on her apron and scrubbed the potatoes her mother handed her. Listening to her mother's chatter, she picked up the paring knife, still sniffling a bit. She cut off a long peel of potato skin.

"*Ach*, surely I have taught you, only pare the eyes, and the bruised part of the potato. No need to peel the entire skin. 'Tis more economical—moreover, the skin contains nutritious vitamins, thus providing a more substantial meal with a truer flavor, when mashed with garlic.

"Now, I shall impart a little anecdote that shall revive your smile," her mother continued, as she lit Nellie's potbellied stove and scalded the milk. "Little Theodora parroted the most adorable...."

Suddenly, her mother interrupted herself and looked at Nellie sharply. "Thrice this fortnight, Cornelia, I have witnessed you in tears!" She charged around the table to her daughter, took her hand and looked her in the eye. Gertrude Entwhistle's face relaxed with comprehension. She drew Nellie to her in a tender embrace.

"I was with *meine Mutter*, when I first realized *I* was with child," Mrs. Entwhistle said into Nellie's hair.

Nellie drew in her breath. *Was it obvious? How could Mutter be so certain when I am so unsure?*

As if in answer to her unspoken question, Mrs. Entwhistle had a smile in her voice when she said, "*Meine Mutter* recognized the signs in me before I myself knew. Oft times the young woman herself is the last to suspect. You might recall a certain series of discussions we Entwhistle women enjoyed, speculating, and opining when your brothers' wives were first in their state of confinement.

"No more sniffles," her mother continued, pulling out her beautifully embroidered lace handkerchief, and gently dabbing Nellie's eyes as if she were still a child. "Or we shall both be sobbing too joyfully to prepare your husband something that shall warm his stomach and sustain him when you divulge the news!"

CHAPTER 10
That's the Way of the World

Sing Sing, New York, April 1853

Nellie was up to her elbows in suds, tears streaming from her face as she scrubbed Obadiah's white shirt up and down on the washboard and threw it into the bluing.

"*Was ist los, mit du*?" Mrs. Entwhistle suddenly appeared at Nellie's sudsy elbow. "What is the matter?" Her mother pulled Cornelia Rose's hands out of the water and folded her daughter into her arms. "Why do you labor at the washing here? I have told you time and again to have your brother Matthias pick up your washing and bring it to my house when he returns from his milk delivery route."

She drew back to arm's length and looked at Nellie.

"*Ach*, you have started. We must send word to Midwife Rafferty!" Mrs. Entwhistle pulled Nellie back into her warm embrace.

"Thank you *Mutter* for acquiescing to my wishes and summoning the midwife and not that vile Doctor Dudley Depew. What unmitigated gall! Denouncing the midwife's value, then horning in on her birthing business, as soon as Depew ascertained delivering babies was a cash cow."

She drew an unsteady breath and groused into her mother's shoulder. "The questionably accredited doctor doubles his bonanza from this new sideline—more coins in his pocket from the purloined work, which coins remain pocketed longer since the new work limits time spent 'bending his elbow'!" *What care I of stupid Doctor Depew? It is as if I can only utter angry words whilst enduring a contraction.*

"On the subject of our town physician's drinking habits we are in complete accord," agreed her mother in her usual matter-of-fact tone. *As if it were the most ordinary thing in the world, talking to her daughter, watching her suffer the throws of contractions.* But she found it rather comforting. Gertrude Entwhistle continued, "*Tsk-tsk*. He does not do his profession any service by frequenting the many local taverns. Nor does he inspire confidence in the soon-to-be mothers."

She dragged Nellie with her as she bustled to the linen closet for one of Nellie's freshly ironed aprons. "The women of the Pffernuss, and even the Entwhistle clan know the old-fashioned method of lying abed anticipating the onslaught of pain worsens the suffering to the point of unbearable."

Nellie smiled outright at her mother's reluctant acknowledgement of the wisdom of her female kinsfolk in-law. *Surely an 'admission against interest' if I ever heard one,* she thought, borrowing one of Obadiah's legal phrases. Her mother commanded, "Continue with your daily business whilst I ensure all is ready for the precious infant's arrival."

In the middle of a painful pull on her abdominal muscles, Nellie actually laughed in response. She took the kettle out of her mother's hands. "Perhaps, since *I* am the one skilled in the business of midwifery, I should make ready the birthing space and *you* can go about the business of seeing that my husband has sufficient food prepared for both his noontime dinner and his supper.... Unless you think my business shall be concluded before then?"

"*Ach du Liebe,*" said her mother, but with a loving smile as she smoothed Nellie's recalcitrant lock of hair from her eyes. "Such wishful thinking!"

They set about their respective tasks. Completing the preparations for her birthing space, Nellie stopped more and more frequently as the contractions intensified. Soon they were less than five minutes apart, and she had trouble concentrating on her knitting.

Obadiah came in, so preoccupied with a letter he held in his hand that he failed to notice Nellie's altered state, or hear Mrs. Entwhistle bustling about in the kitchen. He sighed and twirled his mustache as Nellie set a plate of soup before him. "The trial of the officers of the *Henry Clay* proceeds in fits and starts. We attorneys for the plaintiffs have made quite a convincing case through our witnesses before the Westchester grand jury, but we contest a formidable foe. McMahon, the defense attorney for the ship's officers, revealed a foretaste of his style when he questioned witnesses at the Inquest. His merciless attack on the integrity of our witnesses tipped his hand on the nature of his own character. I anticipate a ruthless, dirty-handed, cockfight of a trial." He took several hurried gulps of soup, still not looking at Nellie.

After a long slurp, just as Nellie was about to mention the onset of her labor, Obadiah continued his stream of thought. "Jessup, the clerk who functioned as acting captain that fateful day, is a wily jack-a-naps, already giving us conflicting statements. Yet, our county prosecutor's feeble efforts at cross-examination fail to elicit the truth from the crew. We need a proper officer-of-the-state with the ability to outmaneuver that bigwig McMahon."

"Why not call upon your acquaintance, the finest 'Philadelphia lawyer', Mr. J. J. Speed?" asked Nellie. "Or mayhap, is he conflicted out of handling the case, as he was a passenger on the *Henry Clay?*"

"Would that we could," replied Obadiah, with a grim expression on his face. "Do you not recall, his body washed up weeks after the disaster, somewhere down river?"

Nellie blanched, but not entirely from sadness at the memory, or its lapse, as Obadiah supposed. She felt another contraction.

"I know," said Obadiah. "'Twas a sad day, and I fear the press did not give his obituary the space it was due, surrounded as it was by the unfolding saga of this disaster. Truly, they gave many details of the process by which Mr. J.J. Speed, Esquire was positively identified, but few particulars of the great man's lifetime of accomplishments."

"Tarry a moment. Did not Thomas Collyer confess to my father *he* was commanding and racing the *Henry Clay?* Can you not have my father swear his testimony and thus establish culpability? I am quite certain *I* recall Mr. Collyer boast words to that effect. Would that I could testify!"

Obadiah shook his head, looking down at his spoon chase a carrot in the soup. "As I have attempted to explain, the intricacies of court procedure often obfuscate the simple truth. I offered this discussion of the facts of this case in the strictest of confidence. Do not worry your pretty little head. We attorneys have our strategy well in hand."

Nellie opened her mouth to reply, but Obadiah threw down his spoon, drank the rest of his soup in one gulp, picked up a roll from the basket and stood up from the table. "I must dash if I am to be home for supper." He gave her a quick peck on the cheek, and hurried down the hallway. "You must rest, you look a tad peaked." His voice floated back.

Nellie burst into almost hysterical laughter. Mid-laugh, she caught her breath as the severity of the next contraction overwhelmed her. Gertrude Entwhistle ran out of the kitchen and helped Nellie back to the settee in front of the fireplace. "In between contractions you must either rest, or otherwise occupy yourself. Our hard work barely begins." She paused and looked at Nellie's expression. "As you well know," she acknowledged Nellie's expertise and soothed Nellie's back with her hand.

Mollified, Nellie submitted to her mother's care.

A big basket of herbs and potions came through the door, followed immediately by Mrs. Rafferty. The very sight of her teacher and mentor calmed Nellie, in spite of the onset of another long, painful contraction.

"Now, breathe!" commanded Mrs. Rafferty, barely inside the doorway. "For the love of Saint Bridget, Cornelia! How many times have you coached patients, instructing them in this very technique? We must breathe and push t' pain away."

Mrs. Rafferty put down the basket and pulled Nellie off her Dessoir settee. "Let's get shinning around," she said. "Time to move to the next stage." She bustled Nellie over to the cot Nellie had readied in her sitting room, and helped Nellie lie down. "'Tis time to rest in between contractions. We must conserve your strength for later."

"How very strange to view the birthing table from this perspective." Nellie gave a weak grin, the intensity of the next contraction already taking its toll on her.

The front door banged open, audible in the lull between contractions. Obadiah called, "Cornelia, I had to hurry back with the good news. We have obtained federal jurisdiction! The *Henry Clay* officers will not be tried for murder in New York state court, but rather be held for manslaughter in the first degree in Federal Court, under the 1838 Steamboat Act. We would never have been able to prove the *mens rea*, the intent to harm, required for a conviction of murder! This indictment most definitely ensures us a guilty verdict and perhaps pecuniary accountability...."

Obadiah's figure appeared in the doorway of the labor room, the word 'accountability' apparently caught in his throat. "Hornswoggling hellfire!" he cussed and turned on his heel. His receding voice echoed along the hallway. "Perhaps I will fill you in on the particulars at another juncture...." The door slammed again.

Nellie, Midwife Rafferty, and Gertrude Entwhistle looked at each other and burst into laughter.

Nellie's laughter spurred another contraction, and they all went back to work.

"Glory and praise to the Lord," whispered Nellie, fourteen hours later, taking the slippery red infant into her arms. She took a long look at the small body taking up so little space in her arms. The strangest thought struck her. "My sweet Emmeline Rose, you look familiar!" she exclaimed out loud. Reluctantly, she gave the baby to Mrs. Rafferty to be bathed and swaddled.

Obadiah rushed into the room.

He sought out Nellie's eyes first, then looked at their cleaned, wrapped baby, nestled in his wife's arms. Nellie observed the amazement and joy on his face at his first look at their daughter. *I shall cherish his look of wonder and awe all the rest of my days,* she vowed.

"My darling," said Obadiah, tenderly, gently, kissing Nellie on the head. "No, no—my darlings!" he corrected himself, even more gently kissing the infant on her head. Emma gave a little sleep smile but did not open her eyes.

Nellie looked up at him. They both had tears in their eyes. *Although in truth, I have journeyed far beyond the 'wonder' portion of this miracle. Now I simply shed tears of exhaustion.* Nellie giggled. The noise turned into laughter and the laughter came faster and faster as she realized she could not stop. Obadiah plopped down on the bed and embraced both mother and daughter.

"Laughter for joy—far better, my Cornelia Rose, than tears of relief," he whispered into her hair. New tears sprang to her eyes at those kind words, but she calmed herself and settled into him, their precious bundle still in angelic repose in her arms. She felt his lips brush her hair, and then her ear, and then her neck. A delighted tingle ran down Nellie's shoulder. *Merciful heavens, the agony is gone. In its stead, warm, wonderful sensations reappear.*

Nellie felt rather than heard Obadiah whisper,

"'I humbly do beseech of your pardon, For too much loving you'."

Obadiah's quote of Shakespeare caps my euphoria.

For a long time, they sat intertwined, feeling the joy, the elation, and the responsibility, of becoming parents.

CHAPTER 11
Stand by Me

Sing Sing, New York, April 1853

Less than two days later, Nellie felt strong enough to venture into her garden. She picked some early spring herbs — the ingredients for a tincture and for good measure, a poultice. The seedtime sun felt warm on her back, but Nellie suffered such anxiety about her new responsibilities the sensation barely registered. With the duties of motherhood far more overwhelming than she imagined, the only rational thought she could muster took the form of a midwife recipe. *Mayhap boosting my sanguinity shall result in greater competence at this task.*

Rushing back into the kitchen, she heaved a huge sigh of relief at the sight of Emmeline Rose sleeping in her bassinet like a cherub. *The line between Emma's existence and her state as a figment of my longing and imagination seems so tentative. Shall I always fret, when out of her presence, even if still within earshot? I suppose I shall become accustomed to motherhood. Howsoever, my present state is rather precarious. My agitated mind conjures all sorts of dreadful happenstances, making me doubt my reasoning. Truly, Emma's very life seems almost hypothetical.*

Nellie turned to a familiar activity. *To ground myself more firmly in the reality of this day, I shall grind some herbs!* She pumped water at her sink and put the kettle on her potbellied stove. *Whilst I wait for the roiling boil needed for my poultice and Emma still sleeps, I can gather two more herbs and formulate the cure for Papa's fresh onset of gout.*

Gertrude Entwhistle bustled through the door, already wearing an apron, carrying a big basket of freshly laundered clothes. "*Was machts du*, Cornelia Rose? Why do you rove about the house instead of resting in bed?" she demanded, drawing Cornelia away from the stove, and sitting her down at the kitchen table.

"Making a poultice for you to take to Papa!" Nellie protested, although, truth be told, she felt a bit weak in the knees. "I shan't rest until his horrible advance of gout retreats. We mustn't allow it, or Papa's arthritis, to wreak havoc on his health."

Nellie did not wait for a response. "*Mutter*, I cannot find the layette for the baby. I must launder it whilst Emma still sleeps. Mercy, I must prepare the poultice so it is ready when you leave, for how else can I ensure Papa receives it with the proper instructions?" Cornelia's eyes began to tear in frustration, but she remained seated.

"At my request, Jerome hauled all your laundry baskets to my house."

Cornelia opened her mouth to protest further. "*Ach du Liebe*," Gertrude Entwhistle held up her hand to stop Cornelia. "You must allow Anastasia the pleasure of fussing over her big sister. *She* insisted we bring all your washing to my big copper kettledrums in the steam-heated laundry room." Her mother smiled.

"In the middle of her last-minute wedding preparations Stasia is worrying about my laundry?" asked Nellie, now openly crying. Mrs. Entwhistle made no reply, she just helped Nellie to her feet and steered her back to her bedroom.

Just then the baby began to cry. Nellie rushed to the crib.

"*Gott im Himmel*, God in heaven, you must resume bed rest," chided her mother, already bending over the crib to pick up the baby. "You must sleep, how else shall you recuperate? *Ach du Liebe*, Emmeline Rose is only two days old. With the first-born, every time the baby sleeps, you must rest! Honestly, up, and about, making poultices, worrying about laundry... tsk, tsk."

"There is no scientific proof the aftereffects of childbirth incapacitate a woman. Nowhere in all my training did I learn labor would make me infirm," Cornelia said. Bursting into fresh tears, she joined her daughter in a loud cry, but obediently shuffled back to her bedroom along with her mother and her daughter.

"*Was ist los mit du?*" Mrs. Entwhistle kept tsk-tsking, even though she knew very well what ailed her daughter as she guided Nellie to bed. Once she got Nellie settled, she gently placed Emma in her arms. The baby stopped crying and looked up at Nellie as soon as she felt her mother's touch.

"Thank you, Lord God Almighty, for *this* blessing," said Nellie. She swiped her tears and some stray hair away with one hand and tugged the corners of her lips into a tiny smile. Gertrude sat down on the edge of the bed and hugged them both. Nellie began to nurse the baby.

After a moment Nellie burst into tears again.

"*Nun! Was ist los?*" Mrs. Entwhistle jumped to her feet in alarm.

"What's wrong? The tragic mistiming of Emmeline Rose's birth!" Nellie sobbed. "Stasia is to wed in less than a fortnight. How *ever* shall I fit into my gown?"

"*Ach du Liebe!*" Mrs. Entwhistle said, smiling, and sitting back down on the edge of the bed. "First of all, I observe you have already regained your figure; the dress shall positively swim on you. Secondly, will you need it now? Is it a sound proposition, traveling all the way to West Point on a steamer for a crossed swords wedding when your baby is less than a month old?"

Nellie burst into tears again.

"You should not even consider that scheme," said Agnes, appearing at the foot of Nellie's bed, carrying a basket of daffodils. "You recall, my little Cuthbert, that rascal of a boy, was inconsolable at frequent, unpredictable intervals throughout the day. A baby shall not endure a separation from its mother for several hours' time, even if the occasion be as grand as a West Point wedding."

"I shall not miss my sister's wedding. Forsooth, I am to stand up for her," wailed Cornelia, as she tried to make sure the baby latched properly on her other side.

"But you can barely stand for yourself," Agnes observed, raising one, annoying, eyebrow.

Anastasia bounced into the room with a bouquet of colorful, exotic tulips. She rushed to the bed and gave Nellie a warm hug. The ladies exclaimed over the baby as Nellie finished nursing.

Nellie rubbed the baby's back until Emma gave a satisfying little burp, which caused exclamations of delight from all the womenfolk. Nellie beamed a broad, proud smile. Then she frowned. "Agnes, were you similarly both overwhelmed and overjoyed at the birth of your child?"

"Mostly overwhelmed," Agnes confessed. "Were it not for your tea supplements to stimulate my lactation efforts, I do believe my nursing would have continued to be ineffective. I felt quite a failure at motherhood when unable to comfort that boy!"

Nellie smiled in appreciation of the compliment. Agnes put her hands on her hips. "Which is why I repeat, 'you cannot stand for Anastasia when you can barely stand for yourself'."

"Nonsense," Nellie replied. She handed the baby carefully to her mother, scooted to the opposite side of the bed, and stood. She wobbled just a bit when her feet first hit the floor, but she turned that wobble into a little flourish of a curtsey.

Nellie appealed to her mother. "*Mutter*, I recall your truly herculean ability to resume normal activities after each childbirth. Why I remember you prepared supper for the family the day Matthias was born! You of all people shall support me, *nicht wahr*?"

Perhaps it was that Nellie asked 'Isn't that true?' in German, or merely that she appealed to her mother's heart and her stalwart principles. In any case, Mrs. Entwhistle said, "*Natürlich*, naturally I shall be blessed to hold your precious little Emma whilst you witness your sister and her groom's exchange of the vows of Holy Matrimony. If we make sure you nurse her immediately prior to the ceremony, I am sure we shall have no interruptions during the Mass."

Cornelia turned to Anastasia, who had remained silent, looking at each of them with a puckered brow. Agnes, with her one eyebrow raised in her trademark expression, still looked disapproving.

Nellie pleaded, "Anastasia, I promise you: I shall be responsible for nary a glitch in your ceremony."

"But hopefully the wedding will *not* go off without a hitch!" Obadiah said in a merry tone as he entered the room.

The silly pun helped ease the tension. The ladies laughed.

"Look!" Nellie said. "I do believe *Emma smiled!*"

Her sisters clustered back around the baby, cooing and fussing, and Nellie slipped back into bed.

Nothing more needs be discussed on this subject. I shall stand witness for my sister — my ability and right to this honor supported by both my husband and my mother.

"Mercy, you mean to say that little angel was in attendance throughout the entire Mass, including exchange of marriage vows?" asked Armistead leaning in his chair and tickling Emma under the chin.

Nellie nodded. "I told you the choir was heavenly. They must have charmed my little one into a deep slumber."

Agnes threw up her hands in agitation, upsetting her plate of petit fours on the edge of the table. "Only you, Cornelia, could lead such a charmed life. Your baby behaves exceptionally, in fact perfectly, at a marriage ceremony. As an infant, Cuthbert refused to nap. In fact, he still does not nap consistently to this day. Sakes alive! Observe his behavior at this very instant."

Nellie looked all around the sumptuous, West Point Hotel hall where they sat, enjoying the wedding feast. She shook her head. Agnes pointed, but Nellie still did not see her nephew. As she opened her mouth to ask, she saw the dessert table's cloth flicker back and forth. Some feet, followed by the back end of a boy, emerged. In two steps, Armistead reached the table, scooped his toddler out from under it and in two steps more, returned to his seat carrying the squirming, protesting boy.

Agnes turned back to Nellie and continued speaking, as if nothing had happened. "But your Emma! Nestled in *Mutter's* arms, she drifted off to sleep without a peep of trouble. I prithee my next one," she pointed to her own protruding midsection, "is Emma's double—an enchanting and enchanted, baby girl."

CHAPTER 12
What a Wonderful World

New York City, Summer 1853

"Dut-da-da dut-da, Tah Tah!" Obadiah trumpeted. "Ladies and... little lady." His beautiful baby, cooing in her cradle, caught his eye. He smiled, momentarily distracted, and reaching out a finger, caressed Emma's soft cheek.

"*Ah-hem.*" He pulled back his hand, remembering his announcement. "The Crystal Palace is open!" Nellie turned from their potbellied stove, rosy red from stirring stew to see her husband's smiling eyes, evening newspaper flicked down on one side revealing half a grinning face. Obadiah winked at her and read aloud from the *Tribune*, "'The grand event on which so many hopes and expectations and anxieties were clustered is at last completed. The great Temple of National Industry has unclosed its portals and displays its treasures to the multitudes.'"

"How I long to attend the opening ceremonies and hobnob with the distinguished guests," hinted Nellie.

"Indubitably. By the looks of the expected attendee list, you join 15,000 other guests and dignitaries who simply *must* attend. President Franklin Pierce shall provide the inaugural address at the opening ceremonies. The formal dinner features Secretary of War Jefferson Davis as the main orator. Guess Old Horace Greeley surely backed a winning horse right out of the starting gate this time."

"Jefferson Davis, Mr. Secretary of War," Nellie giggled. Obadiah looked at her askance. "Every time I hear that man's name I remember my escort at West Point, William T. Magruder's, tales of the exploits of cadet Jeff Davis. His infamous antics as a student!" Nellie raised her hand and ticked her points off on her fingers. "Davis put brandy in the punch at an official's Christmas party and was tried for inciting disorderly conduct." The next finger went down. "He frequented Benny Havens' Tavern and was arrested there more than once. Davis got so drunk one evening he almost fell off the highest cliff in Buttermilk Falls when trying to escape a raid at the Tavern...."

Obadiah caught Cornelia's eye in a malevolent glare. She closed her mouth in consternation. Turning back to the stove, her vision swam with tears. *Does he still begrudge me my memories of youth, simply because he played no part in those comedies?* she wondered.

"How preposterous appears the thought of Colonel Davis as Commander of our Armed Forces," she said aloud.

"One would hope that a certain maturity develops as one ages, sufficient to repent the sins of youth, followed by sincere regret," Obadiah said through tightened lips.

Nellie took the hint and changed the subject. "I read a piece in *Godey's Ladies Magazine* entitled 'On Articles at the Crystal Palace Most Attractive to Ladies'. The author claims there shall be luxuries galore on display, in addition to time-saving devices and clever inventions," she said, excited at the imminent opening of the exhibition. She marshaled her arguments and prepared to petition for frequent visits to the Fair.

Obadiah laughed. "There is no need for coercive or cajoling words to induce my attendance. I am equally enthralled with the prospect of viewing all the innovations, gadgets and indulgences from around the world now on display."

Obadiah lifted his head from his newspaper. "The reviews of the Fair promise excellent and astounding exhibits. This one, in *Prairie Farmer*, argues that the exposition is '...no humbug, but a school of wealth and luxury—of taste and refinement—rather than hard-handed utility'."

"Certainly, if the *Prairie Farmer* confirms the Fair's authenticity, then we must attend *at once*," laughed Cornelia. "What prompted your subscription to the *Prairie Farmer*?"

"That is a discussion best left for another day," said Obadiah. Nellie, poised for argument, instead gave an excited squeal when he took two tickets out of his pocket. He looked at her and smiled. "We attend the great Exposition tomorrow. Anchors aweigh on the steamer at seven bells, docking in The City at the 42nd Street Pier. From there, 'tis a short perambulation to the Sixth Avenue railroad car."

Nellie looked perplexed.

"Are you apprehensive of steamships? 'Tis quite normal to suffer lasting effects from the traumatic *Henry Clay* disaster."

"Not in the slightest. As an immediate result of your efforts with the Coroner's Inquest and the negative press your findings engendered, our legislature outlawed steamboat racing on the Hudson. Furthermore, any ship certified seaworthy and fit by Entwhistle Enterprises engenders my continued confidence in its prowess as a comfortable conveyance."

"Then I confess I cannot fathom the cause of your dreary, foreboding facial expression," said Obadiah, twirling his mustache.

"My contemplation of the preparations for our journey unnerves me. An outing's success resides squarely upon proper planning. I must not neglect any detail or scenario, but rather anticipate all of Emma's needs and prepare accordingly."

A frown hip hopped across her brow as a new worry occurred. "Can our precious little Emma withstand the incessant jolting of the streetcar?" she worried.

"Have no fear, the Sixth Avenue railroad, while still drawn by horses, is pulled along a smooth iron rail, eliminating the unremitting convulsing and jerking suffered by passengers on the rattling omnibuses."

The next day, the railcar deposited them behind the Croton Reservoir, right in front of the Crystal Palace. Joining the crowd of spectators admiring the awe-inspiring building, Nellie felt her excitement and anticipation mount. Resembling a large greenhouse of Moorish architecture, the building was different from any Nellie had ever seen. *So grand, the outside alone is worth the trip to The City.* She leaned her head back and squinted at the imposing structure. The building seemed to sparkle as the sun glittered off the glass.

Enchanting. 'Tis a fairy palace, enticing my entrance. Mercy, with a façade this grand, the treasures lying within must be more fascinating than the tales of Scheherazade!

Obadiah strode toward the front entrance, pulling tickets from his waistcoat pocket, but Cornelia lingered. She deliberately turned her back on the captivating palace, and scrutinized a building directly across the street. The Latting Observatory rose, scraping the sky right in front of her, 315 feet in the air, the tallest building in the world. She stood, cradling Emma, her neck craned, hand shading her eyes, looking all the way up to the top of the iron-braced wooden tower.

"'Tis grand. The rather bizarre octagonal base stands stout and graceless, not built with any regard for beauty of form, but nonetheless, simply grand," whispered Nellie to her daughter, squeezing her little hand. "Just like you, a wonder of the world." The baby cooed back in delight."A capital example of architectural skill," said Nellie, and Emma's fist curled around Nellie's finger as if she appreciated the sophistication of her mother's 'baby talk'.

They handed their tickets to the gatekeeper and walked through the turnstiles, flowing with the crowd into the grand center hall. The large statue of George Washington astride a horse, in the dead center of the building, commanded their attention. Light streamed down upon it, highlighting the fine carving of Baron Carlo Marochetti. As if pulled by its magnetism, the Wrights walked to the featured piece and stopped.

"Spectacular," whispered Cornelia, squeezing Obadiah's hand. He squeezed back. "The architectural features of this rotunda, including the glass which makes the structure appear transparent, are fitting for the Temple of Industry and Art and do *not* disappoint." They stood in that spot, turned their backs to the statue and rotated around its base, scanning the length and breadth of the palace.

Designed in the shape of a Greek cross around the huge domed hall in the center, signs indicating the exhibits hung over each arm. The Wrights looked down each of the four wings' corridors in turn. The exterior of specially tinted glass ensured that the entire palace was drenched in sunlight, making the overabundant displays, spilling into the corridors, dazzle enticingly.

"Mercy, a plethora of items awaits viewing! The aura of excitement alone necessitates a return visit, without considering the overwhelming stimulation of the senses," said Nellie, loosening Emma's bonnet strings, and taking off her little sweater. The child looked around with wide eyes.

Obadiah said, "I have examined Mr. Horace Greeley's *Art and Industry as Represented in the Exhibition at the Crystal Palace in New York* from cover to cover. Our fine *New York Tribune* editor has crafted a quite comprehensive treatise. Using it as a guide to the exhibits, I have determined our course of exploration of these treasures." He smiled down upon her with love in his eyes. "Moreover—yes, in answer to your thinly disguised hint, I concur. The critics *do* advise the wonders are too plentiful to limit one's experience to a single visit. You need not fear, I have already decided: any display we neglect today we shall view at another time. We shall, quite willingly, place money directly in Old Horace's pocket, for as an investor in this special exhibit he stands to profit every day we devote to attending the Fair.

"Let us start at the great display of carved fireplace mantels and parlor furnishings and peruse the perimeter of the dome before we venture down the arms of the edifice to see the entries from other countries." Obadiah drew their path along the floor plan with his finger, and the Wrights started walking.

"Mercy this parlor setting is grand!" exclaimed Nellie. Emma seemed to coo her agreement. "The marble of this fireplace is aglow and its aura is reflected in that enormous gilded mirror to our right."

"Now, now," said Obadiah, gently guiding her by the elbow. "We have much to see. We mustn't linger too long ogling any one particular exhibit."

Nellie allowed herself to be led to a spectacular glass case, which had caught her eye earlier. It appeared to be a pyramid. Upon closer examination, the Wrights discovered it was made, not of bricks, or mortar, but of rope, wound length upon length, crowned at the top with an eagle.

"New fibers for rope," said Obadiah, reading the display information. "I wonder if Entwhistle Enterprises' fleet uses cotton rope like this fine hewn line from Macon, Georgia. It claims cotton's attributes exemplary for ships' moorings. Apparently, cotton fiber has vastly superior qualities to the hemp and twine previously hailed as exclusive roping material."

"The artful arrangement of the cord elevates this display from a mere industrial improvement to an art form," Nellie observed.

Out of the corner of her eye, Nellie saw a lifting platform ascend to the height of the glass-paneled ceiling. It hovered above the second-floor level of the great Crystal Palace. "Ladies and Gentlemen, please direct your attention to a phenomenal improvement to the elevator," shouted a man into a bullhorn. "Introducing Mr. Elisha Otis, the inventor of the safety lift. As you can see, Mr. Otis rises high above us all to demonstrate this mechanical wonder."

As the crowd watched, Otis gave one final tug on the pulley ropes and touched the top of the banner furled over the second floor of the building with a grand flourish. At once, the entire platform began to descend.

Suddenly, Otis took out his sword and slashed the rope. The elevator plunged downward!

Nellie gasped. Some women screamed. Horrified, she held her breath for the inevitable crash.

But Elisha Otis pulled a lever at his right hand and the platform's plunge ceased in just seconds. At the pull of the brake, the elevator slid to a smooth stop after less than a foot of further free-fall. The crowd erupted into applause and shouts of relief.

"I have invented a safety brake for lifts," Otis announced, still bowing, and flourishing his arms. "No longer will elevator use include the risk of rope failure and deadly free-falls."

Nellie's heart still raced a mile a minute as she listened to the crowd exclaiming and laughing. "Simply a spectacular demonstration," she gasped to Obadiah.

"Yes, the inventor is a showman, molded in the cast of P.T. Barnum, but there is no humbug in the value of this invention. I do believe the gentleman's improvement shall pave the way for future buildings to assume greater heights."

"Pun intended," laughed Nellie. "Think how easily the top viewing platform could be obtained with a steam elevator, complete with safety brake, in the Latting Observatory." They turned toward the next exhibit, an elaborate case bearing the name "Tiffany & Co." in gold lettering across its top. Nellie bent to examine the sparkling merchandise.

"The jewelry is enchanting, its bewitchment further enhanced by the novel method of highlighting the gems. 'Tis no wonder Mr. Tiffany won a silver medal at this Fair for the overwhelming beauty of this matching seed pearl brooch, bracelet, necklace, and earrings," said Nellie. She walked around and around the case, looking intently at each item, lingering far beyond the allotted twenty minutes at the Tiffany Bazaar.

Finally, she stepped back, spell broken, thinking, *it is all too grand and glorious for a girl like me!* She caught a glimpse of her reflection in the squeaky-clean glass of the display case and saw her hair was escaping her bun into ringlets, curling tightly in the August humidity. *My efforts to maintain a neat coiffure, all in vain,* she lamented to herself.

Clutching the sleeping Emma, Nellie looked around with a sudden bashful lack of self-assurance, assessing the fashion of the women clustered around the spectacular display. Much to her relief, her attire withstood this comparison. Many of the other coifs in view were now sporting clusters of weather enhanced curls, and the multi-tiered ruffle of the skirt of her dress was similar to the multi-tiered ruffle of the jacket worn by the woman beside her. *Praise the Lord, I do not appear a country bumpkin! Mercy, Mutter was correct — I did not err, and am certainly not overdressed in my lace-trimmed cambric. In fact, I must concede, I blend rather nicely with other well-heeled ladies.*

Self-confidence renewed, Nellie smiled and walked with a spring in her step as they wandered to and from amazing displays and made their way down the hall.

"Pray tell, now who needs to be lured away from a clever casket?" Nellie laughed, after twenty minutes of viewing the Colt revolver display. Obadiah opened his mouth to protest but Nellie laughed again. "I am fully cognizant of the ingenuity of the arrangement of the firearms in the pattern of a coat of arms. It is cunning. Moreover, I can see the superior workmanship and finish of the patented and improved pistols. Howsoever, our patient Emma has fussed repeatedly in the last five minutes, a sure sign she is hungry, and I recall a wise man very recently proclaiming that twenty minutes was the upward limit for gawking at any particular display.

"While I concede, the ingenuity and theatrical showmanship of the novel displays are every bit as captivating as the modern inventions they showcase, we must pause and attend to some basic comforts." Nellie took him by the elbow and pulled him away.

"Let us first take a peek into the hall of machines," said Obadiah, trying to take Nellie's arm to lead her.

"Obadiah, our priority needs be attending to the care and feeding of the baby." Cornelia tried the direct approach. Obadiah frowned at her. She pulled at her stray hair, and shuffled her tired feet, resolute to stand her ground.

Obadiah smiled. "I would not disdain a bit of repast myself. You are wise; the Hall of Machines can wait. Come, let us visit the refreshment rooms inside the palace. We can rest our weary feet and enjoy an inexpensive treat of some oysters."

"Are their saloons genteel enough for a lady and a baby?" fretted Nellie.

"I have it on the best authority that the culinary delicacies, offered in the parlor-like settings, are an important part of a lady's exhibition experience." Obadiah winked at her. "We would not want to miss the opportunity for some ice cream and soda water, would we?"

Gratefully, Nellie allowed Obadiah to take Emma from her tired arms and lead her to the refreshment parlor.

Renewed by their oysters and refreshed by their ice cream and soda, the spring returned to Nellie's step and they turned to the Hall of Machinery.

The flamboyant colors of a woman's sleeves, fluttering around a strange machine on top of a high pavilion, caught her eye. The material of the sleeves on the woman's exquisitely tailored dress fanned out over the edge of the machine, revealing an intricate pattern of colorful strips of fabric. As if pulled by a magnet, Nellie was drawn to the exotic colors.

Upon her approach, the barker shouted, "Observe the Singer machine for sewing, the ultimate labor-saving device! Step right up, get a closer look!"

Obadiah crowded closer to the machine, right alongside Nellie.

"This entire exposition is a showcase of one improvement after another," Obadiah said in a low voice to her, as they watched the woman sew a whole row of stitches in less than a minute.

"Most of these inventions originate in the United States," Nellie replied. "Our nation's showcase documents its leadership in technological ingenuity." Nellie could not take her eyes off the sewing machine. *Imagine the hours saved, sewing a whole seam of fine stitches in less time than it often takes to thread a needle!* "The wonder!" she exclaimed.

"Mark well my words, within the decade these efficient, timesaving devices will be household items," said Obadiah.

People thronging the middle of the hallway between the exhibits suddenly parted. An odd contraption rolled past them as the crowd 'oohed' and 'aahed.'

"Mercy, what in tarnation is that?" Nellie blurted.

Obadiah frowned at her outburst. But a female voice behind Nellie said, "Sakes alive 'tis a quadracycle velocipede—an improvement on the Dandy Horse."

Nellie knew that bossy tone. She whirled around to see her sister Agnes and brother-in-law Armistead craning their necks to see the disappearing contraption. Corporal Armistead Long's head snapped towards them, with military briskness, as the vehicle made its way back in their direction. It seemed he and his wife could not take their eyes off the contraption.

At the surprise encounter, the four exchanged greetings.

"Are not these Dandy Horses usually two-wheeled?" asked Nellie.

"That is the clever part," said Armistead, searching through the crowd for another glimpse of the vehicle. "Not only has this inventor made the two-wheeled contraption more stable with the addition of two smaller wheels, but he also added a pedal mechanism to make the wheels turn, rather than necessitating the rider's feet pushing off the ground."

"It rather resembles a carriage without horses. The contraption is much improved by these additions," said Nellie.

"Perhaps we might purchase one?" Armistead proposed in a jovial tone that was quite a contrast to his soldierly bearing. "It might be just the curiosity we need to become the talk of Chicago!"

Chicago? Nellie echoed in her thoughts, confused.

Agnes's laugh contained a scornful edge, "Sakes alive! We shall be the laughingstock, railroaded out of that frontier town before we are even settled."

"What ever is making you adopt such a cross tone with your lighthearted husband?" whispered Nellie, trying to prevent a scene.

"Has *Mutter* not broadcast our news? We are scheduled to depart for the West—the wild frontier—within the month," harrumphed Agnes. "My dread of this impending disaster quite overwhelms my delicate constitution. It casts a blight upon my life. It hinders my enjoyment of this fine Fair."

"Take heart now, Agnes," said Armistead mildly. "Chicago hardly deserves the moniker 'frontier', these days. The latest Army reports claim there are upwards of five thousand citizens spread around the mighty Lake Michigan."

"Pshaw, call it a muddy swamp then, certainly," said Agnes, not placated for a second.

"There is talk of raising the streets above the mud, and then this little contraption might come in handy. We surely would be the talk of the town," Armistead replied in an even tone.

Mercy, I am in the novel position of pitying my cantankerous sister Agnes. Imagine having to follow one's husband to the far corners of this land, so far from the amenities of civilization. She handed baby Emma to Obadiah and took her sister's hand.

"Pshaw. Imagine having to raise a family of two boys in a one horse, uncivilized, cowpoke of a town," said Agnes, tears welling in her eyes.

"Not so," cried Armistead, rising to the bait. "In 1840 Chicago was the 92nd most populous city in the United States."

"As Mr. Wright has been known to declare: I rest my case," said Agnes, folding her arms across her chest.

Nellie and Obadiah exchanged glances as Obadiah handed Emma back to her. "Armistead's fact does damn his argument with faint praise," whispered Nellie.

"If you will allow me to continue my dear," said Armistead through gritted teeth. "The city is so favorably located, is blessed with so many natural and modern advantages, it is now the ninth most populous city in our country."

Agnes sniffed. "It is still an outpost."

Armistead answered, "With canal systems and the steam locomotive connecting it both East and West, the natural beauty of Lake Michigan, the telegraph... the benefits of the location are quite extensive."

"We are blessed with all those attributes here. Moreover, we have a cultured society. What of music, the arts, the theater? One could not stretch the imagination far enough to suppose anything similar in a town in the middle of nowhere," sniffed Agnes.

Armistead planted his feet, adopting an 'at ease' position. He enlightened his in-laws, "I have received my orders. As an officer of the Army Corps of Engineers I shall review the feasibility of constructing a Toledo to Chicago water passage. Now, my predecessors already dug the Clinton-Kalamazoo canal ditch, but I must assess the viability of reviving and extending this conduit."

Nellie patted little Emma and fiddled with a stray curl. Agnes sniffed.

Nellie cleared her throat and said, "Agnes, you shall storm that town and assume the task of civilizing it." She gave an emphatic nod of her head. "Armistead counsels Chicago is quite the up-and-coming city. You can imbue its citizens with a renewed sense of the fine arts. After all, it is just a float up the Missouri River from the well-established, sophisticated city of New Orleans. You, my dear sister, shall bring Chicago culture."

Encouraged by the support, Armistead said, "Agnes, mark my words. Within a year's time I shall engineer a canal system enabling your whole family to visit with a mere weeklong journey." With this attempt at reassuring his wife, Armistead spun her around and tried to hug her. Agnes submitted to the hug, but not from love, only to avoid making a scene.

Cornelia pulled her sister forward and they walked closer to the velocipede exhibit to examine the vehicle.

"Armistead, inquire as to the expense of this contraption," Cornelia directed. "Agnes, you *shall* wear the mantle 'standard bearer' of our well-bred, sophisticated way of life here in New York. Take comfort in this technology we see amassed around us. Allow it to ease your disquiet. When the entirety of this ingenuity and these time-saving devices are incorporated into our daily lives, it *will* be possible to sail the vast distance to Chicago from New York and I shall surely come a-calling!"

Agnes did not look any happier.

Cornelia tried a different tack. "Anyone for a stop at any one of the fine saloons in and around this palace for a short rest and some refreshing sarsaparilla?" Agnes still looked more dour than usual.

"How about oysters?" Nellie asked, trying again to cheer her sister, this time with the promise of her favorite food. She switched Emma to her other arm and linked her elbow into her sister's. "Come let us discourse on other topics and enjoy this unexpected gift of sharing the marvels of this Exposition together."

The gentlemen followed them to the oyster bar, already deep in their own conversation about the underhanded maneuvers of the defense attorneys in the trial of the officers of the *Henry Clay*.

CHAPTER 13
An Innocent Man

Sing Sing, New York, November 1853

Obadiah put down his fork, frowning at his plate still half full of food. Out of the corner of her eye she saw him put his elbows on the table, rest his head on his hands, and slump forward.

Nellie looked up from the ground carrots and broth she stirred as she fed Emma. *How uncharacteristic — such poor table manners, and a dejected air.*

"My dear Mr. Wright, what causes a distress so deep it obliterates a gentleman's ability to civilly partake in his fine, nighttime repast?" she asked, trying to joke him out of his mood.

Not altering his position in the least, Obadiah said, "The jury returned a verdict today in the trial of *The United States versus Collyer, Tallman, Germain, Hubbard, Jessup, and Elmendorf.*"

Nellie gave a sharp intake of breath and sat up straighter, upsetting Emma's puréed carrots. She ignored the fact that Emma now splashed her hands in her food and waited for Obadiah to continue.

"They deliberated for less than thirty minutes over the accountability of the principles of the *Henry Clay* disaster," he said, still looking down at the table.

Nellie waited.

"Hopping horse feathers, the defense attorneys employed brilliant strategies." Obadiah banged his hand on the table. Emma kept squishing her carrots, unperturbed. "They invented all kinds of fanciful defenses — Collyer was not at the helm, the aft of the ship where the passengers were trapped after being instructed to go there, *could* be safer if there was a danger of the smokestack falling, the shaking of the boat was due solely to the ebb tide and the southerly breeze creating rough water...." Obadiah put his head in his hands.

"Then I take it the verdict was *not guilty?*" asked Nellie, laying her hand on Obadiah's.

He sighed. "It was the inevitable conclusion, based on Judge Ingersoll's direction to the jury. Ingersoll had obviously prejudiced himself and predetermined there was not enough evidence to convict these men of manslaughter."

"But how is that possible? The boat traveled at an unsafe rate of speed, someone jimmied open the steam engine's safety valve, the officers admitted they engaged in racing the *Armenia*, passengers pleaded for caution and warned the officers of impending disaster, there were no fire buckets, there was no line thrown, no direction from the crew, no small boats dispatched...." Nellie slumped back in her chair. Oblivious to Emma's antics, Nellie sat with her mouth open in disbelief at the verdict as the baby smeared her carrots all over the table and the sides of her high chair.

"The jury had to consider the charge of whether the defendants' misconduct, negligence, or inattention to their duty, destroyed the life of any person on board," said Obadiah.

"Most assuredly it did! The crew neglected to release steam at each landing, as required by law," said Nellie. "The steam pressure Patrick recalled seeing, and the newspapers listed, generated by over-stoking their fire, well exceeded the certified amount approved for the vessel."

"How could you know the amount stated on the certificate?" asked Obadiah.

"I recall—I saw the certificate myself!"

"How in tarnation?" Now Obadiah's mouth gaped open.

"I spent time chasing Perpetua around the ladies' cabin. At one point, I leaned against the wall to catch my breath, and avoid *Mutter's* stares of reprobation, and noticed the certificate, hung in its usual place, on the right-hand side of the ladies' parlor. Pshaw, there was a plethora of potential witnesses as to the buildup of steam. Were none of them called? Certainly, Papa could have testified as to the steam pressure."

"The defense lawyers made mince-meat out of most of the witnesses called. They were merciless. They not only attacked the credibility of the witnesses, they criticized and chastised each witness for his response to the disaster. Passenger John H. Gourlie, who testified that none of the accused helped rescue any passengers, was asked why *he* stayed on the beach assisting victims, rather than saving fellow passengers drowning in the water. Gourlie replied, 'I did what humanity required'. Defense Attorney McMahon sneered, 'Humanity, I suppose, did not require you to wet your feet.'"

Nellie winced in empathy for the witness who was forced in the name of justice to relive the disaster and testify truthfully as to specifics, only to be treated so caustically.

Obadiah shook his head. "Make no mistake, prosecutors exhibited flashes of brilliance as well, establishing many key facts which pointed to the defendant's culpability. Passenger James F. DePeyster testified after the 'alarm of fire' was given, the only crewmember he saw during the whole disaster was the man forbidding passengers to go forward on the ship. If the crew had done their duty, he swore, 'they could have escaped as I did.' The DePeyster name is so well established around these parts... blazes! It goes back to the Dutch settlers... the defense did not dare harass him. Howsoever, most of the prosecution's witnesses were attacked, even if just to prove, in the long amount of time since the Inquest, their memories had become vaguer, their eyesight faultier and their ability to identify the defendants more unreliable."

Obadiah shook his head, and his shoulders sank as if the whole burden of the disaster pressed them downward. "The attorneys for the prosecution never stooped to conquer. No foul play sullied their cross examinations. They sought the truth from the defendants, set the bar high, and the defense never rose to meet that standard."

Obadiah remained silent for a moment. *He takes this unfavorable verdict to heart.* Nellie's mind raced, seeking words of consolation, but she could not summon any. She too felt bereft at the injustice of the verdict.

"Passenger Lloyd Minturn is another example—both threatened *and* insulted by defense attorneys." Obadiah raised his head and sketched more details of his grievances with the trial. "After giving testimony that incriminated the defendants on several key points, the defense attorney told Minturn, 'Oh, yes, you are very brave when there is no danger.' Often, it appeared the witnesses were on trial rather than the officers of the ship. I am quite certain this tactic confused the jury. Your father fared better than most, but unfortunately, his testimony on the excessive amount of steam pressure was stricken from the record, as the defense objected that your father had not been established as an expert qualified to comment on the correct amount of pressure required," said Obadiah.

He sighed again. "I suppose the judge is right—the evidence was perhaps not strong enough to prove the causality of their actions. And perhaps, as Judge Ingersoll said on more than one occasion, those accused *have* already suffered huge financial loss, loss of reputation, and public scorn. What is to be gained by sentencing them all to ten years of hard labor?"

"They would have landed right back in Sing Sing where they belong—just a different address," said Nellie.

Obadiah raised an eyebrow in question.

"At Sing Sing Prison," she said, looking at him askance. *'Tis not like Obadiah to miss such an obvious joke. His anger at this inequity overwhelms him.*

Emma squealed in delight. Nellie glanced down at her baby.

"Tarnation!" she exclaimed, catching Emma's hands, preventing the baby from smashing the last bit of puree on the table and sending more sticky mush into the air.

She looked up at Obadiah, seeking his aid, or a towel, or something.

His eyebrows knit in anger, he said, "What sloth is this, enabling our daughter's slovenly mess?"

Nellie dropped Emma's hands in surprise at his hostile reaction. *Mercy, I know full well he detests sticky untidiness, but he must not vent his ill humor on our innocent child!* "I-I beg your pardon. I fear my distress at your news so thoroughly overcame me...."

Thwat! Hands liberated, Emma retrieved some carrot mush from the side of her chair and threw it at Nellie. It smacked her in the face.

Obadiah burst out laughing.

Thank you Lord, she did not throw it at Obadiah. He certainly would not find any amusement in being the receiving end of that prank. She joined his laughter and picked up her messy baby, smothering her with kisses, making herself as carrot smeared as her daughter. *You are the gift of joy, my precious daughter.*

She looked at Obadiah, who was frowning again. "Cornelia Rose, now you are both quite revolting and your person appears quite a repulsive muddle."

"My apron was already smeared, and my face is washable," replied Cornelia. "How very distraught you must indeed be, to call this little, cherubic face revolting, no matter in what it is smeared."

Obadiah looked at them both and his face softened.

"Let us thank God again we were spared the fate of so many of our fellow passengers on the *Henry Clay*," she said. "Moreover, since our judicial system has failed us, let us take heart that the legislative branch of our government, at least, has responded with several pieces of new legislation to ensure this type of disaster never again occurs."

Obadiah still looked doubtful. "Mayhap there is a possibility of appeal," he said.

"In the meantime, I for one, shall delight in our little vaudevillian," Nellie said, hugging Emma tight. Emma cooed with happiness and brushed her sticky hands against Nellie's hair as she reached her arms around Nellie's neck and returned her mother's hug.

Obadiah shook his head.

"My hair is also washable," said Nellie with a smile and a shrug. *Shouldering the burden of all the washing in the world is a mere pittance to pay for my first real embrace from my baby.*

CHAPTER 14
Top of the World

New York City, January 1854

I am standing atop The Latting Observatory. Looking down from the wooden tower. I am perched upon the tallest building in the world! Nellie drew in her breath and felt her stomach do a weird flip-flop. *Tarnation, I must avoid looking directly down. Could I be acrophobic? I suppose I have never experienced elevation quite this high. The top of the Croton Distributing Reservoir seems a tremendous distance below me. I can see across the river, deep into the bucolic beauty of New Jersey. OOOOO.* Nellie felt a wave of dizziness. Her one free hand shot out and clutched at the railing.

"Cornelia, you must be careful — do not approach the edge of the viewing platform," cautioned Obadiah.

"Of course. I shall view from behind the safety of this telescope." Nellie gave a nod, and clasped Emma tighter, stepping back. *This is far superior. I still thrill at the bird's eye view, but avoid the wooziness engendered by the extreme height.* "Pshaw, to think, I imagined I floated in the clouds when we merely stood atop the Murray Hill Reservoir." Nellie giggled to Obadiah.

"I confess, the view does quite take my breath away," Obadiah agreed. "In spite of increasing anticipation as we labored the three-hundred-foot ascent to the top platform of the structure, the vista astounds me. The more fatigued I became, the more determined I grew that the view should be worth the strenuous effort. Still, my enormous expectations did not prepare me for the wonderful panorama that seems to afford a view sixty miles away. There is not a finer, farther view anywhere in the world." Obadiah's head swiveled around, owl-like, as he spoke.

"Unsurpassed, even in London, The Great Wren, or Paris, The City of Light," Nellie agreed, her gaze sweeping to the far reaches of the horizon and then back down on the streets below. *But not directly below,* Nellie cautioned herself, as a wave of nausea threatened again the moment her eyes glanced straight down. "The vast stretches of land are astounding!" she exclaimed. "What a tremendous contrast the grandeur and stillness of nature makes to the teeming human hive crowded in the apiary of streets below."

"Verily," said Obadiah. "The view from the top of the Great Pyramid of Giza holds no candle in comparison to this spectacle." They stood, arm in arm, with Nellie's other arm wrapped around Emma, transfixed, as if memorizing every detail of the scene, from directly below them, to far off in the distance.

At last Obadiah said, "While I am loath to leave this view, I do believe the taxing climb has hastened my digestion. I am quite desirous of a morsel or two. What say you to an early luncheon?"

"I confess an invigorated appetite as well," admitted Cornelia. "But I am averse to averting my eyes from this marvelous sight."

"I agree," said Obadiah. "Therefore, I propose we lunch at the saloon on the middle platform, an impressive 225 feet above street level. Thus, we can return to the peak for another peek before our descent from the heavens to the street."

Nellie giggled at his pun and rhyme in happy agreement. Obadiah kept a firm hand on her arm, supporting her and steering her as they began their descent. "I thought I read a steam elevator was designed for this structure, so that those less hardy could still partake of the view," Nellie said over her shoulder as she carefully placed her feet on the narrow stairs.

"I read that in the *Tribune* as well," confirmed Obadiah, now walking in front of her so he could better lead her down the winding staircase. "But think on it—to date the tallest elevator system can only climb 75 feet. To reach the entire 315-foot zenith of this tower would necessitate installation of several sets of elevators."

"Mayhap Otis' new braking system shall inspire creation of elevators with greater height capacity," replied Nellie to the back of Obadiah's head as they continued down the stairs. She smiled at him as they lingered at a landing. "On second thought, if the steam elevator made the climb for the visitor, there would be no need for the many resting landings, nor any of the pushcarts of enticing merchandise. We must keep in mind, the building was designed not for its architectural beauty but for its commercial purposes."

In short order, the maître d'hôtel seated them at a table, and scurried away to retrieve an appetizer of oysters. Nellie smiled at

Obadiah, watching him hug Emma and look out the large windows at the view from this height. She whispered, "I thank the Lord for all his kindness. I thought my joy would fill the world when we stood on Coney Island looking at the sea. Yet, here we are, two years later, even more rapturous for the miracle of Emma."

Obadiah's eyes glinted with tears as he grasped her hand across the table and drew it to his heart. "My love, my heart responds with an emphatic 'amen'. You are my joy. Moreover, now we are a family. Could any man want more?

"As a small token of my great, ineffable happiness, I present you with a trinket, selected specially to mark the occasion of our second anniversary and the beginning of our blessed little family. Our family will be the indestructible nucleus of our long lives together."

Nellie took the little blue box, noticing the mark of "Tiffany & Co." stamped upon it. She opened it to see a lustrous seed pearl bracelet ensconced in cloudlike white tissue paper.

"Obadiah," she said in a breathy voice. "This is utterly exquisite. Mercy, I recognize it as the bracelet I coveted on display at the Exposition. I am quite taken aback by your extravagance."

"It matches your necklace—my gift on the day we exchanged matrimonial vows." Obadiah beamed.

"How clever of you, my dear Mr. Wright." Nellie laughed. She clasped the bracelet around her slender wrist and admired the fine craftsmanship and the perfectly formed pearls. "Mr. Charles Lewis Tiffany has quite outdone himself. This ornament deserves its acclaim as an award-winning piece of art."

"You noticed it won an award at the Fair," observed Obadiah. "How clever of my reward of a wife!"

Nellie smiled. Obadiah waggled his finger at her and teased, "Although you did spend a fair amount of time hovering over that casket. If you hadn't noticed the accolades for this jewelry, I might have inferred a diminution of your acumen."

After a sumptuous lunch, they once more mounted the heights of the tower and spent another long while drinking in the view, arm in arm while Emma napped peacefully on Cornelia's shoulder.

After they had circled the viewing platform for the third time, and again looked through each of the six telescopes, Cornelia looked down on the Crystal Palace and noticed there was no line of people waiting for entry to the Fair. "We simply must have another look at the marvelous displays in the Exhibition of the Industries of All Nations. As you will recall, the time to view the entries from France or England eluded us; the only in-depth exhibits we saw were from Denmark and Canada."

"The wisdom in paying the entire entry fee for only an afternoon visit escapes me. Think on it. Fifty cents is often the lion's share of a day's wages. Some poor chaps fail to earn even half that in an entire day's work." Obadiah shook his head.

"No, no. We must defer entrance to another day when we have more time. It is foolhardy to pay full price for a half-day admission. Fifty cents saved is fifty cents earned. Furthermore, in this case, two admissions are a dollar saved," Obadiah concluded.

"Yes, Mr. Wright, but Emma's entrance is free, and the low attendance in the afternoon shall facilitate ease of exploration. We may well view more than we could that entire first day, when our movement was often impeded by the crowd." Cornelia was ever reluctant to question Obadiah's decisions, preferences, or opinions. *But the Fair beckoned, from right across the street!* Her tug of the stray strand of hair, perpetually escaping the cluster of curls at the nape of her neck, evidenced her determination to plead her cause.

She said nothing as they wound around and around down the stairway, all the way to the street.

When they were again outside, looking at the entrance to the Fair, she said, "We shall save the transportation costs of another trip into The City if we attend the Fair now, whilst we stand at its front entrance."

Obadiah hesitated. Cornelia stretched her neck and leaned close enough to his ear to kiss him. Obadiah's mouth softened in anticipation. But instead she whispered, "Let us not quarrel over husbandry. My omnipotent love for you makes my heart soar to the heavens every day I dwell with you. Let not our difference of opinion check its flight."

Obadiah blinked, looking hurt. She stood on her tiptoes and gave him a soft, sensuous kiss on the cheek. She stepped back.

Obadiah cleared his throat, looking down at her, and their baby nestled in her arms. "Of course. Howsoever, sometimes we must draw that veil of love aside and get down to brass tacks." Nellie frowned, *Cast our love aside? To better enable acrimonious argument? But our love should always be foremost in our minds to sidestep the confrontation.*

Obadiah gave her a perfunctory peck on her cheek. "Parsimony shall never be your virtue," Obadiah proclaimed, stepping back.

He looked as if he were to begin a lecture on the value of money, when suddenly Anastasia and Zetus distinguished themselves from the small group of people purchasing tickets.

"Nellie, how fortuitous to find you here," Anastasia called out, rushing over and embracing her sister.

"Equally fortuitous for me!" exclaimed Nellie. *At the precise time I crave a smiling, loving face.*

Obadiah shook Zetus' hand. "Neighbor. Is it not enough that we live across the street from you newlyweds? Must we cross paths with you here as well?"

Cornelia and Anastasia looked at each other, miffed.

Hot words rose to Cornelia's mouth. *I must counteract Obadiah's rudeness,* "The talk is of nothing but the Crystal Palace Exhibition! We are all entitled...." But both men broke out in huge guffaws, apparently enjoying the same sense of humor.

"Evidently, we cannot view the phenomena of modern innovation without accompaniment by some member of your family or another," growled Obadiah, but his laughing eyes betrayed his jest.

"Are we not most blessed with good fortune—living in this grand city, full of economic promise and the wonders of convenience, surrounded by a large, loving family?" said Nellie.

"Stasia," she said, taking her sister's hand. "Let the men purchase our tickets, we women...." Nellie hugged the sleeping Emma tighter in her arms. "...shall walk ahead. Thus, when we gain entry we shall make a beeline for the most dazzling of all treasuries at the fair, Phalon's Bowery of Perfume."

Anastasia giggled. "Once we are, quite literally, smelling like roses, we shall feast our eyes again on Phalon's hanging bowers and garlands of flowers *and* ogle the gold-capped glass wonders dubbed flasks of toilette water. Properly fêted, we shall float like princesses to Genin's fashion bazaar to marvel at the ready-made creations of the latest fashion in women's dress. Merely turning within the display shall allow us to next peruse the darling baby furniture, for our princess-in-waiting." She kissed the little hand of Emma, lying on top of her bunting, as the baby slept on. She raised her head and looked at Nellie. "Come, sister, our agenda is set."

The men now exchanged looks. "Perhaps the Fair entrance fee will be best spent if we part ways with the fairer sex upon entry of the building," Obadiah said.

"Indubitably!" seconded Zetus. "The newest combine harvesters and cotton gins hold far more appeal to me than a bunch of fancy olfactory bottles filled with sinus irritating perfume. After all, we are obliged to tender *fifty cents* for our entrance, thus we must ensure we examine every gadget in the machine arcade to garner our money's worth."

Anastasia giggled. Nellie leaned her head in closer and whispered, "Two peas in a pod. Although I must admit, I am impressed with your husband's clever expansion of his lexicon. The new word gadget, from the French *gâchette*, meaning a lock mechanism, has only recently appeared in newspapers and heard in circulation only in the most learned of society."

"Truly, he is rather intelligent, just the right sentimentality for his professorial duties at Sing Sing's Vireum Academy. Howsoever, there is still a boyishness to his nature that is quite endearing." She called to the men. "Do not forget, the world's largest known alligator is exhibited somewhere inside. You gentlemen shall not likely want to neglect that curiosity, howsoever mesmerized by the mechanical contrivances you become," taunted Anastasia.

"You will first have to forcibly remove us from the thirty-one classes of exhibits from the United States Mineral Department," countered Obadiah with a warm laugh.

"Wonders never cease," laughed Cornelia. In a swirl of petticoats and bustles, the giggling ladies swept off to see the marvels of the modern world.

CHAPTER 15
Magic Time

Sing Sing, New York, February 1855

"Wonderful! The site for this year's Sisters of Charity Orphan Aid Ball is the Crystal Palace," exclaimed Nellie, looking up from a beautiful, embossed invitation. "How I have longed to return to that fairytale place the renowned poet Walt Whitman called '...Loftier, fairer, ampler than any yet, Earth's modern wonder, History's Seven out stripping...' in his *Song of The Exposition*."

"What date is the event?" inquired Obadiah.

"In a fortnight's time, on the twentieth of February," Nellie replied, and her face twisted into a wry grimace.

Putting his hand on her shoulder in a gentle restraint, Obadiah said, "I do believe Midwife Rafferty advised extensive travel should be curtailed after this week. The time of your confinement is too near; I am afraid we shall have to decline."

"But the grand charity soiree is held in The City, not in the midst of the wilderness. There shall be no dearth of aid, no lack of resources if suddenly my confinement were to end," exclaimed Nellie. She snapped her mouth shut and grit her teeth.

"Why you wish to socialize with a bunch of businessmen and their valetudinarian wives in the first place, I cannot fathom," Obadiah countered, his head back behind the evening *Republican* newspaper.

"Hypochondriac wives are constantly seeking medical remedies from midwives," retorted Nellie. "I give consultations, earn their confidence, and attain them as my best patients."

Obadiah's temper flared. "Your words force me to infer you find my income lacking and must supplement your household allowance by selling your concoctions of eye of newt and devil's claw!"

Nellie's eyes flashed in return. "At last, you reveal your true opinion of my scientific knowledge."

Obadiah laughed and drew her into his arms, "I knew that would raise your dander." Nellie looked surprised, but still hurt. "My jab was in jest, as revenge for the evident insufficiency of my income, my sweet Rose."

Nellie pulled her lips up in a tight smile, in spite of her anger. Once again, Obadiah had disarmed her and distracted her from the main topic.

"If you merely jest, then you recognize my qualifications for determining my own state of being." Her eyes were set in determination. She tugged on a strand of her hair. "I believe I am in a superior position to discern whether it will be safe to travel at the time of the Ball."

Obadiah took a long look at her, and then squeezed her tighter in his arms. "That determination in your jawline, that set of your face is all too familiar to me," he said softly. "I suppose at this juncture, I have acquired enough wisdom to refrain from contradicting. You possess the knowledge of midwifery; if you think it is safe to stray so far from your home and the womenfolk you know when this birth is imminent, I shall defer to your judgment."

Nellie opened her mouth to speak, but he continued. "Do not permit this isolated incident to spawn a big head. I shall defer to your judgment in this single, solitary, arena *only.*" He sat back down, picked up his newspaper, threw back his head and laughed again. Shaking out the paper's creases, he disappeared behind the news again.

Even though Nellie was quite certain he was dead serious about this last statement, she laughed it off and tried to make the last word on the subject positive. "Then we shall attend the ball for this most worthy charity and enjoy ourselves to the fullest."

"What arrangements shall you make for Emma's care?" asked Obadiah, flicking down a corner of the newsprint to see her face.

Nellie blushed. *Tarnation, I had not considered....* "Why I can leave her with...." Nellie hesitated. Her mother and sisters had all been invited; who would stay with the children? Inspiration struck. "We shall make a grand adventure. The whole family shall spend the night in The City and all the cousins can keep each other company while the adults attend the ball. Surely Theodora is old enough now to shoulder some responsibility, along with the Long's nanny. I'll wear my new hat from John Genin, the award-winning milliner who displayed at the Exhibition. Mercy me! Recalling the Exhibition, the *raison d'être* for the existence of the Crystal Palace, brings to mind a thought of poor Mr. Horace Greeley." This time Cornelia distracted herself.

"Good 'Old Honesty' himself?" asked Obadiah with a wry face. "Greeley proves himself a pillar of morality; the only one of those scallywags financing and promoting the Industrial Exhibition that stood by his deeds and offered accountability to the Fair's participating displayers."

Nellie stamped her foot. "Tarnation, those hornswoggling Frenchmen tricked him into coming to France to make 'repairs' for some minor damage to an exhibitor's displays. What did his honesty gain him? Incarceration in a France jail for lack of payment of some exhibitor's alleged losses!"

"Spoken like a true Philadelphia Lawyer, my Rose." Obadiah smiled in appreciation of Cornelia's passionate defense of one of their heroes.

"You don't see that humbug, Phineas T. Barnum making reparation for anyone's losses, much less than bearing imprisonment. Mercy, Mr. Greeley suffers wrongful imprisonment, simply for accepting responsibility. Through all his undertakings his honor and principles shine. How utterly unjust, the treatment of this noble man!" Nellie wrung her hands in compassion and frustration.

"Mark my words," consoled Obadiah with a quick hug. "Even the French cannot keep our good man down. Once again, Greeley's actions shout his integrity, obviating the necessity for words. Horace Greeley will return, just as honest but more powerful and effective than ever. By gum, I foresee him one day standing for the highest office of our country."

"Truly Obadiah—Mr. Horace Greeley, our President?" asked Nellie with wide eyes.

"His is the voice of reason and morality. Persuasive and influential, 'Old Uncle Horace' stands out as a bona fide leader," Obadiah replied.

Two days before the ball, as Nellie, her sisters, and her friends made final alterations to their newly tailored dresses, she looked out the window and saw a few snowflakes falling.

By the time Obadiah got home for his noontime dinner, a fair coating blanketed the landscape, muffling sounds, and enchanting the view.

The impending storm held no threat for Nellie. She already knew she would miss the Crystal Palace and the fancy charity soiree tomorrow. That message had come from her queasy stomach, roiling from sporadic contractions.

"Obadiah, what say you to a grand adventure at my mother's house for the duration of the snowstorm? I judge it will be quite the tempest."

"Do your midwifery skills also include weather forecasting?" Obadiah joked. But Nellie could see he gleaned her meaning. As Obadiah ate his meal with Emma giggling and nibbling too, Nellie packed some supplies and asked their stable boy to bring around the carriage.

"May we postpone our trip to the Entwhistles' until this evening? Some research requires my immediate attention for a new case before Judge Urmy."

Nellie shook her head no.

Obadiah raised his eyebrows. "At the very least, permit me a foray to Barlow Brother's Hardware store for a sturdier shovel. I must arm myself or lose the battle of a clear path during these perpetual snow storms."

"I fear not," said Nellie, rubbing her protruding abdomen and looking at the rapidly accumulating snow with apprehension. Obadiah shook his head and sauntered to their bedroom to gather some clothing. Nellie tapped her foot, nervous about the storm and, anticipating baby number two might make a more rapid appearance than Emma had, wondered when she should send for Midwife Rafferty.

Why does our horse's step appear so tentative? Nellie looked at Obadiah, wiping snow from his eyes at frequent intervals, clutching the reins and leaning his head over the edge of their buggy to stare ahead. Nellie wrapped the blanket around Emma tighter and fretted, *The trip across Sing Sing may already be too arduous! I prithee Lord, may the full force of the storm remain at bay until we arrive safely at Mutter and Papa's house.*

The swirling snow impeded visibility. The dark cloud of the storm sat low on the town, obliterating its usual glow from the gas-lit streetlights. The trip usually took less than ten minutes by carriage. In fact, it often seemed more expedient to walk, rather than take the time to harness the horse and tether it to the buggy. But not this afternoon. Pedestrians, heads bent low, made no headway in the gale-force wind, and the Wrights' carriage slipped and slid all over the road.

Within the hour, this road will only be navigable by sleigh.

By the time they reached the house, the snow was coming as thickly and quickly as Nellie's contractions.

The Entwhistle valet helped them unload under the cover of the carriage entrance canopy.

Gertrude Entwhistle appeared at the door. "To what do we owe the pleasure...?" she broke off when she saw Cornelia's face. "Emma, *meine kleines Mädchen, komt zu Oma.* Come to your Grandmama, my little girl. I shall take your cloak, and bring you to the nursery, where your cousins are already playing."

"*Oma,* hello!" Emma said and skipped up the stairs to her grandmother.

Mrs. Entwhistle turned to Nellie, struggling to lug a frozen basket of laundry into the house. "*Ach du Liebe,* let the men handle this."

"Do not fuss *Mutter,*" said Nellie, suddenly feeling as if she had jumped the gun on the immediacy of her baby's arrival. "We are only here seeking shelter from the storm in a house equipped with legendary laundry kettles and a drying room. I must ensure a proper supply of clean linens will be at the ready when I feel the onset of true labor."

"Your instinct to travel in advance of this blizzard shall prove both sagacious and prudent. Your presence upon my doorstep already allays my fear that my new grandchild would appear in this world before I could arrive to assist." Gertrude Entwhistle folded Nellie into her arms and scrutinized her daughter's face. "But there will be no use of my laundry room."

Nellie pulled back from her mother's embrace in surprise.

"Daughter, the second child arrives more swiftly than the first, as the path has already been prepared." Mrs. Entwhistle took another hard look at Cornelia and whispered, "*Gott im Himmel, raus mit du.* God in Heaven, we must make haste, we must prepare the birthing chamber immediately."

"Tarnation, I should have requested the midwife meet me here."

"Matthias," Cornelia called. "Send word right now to Midwife Rafferty. She must not delay, but come forthwith."

Mrs. Entwhistle shook her head. "I am afraid we have missed our opportunity. The roads, as you yourself attested, are treacherous.

Matthias shall be hard-pressed to attain the Rafferty residence in this storm, much less than be able to bring the midwife back."

"Tarnation. We must send for her! It is nigh impossible to diagnose myself. Lord have mercy, what shall we do if the midwife cannot get here in time?" gasped Nellie, feeling another contraction, much stronger than the previous ones.

"Your sisters and I are experienced and prepared," said Mrs. Entwhistle. "Fret not you are in the bosom of your family."

Just five short hours later, Obadiah and Emma were invited to the room to meet the newest member of the family, Elizabeth Violet. Emma's solemn eyes took in the squalling red creature Nellie held. She looked at her mother with doubt. "Baby not happy," she said.

Obadiah laughed as Nellie giggled. Obadiah scooped the big sister into his arms and they both sat down on the bed next to Nellie and the baby. "Come to your mama," whispered Nellie. "Together, we shall welcome your new sister."

Obediently, Emma crawled into her mother's outstretched arm and they both held the little baby. Nellie showed Emma how to rub the baby's tummy, and the infant soothed and stopped crying. "Success!" Nellie smiled. She handed the sleeping baby to Obadiah, who held her gingerly, gazing down at the tiny creature in wonder. Nellie wrapped Emma in her arms and buried her nose in her soft lavender-scented hair. "My wonder of an offspring," she whispered in her ear. "You never cease to bring me joy. I am so blessed to call you daughter."

Several hours later, Cornelia woke up from a nap at the baby's cry. They nursed for a bit, and then she grew restless. With the help of her mother, she crept down the stairs, following her new daughter in the arms of Mrs. Entwhistle.

The entire family, seated in the ballroom, paid rapt attention to a large sheet suspended over three of the floor-to-ceiling windows. A man standing behind the group worked a large lantern, pulling tins, cut with shapes, in and out. Actors danced and sang around the images projected on the sheet as a tall man boomed a story in a theatrical voice.

"*Was ist das?*" asked Nellie, as she sank into the first chair in the back of the group, wondering what she was seeing.

"*Ach du Liebe,* that is your father and his boyish enthusiasm for all things technologically novel," whispered her mother, sitting in the chair next to Nellie and handing her baby Elizabeth. "Our evening entertainment is a traveling Magic Lantern show. Your father used his connections to persuade the Magic Lantern Troupe to provide us a preview. And now they must be our overnight guests, as travel tonight remains impossible. The Olive Opera House will host this entertainment tomorrow night, if, of course, the storm has passed. As your father is on the board of directors of a charity raising money for a new Sing Sing hospital, we thought it only fitting we host the dress rehearsal of the Magic Lantern fundraiser performance."

"Since this beautiful baby prevented me from going to one Crystal Palace charity benefit, it seems only fitting I should be in a winter wonderland palace, privy to a preview of the entertainment for another." Nellie smiled.

"After the performance, you must ask your father for an explanation of the technique," whispered Mrs. Entwhistle. "It shall please him to no end. For weeks our dinner conversation has been focused on limelight, hand painted glass slides, and magical smoke effects in anticipation of this event. In fact, I am quite surprised that you have not already been regaled with the technical details of this 'magic'!" Mrs. Entwhistle laughed softly.

"Come to mention it, I *have* heard Papa discourse at length about this magical combination of technology and showmanship," Cornelia said, raising her whisper to normal conversation volume as her whole family burst into song along with the performers. She smiled. The sound of music filled her already happy heart with joy to the bursting point.

The performance engrossed the attention of Nellie's entire family so thoroughly, not even Emma or Obadiah had noticed her entrance into the room. They all sat watching the images projected on the sheets, paying rapt attention to the stories and laughing at the jokes.

Content to be a fringe participant in the comedy mixed with drama and song, Nellie quietly arranged her garments to let the newborn nurse and relaxed back into the chair, watching the antics of the light show through mostly closed eyes. Mrs. Entwhistle squeezed her hand. Nellie returned the squeeze, hoping her mother knew how much Nellie loved and appreciated her. Nellie smiled her gratitude. *The Lord is good; I am truly blessed.*

PART TWO

CHAPTER 16
Cornelia Street

Sing Sing, New York, August 1856

Nellie hummed and sang as she presided over the stove, listening to Emma 'read' to her baby sister. *I must sew Emma another book. She has quite mastered this one.... 'Twill not be much longer before baby Betsy learns to play with her big sister.*

Nellie clapped at Emma's dramatic conclusion to her reading. Opening the lid of her kettle, and adjusting the heat, Nellie crooned, "All around the cobbler's bench, the monkey chased the weasel." She turned around at a commotion: Emma ran around the baby's chair as Elizabeth squealed in delight. *I must capture our family's joy and wonder at this precise moment in time. I read the brilliant photographer, Mr. Matthew Brady, just opened his second portrait shop in The City, using the newest technology in photography to capture images. This modern invention is so far advanced from the painted picture, I have a mind to hire his services. I wonder if Papa could help me arrange a session as a special surprise for Obadiah? Our family, as we truly appear, commemorated forever, not in an old-fashioned painting, full of artistic interpretation, but in a tin daguerreotype or, far superior, a paper photographic portrait. Our two precious jewels, sweet Emma and that little character Betsy shall be captured for all eternity!*

Nellie glanced out the window over her kitchen water pump and basin, observing and absorbing the streets of her childhood she loved so well. *Red sky at night, sailor's delight,* she thought, savoring in the spectacular hues of red and pink streaming through the clouds hovering over the Hudson Highlands across the river. *Tomorrow shall be the perfect morning for a stroll through the woods at Croton Point. Betsy can practice her walking on the sandy beach and Emma can collect oyster shells from the big mounds left by the Sinct Sinct tribe. Mayhap we can start our visit to Lyndhurst Mansion for tea early by joining Mutter and Anastasia in their carriage for the drive. Mutter shall delight at the prospect of holding Elizabeth the entire journey. Emma will be tickled pink as well; I never did think such a fledgling would so adore the company of ladies at tea.*

"Cornelia, a thousand kisses if you can deduce the contents I bear in this appendage." Obadiah snuck up on her while she was feeding the children, wrapped one hand around her waist, and kissed her on top of her head. She tucked her vagrant hair into place and turned into his arms with a smile.

"Papa," shouted both girls in chorus. All the Wright women looked at him with big loving eyes.

"My ladies, now that I command your attention...." Obadiah stepped back, revealed a parcel in his hand, and strode grinning toward the potbellied stove. "I have an announcement to make: I purchased a wonderful new book, hot off the presses, which shall help us prepare for our journey."

"Journey? Whither do we fare?" Cornelia Rose was astounded.

Obadiah stuck out his right leg. Assuming a pose, he tucked his left hand into his lapel and looked off into the distance dreamily.

"Mercy, what is it, Papa? Do not tease so," begged Emma.

"Da da da?" Elizabeth seemed to ask too.

"Go West, young man, go West," announced Obadiah.

The young ladies looked at each other in confusion. Even Nellie found no clues in his dramatic proclamation helpful for solving the riddle.

"'Go West, young man and grow up with the country?' Does not this oft quoted utterance ring a bell?" Obadiah burst out laughing at Nellie's puzzled look. "Have I stupefied thee into silence? It is an incitement to action from our finest of editors in the most accurate of newspapers, 'Old Honesty' himself. We embark upon a journey West, my ladies, as our editor and good neighbor, Horace Greeley has urged."

Nellie blinked back tears as Emma ran giggling into her father's arms.

"Where is my 'Huzzah'?" teased Obadiah gently, looking at her from the joyous hugging of two squirming girls.

"I am rather taken aback! Speechless, in fact," Nellie looked at her husband with startled eyes.

"Never in all my experience have I ever known that to be the case," Obadiah teased gently.

Nellie shook her head. "Go West? How far? To what end? For how long?"

"I propose we go West and make our fortune," Obadiah said with shining eyes.

"Forsake our home, our neighborhood, our community? Ride off into the prairie?"

"The prairie is the Northwest. That territory has long been settled."

"Go farther than Agnes in Chicago? Abandon our current, opulent lives — to live in the woods or on the plains? After all the wonders we witnessed at the great Exposition, inventions that will soon make our lives here even more comfortable and enjoyable? Do you imagine there will be streets to stroll, gas lighting, or even a theater on the frontier? Leave our thriving hometown, with ships that bring us any commodity we need from the four corners of the earth and take us to the greatest commercial metropolis of the nation in one short hour, for parts totally unknown?"

"Come, come, what care we of the great metropolises? We love the open land where our independence, cunning, and fortitude shall allow us to seek our fortune!"

Nellie's head spun. "We have an interest in our fortune vested right here. We've built a cozy home, surrounded and aided by good, God-fearing neighbors. Yet open land aplenty abounds — just look across the river at the majestic mountains. The bounty you cast aside so cavalierly must be delineated: Sing Sing affords us beautiful villas and auspicious, venerable estates, a sophisticated village of thriving shops with any merchandise or service we could desire at our command. Do you not relish the prosperity of this town, with its shipbuilders, manufacturers, venerable boarding schools, and academies?"

"I see you neglect to mention this prosperity's attendant noise, pollution, and debris. I have oft heard your complaint — when the wind blows from the north you cannot abide the stench from the neighbor's privy and livestock," Obadiah reminded her. "Not to mention your dismay at the continuous belch of putrid smoke streaming from the locomotives and factories, polluting the river."

"Abandon our home, and your promising future in your legal career?" Nellie whispered.

"I kept the choicest portion of my announcement until the end. The motivation for our quest is a significant promotion, in the form of an opportunity, that has been bestowed upon me."

Nellie looked at him. Her interest now aroused, in spite of her stomach churning horror at the thought of leaving her home, she said, "Pray tell, hold me in suspense no longer!"

"Right smart. Your instinctive and insatiable inquisitiveness has returned," teased Obadiah.

"Dear husband, your news has dealt quite a jolt to our comfortable scene of domestic tranquility. You have shaken me to my very core. Do not toy further with my mental state," said Cornelia, without a trace of her usual good humor.

"As you wish, Madam Wright," Obadiah said with a flourish and a bow. "Justice Urmay has been instrumental in aiding my procurement of a position as a circuit judge in Utah Territory."

"Utah?" Nellie gasped.

She plopped down on the stool by the stove, as if the wind had been taken from her sails.

"Shucks, where is that bold adventuring lady whom I wed such a short time ago? The wench who said 'whither thou goest, so goest I'?" He smiled and took her in his arms.

Normally, being dubbed a wench would perturb Nellie, but she was too upset to even notice. "Forsake my family, our comfortable life, the streets where we live, our beautiful surroundings? Shall you truly demand this of me? Pull up stakes never to return?" Nellie asked with tears in her eyes.

"You are already in the correct mindset—using slang from the claim digs at the gold mining camps." Obadiah laughed, but Nellie just stared at him. He closed his mouth and returned the stare.

Nellie looked around at her cozy kitchen: the dinner simmering happily on the gleaming black potbellied stove, water pump primed and poised over the basin for a quick dispatch of cooking utensils and dinner dishes, gas light glowing through beautiful sconces, and fire crackling merrily, spreading warmth throughout the room. *This is the very life I have chosen, and I have created, for us. How can I abandon it?*

Suddenly, she had an even more horrible thought, and looked up at Obadiah with fear on her face. "Are we to travel the same trail as the Donner-Reed party?" quivered Nellie.

Obadiah held out his arms. She hesitated at first. *Must I subsume my desires to his? Must I choose between losing my life or forsaking my husband's happiness?* She teetered on the brink of indecision.

...To love, cherish and obey, until death do us part, according to God's ordinance.... She remembered her marriage vows. She hesitated, looking at the floor, listening to her adorable babies' chatter. *Obey? Do I not have a voice?*

She heaved a deep sigh and surrendered into Obadiah's arms.

CHAPTER 17
I Would Do Anything for Love

Sing Sing, New York, September 1856

"I too, am reluctant to witness your departure. But wives must be submissive unto their husbands," her father said with a stern expression on his face. "Your husband has all of t' markings of a fine attorney at law. Would you deny him his dream, for selfish sentimental reasons?"

Selfish? Sentimental?

"This 'dream' of his upends our entire lives. Wrenches us from civilization on a whim!" Nellie cried. "What of my dreams—for my children to know their heritage, and their grandparents? For a life utilizing the comforts of industrialization, rather than a life of deprivation?"

"This assignment is a mere five years' duration. After sowing his oats, yer husband'll likely desire a return to civilization. Surely by that time we should have a navigable channel clear across t' country, and yer *Mutter* and I'll come out to meet ye and bring ye back ourselves."

Nellie frowned, opening her mouth like she would argue that fact. *Certainly, state governments are digging canals all over this land, connecting the Atlantic to many of the great waterways. But all the way across this huge continent? Could that be anything more than a dream, or at most, a remote possibility?*

"Even if not a waterway...." Mr. Entwhistle paused and looked around as if he did not want anyone to overhear this confession, "...that dread locomotive will soon be connecting t' country, sea to sea." Nellie gaped at him in surprise. *Does Papa think rail travel will outdistance water navigation?* James Entwhistle ran his hand over the top of his head and down to the base of his neck, looking sad. "The only good o' that fact is today's yearlong journey over land, or months long dangerous ocean voyage to the Isthmus of Panama, canoe ride across a river, trek across land, and sail up the west coast, will soon take less than a few weeks via rail or inland canal. Moreover, 'tis not a pie in t' sky hope nor a bunch o' Blarney, there's speculation our government has plans in t' works, engineering a canal *through* Panama."

He shook his head. "By the staff of Saint Patrick, there are mighty travel improvements heading down t' 'pike. Come here to me, there's my good wee colleen," he concluded. He wrapped her so tightly in his arms Nellie knew he was not so quite accepting of her husband's decision as he represented.

Cornelia's mother, at least, expressed more sympathy. "*Ach du Liebe*, my heart broke when Agnes uprooted and journeyed to Chicago. Howsoever, I took a modicum of consolation in the realization that Illinois and the Northwest Territory is now within our United States. But Utah Territory, the hotbed of heathens? *Ach*, so far away. *Mein Kind*, my child, all we can do is pray that this bold adventure is short-lived." Gertrude Entwhistle reached out her hand and patted Nellie's stray hair back into her bun.

"Now," Gertrude said briskly, pulling back and re-tying her apron. "We must prepare for our Sunday family picnic. Constantly changing circumstances in life make us all too painfully cognizant of the brevity of time we are allotted to enjoy our abundant blessings."

Nellie scurried around, sorting through her possessions, painfully parting with many things she realized would not serve them on their journey. Ever the scholar, she read every guidebook and newspaper article about the Oregon and California trails. Ever the romantic, she read novels and accounts of the fate of emigrants who traveled before her.

She and Obadiah spent many a night, after her darling daughters were in bed, planning and making lists until the candles burned out and even the gaslight seemed to flicker.

On the previous Saturday, Obadiah, Zetus, and Jerome returned from New Hampshire with two new horses pulling a wagon made of New Hampshire pine so raw it gleamed.

"Cornelia Rose, may I present...." Obadiah stepped aside with a boyish grin and a grand flourish, "...your new Conestoga wagon! 'Tis renowned as the finest wagon made anywhere in the world," Obadiah boasted.

"Originally made only in the Conestoga River Region in Pennsylvania, the best Conestogas are now made in New Hampshire, from New Hampshire pine," said Jerome. "This beauty will hold up to six tons of cargo. There shall be room for little else, but it might just be the right vehicle for all your books, little sister!" He smiled, a broad impish grin that scampered from his face at the site of Cornelia's stormy countenance.

Zetus ran his hand over the gleaming pine. "With this sturdy girl, you'll have enough space for your Julius Dessoir settee!" he said, and turned toward Nellie with a smile. "...By the sword, Nellie, forgive my vagary. I meant no harm." Zetus dropped his hand to his side and hung his head. "'Tis a 'bang up to the elephant' wagon."

Nellie knew the menfolk and Obadiah were right—it *was* the finest, most sturdy conveyance. She had read all the literature too. "Mercy, there is not enough room for even my chest of drawers, much less our potbellied stove," she said, wiping away a tear. Jerome and Zetus vanished with a hastily mumbled, "Adieu."

"Mr. Wright, I wonder at your choice of a Conestoga wagon," Nellie said, hesitant to cross her husband, but incensed that such an important decision was made without consulting her. "The guidebooks I have perused counsel an ordinary farm wagon qualifies for the task better than a Conestoga. A farm wagon's spaciousness and lighter weight makes it far easier for a horse team to pull."

"Why do you presume I have not taken this information under advisement before making my decision?" Obadiah scowled at her. "I knew you would express hostility toward my purchase."

"Your accusation is unjust. I merely believe we could have saved the entire sum of this purchase by simply using a wagon already in our possession. A farm wagon, already equipped with a bench in the front, affords us a convenient perch for our daughters. I despise the thought of our tiny tots walking all the way to Utah Territory."

"'Tis a simple matter to add a bench in the front, complete with a buckboard," said Obadiah, through stiff lips.

"A simple matter? Will it not change the very structure of the Conestoga?" asked Nellie.

"I chose this wagon so you might have maximum capacity for all your prized worldly goods you are loathe to part with.

"Doggone it, Cornelia Rose! If I could but wipe that contentious countenance off your face." Obadiah slapped his hand hard on the tongue of the wagon. The sound reverberated so loudly Emma ran over from her swing to make sure no one was harmed. "Recall your vows— 'wither you go, there goest I'!"

He stormed off towards the barn.

"I shall expect you to soak the canvas cover in linseed oil to waterproof it whilst I construct your precious riding bench." Obadiah threw the words over his shoulder as he strode away. Nellie caught him muttering, "I purchase the finest wagon money can buy, yet she takes umbrage. Impossible to please this choleric woman...."

How preposterously unjust his mumbled accusations! How totally unfair to permit no opportunity for my rebuttal. "All is well, my little angel," Nellie said aloud to her daughter, catching Emma in her arms and kissing the top of Emma's head to hide her own tears.

CHAPTER 18
No Woman No Cry

Hudson River to Erie Canal, New York, October 1856

The steamship, relieved of some freight, yet encumbered with more passengers in Newberg, pulled away from the dock and continued its sail up the Hudson. Cornelia Rose took her customary place at the bow. Her heart lifted with its usual delight as soon as the ship began to move. *Merciful Heavens, the smell of the salt air when the high tide rushes in from the sea cuts a caper of joy in my soul. The caw of the gulls circling overhead warbles like the sweetest of music! Thank you Lord for the still-nurturing warmth of the October sunshine, pouring unobstructed from the sky.*

Her roving eye caught sight of their Conestoga wagon, anchored on the top stern deck of the ship, like some oddity in P.T. Barnum's famous American Museum. The excitement and elation left her body in one fast *whoosh*, like hot air from a balloon stabbed by a pin. *Mayhap if I stare at it long enough, Tom Thumb or the Fiji Mermaid shall appear, confirming 'tis both an apparition and a hoax.*

This is not the beginning of an exhilarating trip on my beloved river. It is the beginning of the end. The end of my time in civilization.

Obadiah and her daughters caught up with her. Emma, now three-and-a half-years-old, and Elizabeth, nineteen months, giggling, ran right into her skirts. She bent to hug them and looked up at her husband. Obadiah's eyes lit up when he saw her look at him.

The love in his eyes and his tender smile warmed the melancholy from her soul.

One of the many things I love about him, his perpetually happy affect, especially when I am lost in the loss of my family. Nellie shook her head, trying to erase the vision of her mother, Anastasia, and her dear friend Augusta, sobbing and waving as they pulled away from the Upper Dock at Sing Sing for the last time.

She smiled at Obadiah, in spite of the tears in her heart. "Your smile excites the most tender of emotions in me," he whispered and kissed her. The soft kiss shot a fire of passion from her cheek into her soul, rekindling her faith in her decision to follow him wherever he led.

The pale sun caught the gold of the autumn leaves, and the silver of the airborne spray flung by the ship's movement. "Look Mama, a fish!" Emma pointed. Cornelia looked over the rail, drinking in the familiar sights and sounds of the Hudson.

"Why do you gaze so intently at the landscape?" Obadiah asked.

Nellie blushed. "I wish to imprint this felicity of nature upon my memory. As the British author Thomas Hamilton wrote, '...add elevation to the mountains and the consequence of the river would be diminished. Increase the expanse of the river and you impair the grandeur of the mountains. As it is, there is a perfect subordination of parts and the result is something on which the eye loves to gaze and the heart to meditate....'" Nellie's voice shook. Tears slowly ran down her cheek. "'...which tinges our dreams with beauty, and... often... in distant lands....'" She choked on a sob, and coughed. "'...will recur, unbidden, to the imagination'."

She stared at the landscape, willing her tears away, trying to regain her composure while absorbing the golden view.

The ship's twenty mile-an-hour speed ensured they would arrive in Albany long before nightfall. *Fast enough!* Ever since the *Henry Clay*, she watched anxiously, monitoring steamship crews' performance of their jobs, even on her father's ships. Once, her report of a pilot calling for an increase in speed when they already traveled at a maximum steam-capacity clip produced her father's public reprimand of that man.

Just after they boarded, she saw Obadiah examine the engine room to ensure there were sufficient fire buckets stacked at its door. She kept her brood at the bow, *the safest part of the ship*, she often reassured herself, and fell into her habit of monitoring the release of steam from the boiler at every familiar stop along their route.

The hill of Albany soon appeared in sight. "Our honeymoon journey comes to mind," said Cornelia, with a briskness that disguised the supreme effort it cost to maintain her positive outlook. The ship nudged the dock and the little girls jumped up and down in anticipation of regaining dry land. Cornelia continued, "The thrill of the voyage, the quaintness of the historic Dutch district in Albany, the wonder of each other and our love...."

"My dearest Cornelia Rose," said Obadiah, catching both her gloved hands in his own. "We are on a journey of a lifetime. Sustained by precious memories already created and fortified by the continued love of those we have left behind, we shall keep our hearts focused on the wonder of new vistas and worlds we shall view, and pioneer forward to create a new existence for ourselves."

He smiled at Nellie with an expectant look.

She stepped to the plate. "In my extensive reading, I have discovered literature from many famous authors, recording their impressions on their Northeast Tours. The romance! The scenery! The commerce! I have long desired a voyage on the modern-day wonder, the Erie Canal. Moreover, with only a few short detours, we can see Niagara Falls and other sights of resplendent natural beauty along our path."

Obadiah frowned. Nellie read his face and knew he would not entertain the thought of detours on their journey. He cleared his throat to speak, but his demeanor communicated all Nellie needed to know.

She rushed on, "The musings of England's Frances Trollope, in particular, come to mind. While she viewed all things American with a critical eye, hence the derogatory title of her book on her travels— *Domestic Manners of the Americans* — her praise for the Trenton Falls was superlative."

"Trollope?" asked Obadiah. "Is she not the woman who praised these Hudson Highlands?" Nellie nodded her affirmation. Obadiah continued, "Whilst you advised me she took umbrage in the 'lack of inspiration' of the names of our landmarks, she certainly praised the landmarks themselves."

"True," Nellie said. "Howsoever, I am sure her heart was set against finding anything notable at all on this continent—preferring instead to sling uncharitable, unforgiving witticisms. Therefore, the fact that she writes solely laudatory descriptions of these Trenton Falls makes me desire a stop in the landlocked city of Utica."

"Nothing is more compelling than a 'declaration against interest'," Obadiah agreed with a smile.

Emboldened Nellie continued, "With a mere fourteen-mile detour we too could be privy to the unparalleled grandeur of the succession of leaps the West Canada Creek takes from platform after platform of rock the Natives call 'Cayoharic'."

Obadiah looked skeptical. Nellie sighed. "That literary giant and my personal acquaintance, Mr. William Cullen Bryant, confessed he scampered about like a little boy enraptured by the beauty of the seventh Fall in the Trenton cascade. So compelled was he by the Fall's splendor, he climbed and tramped through a private ravine, exploring dangerous terrain as the river rushed by in a torrent of perilous rapids. In his zeal to explore the bounty of nature and the majesty of the river, he quite lost track of time. After darkness fell, concerned friends organized a search party with torches. They scoured the area for several hours before Mr. Bryant finally groped his way homewards through the dark forest."

No reaction from Obadiah.

Nellie took a deep breath and continued, hoping to persuade him. "Internationally renowned, Trenton Falls is second in fame only to Niagara Falls. Quite the rare opportunity to view such splendor presents itself. I would not dare trespass upon your goodwill to request the *significant* detour from our route entailed by a visit to Niagara Falls. I only ask for a slight diversion, a fourteen-mile carriage ride on a well-traveled road." Nellie smiled and added a mute appeal through raised eyebrows.

But Obadiah shook his head. "We shall not deviate from our scheduled plan of five days' and four nights' ride on the canal boat. We must get across Lake Erie, and then by land to Chicago before the canal and the lakes freeze and the snows set in.

"But it is late October. We have the entirety of November before we must worry about ice and snow."

"Not in those northern parts of New York State. Meteorological trends indicate snow could commence there at any moment."

Nellie tried one more argument. "Our canal travel is so swift we shall arrive in Sandusky, Ohio, a week and a half earlier than stagecoach travel would have taken us. Surely that affords us some leeway."

"I already calculated that swiftness and economy of travel into our schedule," Obadiah countered. "We must assimilate the wisdom of the guidebooks and adhere to our plans."

He turned on his heel and walked away.

CHAPTER 19
We May Never Pass This Way Again

Erie Canal, New York, October 1856

It seemed to Nellie she had barely closed her eyes when Obadiah caressed her arm and woke her.

"Time to begin the adventure of a lifetime!" He smiled at her in the darkness of their cozy hotel room.

Their pre-dawn activity was filled with the many logistics of the journey. They readied the children, breakfasted, repacked the few things they had needed the previous night and saw their Conestoga wagon, crammed with personal belongings Nellie was loath to leave behind, as well as equipment for their long trek, safely loaded onto a freight boat.

"We shall bypass more than four hundred miles of highways and turnpikes by floating down 'Clinton's Ditch'," marveled Nellie to Obadiah upon boarding the boat. The four Wrights stood on the deck watching the three horses on the side path break into a trot. The boat floated smoothly down the recently widened canal.

"Whilst I do admire your blithe, adventuresome spirit, I remind you of our conversation of yesterday. Be cognizant, always—this is not a holiday, but rather the beginning of a long voyage into the unknown. 'Tis best, I believe, not to tarry sightseeing nor disembark to dine in every town. What's more to the point, of course, is a discussion of the matter of frugality of resources. We must resist the temptation to spend traveling funds before we realize the full extent of expenditure required to provision ourselves for the overland journey. We have already disbursed the entire expense for passage on this boat, the *Storm Queen*, at four cents a mile, including room and board. There is no compelling reason to alter our course."

Nellie sighed. "I am painfully aware we do not embark upon a pleasure cruise. I know full well a tiresome and arduous trek across the wilderness awaits us. Howsoever, as we can already ascertain from our morning's float along this passage, nothing is seen to advantage from this canal." Nellie stared at the swampy land, littered with rotting tree stumps, passing before her eyes. "In point of fact, very little is seen at all. Mayhap you can allow our purse strings to open for just one adventurous journey, such as a trip to Trenton Falls, before we must fully assume the mantle of pioneer."

Obadiah's face looked like a thundercloud.

Nellie sighed. "I am sure the children and I shall find many amusements and diversions simply floating along the canal. Further, I live in hope that as soon as the canal path parallels the Mohawk River the scenery shall improve." With another sigh, this time of resignation, she made a beeline for a chair on the deck, careful not to stray too close to the rail-less edge of the roof of the main cabin upon which they stood. With another look at the swamp around them, she brushed her hair out of her eyes and settled herself with her daughters and her knitting bag. *I shall nip my disappointment in the bud and take consolation in the name of our vessel, the Storm Queen, as it reminds me of my favorite mountain at home, Storm King.*

Nellie listened to the jargon of their captain and the canawlers commandeering the commerce along the canal. She contemplated the new words she had already learned while she knit and enjoyed the autumn sun. Most of the words she could discern from context—*canawlers,* people who worked on the canal; *towpath* or *berm,* the narrow path of earthen embankment that ran the whole length of the canal along which the horses and donkeys walked and pulled the boats; *Lockkeeper; Pathmaster.* She giggled. *By all appearances, the Pathmaster's main mission this morning was shooing the Dutch goose-girl and her geese from the canal towpath.*

Nellie glanced at her daughters, cuddling their dolls on the bench beside her. *All's well. My safety checks must be frequent and thorough, to spot potential dangerous situations before they occur.* With a sigh of relief, she turned her thoughts back to her new vocabulary list.

Nellie loved acquiring new vernacular—*hoggee* meant the boy driving the team, *mung news* meant gossip. Nellie could not fathom why. Besides the usual nautical terms—bow deck, stern deck, tiller, and steersman—a whole new string of words evolved for the breed of boats developed solely for canal travel. *Packets* were boats exclusively for passengers that commanded the right of way; *line-boats* took on both freight and passengers; *counter sterns* seemed to be boats that had two sterns and no bow. *The craft looks confused... or mayhap, as if it travels in continual backwards motion.* Nellie giggled to herself.

Obadiah opened the Albany morning newspaper and perused the front page. Nellie made an attempt to resume pleasantries. "The fresh breeze on the deck shall keep the tenacious autumn mosquitoes at bay. I can save the spicy odor of my stash of pennyroyal leaves for repelling those disease-carrying gall nippers later in our journey."

The children began jumping around her, playing and laughing in the sunshine. Nellie smiled too, until her memories of the *Henry Clay* tragedy threw her into a fretful state. *Mercy, Emma is not yet a confident swimmer and Elizabeth has only begun to learn. Perchance my back shall be turned and they shall slip and fall overboard. Will they have the skill to stay afloat?*

She retrieved a scarf from her bag and tied one end around Elizabeth's waist and held the other firmly in her hand. At Elizabeth's attempt to pull it off, Nellie said, "Now you can scamper about to your heart's content and not tumble overboard. This beautiful fabric shall guarantee my peace of mind." *A small step to alleviate any chance my little darlings might fall to a watery grave.* She put her knitting away and stood up, ready to walk around behind her toddler. Obadiah stood up and stretched.

"Here's an adventurous navigation," snarled a man appearing at Nellie's elbow. "'Tis a triangulation of a murky mud-puddle."

Cornelia and Obadiah swiveled their heads toward the speaker in surprise. A whiskered and wizened old man stood nearby, scowling in the direction of the horse team and the razed forest beyond the berm. "All the dismal swamps and unimpressive scenery that could be found between the glorious Hudson and the vastness of Lake Erie shall be on display during our entire voyage," he said in a querulous tone.

Quite the curmudgeon, thought Nellie. In an attempt at civility and diplomacy she said, "Truly, the canal is still called 'governor's gutter' by some. Howsoever, experience has proved its mettle as quite an efficient and profitable way to move people and freight. In truth, the only way one could travel faster is by sleigh, over snow and ice – an impossible choice on a beautiful autumn day such as this!"

All of a sudden, a dark structure loomed directly in front of them. The barge continued along its conduit, right toward it.

"The railroad will soon overtake...." the curmudgeon began.

"Duck!" shouted Nellie to the grouchy man, as he was now facing toward her and the rear of the boat.

"Madam, do you refer—"

Bam! The stone façade of a low bridge hit the man in the back of the head and he fell forward on top of the crouched Nellie. Nellie fell against the deck. The dark underbelly of the bridge obliterated the sun for thirty seconds while they passed underneath.

Obadiah hurried around Nellie's trapped figure and yanked the inert man off her. Blood dripped from a gash across the back of his head, and Nellie's heart skipped a beat. *Was he fatally injured?*

Handing Obadiah the scarf still attached to Elizabeth, Nellie turned to the stricken man. She pulled smelling salts out of her bulging handbag and stuck them under the man's nose as her other hand reached for the side of his neck to check his pulse. *He still has a heartbeat,* she thought with relief, as she passed the salts back and forth with one hand and chafed his hand with the other.

At last, his eyes flew open. With a dazed expression on his face, the old man looked up at them in terror. "What's happened?"

"'Tis most fortuitous that my wife shouted a 'low bridge' warning at that precise moment," said Obadiah. "It afforded me, and the rest of the passengers on deck, sufficient time to stoop, sparing our heads. You, Sir, have been lucky as well, as you bent slightly toward her seeking an explanation of her brazen command, and fell directly upon her, which cushioned your fall. But for that, you might have been knocked off the boat, or killed."

The old man lay there, rubbing his head, and looking dazed.

"In other words," said a fellow passenger. "We thought the atoms in your head were rearranged for you." Nellie and Obadiah stifled smiles.

One of the crew came forward and led the man down to the multipurpose room below.

"Mercy," said Nellie, from her prone position on the hot deck floor, after yet another low bridge. "The numerous bridges could, in fact, seem quite the nuisance. The arches of most are barely high enough to admit the passage of the boat. They leave us no option but to descend from our seats and drop to the deck, every time we approach one, or be swept summarily into the drink!"

She looked at her daughters and laughed. They skipped around, enjoying the sudden changes of position.

Obadiah laughed too. "Seen through younger eyes, 'tis merely a game. Bobbing one's self down at randomly spaced bridges is stimulating."

Nellie said, "In this spirit, the next time we are forced to prostrate ourselves in homage to the lack of clearance, I shall peep around to see if everyone else looks as comic as I feel."

She did not have long to wait. Gliding under the next low bridge, Nellie convulsed with laughter at the sight of a young boy sprawled on his ear, a portly gentleman hugging the deck, and a middle-aged matron lying on her side, still talking to her companion, who was on her hands and knees. From these strange positions, the two women continued their conversation as if there were no reason to pause.

The Wrights spent a pleasant morning on deck watching dark dense forests, small log-cottages, farmhouses, and the occasional church-spire float by. A professor from Union College and his wife got on in Schenectady. They were on a holiday to Niagara Falls. Nellie found pleasure in their company.

This pleasure was increased by her secret joy in overhearing the professor remark to Obadiah, "Good Sir, you most emphatically and categorically should take the requisite time to detour to Niagara Falls. This is the second trip for the missus and me. The magnificence of the Falls astounds the visitor and compels one to return to its beauty. Many a dignitary, quite a few foreigners, and even some royalty travel from all ends of the earth to see these Falls, claiming their splendor without parallel anywhere in the world. Yet you, Sir, ignore them as an unnecessary detour! The Northern Tour has become quite fashionable, thanks to Niagara Falls, and the ease of travel of our old Erie Canal. Tourism is another form of the commerce this manmade seaway nurtures."

But Obadiah remained resolute in his desire to press on, without sightseeing detours.

The professor shook his head as if in dismay at Obadiah's foolishness. "My wife and I have the luxury of traveling again to the Falls. In fact, we could foreseeably take this journey every summer, when Union term is on holiday. But you, my good fellow? With the goals and parameters of the journey you've articulated, shall you ever pass this way again?"

These words burned into Nellie's soul, and she remembered them long after. *Shall I ever pass this way again?* She wondered afresh at each new sight in their journey. The subject of the conversation switched with no further memorable words from either man. Nellie only listened with half an ear to the merits of Union College, its learned staff, and varied curriculum.

"Our venerable Board of Trustees at Union College now offer a civil engineering degree," the professor said with pride. Nellie turned two ears of attention back to the conversation. "We are the *first* institution of higher learning to offer this training," boasted the professor.

"I beg to differ," Nellie interrupted. "West Point Military Academy has offered civil engineering training since its inception." Both men looked at her with raised eyebrows and open mouths. *Must I not interject my knowledgeable opinion simply because I am a lady?* she wondered.

"My word! You Yankees are a feisty, opinionated bunch," said the professor, but with a jovial smile. He and Obadiah gave hearty laughs. The professor cleared his throat. "Hopping horse feathers, Union College has one of the largest faculties in American higher education and an enrollment surpassed only by the esteemed Yale University. Only a native New Yorker would have the temerity to question our accolades. Howsoever, I shall concede, West Point commands the honorable achievement of 'first' technical college in the States. Nevertheless, Union College does lay claim to the first successful attempt in America to raise applied science and technology to a collegiate level."

"One of the first, but well after West Point," amended Nellie with a laugh. *My heart capers with joy at the reception my contribution to the sport and stimulation of conversation receives.*

The professor blushed, nodded, and resumed his thought. "Ever since those chaps completed the Erie Canal, the rest of the nation desires its own canals too. We need more engineers. Never you mind that most of the men designing the Canal had little or no formal engineering training. Now, I am not one to cast aspersions, but perhaps that lack of book learning is the reason for erosion of the banks and silt formation in the canal, right from the get go."

He cocked his head to the side and mumbled to himself, "Or it could be just as critics' claim, the wake from swiftly moving vessels dislodges the dirt from the canal banks, and the displaced dirt accumulates on the bottom of the canal creating shallow areas that ground boats and slow traffic." The man shook his big shaggy-haired head again and said louder, "Yes sir, our country needs more engineers.

Moreover, that need shall only intensify. A project to widen the canal began way back in 1836. That venture needs more engineering minds, if it is ever to be completed."

"Tummy hungry. Eat breakfast. Now?" asked Elizabeth.

They all laughed.

"Certainly, my tummy says it is time for dinner too," said Nellie and gave Elizabeth a hug. They went below deck, both girls hungry and tired from skipping around every time a bridge loomed overhead. They saw the kitchen staff elongate the table in the center of the sitting cabin. Soon the table was filled with fresh-caught bass, cucumber, tomatoes, hot fluffy biscuits, smooth churned butter, ale, iced water with lemon, and tea.

"Yum, yum," said Elizabeth.

Their supper later that day was equally delicious; a soup of ham and potatoes, honey cakes, cornbread, and jam.

At eight o'clock, supper concluded, the multipurpose room was once again converted, but this time into a dormitory. Nellie and her family looked on in amazement as the crew transformed the cushioned benches into beds.

"Mama, look!" said Emma. "The settee that goes the whole length of the boat right up to the kitchen unfolds into a cot!"

"Yes," said Nellie. "I have read of the remarkably efficient use of the sparse space inside these packet boats, but the sight exceeds expectations."

"Just wait until you see the source of the rest of the beds," said Obadiah.

The crew stuck the long end of frames into sockets arranged in pairs, one above the other, along the walls over each of the newly made beds. Next, they attached two cords to hooks in the ceiling and then secured them, one at the head of the bed frame and one at the foot, on the side of each frame that stuck out into the room. Finally, they placed pallet bedding and a thin pillow across each frame.

"*Voila!*" exclaimed Obadiah, as if he had invented the design himself.

"The space between the berths is barely sufficient for a man to crawl in," worried Nellie.

"We will sleep on those shelves?" asked Emma.

"Do you not entertain apprehension of asphyxiation, lest the cords should break?" Nellie mouthed the words behind her hand, to prevent the children and other passengers from hearing her anxiety.

"Such fears are groundless. These berths have been engineered rather cunningly, as I am sure our good professor from Union College will attest." Obadiah patted Nellie's hand reassuringly, as she did the same for Emma.

"Mayhap that gentleman...." Nellie looked over at a portly man, still munching on a second piece of cake from their supper, "...would feel most comfortable on the lowest bed, or even a pallet on the floor." Obadiah looked at her in surprise.

Nellie blushed. "I apologize for my uncharitable remark. 'Twas truly unchristian to call attention to his jollocks. I do believe this journey beyond civilization already triggers a lapse in my manners," she said. *What an unkind thing, underscoring a man's excessive weight in front of my daughters.*

They walked in between the rows of bunk beds.

"I have selected this berth for its location, directly adjacent to my bunk on the other side of the curtain divide," said Obadiah. He put Nellie's small traveling case on top of the lowest bunk bed. "With you and the girls snug-a-bug in this innermost berth in the ladies' section, our heads shall almost touch when we are sleeping!"

The girls giggled at the thought.

The crimson curtain dropped, dividing the men from the women. With a quick kiss for each, Obadiah lifted the curtain and disappeared behind it.

Nellie helped her chatting daughters into their nightdresses, and then lay on the bunk with them, fully clothed, one nestled in each arm. The girls snuggled in and with just a minimum of tossing and wriggling, fell asleep.

But Nellie lay awake, at rigid attention. *The jerk and pull of the horses powering this barge is an impediment to sleep. The notion that this uneven movement would inhibit the onset of slumber never crossed my mind. I have always delighted in the gentle, or even rough, motion of our Hudson River. 'Tis quite unexpected the mere floating of this vessel does anything other than instantly lull one to sleep....* Nellie suddenly giggled to herself. *Mais oui! I cannot sleep because our ship performs a 'triangulation of a mud puddle'!*

"Shhhhh," hissed a warning from below her.

Tarnation! Now I am too irked for slumber. Mayhap a perambulation upon the stern deck will ease my tension whilst I enjoy a view of the canal at night.

The lantern at the end of the stern lit the faces of two men, deep in conversation. Nellie was delighted to discover Obadiah talking to the steersman. He held out his hand for her and she joined them.

"Halloo!" called the steersman, pointing and waving at a craft behind them. "That there is the *Starry Flag,* a freight boat licensed for perishables and only four passengers. You see there, Captain Angus Robie commanding the helm. A more macaroni and personable seaman you won't be easily finding on this here canal."

A companionable silence fell. The Wrights looked at their boat's wake, and the scenery they had just passed, and after a moment, wished the steersman good night. Strolling arm in arm, they walked back toward the cabin door. Obadiah paused, drew Cornelia around to face him and said, "A breath of fresh air on the top deck, whilst our babies sleep might prove just the elixir we need to refresh our sense of adventure."

They scrambled up the ladder to the roof of the cabin, and looked out over the water.

"I must confess, the lanterns of the approaching boats look like fairy lights. 'Tis quite the romantic view of the canal—mud puddle or not." Nellie laughed.

"Keep your eyes trained on the canal ahead then," Obadiah replied, standing behind her, wrapping his arms around her waist, nestling his chin on her shoulder and planting his feet to keep her looking forward. "Do not turn to see the ruined white cedar and black ash to our right, past the berm. 'Tis ghost-like in the extreme. This seems the very land of unsubstantial things. Therefore, I shall dwell upon your romantic fairies and not give another thought to the ghastly ghosts of tree stumps that surround us."

The couple enjoyed a few minutes of serenity. Nellie leaned back against Obadiah's solid warm body, watching the lighted boats glide past, viewing the stars up above. Just as Nellie thought, *'Tis so refreshing and romantic out here, I might not choose to re-enter that stuffy cabin at all tonight,* she heard a faint *low bridge* warning, and threw herself prostrate on the deck.

Obadiah bent down over her. "Mayhap you have overreacted? No bridge would be that low."

But as Nellie lay there, they heard the warning again. She sat up and then lay back down, pulling Obadiah down with her.

"Golly," he said. "I stand corrected."

"No," Nellie said, giggling. "You lay, corrected!"

In the darkness, from his prone position, Obadiah kissed her. Nellie opened her eyes and looked at the starry night. Obadiah nibbled on her ear.

"Goodness! Obadiah, we must save these romances for our bedroom," Nellie said, trying to sit up and look proper.

Obadiah pulled her back down. "There is no bedroom, just a multipurpose room with shelf berths!" He kissed her again, sliding his lips from her cheek to her mouth. His warm, tender lips lingered, kissing her again and again. Nellie felt the familiar tingle of anticipation and reached her hand around him to run it through his silky hair.

Obadiah kissed her chin, his lips soft under his mustache, his breath warm on her cheek. "'Tis heavenly," whispered Nellie, snuggling under his arm, kissing him passionately in return.

He kissed her briskly and pulled her upright. She looked at him in surprise.

He laughed, and she saw his rueful look clearly in the moonlight. "I must remind us both — we are bereft of a bedroom!"

They made their way down the ladder and stood in front of the cabin door. Nellie realized anew, with an unpleasant jolt, they must part for the night. She gave Obadiah a self-conscious peck on his cheek.

She entered the ladies' section but still did not disrobe. She climbed up to her middle berth and then knelt on its edge. She re-tightened the scarf she had strung from cord to cord down the length of her daughters' bed and tucked its edge under their pallet to prevent them from rolling out and dropping onto the floor. She tugged it to make sure it was taut, and then fell back onto her shelf, her muscles tense and tight.

Eventually, she found sleep, rocked gently enough to elude consciousness by the barge floating along, all night, through the muddy canal.

CHAPTER 20
What a Difference a Day Makes

Erie Canal, Herkimer to Rochester, New York, October 1856

The morning brought a confusion of arms, legs, and dresses flying about as all the inhabitants of the ladies' cabin tried to get ready for the day at the same time.

"We are so mixed up, I can't pick myself out!" laughed Emma. The women nearby smiled, confirming the jovial mood with their own laughter.

The good nature of this company is our saving grace. In all the commotion of these cramped quarters, not a cross word heard, not a sourpuss scowl seen.

"How sleep, Papa?" asked Elizabeth, when they found Obadiah on the stern deck. Nellie and Emma hugged him good morning.

"I did doubt I would acquire any rest at all—one of twenty men lying like a pack of herring in a barrel. In addition to the berths, men lay end to end on the floor. When the boat thumped against a lock, I constantly worried I would be tossed from my bed and land on the sternum of an unsuspecting fellow sleeper. Howsoever, I do believe my repose was fairly adequate."

"Mama, have we been to this town before?" asked Emma, pointing to the stone houses, taverns, shops, and churches.

"I believe this is the hamlet of Herkimer," said Nellie. *But tarry a moment. These quays and the harbor bustle so, could we be in the inland city, Utica? No, no, that would require docking.* "I must confess each small town, so recently hatched along this canal, seems much the same to me too, my little pumpkin." She held both her daughters' hands as they watched the town float by.

"The only difference is how many locks and docks," agreed Emma, and Nellie marveled at the astuteness of her observation.

Drawn forward by their three horses, they floated along the canal section dubbed the 'Black Snake', due to the winding course dug for this part of the channel. Their forward progress quickened in this serpentine section from Utica to Syracuse, however, because this long level part of the canal contained no locks. Speed unimpeded by gates, they sailed on.

Obadiah jumped off the boat onto the towpath and, matching his pace to their packet's travel, walked alongside them. The girls jumped up and down on the deck, calling to him.

"Your walk is a brisk four miles per hour," Nellie called to Obadiah, and his daughters applauded.

"From whence did you obtain that information?" Obadiah called back.

"The steersman told me that is the usual speed of the packet," Nellie replied.

"Horse feathers!" said Obadiah. "One would imagine that with three horse-power a small vessel like this packet could go faster than that."

"Whoa, hoggee,"called the steersman. The boy leading the horses stopped in front of a fresh pack of horses. The second he stopped walking, the boy and the land agent who brought the new horses started unbuckling harnesses. During the process of unhitching the old pack, one of the crew pulled the ship closer to the berm and Nellie and her daughters disembarked. The girls ran to Obadiah, hugging his legs. Several other passengers poured off the boat behind them.

Splash!

A man, dressed in his Sunday best, fell into the muddy canal. All the ladies gasped and Nellie feared for his safety. *Can he swim?* she wondered, scenes of the horrible disaster of the *Henry Clay* flashing before her eyes. His head underwater, he floundered for a second in the dank, murky water.

At last he raised his head, gasping for breath, flailing his arms in a desperate attempt to stay afloat.

"On yer feet, man!" shouted the steersman. "'Tis only four feet of water still in this part."

The man stood up, sputtering. The murky water only came up to his waistcoat. All those safe and dry, both onboard and on land, laughed and applauded this comic entertainment. The man flushed the crimson of his cummerbund.

Goodness, Nellie thought, relief washing over her like the refreshing shower she was sure the man now coveted.

The moment her terror subsided, however, a more mundane fear crossed her mind. *That crimson velvet of his cummerbund might just remain brown as there is a dearth of fresh water for scrubbing onboard.* She shook her head in dismay. *That laundering cannot wait until he reaches his destination.*

Obadiah saw the steersman, now enjoying a stint on land while they swapped horse teams, was the same man with whom he had conversed the night before. "Why does the packet travel at a mere four miles per hour? Is this vessel not capable of a faster speed?" he asked.

The steersman turned red and sputtered, "This little ship is fleet and yar as they come. 'Tis the high mucky-mucks of the Canal Commission, deciding fast travel causes damage to our canal—them are the geniuses that put a four mile per hour speed cap on our travel." The man shook his head in disgust. "Let 'em come here and ask me. I'll tell 'em what *truly* causes damage...." He shook his fist in a menacing gesture and Obadiah did not pursue it further.

The hoggee and the land agent finished harnessing the fresh trio of horses. Nellie and the girls prepared to go back onboard. Carefully gauging the distance across the watery gap between the towpath and the boat, Nellie judged it as an easy step. Clutching her shawl tightly to her, she extended her leg. In the middle of her stride, the boat lurched away from the land. Already committed to the motion, she turned the step into a leap. Determined not to fall into the water like her hapless fellow traveler, Nellie exerted a bit too much forward motion and found herself sprawling headlong on the deck. *It is very hard to maintain one's dignity on this infernal packet,* she thought, checking her hands for splinters as she righted herself.

Obadiah handed each girl over the watery gap, seconds before the hoggee called 'gee up' to the horses. Nellie hugged them to her, glad they safely averted yet another opportunity for a watery disaster. Obadiah continued his journey on foot.

"Papa, shall you walk all the way to Buffalo?" asked Emma.

"No. Just wait and see," replied Obadiah. They watched him walk along beside them, whistling a merry tune. The girls sang along. At the sight of the next low bridge, Obadiah ran ahead. The girls watched him scramble up the bank. As they all scrunched down, Obadiah jumped off the bridge and landed on the deck, immediately crouching down with them. The boat slid smoothly under the low overhang.

"Mercy, quite the daring stunt, Papa!" Emma giggled.

Nellie wondered why he did not jump from the other side of the bridge, after the boat emerged from the low overpass. "Pshaw, you say *I* have a penchant for drama!" she said. But Obadiah winked with a merry expression. "Just attempting levity and a bit of sport," he said.

That second night they floated by yet another forest decimated during the widening of the canal. Stumps of trees stood clustered like bewitched statues in grotesque positions. During the day, the stumps appeared petrified, as if unable to recuperate from man's intrusion into their domain. But at night, these stumps glowed with an eerie phosphorescence.

A long melancholy horn sounded in the distance, and bounced off the ruined trees, further contributing to the spooky scene.

"Is it this eerie forest which gives the canal its name?" asked Emma.

Cornelia could not restrain herself; she joined Obadiah and some eavesdropping passengers in a hearty chuckle.

Emma looked crestfallen. Nellie quickly engulfed her in a reassuring hug. "We are laughing because your explanation makes so much sense, I wonder I did not think of it myself. The glowing trees make the scene an eerie night on the Erie Canal."

"That is quite solid deductive reasoning," her father reassured Emma. "Howsoever, I do believe the canal was named for the Erie Indians, native to this area. When you learn how to spell words, you will see Erie Indians are written differently than an eerie forest."

"Furthermore, the unnerving sound of the horn is probably a packet traveling ahead of us, calling some land agent, watching in the wilderness, to ready the fresh horses," Nellie said.

"I cannot wait to spell," said Emma. Nellie smiled in the darkness and gave her daughter another hug.

"Low bridge, everybody down!" shouted Elizabeth, jumping off her chair on the top deck. The other passengers obediently jumped down too.

Low bridge, everybody down. Low bridge, we're coming to a town," the two girls sang. "Much fun," Elizabeth said, from her crouching position on the deck, even though for this bridge at least, *she* could have stayed standing. The bottom of the bridge cast its shadow over them as the packet boat slid underneath. "Can we play this at home too?" asked Emma.

Home. Nellie felt a pang of longing for the place to which she might never return.

One of the staff offered them drinks from a tray.

"Mama, iced water with lemon juice, again," said Emma. "But where do they keep the icehouse?"

Nellie suppressed a grin and explained, "The canawlers pack enough food and supplies for the journey. I am sure they engineered enough room for ice, both as a preservative of perishables and a complement to our beverages."

The steward overheard her. "Little Ladies, yer in for a treat. Yep, yer mama's right, we carry our supplies with us, but not a hold-full for the entire journey. You'll be seeing the farm urchins, in their bateaus, sidling up to our packet. They'll be hawking their fresh produce, and fresh caught game."

Just as he finished speaking they heard a shrill, "Halloo!" from the water below. The Wright women looked down and saw a group of children on a flat-bottomed rowboat holding up quail, partridge, and pigeon, as well as bunches of carrots, lettuce, and radishes. As they floated onward, the steward jumped from their packet onto the children's boat. Nellie and her daughters looked on in amusement as the man haggled for the best price and then bought sixteen quail for their dinner.

"Mama, on land, we travel to the market. On the canal, the market travels to us!" said Emma. Nellie smiled.

The steward threw his bartered bundle on deck and then clambered back onboard. As the children's rowboat slipped back behind them, the sky darkened. The beautiful autumn day vanished behind a thick black cloud.

CRACCCK! A loud clap of thunder seemed to rumble right behind them.

"Best be heading below, Miss," said the steward. "Ye won't want to be out on deck in a thunderstorm."

Emma looked down the canal and along the berm behind them. "Where did those children go? They mustn't be out in a storm either."

"We haven't yet seen lightning. The storm must still be miles away." Nellie said, with a soothing hand on Emma's head. "Furthermore, I am sure any children smart enough to barter with a canal steward aboard a fancy packet boat will be smart enough to vacate the canal in a thunderstorm."

But as she shepherded the children to the hold below, her eyes scanned up and down the canal. *Nowhere to be seen. I hope they arrived safely at their home. I, too, tremble at the thought of children out on the water in a storm.* She shuddered, picturing the drowned children washed ashore from the *Henry Clay* disaster and then laid out in a dignified manner on the beach by Agnes. She clutched at her heart, renewing her vow to spare no effort in keeping her children safe from harm.

Suddenly, a bolt of lightning sent a jagged streak across the dark sky.

"Mercy, that was near!" Cornelia exclaimed as she hurried the girls into the sitting parlor.

Thunder boomed through the air, just as they seated themselves in the passenger cabin. "That noise was as loud as a cannon," cried Emma. Nellie threw protective arms around both her daughters.

A bolt of lightning flashed so brilliantly, it appeared to be inside the cabin. Both girls' cries joined the screams of the other ladies surrounding them. Nellie hugged her daughters again. Obadiah joined them on the bench as thunder banged and lightning flashed. Cornelia's anxious eyes found her husbands' and she thought, *Merciful Lord, protect us.*

After another volley of thunder and lightning, the sky brightened. *Has the storm ceased its fury?* Curious, Nellie rose to peer out the window, to see if the storm clouds had passed.

Without warning, the boat jolted. Cornelia lurched with the boat and nearly lost her footing.

Another boat floated within arm's length of their packet, and she stared into its cabin. Chaos visibly erupted among the passengers, but no sound was heard through both sets of closed windows.

"What's happened?" Nellie reached her arm out to the first mate as he hurried through.

"That packet..." he said, jerking his thumb toward the window, continuing to walk. "The *Chief Engineer,* just had two horses kilt and its hoggee stunned by an electron from this here lightning."

Lightning flashed again.

The man hurried away.

Emma tugged Nellie's skirt. With eyes as wide as teacup saucers, Emma asked, "Is lightning going to strike us, too?"

CHAPTER 21
Sittin' on the Dock of the Bay

Erie Canal, Rochester, New York to Towanda, Pennsylvania, November 1856

The stone passageway of the aqueduct towered in the near distance. Nellie could see it clearly from her perch on the rooftop deck, around a curve in the canal. *I'll not miss this ingenious conduit,* she vowed. When they had traversed the Weedsport Aqueduct, Nellie had been occupied putting her daughters to bed. She had been unaware of the great engineering feat over which she traveled. *I am attentive and ready for this marvel, worthy of display at the Exhibition of the Industries of All Nations. The aqueduct's arches lift canal commerce twenty-six feet in the air over the bustling Genesee River, right in the middle of the town of Rochester. What a wonder!*

They rounded the curved entry from the east, and their boat climbed the trough supported by two massive stone arches. Now they were on the 444-foot long central trunk of the aqueduct, directly over the rushing river. Nellie looked down from the dizzying height of the boat on top of the water and felt as nauseous as if she were back on the Latting Observatory, looking straight down at the streets of Manhattan. She saw Obadiah try to count the arches as they floated past. *Mercy, the massiveness of the fifty-two foot pillars is intimidating, even from this vast height. Yet that very massive girth provides comfort in its superlative support of this waterway.*

"I understand this aqueduct replaced the original that leaked like a sieve," said Obadiah.

"Yes, I read that too," said Nellie. "This 'new' conduit was completed back in '42, engineered by Josiah Bissell, and hasn't leaked a drop."

Obadiah leaned over and kissed her. "Mercy! In public?" Nellie whispered, with a pleased blush.

"That was a reward for your resourcefulness in keeping well-informed in spite of your expanded duties," Obadiah said. They sailed through the streets of Rochester, into a bustling harbor, and docked at a busy quay.

My word, this town deserves its reputation as 'an emporium of mud and outcasts'. Nellie sniffed in dismay. *The elevated aqueduct is its only salient feature.* She giggled. *We shall hope the canal can one day elevate the rest of this town to a larger, more engaging city.*

By now they were accustomed to the business of the harbor — the disembarkation of passengers, the replenishment of supplies, and the boarding of new travelers. After what seemed like only a moment to stretch their legs, the *Storm Queen,* pulled by fresh horses, floated out of town.

Their packet was in the 'long level' now, the last lockless leg of sixty-three miles extending from Rochester to the stepped locks of Lockport. Nellie felt the pace of the journey quicken, ever so slightly, and she surmised the captain fully intended to take advantage of travel without interruption, but for a change of horses.

"After our three days and nights on the canal, I quite comprehend the appeal of having neither lock, block, nor stay of travel, to impede our progress," Nellie said. "But should we so cavalierly neglect honoring the Lord's Day?"

They sat at the breakfast table enjoying coffee and fresh farm eggs fried with a round of crisped pork, bartered yesterday from a farmer's barge.

An earnest-looking man, with spectacles that made him look pensive, said, "The packet boat is the cock-a-hoop high-mightiness of the Erie Canal. She alone can break God's holy law at four miles-per-hour, through special privilege granted by the Canal Commission."

Nellie nodded her thanks for the information and turned away from the speaker to cut some pork for Elizabeth. The pensive man cleared his throat and again addressed her, "Madam?" Nellie looked at him again with quizzical eyes.

"In light of this information, I expect you will attend my preaching later this morning, Madam?" The man tipped his hat to her.

Nellie recoiled. "But I..."

"This modern era affords us opportunity to worship *whilst* traveling. In point of fact, I believe we are called to consecrate our life's journey as an unending, continued worship of the Lord God Almighty," the preacher continued, bowing his head.

Nellie blushed and looked at Obadiah, who glared back, angry at the thought of coerced worship.

"With all due respect, Sir, I am a Catholic and I...." Cornelia Rose began.

"Then you should have taken advantage of the stop at Rochester. Just a short trek up the path from the berm they've got a pretty little Catholic Church. Saint Patrick's I do believe. Tsk, tsk, tsk. 'Tis inevitable now you shall neglect your obligation to attend Mass. There ain't no other *Catholic* Church until Medina. Furthermore, we shall not arrive at that dock until eight o'clock this evening, at which point you will have committed mortal sin, if memory of your Papist rules proves correct."

Nellie was flabbergasted. *I am quite certain this arduous traveling gives us dispensation.* She put her hand under her chin to close her gaping mouth.

Obadiah pulled her back around and gave her a fierce whisper. "Curb thy tongue! Your idle chatter has placed us in an untenable position. We must either disembark and walk back to Rochester, lose time at Church, and then organize our continued passage on the next packet — or attend this know-nothing's preaching."

Tears stinging her eyes, Nellie made an attempt to defend herself against his harsh criticism. "I petition you grant my fervent wish for no delay to our progress. Postponing my long-awaited reunion this very evening with my dear friend and fellow midwife shall trigger my profound grief."

Like recalcitrant children doing penance, Obadiah and Nellie sat listening to the assertive preacher's sermon. The girls, ordinarily well behaved in Church, squirmed under the preacher's rantings. Emma stood up and sat down, bounced from side to side and whispered to Elizabeth. Elizabeth shouted her replies and pulled away from Nellie's grasp. "Shh! Shush!" whispered Nellie, again and again. *Mercy, can my rebelliousness at the underhanded ensnarement of my person at this service instigate poor behavior in my daughters?* Nellie wondered.

She stole a glance at Obadiah. He seemed not at all concerned by his daughters' antics. He sat with an amused expression on his face. Nellie tried to return her attention to the preacher, who rambled and raved about 'fire and brimstone' and pounded his fist.

Elizabeth jumped up and shouted, "No".

My daughter rejects fire and brimstone? Nellie and Obadiah stood, as of one accord, whispered apologies to the people sitting next to them and removed themselves from the area. All eyes turned to stare at them.

The Wrights escaped outside. Nellie and her daughters looked apprehensively at Obadiah when Nellie closed the door behind them. "That's quite enough of that," he said. The girls looked uncertainly at Nellie. She smiled. Obadiah laughed and opened his arms. Nellie joined his laughter. His daughters ran to Obadiah, and covered him with kisses. They climbed to the top deck for repose on the packet's benches and the calisthenics of jumping down at the call of 'low bridge'.

"At a minimum, the preacher could have had a lap organ to provide relief, and arm us with ammunition to resist our sermon-induced stupor," said Obadiah with his good-humored grin.

"We certainly were subjected to a healthy dose of hell fire and eternal damnation," agreed Nellie.

A church bell chimed as they passed through the town of Spencerport.

"Ten o'clock, Methodist time," Obadiah said with a wicked grin. He and Nellie laughed and settled in to enjoy the crisp fall air and the golden sunshine. Obadiah opened the Rochester *Telegraph*, hawked while their boat floated in the quay, and Nellie began knitting a new pair of mittens for Emma.

At last the spacing of occupation bridges became so thickly clustered that the girls' song lyrics proved true — they came to the town of Lockport, and its famous stairway of five locks.

Nellie could not believe her eyes. Her friend Clara Rafferty Otis stood on the towpath well before the entrance to the first lock, scanning all the passengers on *Young Lion of the West*, the packet lining up ahead of them for the flight of locks, looking for her.

"Halloooo! Here!" Nellie shouted. "We are here, in the next boat!" She blushed. She could just hear her mother's chastisement, *'One week in the wilderness and you are shouting like a tenement dweller calling her children home for supper'*. Tears popped out of her eyes. *Ach, Mutter! Her frequent admonitions have been drilled into my manner and the memory of her words shall keep her close to my heart.*

"Clara!" Nellie shouted again. Her daughters jumped up and down and shouted with her. "We are on the *Storm Queen*."

"Obadiah, I see Clara," Nellie jumped into his arms, in her excitement.

"And I see her husband," Obadiah replied with a grin.

Nellie felt the wind leave her sails.

"Mercy, did you not expect to see your former beau, *and* dear friend's husband, Elmer P. Otis?" Obadiah teased.

"I deluded myself with the hope he would be deployed on an Army Corps of Engineers' assignment," replied Nellie, head hanging down. "Moreover," she stamped her foot, her elation gone. "He was *never* my beau!"

Moments later, Nellie jumped out of their boat and into the arms of her childhood friend. After a long hug, she turned to introduce Clara to her children. So excited, Nellie knocked Elizabeth with her skirt and sent her stumbling headlong towards the canal. She reached out and caught her daughter seconds before the toddler toppled sideways into the churning water.

"Thank the Lord you have retained your excellent reflexes," said Clara. The women laughed and hugged each other again. It took several more hugs and excited chatter before they walked up the incline from the towpath, toward the shops and taverns of the town.

Nellie peppered her friend with scores of questions.

"When I first arrived, I do confess, I thought Lockport a most peculiar place," said Clara. "The stumps of newly felled trees predominated the landscape, resting side by side with the new factory buildings that gradually replaced the forest. Francis Trollope's snide remark that my town '...looks as if the demon of machinery, having invaded the peaceful realms of nature, had fixed on Lockport as the battleground on which they should strive for mastery...' was not far off the mark. Now however, the poor forest has quite conceded defeat, and civilization has taken its firm hold. We have sixteen hotels...."

As her friend listed the 'improvements' to the town, Nellie could not help but wonder if this unbridled commerce was truly progress.

The town retains a frontier look, in spite of the plethora of shops, hotels, and taverns, Cornelia noticed. The stores displayed fine goods in their windows, but the architecture seemed straight out of a photograph of the Wild West. She listened to her friend with one ear as they walked along, the other ear monitoring her little girls skipping and jumping. After four solid days and three nights of floating along the canal, the children's relief at leaving the cramped packet expressed itself in running races. Nellie smiled at their antics.

Clara frowned. "I do apologize for the logjam of traffic. Since the Sabbath prevents the freight boats from locking through, yesterday all other boats were given priority over packets, which has caused a bit of a delay. I am sorry to report your boat could be tied up locking for hours."

Nellie looked surprised. The Wright family happily availed themselves of every opportunity to go ashore while the packet boat waited in line for its turn in every lock. She said, "The interval affords the real pleasure of a fine, leisurely walk. An extended stroll through your growing town provides quite the luxury for us. Yet my paramount pleasure resides in the fact that our visit shall not conclude when our boat descends to the lowest level. Rather, we shall prolong our companionship whilst you join us on the packet for your overnight trip to Towanda."

With happy smiles, the two women watched in delight as the little girls frolicked and laughed their way across the 'widest bridge in the world', enjoying the feel of a non-rocking surface. The bridge, a touted feature of the town, hosted two taverns, a hotel, and some shops, in addition to carrying Lockport's Main Street over the canal.

Nellie looked behind them in search of Obadiah. He followed a few paces behind, deep in conversation with Clara's husband. *Thank you, Obadiah, for sparing me from a tête-á-tête with Elmer Petulant Otis, my former suitor.* Nellie could hear Obadiah asking questions about the 19th century engineering wonder, the unique flight of five double locks performing its mighty task right below them. She looked over the bridge's railing and watched the water rush in on one side of the double lock and empty on the other.

"I rather like this bird's-eye view," she said to Clara. They stared down at the ingenious lock system. The canal here divided in two. Five levels of locks were placed side-by-side, one set for elevating eastbound traffic and the other for lowering boats heading west. Both sides had long lines of vessels, waiting to be transported the sixty-foot height differential.

The workings of the locks blurred and faded from her consciousness. Her happiness at seeing her old friend made her giddy and unable to concentrate on anything else but the joy of the reunion.

"I fretted our time together would be truncated by your desire to remain onboard as your packet traveled this engineering marvel, whilst I may not board until the ship has locked through," said Clara.

"Fret not, my dear companion, all the engineering wonders of the world could not wrench me from your company. We Wrights remained onboard through the full panoply of the other seventy-eight locks along the way, experiencing firsthand the modern feats of engineering they embodied. Our frequent locking somewhat diminishes the Lockport steps' novelty and marvel. Moreover, we likewise rode the aqueducts carrying the canals over the rivers, astonished at the design ingenuity. You might say we experienced every canal pleasure and treasure."

"Mercy, riding seems contrary to your ever-locomotive nature, Cornelia. Have you never walked along the towpath?" asked Clara.

Nellie laughed. "Of course. We took advantage of every daytime change of horses, and any equipment delays. We simply chose to float onboard through all the engineering wonders.

"Now, not another moment's delay. We must engage in a 'mung-meeting'. I must impart the news of your mother and my family," said Nellie, linking her arm with Clara and bending her head toward her friend.

"How I have missed your delightful wordsmith-ing. It does my heart good to hear and remember this bit of my childhood. 'Mung-meeting'! Canalese for gossip—you have become a regular canawler," said Clara.

"If my word choice so delights you, my actual news of your loved ones shall transport you to the moon with happiness," Nellie replied. They walked deep in conversation for many delightful moments, discussing all of their mutual acquaintances.

But neither Nellie's many tête-à-têtes with Clara, nor Obadiah's diversion tactics prevented the inevitable awkward encounter with Elmer.

Elmer found his opportunity while the rest of the family gazed in wonder at the mechanics of the lock system, housed in a building in the middle of the lock stairs. He cornered her behind a tall gearbox and leaned a little too close to Nellie.

Elmer whispered, "May I say you look resplendent in that gown, Cornelia Rose, as lovely as the day I spurned you for another."

Nellie wrinkled her nose at his acrid, sweaty scent, and his close proximity, and blushed crimson with fury. *Why, you deceitful little weasel!* "No. In fact, you may *not* say. History most accurately confirms, as we *both* are fully cognizant, I rejected *you*," Cornelia said.

At the sight of Otis's crumpled face, she immediately regretted her words. "Mercy," Nellie tried to make amends, touching him lightly on the arm. "I did not mean to hurt...."

Elmer stiffened and pulled his arm away. "Mrs. Otis and I are quite happy, thank you very much for asking."

Nellie realized she must ignore her pride and overlook Otis' attempt to re-write history. "I ascertained my dear companion Clara was content and pleased the moment I saw you both standing at the dock. Truly, you make a worthy couple."

"Yessiree," Otis said. "I am quite the catch. They say you missed the boat when you failed to reel me in, Cornelia Rose."

Nellie grit her teeth. *As if his conceit were not irritating enough, he insists on mixing his metaphors....* Her new resolve to overlook her anger crumbled.

She was spared formulating a reply, however, when Obadiah strode forward and clapped Elmer on the back. *Thank you Lord for the interruption.* She smiled at her husband with big, loving eyes. *Once again, my knight in shining armor has come to my rescue.*

"Otis, you've had a hand in engineering quite the little beauty of a canal," Obadiah said with a jocund expression on his face. Nellie stifled a giggle. *Elmer puffs his chest as though he were personally responsible for excogitating and digging the entire canal!*

"Yessiree," said Elmer, clamping Obadiah back, and then standing awkwardly on his tiptoes to keep his arm around Obadiah's shoulders. "Hewn out of stone, she's not only a wonder of the world and a thing of beauty, but she is worth her weight in gold. Ever since she opened, farmers in central Georgia are complaining that wheat from this western part of the great Empire State is selling in Savannah *cheaper* than their own Georgian wheat!"

Obadiah grinned and stepped back, permitting Otis to drop his arm.

Elmer slapped his thigh.

Why he seems to be reviving the feeling in his arm and his limb. Nellie giggled to herself.

"Yessir," Elmer said again, with another slap, as if to prove he was only doing it to emphasize the importance of his proclamations. "This here canal is what made New York City the biggest port city in the nation. As well it should, what with the *en*-tire construction funded solely by the great state of New York, without any U. S. Treasury money at all. The Federals are crying in their beers now. It's got them folks in Boston and Philly all fired up, but they still don't know what hit 'em. They're going to have to acknowledge the corn and watch their own ports play second fiddle."

"Or build their own canals." said Obadiah with a laugh.

"Well, *this* here canal is the Gateway to the West! Furthermore, and it's almost against my interest to admit this, the original brains behind the famed flight of five double lock systems was Nathan Roberts, a man bereft of a formal West Point engineering education. So, logic would imply any new canal, built by a *trained* engineer, could provide us pretty stiff competition.

"Yessiree. But no one's built anything like this yet. To my way of thinking, it's Roberts' fresh perspective, what provided the breakthrough. Roberts was a teacher by trade. The second in command, Amasa Drake, learned on the job as well. On a lark in 1817, Roberts joined the original survey team. After scouting out the route, he submitted the winning lock design that solved the problem of ascending the Niagara escarpment. He was self-taught and genius-like and sought little aid from even published works on the subject of engineering."

"If that don't beat the Dutch!" said Obadiah.

Elmer slapped his leg again and agreed. "Yessir, Cornelia, your pappy must be so proud, what with him a self-taught engineer too, and Irish to boot, like the lot of workers whose sweat and tears actually dug those ditches."

Nellie, surprised at the laudatory compliment to her father, felt unbidden tears come to her eyes.

Elmer didn't notice. But Clara did. She gave Nellie a hug as her husband continued. "So go on now, and copy it, I say. Old Thomas Evershed from England is still head engineer on the enlargement project, and he'll personally guarantee the entirety of the canal channel will soon be bigger and better than ever. But let the old Erie give them other states a leg up on their own canals. My canal is responsible for Ohio, Illinois...." Elmer held up a stubby hand and ticked the names off on his fingers, "...Indiana, Wisconsin, *and* Michigan's economic ties to the East. She also conveys a considerable number of folks like you out West, *and* connects you with a market once you get there," Elmer paused.

Is it too much to hope he has exhausted this subject?

"Might I offer you the finest anti-fogmatic money can buy around these parts?" he asked, with a slight flourish.

"No, no, Elmer," said Clara, joining the conversation, with each of Nellie's daughters holding one of her hands. "Mr. Wright cannot imbibe that raw whiskey. We must offer him some of our finer spirits."

"Pshaw, he won't let it put a brick in his hat," scoffed Elmer. "Unless you don't set by this here type of refreshment."

Obadiah shook his head 'no' and Nellie turned the girls away.

"All right then, no offense taken," said Elmer, taking a swig from the bottle. "Come over this-a-way. There's a fine view of the lock tenders putting our machinery through its paces. I'm sure you won't want to miss that." He threw his arm around Obadiah's shoulders and, on tiptoes again, dragged him off, leaving Nellie and Clara free to explore the town with the two little girls.

"I must say...." Nellie giggled to Clara. "Your midwifery remedies have done wonders. I remember when your strapping husband was a wimpy, whiny boy."

Clara looked a bit irked, but smiled and said, "Well at least you didn't call him a 'weakling dandiprat' again."

Nellie's face turned an alarming shade of magenta. "Mercy, Clara, that was a long time ago, before he turned his attentions to you. I humbly apologize, I meant only to compliment you. I meant no slight, nor criticism."

Clara laughed. "I well remember, when Otis pursued your hand, how often you despaired 'that sickly ruffleshirt' was your suitor." Nellie opened her mouth to protest. Clara held up her hand to stop her. "But *I* could see his mettle beneath the ruffles. Furthermore, I knew *I* held the magic elixir."

"The elixir, not just of herbs and tinctures for wellness, but the magic of love," agreed Nellie. She put her arm around Clara. They smiled and continued their walk.

"For the first time on our canal trip, I do hope locking through takes a long time!" Nellie exclaimed. But instead, it felt like time accelerated as she enjoyed her friend's company. In just the tick of a clock, the packet had locked through the steps and they returned to board the boat.

Clara ducked into the gate cabinet next to the building that housed the lock mechanism and jumped aboard their packet carrying a small overnight bag.

Nellie breathed a sigh of relief. Duty prevented Elmer from joining their journey. She blithely waved goodbye as he left to report to the superintendent at the locks. Only Clara would ride with them to visit her friends a few towns up the canal in the last city before their terminus in Buffalo at Lake Erie.

"Fresh pike and baked jacket potatoes for dinner," Obadiah advised. "And do I smell a molasses and four egg cake for dessert?"

Nellie felt like joining her daughters, jumping up and down in happiness.

The evening flew by. The two women talked and laughed. The feeling of *gemütlickheit*, her mother's German for 'wellbeing' and 'coziness' overtook her. For the first time since they had left home, she felt content.

Happy to have a kindred spirit, Nellie confided, "Eau de Cologne and feather fans have been my salvation in these close quarters. Even at the end of October the atmosphere in the lounge, with all these bodies pressed so tightly together, can be stifling."

Soon, the now familiar scene of converting the day lounge into sleeping quarters unfolded before her eyes, as she sat, lazily talking to her friend over biscuits and tea.

The staff shooed her to readiness. Obadiah said his goodnights to each of the ladies. The red curtain dropped between the men's and women's quarters.

"Even on the fourth night, I still find it quite disconcerting to disrobe under these circumstances," Nellie whispered to Clara as she stowed her two little girls on the shelf above her and strung and tacked the colorful scarf she used as a bed railing into place. "In fact, before you joined us, I slept fully clothed."

"Including your corset?" Clara whispered back. "How dreadfully uncomfortable."

"Obadiah confirmed — the slightest sound is heard by the men on the other side of this divide. He found the noises rather disconcerting too, as if his ears became his eyes, and he could see laces loosened, stockings rolled down over shapely legs, heavy dresses pulled overhead revealing...."

Clara giggled quietly into Nellie's ear. "Our fairer sex shall never control the thoughts and imaginations of these beastly men. Best not to speculate what their ears do with the information so voyeuristically gleaned!"

"I am in complete accord." said Nellie and gave her own giggle.

"Shhh!" hissed several voices from the surrounding berths. Nellie put her knee on the middle berth and pulled herself up to the lip of the shelf above it to reach the top bunk. She kissed her girls on their soft cheeks as she tucked their blanket up to their sleeping faces. She ducked down to the shelf below and Clara tumbled into that middle shelf behind her.

"I realize this shelf has the width of a coffin, but I thought perhaps these tight quarters would give us a few more moments to whisper together," said Nellie.

"I was wondering how we might arrange additional private conversation," whispered Clara back. "The demands upon our time are far greater than when we were mere buds on the stem."

Nellie and Clara lay with their arms around each other, nose to nose, exchanging confidences. They enjoyed silent laughter, and a few tears.

A loud snort, and sonorous snoring from the men's section behind the crimson curtain interrupted their tears, engendered by Nellie's sad story of her brother Matthias' misfortune in love.

Both misty-eyed women giggled.

"In my experience, the loudest snores emanate from the people quietest during the day." Giggled Clara. They held each other close as the boat continued its steady progress, lulled to sleep by the comforting nighttime sounds of water lapping, rain tapping, and an occasional horse whinny.

Suddenly, Nellie's sleep was disrupted. *But what has transpired? I did not hear anything alarming. Oh, Mercy, our movement has ceased!*

"Why have we pulled toward the berm? What could be amiss?" Nellie asked Clara.

"Shh, listen," said Clara. They could hear talking and commotion.

The solitary *night I disrobe for sleep,* Nellie grumbled to herself. She jumped down and scrambled to pull her dress on over her nightgown. Nellie stuck her head out of the opening in the women's section just in time to see Obadiah hurry by.

"Stay here, you are not properly dressed. I will ascertain the emergency and report back immediately." He threw the words over his shoulder as he went by.

Clara stepped around Nellie. "I shall investigate," she said. "*My husband is not here to chastise me about the inappropriateness of my appearance.*"

Clara was back in less time than it took Nellie to go back to her row of shelves and check on her children.

"'Tis a mercy I reconnoitered, so you could receive the news immediately," said Clara. "Your husband remains on deck, toying with the notion of joining the 'hurry up' boat. There is speculation that a bank of the canal collapsed. All hands must be on deck to mend a breached wall."

Nellie shook her head to see if that would help her make sense of this information.

Clara laughed. "My apologies. We are merely pulled over to the berm to allow the hurry up boat to sail through."

"The constant overtaking and passing other vessels has been a noticeable singularity of our voyage. Throughout the entirety of our journey we have been given right of way, in addition to being allowed to travel on the Sabbath, unlike the freight and line boats," said Nellie. "Why are we ceding precedence of travel now?"

"'Tis a hurry up boat, coming down the canal towards us," said Clara, looking at her as if Nellie had lost some of her hearing.

"What in tarnation is that?" Nellie asked, surprised to learn some new canal lingo this far into their journey.

Clara frowned. "I am afraid it means there is trouble down the line. The *hurry up boat* is a thin, narrow needle shaped boat that squeezes between the other boats on the canal to help any boat stopped, grounded, or otherwise distressed. I do hope there are no injuries. I wonder if my medical services will be required."

Nellie and Clara went to the entry of the ladies' section. Once again, as if on cue, Obadiah appeared.

"The hurry up boat is bound for trouble behind us. There is naught we can do; no aid we can provide at this time," Obadiah reported.

"But what is the difficulty?" both Cornelia and Clara asked.

"A boat with bilge water waist high to its helmsman, marooned right in the middle of the canal a few miles back. It's choking the canal and halting traffic all the way back to Lockport," he replied.

"Mercy, thank goodness!" exclaimed Clara, breathing in deeply with her hand over her heart.

Nellie and Obadiah looked at her in surprise.

She lifted round apologetic eyes to them. "Pshaw, 'tis not good there is a distressed boat, truly. But it came to my mind that the worst of all canal disasters occurred—a breach!" She patted herself on her chest and drew a deep breath, as if to calm herself. "I thought land cascaded into the canal, filling it with dirt and grounding every boat in its path. Inhibiting and repairing a breech is dangerous work—all manner of men felling trees to make retaining gates, repack the dirt and rebuild the dam. 'Twould have ground all the traffic to a halt, mayhap for days, whilst they re-excavated the canal. Mercy, I thank the Lord Mr. Otis was spared a night's rough work!"

Cornelia and Obadiah looked at each other. Obadiah shrugged. "I do believe the emergency is well in hand here, at least for the time being. We'd best get a bit more shut-eye. We arrive in Towanda with the first light of the morning."

It was heart wrenching to say goodbye to Clara. They barely had time to finish the sumptuous breakfast, consisting of rashers of bacon with fluffy scrambled eggs, before they heard the announcement of their impending arrival.

"Goose-girl?" asked Elizabeth.

"Are these eggs from the goose-girl?" translated Nellie. Clara laughed and said, "Maybe not the girl you saw but someone's goose or chicken-girl, anyway."

After what seemed like mere seconds at the wharf in Towanda, the crew shouted the warning for departure.

Nellie clung to Clara, hugging her one more time. She thrust a bundle of silk into Clara's hands and jumped back onboard their packet.

"What is this?" called Clara. "'Tis is no occasion for gifts."

Nellie laughed. "'Tis my hoop form, wrapped in a silk nightgown."

"But I cannot accept this," protested Clara, making as if to lean across the gap between the boat and the wharf and throw it back.

"I shall not accept your protestations. You simply must," said Nellie, stepping back and holding up her hands. "Other than at Agnes' house in Chicago, there shall be no occasion to wear either of them."

The horses began to pull, and the boat slipped from its mooring.

"Then give it to Agnes," Clara called, walking alongside the boat, now tugged along the towpath.

"I have yet another for her. As you can see, there is not enough space for hooped skirts, even on this boat. Hoops shall be hopelessly out of place on the plains. I have already shortened the hem on half of my gowns to accommodate the lack of hoops," Nellie replied. "I have reconciled myself to the loss of civilized fashion for the duration of my time on the Overland Trail. I only hope this loss of style is temporary."

"I do believe you are correct. I have seen more than a few women headed West pass through wearing bloomer garments. You might contemplate adopting that fashion," said Clara, continuing to walk alongside the boat.

"Mercy! That is perhaps a bit too much of a nod to the lack of civilization I expect to find west of here. The most I shall concede is a bifurcated skirt.

"Now, wear those niceties in good health. I shall think of you often, and of course, correspond when I can," said Nellie.

Clara nodded and stopped walking, clutching the silk parcel to her.

Nellie felt as if she were leaving another piece of her heart behind as she waved her handkerchief at Clara's receding figure.

As if she had heard her thoughts, Clara put the parcel under her arm, made a catching gesture, and placed her hands over her heart. Then she pulled them away again and threw them open, sending a piece of *her* heart back to Nellie.

Nellie caught it, placed her hands on her heart, and stifled a tear.

CHAPTER 22
It's Beginning to Look a lot like Christmas

Sandusky, Ohio to Chicago, Illinois, November 1856

"This is the longest portage in the world," grumbled Cornelia. "What has addled the abilities of Mr. Armistead Long that he could not fully champion the building of a canal from Toledo to Chicago? He must end his befuddlement and advocate the Corps of Engineers begin construction. This walk shall never end!"

"But Mama, we at last get to ride in our wagon," said Emma.

"Yes," seconded Elizabeth. "Wagon fun!"

"My little angels, you are wise to encourage me to higher spirits. I shall abandon this melancholy." Nellie laughed and looked at Obadiah as they trudged along next to their horses. "After all, our dear brother-in-law, Armistead Long, is simply acting true to form. Waffling and 'backing and filling' on an issue have become his forte."

Obadiah smiled and reached his hand to catch her stray hair and tuck it behind her ear. His hand lingered on her chin. The floodgates of love and good feeling opened once again in Nellie's heart and she forgot her disgruntlement.

Nellie smiled at her daughters perched atop the wagon bench. Not content to remain distant, she jumped up next to them and sat on the seat, giving Emma a hug and tickling Elizabeth. *I believe I shall appreciate this seat anew every time I sit upon it*, she thought, wiggling herself in like a kid settling into his parent's lap. *Thank the Lord Obadiah heeded my request and added this feature to our Conestoga.*

"The view from this bench is simply grand. We shall enjoy discovering the Overland Trail from this perch." She hugged both her daughters and continued, "This passage is but a presage of our adventurous journey. Howsoever, before we fully don the mantle of 'pioneers and explorers', we shall visit Aunt Agnes in her house in Chicago."

"Then it will be Christmas!" shouted Emma. Elizabeth echoed, "Kissmiss."

Obadiah jumped up into the wagon seat with them, shouting, "Steady on now boys," to the horses.

"My Cornelia Rose, I am happy you abandoned your grousing tone. I for one, have been longing to test our workhorses and set sail on our own prairie schooner.

"And look, little ladies," he flicked his whip on the team lightly. "These old horses are so strong, they can pull this heavy wagon unaided. Of course, our Conestoga is only three quarters filled with a light load, and this path is packed down like our roads at home—unlike the rough terrain through the plains and the mountains up ahead."

Nellie smiled, good humor restored. *After all, two months frolic and detour with dear sister Agnes begins after completion of just a little more than a day's journey.* "I am mindful of your barely restrained enthusiasm to travel under our own steam. You have been chomping at the bit. I'll allow, you do not find sailing nearly as charming as I do." She laughed. "Howsoever, we shall rely on this point of agreement—the definition of sailing, or even boating for that matter, cannot possibly encompass floating down a muddy canal behind three trudging horses!"

Obadiah joined in her merriment. "I, for my part shall confess, I did rather enjoy the sail across vast Lake Erie after we abandoned that abysmal canal barge in Buffalo. In fact, you are correct, the 'sailing' was positively charming."

As their wagon rolled into the town of Chicago, Nellie and her family observed the familiar signs of civilization. *Civilized, but still raw, rustic, and rough around the edges,* Cornelia thought, observing the swinging doors on the tavern and the wooden façades of the stores. *Pshaw, every commercial establishment in New York City, and most fine houses, are built of brick these days. Even in our little village of Sing Sing, we construct new buildings of brick. The only wood structure I can recall still extant is the old Buckout livery. But I shall not sound a sour note by voicing my disparagement of the architecture.*

"Mama, why are some streets way up high and some down low?" asked Emma, demonstrating with her hands.

"Room for air underneath?" asked Elizabeth.

"These are excellent questions, the answers to which I am sure shall be provided, posthaste, by your Uncle Armistead," replied Obadiah.

Nellie laughed. "Yes, I am sure Mr. Long and his Corps of Engineers had a hand in this undertaking." They turned a corner, and Nellie spotted a numbered house. "We are just a few houses away!"

Whooping and hollering, three boys emerged from a large house and ran towards their wagon. Two adults appeared in the doorway and watched them pull the wagon up the drive.

The Wright ensemble hesitated before disembarking. *Even our horses look uncertain as to how to interpret this reception.*

"Uncle Armistead Long, why dirt here?" called Elizabeth, pointing to a pile of sticks, stones, and mud.

The adults all laughed. Emboldened, Emma asked, "Why is your house suspended in the air on big blocks?"

"They are *raising* the streets," said Agnes as she ran forward. "Literally elevating them directly from this God-forsaken swamp on the edge of Lake Michigan."

Nellie jumped out of the wagon, ran to her sister, and swung her around in a big embrace. Her sister returned the hug.

"Mercy, you are a bright young thing, ain't ya? And right purdy too!" drawled Armistead Long. "Now consider yourselves at home and run off and play with your cousins."

Emma and Elizabeth looked at each other uncertainly. Emma said, "If it is acceptable to you, Uncle Armistead, I do believe my sister and I would feel far more *at home* having tea with the adults."

Nellie gasped. *Agnes will dispense a tongue lashing for that, no doubt! Tarnation! We have not put our best foot forward.*

But Agnes looked extremely pleased for some reason. And Armistead threw back his head and laughed.

"In point of fact," said Agnes, arms crossed in front of her chest, looking like a drill sergeant. Nellie cringed, awaiting a lecture. "It plumb tickles me pink, having some fine young ladies from the East join us at a proper tea." Agnes gave a huge, uncharacteristic smile that lit up her face and increased her beauty one hundredfold. Nellie stood stock-still, dumbfounded. Agnes took Nellie's arm and gave her another hug. "I have long held the sentiment our home would feel more civilized if I had a little angel of a daughter to keep me company. Now *two* such angels arrive at my doorstep. No longer am I the lone female tackling the herculean task of instilling the civility I was bred to practice into a family of rough and tumble men. I have been given a reprieve!"

Relief broke over Nellie's face like the sun breaking out from behind a cloud. "Perhaps this situation is a foretaste of your life to come." She squeezed her sister's arm.

"If it please the Lord, Amen," said Agnes. "Sakes alive, it does my heart good to see you."

Nellie laughed. *Loneliness certainly blunted that sharp tongue of my sister's.*

But she praised her sister too soon.

"The deprivations and the trials I have had to endure in this *God*-forsaken swamp they have the audacity to call a 'city', are more than a decent soul should bear!" Agnes' face resumed its usual dour expression and she wrung her hands.

"Yet, you call *me* dramatic," said Nellie with a laugh. At the thunderous look on her sister's face, Nellie gave Agnes another hug.

"Now, my little short-sweetenin'," said Armistead in a soothing voice. "As I just explained to our nieces, Chicago shall soon be, quite literally, lifted from this swamp and constructed into a great city."

I'll wager Armistead's soothing tone grows more and more polished through daily use, Nellie smiled to herself.

A loud *whoop whoop* cough caught Nellie's ear.

The three boys ran to the far side of the garden. The distress of Agnes' youngest son's loud whooping cough distracted Nellie. She held up her hand and interrupted further conversation.

"Yes, I know," Agnes wrung her hands again. "Dagobert had the whooping cough."

"Had?" asked Cornelia. "He still sounds afflicted to me."

"He is much restored. Observe—he is out of bed and running around." Agnes defended her diagnosis.

"The sound of that wracking cough disturbs me," said Cornelia. "We must address this lingering symptom. I shall concoct several diverse elixirs, each addressing a different one of the myriad causes of the persistent cough. We must not allow this illness to fester into a relapse. Or, far worse, in his weakened condition, allow it to degenerate into consumption."

Agnes led her up the stairs of their grand entrance. "Your mere arrival restores me to better humor straightaway. The joy of my relief at no longer functioning as the sole guardian of the health of my brood is quite euphoric. 'Tis unfathomable, the burden I alone shoulder, to maintain and ensure the vigor and well-being of this motley clutch of heathens."

Nellie grinned, glad to her core that she had insisted on including a visit to Agnes on their journey's route. She had been unsure until just this moment whether Agnes's acid tongue and critical nature would make her regret this detour. *At this compliment to my heretofore-unrecognized medical knowledge, and her endearing terms for my daughters, my heart rejoices! My bond with my sister strengthens tenfold. We are kindred spirits – both lonely walkers through this new world.*

"I am pleased as punch to hear my midwifery can aid you, rather than continue to be a thorn in your side," she replied with a mischievous smile.

Agnes snatched her arm from Nellie's and puckered her face in preparation for an unkind retort. Nellie laughed and folded her sister's arm back under her own. "Hush! My midwifery skills shall be entirely at your disposal for my entire stay. I look forward to a new chapter in our relationship." They walked through the front double doors into a grandiose foyer.

"Mercy!" Nellie exclaimed, pulling away. "I forgot. We must unload the wagon."

This time Agnes pulled Nellie's arm back. "The wagon *and* its contents shall remain unharmed where they landed until *after* we have tea and you have refreshed yourself."

But Nellie evaded her grasp and ran back to the wagon. "There is just one thing I simply must retrieve. I'll be back in a thrice," she called. Before Agnes could shout any reply, Nellie climbed into the back opening of the wagon and practically dove inside.

Her head reappeared an instant later, followed by the rest of her as she jumped back down, cradling something in her arms. She ran across the garden, and up the front steps.

"What in all the world is...." began Agnes.

Breathless, Nellie, already back at Agnes's side panted, "This would... not wait... one millisecond longer... I must present it to you now." She thrust the parcel at her sister.

Untying the string, Agnes muttered, "Sakes alive," as she tore off the paper, revealing a large pineapple, slightly browned on one side. She held it up to her nose and sniffed it.

"You see... it could... barely wait to get here," Nellie said, still panting. "I worried constantly it would ripen too rapidly, or that *someone*...." She glared at Obadiah and her girls. "...would purloin and devour it, as every time they approached the wagon they claimed they could smell its enticing sweetness."

Agnes inhaled deeply, smelling it again. "Visions of the mighty Hudson River swim before my eyes. I can hear the beat of the seagulls' wings. I can feel my own sticky fingers." But she raised troubled eyes to her sister. "By the horn spoon, no! According to the New England shipping communities, *I* am required to set out the pineapple to welcome *you*," she fretted.

Nellie put her arm around Agnes's shoulders, saying, "No, no. Now that we have arrived from afar, the pineapple can be placed at your door, so that all your friends and neighbors know your 'sea captain'...." Nellie winked, "...or, in this case, your 'ship' of loved ones, has arrived. Local visitors are now welcome." Agnes did not react. Nellie tried further explanation. "Thus, you no longer await, anxiously, adverse to callers. *That* is the old New England tradition."

Agnes stood speechless, holding the pineapple to her nose, sniffling.

Nellie tensed and took her arm off her sister's stiff shoulders. *Has this gift somehow offended my sister?* "I am aware that a good many years must still pass before your husband's Corps of Engineers can construct a canal between Chicago and Toledo," she offered "...if at all. It felt unchristian to deprive you of pineapple fresh shipped from the West Indies until then."

Agnes remained still, eyes and nose on the pineapple, looking cross-eyed.

Maybe she perceives the brown spot as distasteful? Mayhap the extreme ripeness of the fruit is offensive to her sensibilities? Nellie gulped and said, "I had hoped the pineapple would keep until it was time to make the Yuletide wassail, but I am afraid it is rather past its peak ripeness."

Agnes opened her mouth, and then closed it again. She burst into tears.

"I fear I have deeply offended you!" Nellie cried in alarm.

"Nooooo," wailed Agnes, cradling the pineapple in her arms. "I ache for our hometown and my family so severely I do believe I have a physical pain in my heart." Nellie put her arm back around her sister. Agnes shook her head and took one more sniff of the pineapple. Her voice, albeit just a bit shaky, took on its familiar, authoritarian tone. "Mark my words, this coarse, uncivilized existence is simply untenable and unsustainable. I daily resist the urge to pack up and journey back to Sing Sing."

Nellie looked around at her sister's grandiose house, perched atop newly packed dirt already cultivated into a garden, with a fine view of a developing city and vast Lake Michigan. *Mercy, Agnes thinks* this *is uncivilized? What of my lot and portion? I fear my future holds only serious deprivations in store, loneliness being the worst curse of all.* Tears welled in Cornelia's eyes. *Poppycock.* She shook herself. *I travel with those I love most in this world. We are our own hardy band of love, warmth, and comfort. We are a self-contained little civilization. We shall not only endure, we shall excel and be prosperous.*

Nellie gave Agnes a hug. She was at a loss for words as to how to comfort her sister, so she said, "Mayhap if we squeeze the pineapple now, collecting its juice for the wassail, it shall outlive these last two weeks until Christmas. A springhouse would aid this endeavor. Has Armistead constructed one?"

Agnes collected herself and said through gritted teeth, "No. He has not. My engineer is far too busy. But that is a subject for another conversation.

"There shall be no wasting this precious fruit as a door decoration, custom or not. Nor will we fritter it away on wassail. We shall slice it immediately and savor its succulent juices before our tea."

Nellie opened her mouth to protest. But Agnes did not notice. "The tea has long since grown too cold, in any case," she said.

She glared at Nellie, who somehow now felt guilty for ruining her sister's tea.

"Furthermore," her sister continued, "Mother Long has imparted her old English recipe for wassail, claiming it is quite superior." Agnes sniffed. "I confess I was pleasantly surprised to find her recipes contained some valuable information for utilizing the few vegetables and fruits in plenty here, in unique dishes. Quite tasty, in point of fact. It has certainly pleased Armistead that I have endeavored to recreate some of his mother's southern cooking. In any case, Mother Long has forced me to concede that wassail more properly *should* be made the old English way, with tart apples instead of pineapple juice."

Nellie nodded her affirmation.

"Do not tell Armistead that I only concede this point out of necessity — due to the scarcity of pineapple around these parts."

Nellie laughed at her sister's attempt at levity. "Then it is settled. Sharpen your best knife," she declared. Agnes led Nellie and her daughters through the beautiful foyer, straight into the large, well-appointed kitchen.

The Long boys ran into the room, marveling and shouting at the appearance of the pineapple. Each boy declared he wanted the first piece.

Emma and Elizabeth stood on either side of Nellie eyeing their cousins as visitors might watch wild animals in a zoo. The menfolk entered the kitchen.

"What have we here?" asked Armistead, with a big grin. Cuthbert, the oldest boy, climbed up the sink and jumped on Armistead's back as he approached the group. Both families surrounded the big table and watched solemnly as Agnes sliced the pineapple.

"Mama, Egbert has crooked-y legs. Do you think he has rickets?" Emma asked, neatly nibbling her slice.

Elizabeth nodded her head, 'yes' making pineapple juice dribble down her chin. She caught it with her finger and sucked it back into her mouth as she said, "Yeth, rick-ith."

Nellie looked at her sister, dismayed at her daughters' bad manners.

"Not full on!" said Agnes, putting her hand, still clutching the knife, on her hip and turning to Elizabeth as if to debate the point. At the sight of the adorable little girl looking up at her, with one edge of her bonnet drooping over her eye and a sticky-mouth smile, she softened. She looked over at Nellie. "I do fear he may be advancing down that slippery slope."

Nellie, her own delicious slice already consumed, *Lord knows I attempted to savor it, knowing full well I may never eat pineapple again,* stooped and looked under the table at her nephews' legs. One set of little boy legs did look slightly malformed.

"We shall begin treatment today," said Cornelia, righting herself.

"Cornelia, 'tis incomprehensible your pineapple-toting Conestoga wagon also secretes every remedy for any malady," Agnes huffed, now both hands on her hips. "Sakes alive, how was there room for the rest of you to fit?"

"I'll grant, I did not transport *every* therapy. Fret not, however. Any herb deficiency shall be readily rectified by a trip to the market in a sprawling city such as your Chicago. But most likely you have some of these very necessities in the harvest from your lovely garden."

Placated, Agnes smiled. "There is one more concern, however."

"Don't tell me Cuthbert has some disease as well?"

"None of my boys are *diseased!* We simply fight the plagues rampant in this swamp of a town," Agnes retorted.

Agnes washed the big knife and hung it out of harm's reach. The two women left the kitchen, leaving the children laughing and licking the cutting board and table in search of remnants of pineapple juice. "Make sure you do not touch the slices for your fathers," warned Agnes in a stage whisper, as the men continued to talk, oblivious to their children's antics.

"What illness do you suspect troubles Cuthbert?" asked Cornelia, already walking back down the long hall to the front door to retrieve her medicine chest.

"He has such severe gnawing pain in the intestinal area upon occasion, I quite fear he has a case of pinworms," Agnes confessed, accompanying her to the wagon.

"Is his breath offensive? Does he have a voracious appetite?" asked Nellie as they walked back outside. Agnes nodded in the affirmative and Nellie said, "I am in accord with your diagnosis. Howsoever, do not be vexed. One short course of garlic, Carolina Pink Root, and molasses shall provide an excellent anthelmintic that shall cure Cuthbert within the week. In the meantime, we shall ensure your other sons, in fact all the children, eat some brown bread and molasses as a preventative."

"Mercy, I am a failure as a mother. I am unable to keep my brood safe." Agnes looked as if she would cry.

"Nonsense," said Cornelia, with a firm, reassuring pat on her sister's back. "These diseases plague us all. We cannot expect to shield our children from all ills. We must practice constant vigilance and take tried-and-true steps to help them defeat the maladies. Your boys derive from good stock. With my remedies and the good food you provide, we shall guarantee these ailments are fleeting in duration. Furthermore, they already appear the picture of well-being, cavorting about, running, and playing like healthy heifers. This natural energy shall aid their return to full vigor."

Cornelia dove back into the wagon and reappeared with a large chest.

The children burst out the front door and ran towards the back. "Listen to them holler and whoop!" laughed Nellie.

"Whoop? Truly, Cornelia, sometimes your puns can be so insensitive," Agnes picked up her skirts and stormed back inside.

"Find me some horseradish and some horehound," Nellie shouted after her, already inventorying her supplies as she walked to the house. Her pace quickened in the suddenly bitter cold wind. "I used my cache of each remedying a cold so tenacious, neither daughter could escape its grip. Have you any fall rhubarb left?"

Agnes appeared at the doorway, "Sakes alive, *do* come *in* before you once again allow our tea to freeze. I shall *not* reheat this kettle again!"

CHAPTER 23
There's No Place like Home for the Holidays

Chicago, Illinois, December 1856

"It fills my heart with happiness to be surrounded by family during our Yuletide season," said Agnes, as the sisters watched the children hang their stockings.

Nellie laughed. "My cup runneth over as well," she replied. "I do seem to recall Christmastime is your favorite season of the year."

"Sakes alive, Cornelia, I am fully cognizant of your preference for celebrations at the big house in Sing Sing, caroling around the *Tannenbaum* with our parents and the rest of our siblings."

Nellie looked at her, startled. "Mercy, no, I did *not*—"

"Nonsense," interrupted Agnes. "'*Tis my preference as well!* To spend my days, all my born days, in this lonely swamp of a one-horse town, pining for my family...."

Cornelia's spirits sank at these words. *This thriving city, within the boundary of the United States, a one-horse town? What would one call Salt Lake City then? Have I foolishly committed myself to a lonely life?*

Agnes threw her arm around Nellie's shoulders and gave her a warm hug. "I appreciate *and cherish* the opportunity to spend the Solemnity of the Nativity with you. Together we can create new memories as we revive and relive the Christmases of our childhood."

Nellie smiled her appreciation of her sister's convivial words.

Obadiah tapped Nellie on the shoulder and beckoned her to a corner of the room. "Before we exchange commemoratives with the rest of the family, I wish to present a special gift I have thoughtfully chosen for my sweet Cornelia Rose."

Nellie inhaled his excitement, and felt her heart flutter with anticipation.

"Close your eyes and open your hands," Obadiah commanded, with a laugh.

Nellie complied. The package thrust into her hands was so heavy she dropped it. It smashed painfully upon her foot. "Mercy!" she gasped.

Obadiah bent to retrieve it. "Exercise more care this time," he said.

Nellie grimaced and stared at the heavy package in her husband's hands. *This mysterious package contains no jewelry, of that I am certain. Mayhap some books? But it is far too awkwardly shaped....*

"Cornelia, make haste, whilst the children are suitably occupied," Obadiah said, and thrust the package into her hands.

Nellie glanced at the fireplace. The children were throwing pinecones and twigs into the fire and watching them crackle and pop. *Suitably occupied playing with fire?* she wondered, untying the string, and opening the brown paper.

A short-handled shovel slipped from the paper and would have dropped again had Obadiah not stuck out his hand and caught it. He handed it to Cornelia.

She blinked, and tugged her stray strand of hair, speechless.

"Isn't she a beauty?" Obadiah gloated. "Real shiny, genuine metal with a beautifully hewn short handle. Perfect size for a little lady, the salesman assured me."

"Mercy," said Nellie, grabbing it with two hands and dutifully turning it over to admire the handle.

"It shall make the trenches you must dig each night for a cooking fire practically dig themselves." Obadiah smiled at her, waiting for a response.

Nellie gulped some air. "Adequate words escape me," she whispered.

"As if it were not special enough, I etched your initials on the handle." Obadiah grabbed the shovel and turned it over to show Nellie the 'C. R. E. W' whittled into the wood. She almost snorted, thinking, *unintentionally apt — I am the sum and substance of our crew.*

Obadiah laughed. "No words of gratitude are necessary. I can see your happiness in your expression."

Nellie looked down at the shovel, willing her eyes to remain dry. *Not only is my treasured gift a shovel, I am to dig ditches every night on our journey, in addition to my other responsibilities.*

Obadiah lifted her chin, and his laughing, dancing eyes met hers. "Once you master the trench, you can advance to excavating a privy."

Nellie did not trust herself to reply. Obadiah stood there watching her, smiling proudly at his own cleverness.

Nellie opened her mouth and then closed it again. *This... this... ditch digging shovel is his special, thoughtful, gift? The summation of his affection?*

He shook his head. "Great shakes, it almost slipped my mind. There are three other little, inconsequential items in the parcel that go along with your priceless spade," he whispered. "Advance apologies are required, however, for I am quite certain they cannot compare in grandeur to your new shovel."

Nellie was tempted to let the shovel slip from her hands and clatter to the floor but she did not want to scratch Agnes's fine wood finish. She retrieved the brown paper at her feet and laid the shovel in its place. Unwrapping it carefully, to protect her foot from further injury, she gasped.

A feather quill lay atop a beautiful leather-bound journal. She dropped the brown paper again.

"Obadiah, you devil!" she exclaimed.

"Tarry a moment, there is more," Obadiah grinned so broadly his mustache over his smile seemed to touch his ears. "I put your initials on the cover."

Tarnation! He whittled the leather? Nellie flipped over the book, and sighed with relief. In beautiful gold-leaf, someone skilled engraved her initials, encircled by a rose. "Praise the Lord, 'tis beyond beautiful," she whispered.

"A journal for you to chronicle our journey, or document cures in your midwifery practice. The possibilities proffered by the blank page are endless," Obadiah said, beaming at her.

"Your thoughtfulness continues to overwhelm me," said Nellie.

"The parcel contains yet another trinket," said Obadiah, pointing at the brown paper on the floor.

Nellie put the journal down and picked up the paper again. Buried in the folds was a miniature leather-bound book. She read the binding and raised her joyous face. "*The Tempest*," she whispered. "My favorite play by William Shakespeare."

"I was taken by the size of the volume," Obadiah said.

Nellie closed her hand around the little palm-sized book and threw her arms around her husband, "Thank you, my dearest, rogue husband." She stepped back, for Obadiah had not returned her embrace.

"What do you reckon I have concealed behind my back?" Obadiah teased.

"A pick ax as an accompaniment to my shovel?" Nellie asked, with feigned innocence.

Obadiah laughed so loud everyone in the room looked at them. "My wife exhibits a keen sense of humor. I shall enlighten you all at a later time," he announced to his in-laws. The children shook their heads and resumed throwing things into the fire. Agnes and Armistead bent their heads together, resuming their private conversation.

"Mercifully, there is an extreme dearth of curiosity in this gathering. Howsoever, I should have restrained myself," Obadiah said. "I do not wish the children to clamor for their gifts. Hopping horse feathers, I am delighted by your response. You may open this now." He handed her an oblong, narrow wooden crate with brown paper tied to the top.

Nellie opened it and stared at a complete set of Shakespeare's works, in miniature volumes. Now she permitted the tears to flow. "Obadiah, my love," she whispered.

"I know full well you were forced to leave your treasured library behind in Sing Sing. I recognize your sacrifice and hope this gift compensates in small part for all you have forsaken in New York."

"Your generosity exceeds itself," Nellie said through her tears of joy. "My heart soars at the love and thoughtfulness contained in these gifts."

"Even the shovel?" teased Obadiah.

"Even the shovel." Nellie laughed. "Why did you not present this plethora of gifts on the morrow, during our Christmas Day festivities?"

"I was loath to risk missing every detail of your countenance as you first gazed upon the shovel. 'Twould have been a tragedy if you opened it whilst I was engaged in the Christmas stocking excitement of the children. Your face whilst you struggled between your disappointment and your courteous nature shall bring me laughter each time I think upon it. 'Tis priceless to me, my precious Rose."

Nellie threw her arms around his neck and he squeezed her tight in his arms. Obadiah whispered, "I hope to compensate for the anticipated lack of literature on our journey by filling your eyes with the beauty of our surroundings and your ears with the poetry of my heart."

Nellie thought her heart would burst from an excess of love and happiness. As she drew back to pour her own words of love into Obadiah's ears, she felt a tug on her skirt. She looked down at Emma's upturned face, pinched with worry.

"Dagobert is daring Elizabeth to put her ribbons in the fire to see if the red ribbon makes a different colored fire from the yellow one," said Emma.

Nellie rushed to the hearth and pulled Elizabeth away before Emma finished the sentence.

"Let's pop some corn," said Nellie, hoping that proposing a safer activity might divert the boys from their pyromania. The popping of corn soon joined the sound of the merrily crackling fire. The children gobbled it as fast as it popped. While they ate, the boys played one impish prank after another. All the children tried their hand at tall tales, keeping the whole family giggling. After several batches, the boys rubbed their full stomachs.

"Full stomach, light head," said Agnes.

Nellie looked at her. "I am familiar with the sentiment, but that phrase is not a common expression."

Agnes laughed merrily. "You fail to recognize *Mutter's* sayings simply because I say them in English?"

"*Ach du Liebe! Volles Magen, leichtes Kopft!*" exclaimed Nellie, giggling. "Why did you not say so?"

"I'd say those children are all full of beans," Obadiah joined in the conversation.

"Your father would say 'full o' Blarney,'" said Armistead. Nellie and Agnes collapsed in giggles at the sound of an Irish brogue overlaid on Armistead's southern drawl.

Obadiah stood, kissed Nellie on the top of her head and then sat back down next to Armistead. Not to be outdone, Armistead popped up and kissed Agnes on the mouth.

"Scandalous," sputtered Agnes. "In front of our guests?"

Nellie, laughing so hard she could barely pronounce the words, said, "Agnes, don't carry on so. We are all family."

"Truly," assured Obadiah. "What is a little passion among family?" He jumped back up, swept Nellie off her feet and kissed her soundly on the lips.

Nellie gasped, but then laughed.

Agnes held up her hand as Armistead rose again. "I think this charade has gone far enough."

Armistead went to her and took her hand. "I shall cease only when you smile and confess your continued amorous feelings to me."

Agnes looked as if she would object, but she said, "My truest love, you ever elicit amorous feelings and ones of good humor in me, for which I am eternally grateful."

Agnes must have a full stomach and a light head indeed to play along.

The families talked, laughed, and played until the two youngest, Elizabeth and Dagobert, rubbed their eyes and yawned. Nellie and Agnes noticed, but the men kept laughing and dipping into the wassail bowl.

"You are right," Nellie murmured to Agnes. "This old English recipe for wassail is every bit as good as our Yankee pineapple one." Nellie stared at the fire, wishing this cozy evening would never end.

"Time for bed," announced Agnes suddenly. Nellie jumped, feeling guilty. *Mercy, surely Agnes does not mean to chastise me?* Like a drill sergeant, Agnes rousted the children from their comfy cushions and Nellie breathed a sigh of relief. And then laughed at herself. *Old habits die hard....*

"No!" shouted Egbert, jumping up, glaring with defiance. "It is Christmas Eve and we have not sung a single carol."

Agnes softened and glanced at Nellie, who nodded her agreement at the implicit question. "Egbert, you are correct, 'tis truly a time for rejoicing and caroling. We must treasure each moment together with our cousins."

My word, once again Agnes reveals her soft side. I'll be a cocked hat! Before her sister began to cry, she opened her mouth and sang, "O Holy Night, the stars are brightly shining...."

The sweet voices of the children warbled right in, more or less in tune, in a middle range between Nellie's alto and Agnes's soprano. The men raised their own voices, rounding the melody with Obadiah's strong tenor and Armistead's baritone.

Our choir is nicely balanced. Nellie smiled at her sister, and squeezed her hand, tears of joy springing to her eyes.

Before the last notes faded away, Obadiah sprinted to the door. Dagobert and Emma began, *"O Tannenbaum, o Tannenbaum, wie tru sind deiner Blättern...."*

Obadiah reappeared with his fiddle, and the choir enjoyed some melodious accompaniment. Nellie looked at the fire in the huge hearth, casting a gleam on the children's happy faces. She settled into the cozy chaise and gazed around the room, noting all the beautifully designed comforts of the Long's home. Her heart glowed at the features of Obadiah as he coaxed music from the instrument's strings, and she smiled at her sister and brother-in-law holding hands and singing. *I shall treasure the peace and joy of this moment in my heart always, made all the more precious by my cognizance of its transience.*

The song ended with the children clapping and running around the room, shouting suggestions for the next musical number.

A line from Shakespeare popped into Nellie's head as she blissfully recalled the new treasure Obadiah just bestowed upon her. She leaned toward her sister, Armistead and her husband and quoted, "'What win I, if I gain the thing I seek? A dream, a breath, a froth of fleeting joy....' How apt these lines, how fittingly they resonate with my sentiment tonight. So blessed are we that we share this holiest of all holidays together. We must cherish our 'froths of fleeting joy' in each other's companionship...."

She and Obadiah exchanged a smile. *He knows I shall cherish his magnanimous gift.*

"Cornelia!" exclaimed Agnes with a sharp edge to her voice.

Nellie's eyes startled at the reproof in her tone. "Mercy, a thousand pardons, Agnes, I only meant...."

"I know well what you meant," Agnes said in an angry voice. Then her voice broke. "I wish your words did not provoke the tears of bittersweet joy I labor so desperately to control."

Nellie scrambled out of the chaise and rushed to hug her sister. "Forgive me...."

"Hush Nellie," whispered Agnes. "My darling sister with the silver tongue and the penchant for drama! I cherish your company, your knowledge, and your sisterly warm love. Always. Even if my own sharp tongue shall never again acknowledge...." Agnes burst into a fresh shower of tears.

Nellie hugged her sister harder and whispered into her hair. "I love you dear sister, sharp tongue notwithstanding." *'Tis quite the evening for joyous surprises.*

After a blissful concert of ten more carols, all the children rubbed their eyes, the older ones hiding yawns behind their hands. Agnes pulled herself out of her chair and said, "Now children...."

"No, no," protested the children. A thunderous look stormed over Agnes' face. *Great shakes! She surely shall lose her temper now, fatigue running high and patience wearing thin.*

Cornelia sighed and roused herself from her own comfortable position, nestled deep in the overstuffed chaise. *It is rather more difficult to extract oneself from this state of recline. 'Tis no wonder protocol demands I sit erect in a hard-backed chair.* She cleared her throat and stepped to the plate. "If everyone scrubs their hands and faces *and* dons their nightshirts within *five minutes,* I shall recite *'Twas the Night Before Christmas* from the foot of the boy's big bed." Nellie pulled her beautiful Swiss pendant watch from her waistband and looked at the time.

The children shrieked with excitement, scrambled out of their chairs, and bolted away. Their footsteps audible, they clattered across the large parlor.

"But *everyone* must be ready or Aunt Cornelia shan't perform the story," warned Agnes, shouting at their retreating backs. Cuthbert's biggest feet scurried faster. Emma giggled, scampering behind the boys. Elizabeth screamed, running last. She caught up to the rest at the stairs. They stampeded upstairs, and in seconds the rafters shook overhead with the energy of their footsteps.

Agnes turned to Nellie, "Have you forgotten your grudge against the Knickerbockers? Have you forgiven Clement C. More for changing Papa's *Daidí na Nollag* and *Mutter's das Christkind* into the jolly Dutch burger Saint Nick?"

"*Ach du Liebe!*" said Nellie. "I no longer allow myself to associate *Santa Nicklaus* with that Knickerbocker gang of fable thieves. I confess you have accurately recalled my reaction when I made the connection between the Knickerbockers and the re-imagined figure so loosely derived from *Mutter* and Papa's traditions from the old country. Howsoever, I long ago experienced a change of heart. The poem is a treasure from our childhood, written by a man from our own hometown of Sing Sing. Papa himself read us that story every Christmas Eve."

Nellie hugged Agnes as tears again dampened Agnes' face. "How *are* the Moores?" Agnes asked. "How *is* Mr. Clement C.? And his lovely wife? Are they keeping well?"

Nellie smiled. "When last I saw Mr. Moore, at a splendid tea Mrs. Moore hosted at Moorehaven, the estate looked well-maintained and the couple seemed in good health. Although Mrs. Moore still pines for word from her adult children and Mr. Moore complains of the gout, they are in good spirits, enjoying their daily constitutionals through their garden along the Hudson River."

"What news of Bishop Benjamin Moore, Mr. Clement's father? Is he still president at Columbia College?"

"Mercy, no! Agnes, I believe he retired before you even left Sing Sing," Nellie replied.

Agnes caught Nellie's hand, and they walked up the stairs to the bedrooms. "It is a good thing we have interminable winters in this God-forsaken one-cow town," Agnes said.

Nellie drew back in surprise. "Why ever for?"

"It will ensure we have months to visit before you can continue this ill-advised migration to parts unknown, and I shall have leisure to inquire after the welfare of each and every friend and neighbor I forsook in Sing Sing," Agnes replied.

Nellie laughed. *Lost in the midst of a plethora of criticism and disapproval is a request for gossip from home and a warmhearted welcome for me to linger here an indefinite period of time.*

"This shall prove an exquisite Yuletide season," Nellie said aloud and squeezed her sister's hand.

At the top of the stairs, they entered the boy's room. There was a mad scramble of legs and arms as the children all jumped into the big bed.

Nellie and Agnes giggled. The children pulled the patchwork quilt over their bodies and froze, as if their petrified cessation of motion could be mistaken for sleeping.

Still giggling, Nellie began, in a dramatic whisper, "'Twas the night before Christmas....'"

She tiptoed closer to the bed.

"...When all through the house, not a creature was stirring'," Nellie paused, holding her hand to her ear, as if listening. She sat on the coverlet and leaned forward. "'Not *even* a mouse.'"

Agnes followed, grabbed her elbow, and whispered directly in her ear. "I sorely missed your penchant for drama," she said.

Hence your adoption of the technique yourself? My, she truly is homesick. A fresh wave of sympathy for her ornery sister flooded her with compassion.

"'The stockings were hung, by the chimney with care, in hopes that Saint Nicholas'....'"

Agnes pulled out her fine, embroidered handkerchief, dabbed her eyes and settled into the rocking chair, joining Nellie's audience.

CHAPTER 24
I Try to Say Goodbye and I Choke

Chicago, Illinois, March 1857

"I am reluctant to advise you." Armistead actually looked nervous as he spoke.

"Why, whatever ails you?" Nellie reached out a reassuring hand.

"Not a single matter, I am quite the picture of health."

"Mercy, then whatever is amiss?" Nellie's hand shot up to her heart.

"'This shall stick in your throat like a hair in a biscuit," said Armistead, shaking his head.

Nellie shook her own head in confusion. "What in tarnation is wrong?"

"This announcement gives me a case of the jibblies," Armistead fretted. "I feel as nervous as a cat in a room full of rocking chairs."

"Armistead Lindsey Long, I doubt any announcement shall make me as irritated as your 'backing and filling'!" Nellie put her hands on her hips.

Armistead hung his head. "I simply fear you shall not take kindly to my news."

"Cease toying with my curiosity, and further testing my patience." Nellie frowned, her foot tapping impatiently, her hand straying upwards to tug on her recalcitrant forelock.

Armistead took a deep breath and blurted, "The Illinois / Michigan canal no longer takes passengers on its barges. Only freight now, since the railroad's been completed." He took a step away from her.

"But the canal still functions," Nellie sputtered. "Why, I read just last week in your fine *Tribune* newspaper—the quantity of goods shipped North on the canal from towns and farms along the Mississippi increases exponentially each week."

"Goods." Obadiah stepped into the fray. "Not passengers."

Nellie grabbed Armistead's hand and gave it a tug. "Surely, you can use your influence as one of the chief engineers in the prestigious Army Corps of Engineers to secure us an exception, and a passage?" Nellie wrung her hands, every bit as overwrought as Armistead predicted.

"We must accompany our wagon," Nellie pleaded. "We require only the meanest of accommodations—why, we can sleep inside the wagon! They shall hardly notice we are there."

"Why should we not send our wagon by freight barge and ride in comfort on the locomotive?" Obadiah reasoned.

"Firstly, the appellation 'comfortable' shall never be an apt descriptor for travel in a smoky, belching railroad car. Secondly, after the tribulations we endured, painstakingly ascertaining, procuring, and packing only the precise provisions essential for the onerous journey ahead, the thought of trusting the safe passage of all our worldly possessions, our only remaining valuables, and our sole conveyance, which, dare I mention, shall be our only home for the next several months, to the good will of common barge hands is most disquieting. Moreover, the thought further heightens my trepidation for the actual journey itself...."

Obadiah held up his hand to stem the flow of Cornelia's outburst.

"Armistead," he said, clamping his brother-in-law on the back. "Let us explore the possibilities for circumventing this situation. After all, 'tis a mere 300-mile trip, just a short three-night duration."

"'Tis a subject left to discussion for another time," said Agnes, practically shooing Nellie back into the kitchen to prevent the conversation from continuing. "Lake Michigan remains far too frozen to even contemplate travel."

The others stared at her blankly. She stared back with defiance in her eyes. "I am quite certain if the vast lake of Michigan is frozen, the small river Illinois is also un-navigable. Why, last year we had snowstorms and blizzards well into April."

Obadiah and Nellie exchanged looks. *Obadiah has expressed his desire to depart in April. Mayhap the weather shall not cooperate. If I had my druthers, I suppose I would choose to delay this trip indefinitely.* But she could tell from Obadiah's look that he would not be deterred from travel much longer.

The weeks spun by quickly as Obadiah made arrangements for the next leg of their journey. He traded one of their horses for two sturdy oxen, and took charge of inventorying and then procuring any hardware staples missing from their provisions. Nellie and Agnes giggled at Armistead and Obadiah deep in discussion over whether tin or gutta percha made the best type of water bucket and where to purchase the best king-bolts and extra links for repairing chain. Cornelia made daily forays to the markets, gathering sugar, flour, tea and other perishables.

"How much longer shall you be staying?" Agnes asked, one afternoon, as the March wind howled outside and gusted into the room through the fireplace flue. Nellie looked up from plucking feathers from their dinner fowl, startled at the mention of imminent departure.

"Do not take offense, Cornelia," Agnes said quickly. "I have treasured this time together." She sighed. "The Lord only knows when I can again expect to see another familiar face."

Nellie looked around the cozy kitchen. The children sprawled on the floor, playing with the boys' tin figures. Early spring rain beat drowsily upon the roof. Agnes ground coffee to brew another pot, and Cornelia alternated between preparing the partridge and rolling dough for the biscuits for their dinner. The fire crackled, the stove emulated warmth, and the clock atop the fine china hutch ticked reassuringly.

Determined not to sound melancholy, Nellie said, "We are waiting for the grass to grow."

Agnes looked hurt.

"Tarnation, I apologize for my flippant reply," Nellie said and scuttled over to her sister to give her a hug. "You know I am loath to leave... for more reasons than I can adequately express." Nellie forced a smile. "I must at least continue our visit long enough to ensure my prescriptives cure your sons' various ailments completely."

Agnes had tears in her eyes. Nellie blinked rapidly and tried to joke again. "But mostly I am waiting for the grass to grow."

Nellie laughed at Agnes' confused look. "Grass shall be the only available feed for our livestock, after crossing to the west side of the Missouri River."

Agnes brushed her tears away and spoke of practicalities, too. "Sakes alive, I never considered all the comestibles you must transport. After all, not only are you leaving civilization, you are also leaving vegetable gardens behind."

"I have not lain idle during our delightful visit. Slowly and steadily I accumulate the necessities. I have cured bacon, packed in boxes with bran surrounding to prevent the fat from melting away. I have sugar well secured in India-rubber sacks and butter boiled, placed in tin canisters and soldered up. The flour is well sewn into double canvas sacks, and it is all stored in the bottom of the wagon, ensuring it is kept cool and dry.

"Why do you think I concoct this hard tack alongside our supper biscuits?" Nellie lifted her hands from the flour, salt, and water she had started mixing as soon as the biscuits went into the polished black oven. "Crackers dried to the consistency of fired bricks certainly pale in comparison to any of the fine biscuits or breads we have baked together and enjoyed here. Yet they are a necessity." She sighed.

"Unlike our fine biscuits, my technique for kneading this mixture shall hardly aid its appeal. Be forewarned: I shall purloin one of your tins and stuff it with some real biscuits, rationing them, savoring them. With every bite, I shall picture and relive our precious moments here." Nellie winked.

Agnes smiled. "This entire visit elicits bittersweet sentiments in my heart. To aid your remembrances, I offer you one of my treasured tins. I have several beautiful ones from our Grandmama's collection."

How did Agnes get 'several' of Grandmama's beautiful tins from Austria? No one offered any to me. Nellie's envious thoughts rose before she could staunch them. *Stubbs of candles and broken candlesticks were all I received.* She shook her head. *Revisiting petty jealousies? One would hope I had matured beyond this feminine foible. Furthermore, Agnes just offered me a keepsake for my own.*

She forced a smile of gratitude. Putting her enmity aside, Nellie said, "I accept your most generous gift. I shall treasure it always, especially since scarcity of space prevented my transport of many of my treasures on this journey.

Nellie shook her head. "Mercy! I've placed a huckleberry above a persimmon and failed to provide an answer to your question. We shall leave within the week. Therefore, the little time remaining I shall utilize in preparing more staples and purchasing the necessary supplies we dared not carry all the way from Sing Sing."

"If I can be of any assistance?" Agnes asked. "Although I doubt...."

"Fear not! As you know I pickled my own cucumbers and potatoes last week, and preserved a batch for you as well. All I request is your aide in determining the best market or source for the remaining perishables that I have been to date unable to procure."

"Such as?"

"In addition to the actual vegetables I have prepared, I shall require more salt, vinegar, horseradish...."

Agnes just looked at her.

"The bottom fact—I have scribed quite a comprehensive list. It helped me pass the time floating through the muddy puddle commonly known as the Erie Canal. I have not mindlessly frittered my time away, dilly-dallying and delaying my crucial preparations. As I said, I have already procured most items and organized them securely and neatly in the Conestoga. Under your tutelage, I am certain I can quickly secure the remaining ingredients from your 'big city' marketplace," said Nellie with a smile.

Elizabeth darted into the room, screaming. Nellie tried to grab her but all she succeeded in doing was derail her path so that the girl floundered to the side, bumped into Agnes, and stepped directly on Agnes's toe before dashing out the backdoor.

Agnes stood, spoon suspended in the air, speechless.

"What in tarnation?" gasped Nellie, as Dagobert, Egbert, and Cuthbert rushed past, brandishing popguns. Emma ran by, right behind them.

Emma? Acting like a wild turkey? Cornelia thought, grabbing her oldest daughter's arm. "Where's the fire?" she asked.

Emma stopped and straightened her bonnet, laughing. "There is no fire. We are just playing 'hare and hounds'."

"Let me guess," said Agnes, laughing. "Elizabeth is the hare?"

"Yes," said Emma. "She is most effective at eluding her cousins!"

"You may continue." Nellie laughed.

Emma fled to catch up to her clan.

"Maybe it would *not* be much different, having a daughter, if my motley crew of sons ensnares her in their play."

"Even Emma has been *Chicagoed!*" Nellie kept laughing, almost on the verge of tears.

Agnes gave her a hug. Nellie caught her breath and pushed the sadness away. The two women turned to face the next kitchen chore, grateful for each other's companionship and solidarity.

Their last week together passed in a blur of wonderful family meals, camaraderie, laughter, love, and final preparations.

All too soon, Nellie stood looking forlornly at the lovely four-poster bed in which she and Obadiah had snuggled for the last three months as she tied her bonnet, and closed her bag.

Obadiah leaned in and hugged her from behind. Nellie reached her hand back and rubbed his head with affection. She blinked back tears and sighed, "We'd best be off, as we are both quite cognizant of my sister's deliberations on company...." Nellie turned in his arms, sighed into his chest, and gave a tremulous smile. At Obadiah's blank stare, Nellie elaborated, "Agnes wholeheartedly espouses the maxim 'company is like fish, it stinks after just a few days'! I am sure her loneliness lessened that sentiment somewhat, but having visited and tarried here lo these past three months, I am quite certain we have well overstayed our welcome."

She broke from his embrace, scooped up her bag, and ran down the grand staircase.

"I am certain Papa and *Mutter* shall honor their promise to visit and will commence the journey soon, once the weather turns to spring." Nellie clasped her sister to her and stood for a long moment, hugging Agnes as if she could include all of her beloved family members, left far behind, in her embrace.

Agnes must have clung to Nellie for the same reason. At last she pulled back, just far enough to look Cornelia in the eyes, still hugging her tightly. "Their visit would be proved beyond cavil if that cotton-picking canal connecting us to Sandusky, Ohio had already been built." Agnes shook her head. "I cannot see our seafaring father condescending to stagecoach, or worse yet, locomotive travel, for the last leg of the otherwise smooth sailing journey."

Emma and Elizabeth cried and hugged their cousins. Agnes' rough and tumble boys looked sad to see them go. As Armistead grabbed Obadiah in a bear hug, Egbert handed Emma a corn-silk doll. "I made this for you, to 'member us by," he said.

Emma smiled through her tears and hugged Egbert hard. "And of course, you shall always think of me when you gaze upon your lovingly mended coverlet. Don't forget, I embroidered your initials on the back, in your favorite color wool."

"You told me you mended that coverlet yourself, Egbert, as I had instructed you," Agnes scolded.

Egbert looked at Emma and said, "Mother, that would have been foolish! If I had obeyed you, my coverlet would still be just a rag, with twine sewn through it, and I would have nothing to remind me of my sweet cousin."

Silence reigned as everyone held his breath for Agnes's reply.

"Hug Lisbet?" asked Elizabeth. Everyone laughed through their tears, as the brothers all rushed to hug the little girl.

Dagobert thrust a small, crudely whittled sailboat into Elizabeth's little hands. "This is the one we was whittling together. Cuthbert finished the trim for us. See, here's the piece of fabric you hung on the wood post as a sail."

Elizabeth clutched it to her chest and cried, "Thank you. Lisbet keep."

Cornelia and Agnes viewed these exchanges from their continued embrace. Nellie tried to blink back her tears as she clung to her sister, reluctant to let her go.

CHAPTER 25
I Don't Know Where I'm Going but
I'm on My Way

Illinois River to the Mississippi River to the Missouri River, March 1857

"I thank the Lord we have seen the last of the Illinois and Michigan Canal. I grew weary of the calisthenics required to prevent concussions passing under each bridge. Further, I do confess, the stench of the foul waste of Chicago seemed to follow us all the way down that canal to the Illinois River," said Nellie.

Obadiah grinned at her. "Most assuredly it did. Armistead expounded, in great length and on many occasions, about the sanitation woes of Chicago. Right now, the Illinois River flows *to* Chicago, connects to the Illinois and Michigan Canal and dumps its water, containing waste and discarded detritus and debris, into Lake Michigan. Recall the stench of that august body of water when the Lake was calm?"

Elizabeth held her nose. Everyone laughed.

Obadiah swung Elizabeth's hand and continued, "As foul as the odor was, soon, the stench shall worsen. According to Uncle Armistead's proposal, the Army Corps of Engineers plans to dig a sanitation canal, deeper than the current freight canal, to reverse the flow of the Illinois River. 'Twill be a tremendous engineering feat. Howsoever, I am afraid the stench of *that* canal will be far more malodorous. The waste, now dumped in Lake Michigan, shall stream the opposite way into the new canal, thus transporting all Chicago's sewage to the Illinois River, disbursing and distributing filth all along its flow."

Nellie looked at her husband in disbelief. "Surely this will cause much distress amongst the city's southerly neighbors. I imagine sending this waste, publicized by its foul odor, down the river, shall foster grave displeasure, not to mention cholera! Will the town counsel seek the consent of those affected before commencing this feat?"

Obadiah shook his head. "Highly unlikely. That's more fodder feeding the legal machine and clogging the district courts."

Cornelia replied, "Chicagoans need summon my father to appear and engineer a replica of the Croton Aqueduct to ensure clean drinking water. He shall find an alternative source of potable water to Lake Michigan."

Obadiah gave her a mock stern look. "Did you not heed our Engineer Long? There can be no superior strategy. Chicago will rid itself of sewage. The Lake shall be salvaged by this ingenious scheme — the drinking water will be recertified as pure. No need for further engineering. Armistead and his corps shall save the city from typhoid and cholera."

"Ensuring everyone south of the city will 'be Chicagoed!'" Nellie pointed her index finger to the sky to emphasize her joke, and giggled when Obadiah laughed.

"'Way down upon the Suwanee River, far, far away,'" sang Obadiah.

"'There's where my heart is turning ever....'" sang Elizabeth in reply.

The little girls jumped up and down with glee.

"Let us sing, Father, just the way Grandpapa always sang with us," said Emma.

Nellie burst into tears. *Shall I ever be blessed with the presence of Papa again? Shall I ever again feel the joy and relief of one of his treasured embraces?*

Obadiah leaned in and took her hand, while her daughters gawked, wide-eyed at the sight of their infallible mother crying.

Now that we have left Agnes and her family behind, I can no longer pretend this journey is merely a capricious lark, spurred by the need to provide aid and comfort to my lonely sister residing at the edge of civilization.

"Cornelia Rose, heed my words," Obadiah said, raising Cornelia's chin so he could look into her eyes. "We must view this as a grand adventure, much like life itself. Observe," he commanded and turned her face toward the wind. "Survey this beautiful, pristine landscape. Our family constitutes a hardy little band of explorers, roaming far afield to discover the world. We are pioneers! We shall attain our destination. We have ensured our survival, nay, we have *guaranteed* a triumphal, successful journey, through our procurement, and now transportation of apposite provisions."

Nellie sniffed and tried a smile. *I suppose one could confect this interpretation of our situation.*

Encouraged, Obadiah continued, "My dearest Rose, our wagon overspills with every conceivable necessity. We have not undertaken this journey blithely. I scoured every piece of literature available, from guidebooks and waybills to newspaper reports, and educated us about the Overland Trail. I read every government directive, every book or pamphlet and even interrogated every experienced pioneer I could cross-examine, seeking firsthand accounts of the perils, in order to map our safest route. We are exceptionally well versed on the journey's hazards. Armed with this knowledge, together we shall surmount each and every difficulty. The emigration path to The Great Salt Lake City is now well traveled. Furthermore, the worst parts of both the California and Oregon Trails are from Salt Lake across three deserts and several mountain ranges to the West Coast. These parts we shall bypass completely. Now all that remains is for us to walk the trail."

The floodgates opened, and she felt their immense love for each other wash over her. "My dearest Mr. Wright, your words tender the *tenderest* of caresses," she said.

His smile acknowledged her word play.

Together we shall embark upon this grand new adventure, shielded by our love, strengthened by our companionship, sheltered by our numbers, ensuring our safe harbor wherever we might journey. She raised eyes full of love and trust to his. *Together we shall walk in love.*

"Mama, there is the mouth of the Missouri River! I'm quite certain. The first mate did tell me to be on the lookout for it. He said we would only steam along the Mississippi for a short distance," said Emma, tugging at her skirt.

"Are we new home?" asked Elizabeth.

Nellie could not suppress a forlorn grin. "Hardly! Utah Territory remains a remote terminus, my little pumpkins. Why even the town in which we end our water navigation is hardly near. We next experience the meandering of the Missouri River, winding and wandering through the countryside like a bunny nibbling his way through the succulent carrot leaves in my garden." She watched the sad expressions of her daughters brighten at the thought of a cottontail hopping through their Sing Sing backyard.

"We soon embark upon the leg of our journey wherein we carry our home with us," said Nellie, assuming a cheerful attitude.

"Like the snails that lived among the rocks on the shore of the Hudson that we watched creep from spot to spot?" asked Emma.

Nellie smiled at her daughter's memory. "Precisely. However, we shall endeavor an execution of our journey at a more rapid pace than a snail."

"Where beds?" asked Elizabeth.

"We sleep in our wagon, utilizing the wagon bed as our bed."

"Like oysters?" asked Emma.

Nellie laughed. "Yes, we shall lie like the oysters that abound in their shell beds along the mighty Hudson River."

Obadiah frowned at Nellie's simile. But their daughters' attention had already shifted upriver to the city emerging into view.

"May we disembark in the big town of Saint Louis?" asked Emma.

"No," answered Obadiah. "This steamboat rounds the peninsula jutting into the intersection of the two rivers just a little north of Saint Louis. We take this ship all the way to Independence, Missouri."

The little girls let out small sighs of dismay. "But it looks like home," said Emma.

Nellie realized the many similarities between the bustle of Saint Louis's wharfs and the docksides of Sing Sing. *How prescient Emma's correlation. The similarities tug my heartstrings as well.*

Obadiah tried to placate their daughters' disappointment. "We can wave to Saint Louis as we steam past."

Later in the day, propped on the ship's railing, Nellie mused, *the interminable Missouri does most assuredly ramble through vast countryside, just as our map promised, yet with little or no perceptible change of scenery.*

Whenever shall we arrive at the edge of the prairie? She grew impatient to be on the next leg of their journey, like her daughters.

"Land ho!" shouted Emma with Elizabeth echoing the words a second later.

Nellie giggled. *Land remained in view the whole journey. 'Destination ho!' was far more apt.*

Now that the end of their water voyage was in sight, Nellie's heart dropped at the thought of actually starting their walk on the rough trail ahead. *Mayhap I can convince Obadiah to delay our foot journey just a trifle longer, whilst still making progress toward our destination,* she schemed.

Nellie marshaled her arguments and approached her husband. "Obadiah, we shall never be able to procure the few supplies we lack at this location. Emigrants run rampant in Independence, like locusts consuming all the comestibles, according to the guidebooks. Furthermore, in conversation with the steamer's captain, I perceived 'tis but a short float further to Council Bluffs, Iowa. From there, only 183 miles to Fort Kearny, versus if we disembarked here, we would be forced to walk 322 miles to that same Fort along the Oregon Trail. Think of the almost two hundred miles of toil our feet avoid, much less the sweat and labor of the oxen spared!"

"Not to mention stave off the land journey, and its attendant difficulties and privations, just a fraction longer?" Obadiah teased her.

"The purser confided, there shall be *no* additional fare. Since we paid the maximum tariff for our tickets, the price already includes the entirety of miles the boat travels." Nellie smiled back, thinking, *my trump card, appealing to your frugal nature! You have taught me a more strategic way to debate my precious husband, through your example.*

"How is that possible?" wondered Obadiah.

"We are now privy to information little known by most passengers," said Nellie.

"I must re-examine the fine print of our ticket contract," said Obadiah.

"Mayhap you should ascertain the veracity of the purser's statement for yourself," counseled Nellie.

Obadiah took her in his arms and beamed his warmest smile upon her. "My sweet Cornelia," he murmured into her hair.

Mercy, the sweetest of embraces, Cornelia thought. "An additional thought, the Missouri River and this boat's journey do not end in Council Bluffs. Perhaps we can save even further costs by sailing to this ship's terminus," she said, with a sweet smile.

"I have studied the map of the Missouri River. As you are well aware, its course meanders like a cock-eyed sailor on a weekend furlough. The river bends far too north to gain us any further advantage on our destination." Obadiah shook his head and irritation crept into his voice. "I shall consider one leg more, and then no further."

He stepped away to the business of the arrangements with one parting shot. "Steam all the way to Iowa? I shall heed your council now, but be advised, when we join our wagon train, *only the menfolk* make decisions."

CHAPTER 26
Stranded

Council Bluffs, Iowa, March, 1857

The two little girls bobbed up and down, chattering in anticipation of their foray into the new city as the steamship blasted its horn and docked at Council Bluffs.

"It looks like home here too, Mama!" said Emma. Elizabeth nodded. "Different home?" she asked.

Nellie laughed. "Yes, many different homes!"

People swarmed everywhere. The wharf was bursting at its seams; people, produce, conveyances, animals, and even birds abounded, rushing, and pouring in all directions, spilling sounds and smells into the river.

They scrambled down the gangplank, anxious to stretch their legs on shore. Nellie's daughters swayed on the dock, walking with tentative steps, trying to adjust their gait to solid, motionless, ground. She grasped each of their hands with a firm grip, determined to hold them tight amidst the chaos of the other emigrants streaming off the ships. Her daughters' wobbly walking, combined with their intimidation at the teeming throngs of people, ensured they stayed glued to Nellie's side.

When the steamboat sounded the three short whistles advertising its impending departure, Nellie's heart sank. *At least the ship flags, flapping noisily in the wind, are waving goodbye. Lord, help me! The last vestige of all I have known, the steamboat, cruises on ahead, leaving me stranded at the edge of civilization.*

Nellie deliberately turned her back on the departing steamboat that served as their home for the past week. She fixed her gaze on the bustle of activity on the wharf at Council Bluffs. *Pshaw. I clutched this boat trip, clinging to it like a life preserver, as long as I was able. I must acclimate myself to the next phase of our journey, finding consolation in my current surroundings.*

The dock teamed with the usual seafaring activity; sailors swabbed decks, day laborers unloaded cargo, farmers carted vegetables, and merchants bartered. *I must embrace this purposeful activity within my regard, for it hardly warrants the nomenclature 'uncivilized.'* In addition to these familiar sights and sounds of the river's edge, hawkers solicited members for wagon train companies and touted supplies and necessities for emigrants' journeys.

"The amount of malarkey thrown about here on poor unsuspecting folk, hoping for a better life, is simply unconscionable," Obadiah said in Nellie's ear as they rolled through the town in their Conestoga, pulling their horse behind. "We must remain firm in our resolve and ignore the bold promises of these outfitters' salesmen promising easy journeys." Obadiah shook his head, grim-faced. "It gives me pause to watch men beguiled by this propaganda. The gall of these hawkers, pledging hyperboles of wealth-beyond-imagination and verdant crops that bloom without tending in the golden state of California."

Both their heads swiveled to the right as they stared at a man untying his billfold, unwittingly revealing its plenty to the world. Engrossed in negotiation with an unsavory-looking man pawning a well-worn harness, the emigrant's trusting face, as open as his wallet, gave him all the indicia of an easy mark.

"Another stranger duped," lamented Obadiah.

"Nefarious activity runs rampant through this town," observed Nellie, nodding her head toward another man, presiding over a blanket full of pistols, shouting about the dangers lurking on the trail ahead and the need to arm oneself accordingly. "I realize a new appreciation for your decision to purchase our oxen in Chicago, in spite of the length of our boat passage. We were assured fair value in all we obtained in Chicago. There shall be no such assurances found in supplies we acquire here."

Within minutes, they drove past the commercial area that seemed to mark the town limits, but the throngs of people did not dissipate. Wagons, people, and livestock littered the landscape everywhere.

"California and Oregon emigrants and their encampments fill the whole countryside along the Missouri River, from Independence Landing and Saint Joseph in Missouri to here in Kanesville... correction, now christened Council Bluffs, Iowa," Cornelia observed. "'Tis a wonder some of these multitudes are not dissuaded from the journey by all this commotion, not to mention the audible dire warnings.

"Truly, I am quite alarmed at the rhetoric of the hawkers and salesmen," Nellie continued in a lower voice, with an eye on her daughters. They were so busy gawking at all the activity and soaking in the character of the frontier town, they paid no attention to their parents' conversation.

"Did you read the flyer thrust upon us, advising of the depredations from the Sioux and Pawnee tribes?" quivered Nellie.

"Alarmists' propaganda," dismissed Obadiah. "The native people are besieged by emigrants traipsing through their land. Most literature on the subject supports my conclusion they are peaceable people, and simply require the respect they deserve. I have also read they are able traders. You shall recall we packed a fair number of curiosities, thus arming ourselves for bartering perishables along the trail in exchange for needles and thread, small mirrors in gilt frames, and other novelties."

"Even so," conceded Cornelia. "I do believe we would be well advised to join a wagon train. A big company, consisting of families with differing skills, shall contribute to our mutual protection from the perils of this undertaking."

"I concur with your consummate reasoning," agreed Obadiah with a smile. "Once we have established our wagon in an apposite spot to encamp for the night, I shall venture back to the commercial area to ascertain our options for amalgamating with a company."

But as they made their way along the riverbank, all sorts of seedy, sleazy men bombarded their wagon with solicitations, peddling wares and advertising companies and campsites. Overwhelming and intimidating, the constant barrage hampered their search for a comfortable, available piece of land to set up camp.

"'Tis hard to imagine a more unsavory place," said Nellie. "Are *all* these people seeking gold in California?"

"No, some itinerants are members of the Church of the Latter-day Saints. This spot is the trailhead for Mormon emigration too. Once we skirt these scalawags...."

"How do you propose we achieve that goalmouth? These streets are so crowded we can barely proceed forward. We are amongst thousands seeking refuge before the journey," fretted Nellie.

"What is a Mormon?" asked Emma, resurfacing from her conversation with Elizabeth. Cornelia and Obadiah looked at each other, each hoping the other would field the question.

"Cornelia Rose Entwhistle?" a voice hollered. Nellie turned her head in the direction of the shout.

"Who in all tarnation could I possibly know in this Godforsaken place?" she whispered.

A big hand appeared out of the crowd and grabbed Nellie's arm. A grizzled face peered at Nellie. "Want to buy some feed for yer stock?"

"Merciful heavens!" Nellie gasped and pulled with all of her might to escape the dirty digits that clutched her. Obadiah whipped the oxen and their cart lurched forward, freeing Nellie from the peddler's grasp.

As if by magic, the passage cleared for their wagon to break away from the throng.

"Who was that?" asked Obadiah.

"I cannot fathom for love nor money!" exclaimed Nellie.

"Cornelia Rose Entwhistle, wait!" an authoritative voice commanded.

A bugle blew. The crowd near them quieted, and all heads turned toward the sound. A uniformed soldier mounted on a fine horse drew up to their wagon. The imposing rider swept off his captain's hat and bowed his head.

"Nellie! Captain William T. Magruder here, at your service," the man said.

Nellie looked at Obadiah, whose mouth hung open. Blood rushed to her cheeks and she felt a tingle of excitement. *An acquaintance from home? What joy!* But she caught herself before she said anything. *Mercy, I am a respectable married woman and a mother of two! I should not react to the sound of a familiar male voice like the flirtatious debutante I once was.*

"This indubitably beats the Dutch! How in name of Beelzebub do you find yourself here?" Magruder pressed his horse closer to the wagon.

Nellie was at a loss for words. Obadiah growled at her, "An old beau, I presume, Cornelia?" All she could manage was a silent nod.

Obadiah's countenance relaxed into a smile. "One's past oft does come back to haunt one." Obadiah and Captain Magruder extended their hands for a friendly greeting at the same moment.

"Come," said Magruder. "Follow me to this side street, away from this swarming crowd. It's a miracle no one has yet pinched your horse in this town of ruffians."

There was no argument from Obadiah or Nellie. "This far from home, any familiar face assumes the moniker of a long-lost friend," she murmured. Obadiah pulled the lead on the oxen and coaxed them to follow Magruder.

"I am of like mind," said Obadiah. "Even an old beau of yours feigns the aspect of a tried-and-true comrade."

"'Tis settled — any old port in a storm," she whispered back with a smile. "Although probably it would be far more desirable to encounter any other ex-suitor than Magruder."

"Be careful what you wish for," Obadiah said with a wink. He jumped out of the wagon, yanked the yoke of the oxen, pulling them in the right direction, and mounted their horse, spurring it ahead before Magruder disappeared from sight.

"Who is that gentleman, Mama?" asked Emma, both girls sidling closer to her as she assumed the reins.

Nellie smiled, she was almost giddy with joy. *An ally here in this wild, chaotic place! Although braggart and windbag are numbered among Magruder's personality traits, his exceptional military prowess should provide us some guidance in navigating this squalid little town.* "Just an acquaintance from my childhood in New York," she said.

"Does Papa knowed him?" asked Elizabeth.

Cornelia hesitated. "Not directly," she finally answered. "Only through my introduction." The two girls seemed satisfied with that explanation.

Cornelia was surprised to see Obadiah and Magruder strike up a friendly exchange in spite of the awkwardness of the situation.

Magruder was all too happy to represent himself as an expert on Iowa and this part of the Northwest territory, and Obadiah was a big enough man to take the situation as it presented, using the opportunity to bolster his arsenal of knowledge of the new territory and strategize for their impending trip.

They stood talking in the middle of a small square in front of a trough where the oxen, their horse, and Magruder's, drank. Nellie anxiously scanned their surroundings. This square, flanked by shops and people with baskets selling vegetables, was not nearly as squalid or chaotic as the main street. She let out her breath, which she suddenly realized she had been holding, and relaxed her guard, just a smidge.

"I expect you've caught the gold rush fever and joined the frenzy heading to California?" asked Magruder.

Obadiah and Nellie shook their heads no, while Nellie thought, *Mercy, I had forgotten how large a man he is. Quite commanding in his captain's uniform....*

"Lookie here, yer too late for the Oregon Territory Donation Land Act. All the free land, every 160-acres-a-person parcel, plus the additional 160 for the little ladies, is all doled out. That law expired in 1854." Captain Magruder pushed his hat up further on his head and frowned.

"'Tis a pity too," said Nellie. "For the United States Government, in its haste to inhabit Oregon, allowed married women to claim title to land in their own names, a major step in women's rights."

Magruder seemed a bit dumbfounded at that news.

"You could not possibly be one of them Mormons, heading out to Utah Territory?" Magruder pushed his cap back up on his head in disbelief.

"We *are* headed to Utah," began Obadiah.

"Most indubitably, we are not Saints!" blurted Nellie.

Magruder laughed. "True. 'Tis hardly an apt descriptor for *you*, little Lady."

Nellie blushed furiously at the double entendre, too flustered to reply.

"The intended import of my *wife's* declaration was to dispel your possible misunderstanding," corrected Obadiah, through clenched teeth. He put a hand on his lapel and leaned toward Magruder, with menace in his eyes. "We are not members of the Church of Latter-day Saints. The impetus for our journey is my new position as Federal Circuit Judge in Utah Territory. We seek not a new fortune, civilization, or order, but rather an extension of our current one."

"Thundering cannons, your choice of watering hole for arresting your journey's progress is dead-on," said Magruder, hitching up his pants and tipping his hat to Nellie. "It is my grave responsibility, it is my main charge, it is my *raison d'etre*, to protect the emigrant. You are under my auspices now."

Obadiah raised his eyebrows and gave a slight grin. "Is that the bottom fact? No matter. We seek a campsite. We shall dally awhile, affording me time to establish a wagon train suitable for our affiliation on the westward passage."

"Sparing you much travail and misery, I advise: you shall find it far more efficacious to cast your lot with prospectors and their families than contracting with a Mormon group." Magruder had the audacity to wink. "You won't have to guard yer white women, iffn ye ken my speak."

Nellie and Obadiah exchanged glances.

"Aye, you'll soon learn of their strange ways. Howsoever, I have it within my purview to associate ye with a company that organizes hundreds of trains a day. They have a practiced hand and will steer ye right." Magruder looked Obadiah in the eye as he picked up Nellie's gloved hand and kissed it.

Magruder smiled at Nellie. "Come camp with my troop of men! We have a fine campsite, northeast of this flea-bitten town. I can nestle ye for a bit with us, have ye avoid the thieving townsmen and the restless Ote who prey on the tenderfoots from the East."

He turned to Obadiah. "I'd whip my weight in wildcats before I'd let anything happen to Nell while ye was under my jurisdiction. Since hundreds of trains leave daily, I can use my influence to obtain your passage with a suitable company. Yea, 'tis truly yer good fortune ye chose this, my town, as the locale for yer departure from the United States," said Magruder.

Cornelia and Obadiah looked at each other, this time skeptically. Obadiah said, "I do believe the weather and the traveling conditions conspire against us. I am afraid our scheduled departure is as imminent as upon the morrow. With regrets, we must forgo your hospitable offer."

Magruder's face fell. Suddenly, he looked like a little boy who dropped his lollipop. "It's not every day in this wilderness that a kindred spirit materializes out of thin air. 'Twould have been an unearned bounty to have kinfolk like yerselves around my fireplace." He brightened. "But, no matter. What say we compromise? We could hitch ye up to a wagon train tonight and ye can be off in the morning after a night of merrymaking."

Nellie and Obadiah exchanged yet another doubt-filled glance.

The wind completely left Magruder's sails. "In this lonely, uncivilized frontier, I humbly request the pleasure of one fine, proper dinner before ye settle in for the night."

Humbly? Pshaw, he's the farthest cry from humble... however, mayhap a night with a familiar face is not unwelcome.

Cornelia gave a small nod of consent and Magruder hooted happily before Obadiah could say anything to contradict her.

"I'll grant ye; 'tis not the social deference you most assuredly are due," Magruder said, rubbing his gloved hands in satisfaction. "But we shall embrace the opportunity and pull out all the stops."

Emma tugged on Nellie's dress. "That man has his own organ? Mercy," she whispered. "He must be important! We've seen no churches in this city."

Nellie smiled, leaned down and whispered, "The Captain is not talking about pulling out the stops of a real organ's pipes. He uses the expression to mean he shall not spare any effort in providing us hospitality." *Although Magruder believes himself quite important enough to posses such an expensive musical instrument,* she thought, still smiling.

Emma grinned. "Silly!"

Straightening, Nellie said, "As for you, Captain Magruder, how did you come to be assigned military duty here?"

"As a soldier, I go hither and yon at the whim of the United States Army and my superior officers. As I believe I have already divulged, my assignment here began a few years ago. I gladly perform my sworn duty — protection of the many settlers and travelers who pass through this region. I send search parties for cattle and livestock separated from their rightful Eastern owners by conniving and devious Natives... I am fighting savages, Nellie, just like I promised." He laughed.

Cornelia frowned and pursed her lips. "Such contemptible bigotry is not suitable parlance before little ladies."

"Always the proper gentry, Mistress Entwhistle. Yer deportment, and may I say yer figure, present no sign of alteration." Magruder gave a devilish grin.

"No, you shan't be permitted that liberty, Magruder, for as any fool can see, Cornelia *has* changed," said Obadiah. Magruder looked confused. "She is now my wife, and I will thank you to abandon this familiar tone with *us.*"

Magruder dropped Nellie's hand.

In the awkward silence, Nellie said, "This is most troublesome." Both men looked at her askance. She rushed to blurt the rest of her thought; "I find the turbulence between our nation and the native peoples of this land most disquieting. In my judgment, both sides have committed grievous wrongdoing."

"A local tribe staged a raid on an encampment of emigrants just a fortnight ago," Magruder advised. "Those Ote braves stole five head of horses and a bunch of cattle. Armed with rifles, they intimidated a whole company, and the pioneers scattered. Only a few valiant settlers, sporting brand new pistols, pursued. The settlers tried to keep the horse thieves in sight as they fled through the woods. We sent out reinforcements... but so did the Indians. By hook or by crook, in the end, we salvaged our people." Magruder shook his head. "There were a warrant out for the arrest of the white men that kilt some of 'em. But even the Indian Chief said, 'Them palefaces have served us right.' He acknowledged his boys had no business on this side of the Missouri River, molesting emigrants."

Nellie's head hurt and she felt a bit squeamish.

Magruder seemed to notice and changed the subject. "There are fellow graduates of West Point Military Academy scattered all about these here parts. Perhaps you remember Cadet Lawrence Baker? He was in the class below me... and most assuredly he remains a class below!" he punned.

Nellie blushed.

"Must our path west be strewn with your former beaus?" growled Obadiah.

"I am quite shocked at the audibility of that remark," whispered Nellie to Obadiah, as Magruder continued.

"I came upon Baker's whereabouts quite accidentally. He is working with Grenville Dodge, a railroad surveyor who has been quite instrumental in Council Bluffs, even before '53 when he established his family in residence here."

"As a mere point of curiosity, whither is Baker stationed?" asked Nellie.

Magruder replied, "He is currently stationed out in New Fort Kearny. When I am not here, pow-wowing with Billy Caldwell," Magruder paused at their blank expressions. "Excuse me, Chief Sauganash of the Potawatomi Indian tribe, my troops and I are out at Kearny with Baker waging...." Magruder looked at the little girls, who stared up at him in wide-eyed, rapt attention. "...Ahem... keeping the peace, you might say, shoulder to shoulder with Baker."

Cornelia and Obadiah exchanged glances, but they were spared a reply. Emma leaned over the tongue of the wagon and asked, "What does 'Sauganash' mean?"

"It is the Chief's name," answered Nellie, secretly delighted at the intelligence of Emma's inquiry.

"But what does it mean?"

"Right smart little lady," said Magruder. "Ye take after yer Ma! It means 'one who speaks English'."

Satisfied, the two girls resumed their play.

Obadiah looked at Nellie, and then nodded to Magruder. "I think we *shall* take you up on that most generous offer—furnishing a suitable spot for making camp tonight."

"Right, ho," said Magruder. "Your livestock will be safely pastured for the night, and you will all be comfortably bedded." He winked at Nellie, who blushed at his double entendre.

"Fall in behind now," Magruder commanded, pleased to have unbalanced Nellie again. "If I cannot slow my horse sufficiently to keep pace with them oxen, ye'll find my troops camped right near the old Caldwell Camp. Any of the townsfolk can tell ye where it is."

"But *what* is it?" asked Nellie.

Magruder laughed. "Still the enquiring student, I see." Obadiah threw him a look and Magruder changed his familiar tone. "Fiddlesticks, it is nothing but available land right now. A few years back, it served as the settlement of the Potawatomi after the Treaty of Chicago. They've vacated camp now, led by Billy Caldwell. Like I told ye, that's the English name of the half-breed, the aforementioned Chief Sauganash. Yep, we pushed 'em further west."

As they drove to the camp, Nellie whispered to Obadiah, "I fervently pray that our stay here, surrounded by donkey jockeys, gamblers, and thieves, will be short-lived." Nellie looked from side to side as she drove the wagon, grateful that Obadiah kept his horse creeping at their side.

"Neglect not mention of the assassins," said Obadiah. Nellie looked at him aghast. He nodded his head toward a particularly unsavory, grizzled man, six-gun belted at his waist, rifle slung across his back. Obadiah laughed and promised, "You'll have a tougher skin after just a few weeks into our land journey."

Forsooth, I discern no desirable benefits of such a state; how could callousness benefit my shrewdness? Is Mr. Wright intimating the presence of so many perils, so many terrors in our passage, I shall simply become impervious? Nellie shuddered.

"May I and your daughters accompany you on your reconnoiter of the wagons?" asked Cornelia.

Obadiah frowned. "My scouting shall be more expeditious and efficacious conducted alone. You must remain with the wagon and set up camp. I envision the inauguration of your Christmas shovel! Mayhap you can instigate some limb stretching for our fair daughters in between inventorying our supplies."

Nellie sighed. *I am surprised he so unreservedly abandons me to the company of Magruder. Yet, his reasoning is undoubtedly sound. In all probability, we have less to fear from a former beau than a town of ruthless and predatory fortune hunters.* She sighed again. *My husband speaks the truth. There are, always, so many details to attend. The animals need picketing and watering. Elizabeth has ripped her petticoat, and it must be mended today, for she has no other. Emma's shoes need evaluation — we cannot very well begin our journey walking to Utah Territory in ill-fitting footwear.*

Upon their arrival at the camp of Magruder and his troops, Nellie gave a silent squeal of delight. Magruder leased a property containing two cottages, in addition to the wide-open land for housing tents. He generously offered his own cottage to the Entwhistles, for the duration of their stay, saying he would bunk with his second in command.

"Mama, look at the teepees!" said Emma, clasping her hands.

Magruder laughed, "Yup, ye'll see plenty of upturned sod and buffalo skin stretched over poles still standing in Caldwell's camp." He winked at Cornelia. "'Tis quite picturesque."

"But girls, what causes your look of disappointment?" asked Nellie. "The cottage is lovely. Why, it even contains two beds! Most assuredly luxurious accommodations, especially when compared to our last travel dwelling, the house outside of Toledo."

"We left home *years* ago," said Emma. "But we have yet to camp in our wagon."

Nellie laughed. "'Tis well our anticipation remains at peak. We haven't half begun our journey."

CHAPTER 27
Stop! In the Name of Love

Council Bluffs, Iowa, April 1857

Obadiah secured them a place in a wagon train of speculators, homesteaders and prospectors leaving for California in two days.

"I thought we preferred an immediate departure?" Nellie asked.

"We shan't let our personal discomfiture at accepting Magruder's hospitality elicit a rash decision. A capable man named Hines spearheads the organization of this particular train's fifty wagons. I have it on good authority; he is an experienced pioneer, having thrice made the journey. As our provisional captain, he makes preparations for a Wednesday exodus," Obadiah explained.

Magruder approached them in time to hear their plan for departure.

"By the great horn spoon!" cried Magruder. "Two days shall ensure time to settle yer hash *and* partake in some of our cultured social activities. Hobnobbing with high society being yer forté, if'n I remember, Nellie. Tonight, we dine at Grenville Dodge's, the aforementioned highly regarded *and* highly reputable citizen. After a wide-ranging and comprehensive survey of this area, Dodge selected Council Bluffs, at that time known as Kanesville, as a suitable terminus for the Rock Island Railroad. Not content to rest on them laurels, he's established a banking house that finances any and all construction around these parts."

Nellie remained unimpressed. *Mercy, half our neighbors back in Sing Sing claim the prominence of bankers, lawyers, or editors of New York City newspapers. Why thinks he this is noteworthy?*

"Yep, Dodge is a banker now. He's got the prettiest wife in Council Bluffs. Although, Nell, ye'll give her a run for the money!" Magruder winked and Nellie blushed. *Confound that man, he still makes me blush like a schoolgirl.* "Yessir, his soirees are the talk of the town. Now it just so happens, by the by, I have been invited for dinner there tonight, and my hint to the hostess shall surely result in an extension of the invitation to include two more persons."

"Four more persons," corrected Cornelia.

Magruder took a step back in surprise. He raised his eyebrows. A light dawned in his face and he said, "One of my men would be happy to entertain yer little ladies for the evening while we dine."

"Out of the question," snapped Nellie. "Goodness! I shan't even humor such a preposterous notion. I suppose we must simply miss the finest social opportunity of this town." She shook her head.

Magruder leaned in towards her, just a little too close. "Fiddlesticks, Cornelia Rose, don't carry on so. For old time's sake, I was jest trying to give ye what might be yer last taste of society for a long time to come."

Nellie blushed again. "Captain Magruder, I do apologize. I have been remiss in employing my manners. Undoubtedly, I appreciate your gallant efforts to entertain me. I take myself to task for failing to grasp a bachelor would have no understanding of a mother's reticence to leave her children in parts unknown, with whom-knows-who, to attend a social occasion, no matter how fine."

Magruder bowed stiffly and said through pursed lips, "I would have entrusted no one but my aide-de-camp—an upright gentleman hardly deserving a 'who-knows-who' moniker. Howsoever, 'nuf said." He forced a smile. "It is always a delight to entertain ye my dear."

Magruder hung his head and shook it sadly. "Yer don't know it, but yer passing up some pumpkins. I don't like to blow my own horn...." Suddenly he grinned, his old spirit returning in a flash. "But there is no one present to vouch for me! I am an influential man—very well connected. Not just in Council Bluffs, but in all of Iowa and half of Nebraska Territory. I don't need to ride on old Grenville Dodge's coattails; I have earned quite the prestigious reputation myself. I guarantee the finest company, victuals, and entertainment, if ye join me."

Nellie's face softened, but she did not soften her resolve. "I tender my most sincere regrets, I cannot attend without my children."

Apparently Magruder's need for old friends outweighs his desire to be the talk of the town, Nellie thought to herself, when Magruder's aid presented her a handwritten invitation, addressed to each member of the Wright family, to dine at Captain Magruder's house for dinner. *I am quite certain my charming daughters shall affirm to the dear captain he made the correct decision.*

That night's sleeping accommodations were as comfortable as Agnes' huge house in Chicago. The next morning, Nellie permitted herself an additional moment of luxurious stretching before jumping out of bed to see about breakfast preparations. *I must confess, the thought of sleeping another night in a real feather bed is simply delightful. I shall savor the comfort! Surely a multitude of months shall pass before I am again favored with that pleasure.*

The day flew by in a rush of final preparations. After she and Obadiah obtained the last few requirements for their journey, Nellie and her daughters left him haggling over a purchase price for three head of cattle. They set off for Edwin Carter's dry goods store. Trained as the army post's sutler, Mr. Carter had perfected his ability to barter. The three Wright women *oohed* and *aahed* over the array of fine goods displayed, and Mr. Carter prepared for battle.

Longingly, Nellie fingered the one bolt of velvet cloth on display.

"I can picture that cloth, all done up right purdy, on you now, little lady," said Mr. Carter, his voice oily with slick salesmanship. "For just two dollars you can take it home with you right now."

"Two dollars?" asked Nellie, aghast. She dropped the cloth as if it burned her fingers.

Mr. Carter scratched his head, assuming an injured air. "What a hard bargain you drive!" He smiled an oily smile. "Doggone it! But for you, little lady, the whole piece for just one dollar and fifty cents. Just take it and walk out that door back home."

Nellie fingered the material again. It was a deep scarlet red, her favorite color, and she could picture it, sewn with a flounced skirt and a bright white lace collar and cuffs. *Mercy, what occasion in the prairie wilderness would ever necessitate such attire? Furthermore,* she told herself, *I already have my green velvet gown tucked around some precious jewelry for just such an imaginary occasion. I must be practical.* She sighed and swept a loose strand of hair from her eyes. "I am afraid my home is too far away to make that proposition practical." She turned away and walked toward the back of the store.

Her girls ran from the pickle barrel, around the shovels, picks and axes, past the bins of brick-a-brack, pins and needles and back to the cash register, exclaiming over all the beautiful merchandise, pretending they were purchasing one of every good in the store. Nellie smiled, finding happiness in their simple joy. While selecting some cheesecloth for her butter making, a long strip of white linen in the remnant bin caught her eye.

She jumped. Mr. Carter had snuck up behind her while she pawed through the remnants and examined the linen.

"Aw heck," said Mr. Carter. "That bit o' cloth won't nearly do you justice. But it just so happens...." He gave a wink. "It'll make some mighty fine collars and cuffs. Just for you now, my little lady, I'll let it slip through my fingers for twenty cents."

Mayhap, far more accurately, slip through your greedy clutches. Nellie tugged at a stray strand of hair, hesitating.

"Dad-blame it, I'll hang up my fiddle," said Mr. Carter. He looked right and left, as if to confirm no one else in the store was within earshot. He whispered, "I'll give you the whole piece for a nickel."

Impulsively, she purchased it. *Mercy, 'tis still highway robbery! Peter Stuyvesant bought the whole island of Manhattan for only sixty guilders, and some of that value was in trade!* Before she could suffer more buyers' remorse, she hurried her two girls back to their temporary home for a short rest.

While her girls lay sleeping, she cut the linen into squares for handkerchiefs. *With a little lace, this cloth shall be big enough for five handkerchiefs.* She took the largest one, crocheted a border of edging, and embroidered the initials WTM.

She was just knotting her thread when Emma awoke and exclaimed, "You've already made a new handkerchief for Papa, 'cause Devil, the ox, put a horn through his old one!"

Nellie blushed. *Mercy, when did that mishap occur? I hadn't even noticed.*

"No, I shall crochet the edge on one for your father as we travel," answered Nell. "It is a thank you gift for Captain Magruder. One must never accept hospitality without a proper and fitting expression of gratitude."

Emma nodded gravely, and Nellie blushed again.

The day of their wagon train departure dawned. The Wright family arrived at the trailhead. In the uncertain light of early morning, Nellie watched with dismay as disheveled figures scrambled to assemble livestock and belongings. *The company consists mostly of men. The scarcity of women in this pack of grizzled fortune seekers is most disheartening. Are so few women hardy enough to undertake this adventure?*

Obadiah scurried around, feeding the oxen, chatting with Captain Hines, and saddling his horse. Nellie, fully packed and ready to go, stood observing the activities of her fellow travelers.

Suddenly, Magruder materialized from behind a tree and stood right in front of her. "You were sadly mistaken, Mistress Entwhistle, if you were under the impression it was acceptable to quit the most important man in Council Bluffs without a proper goodbye," he said, feigning anger. He put his hand on her arm.

"Why, I left you a note, containing a little remembrance, in appreciation of your hospitality," Nellie protested.

"Perhaps 'proper' was not the correct word. In fact, perhaps your adieu was too proper," he said. He took a quick look around him. Ascertaining no one observed them, he stepped in and kissed Nellie directly on the lips. "A lady does not embroider a handkerchief for a gentleman for whom she cares naught. I understand your meaning—I shall await your return," he whispered.

A fellow traveler ran by, chasing a chicken. Nellie jumped backwards, using the squawking commotion to recover her composure.

She tugged at a strand of her hair, uncertain as to how to diplomatically handle this unexpected ambush.

Magruder advanced toward her again. "Thank you kindly for this fine handkerchief. I shall keep it close to my heart.... "He put it in his breast pocket. "Not to use... but to treasure, for it possesses your spirit, retaining you nearby until the day we meet again."

Before Nellie could disillusion Magruder, he picked up her gloved hand, kissed it, turned on his heel, and marched back to his horse.

He jumped in his saddle, raised his hand in salute, and turned his horse away. Nellie nodded politely to his retreating back. He glanced back, saw her still watching, pulled his hat off, whooped, and galloped away.

Not only is he a braggadocio, he's a theatrical one at that. Nellie burst out laughing.

She was still in fine spirits as Captain Hines, commandeering the first wagon in the train, raised his hand, gestured forward, and moved his team onto the road.

Obadiah shouted, "Giddy *up!*" and they pulled to their place behind the tenth wagon. Nellie giggled at the rear view of the overflowing wagon ahead. Pots and barrels swung, suspended off the wagon's sides, bits of material and furniture protruded from the opening in the back and scores of children ran around it. *Emma and Elizabeth might find gainful employment, retrieving fallen items from this burgeoning prairie schooner.*

Nellie noticed an impressive granite building as they trundled along the road, and pointed it out to Obadiah.

"Behold the Kanesville Tabernacle," he said. "The Latter-day Saints founded this town as its winter quarters during The Great Mormon Migration of 1846. Quite a large community of Saints dwelt here, but now they have piled all their worldly possession in handcarts and joined us on the trail to The Great Salt Lake City."

CHAPTER 28
Bright Side of the Road

Merging Trails, Nebraska Territory, April 1857

I do believe the terrain changed the minute we left Council Bluffs, Iowa. Truly, when we crossed the Missouri River at Bullard's Ferry, left the United States and stepped foot in Nebraska Territory, the forests disappeared. Tall grass waved as far as the eye could see. The sound of the wind escalated from barely audible to a noticeable murmur. The expanse of this plain stretches so tremendously, I feel like a mere speck on the face of the earth!

Nellie walked beside the oxen, nudging them every once in a while, guiding them on the path. Obadiah rode up, his stint at herding and guarding the train's livestock concluded for the day. He hitched his horse behind their rolling wagon and joined Nellie. As they trudged alongside their wagon, one of the wagoneers approached Obadiah. Without any introduction or preamble, the man said, "The security of our entire party depends upon the judicious selection of a campsite."

Obadiah and Nellie exchanged glances.

Obadiah cleared his throat, nodded, and said, "I am certain you are quite right, my good man."

The man nodded back. "In this hostile Indian Territory, our first inquiry should be ascertaining a locality with defense capacity. A concave bend in the river stream, with deep water and a soft alluvial bed, enclosed by high and abrupt banks will be the most defensible."

Obadiah and Nellie exchanged another glance, this time with raised eyebrows and uplifted corners of their mouths. "I am uncertain as to whether that particular topography presents itself along this section of the trail," Obadiah said.

The man shoved his oversized hat back above his eyebrows and continued as if he had not heard. "All the more should the concavity form a peninsula. The advantages of such a position are obvious to the skilled pioneer—a diminished need for sentinels, a defense of crossed fire in case of attack on the exposed side. Furthermore, the bend of the stream will form an excellent corral, thus preventing a stampede of the animals."

"Stampede?" said Emma, eyes wide with fright. Elizabeth burst into tears. Obadiah and Nellie immediately scooped the children off the wagon bench and into their arms, all the while walking forward.

Still talking, the man fell back and directed his stream of thought to the next party.

"An odd fellow, by all accounts," said Nellie, over the top of Elizabeth's head, as she hugged her tight.

"Methinks he quoted directly from a guidebook. He hardly looked the part of an experienced pioneer," replied Obadiah with a grin.

"Did his shiny new boots reveal his rawness?" asked Nellie with a giggle. "Or was it his fear-filled eyes, peeping out from underneath the ill-fitted new hat?"

"One might have overlooked those oddities, had one not noticed his strange method of carrying, and his frequent caressing, his shiny new breech-loading Winchester rifle." He lowered his head and touched his nose to Emma, whom he still held tight in his arms. "My two cherished cherubs, listen, we have embarked upon the greatest of all adventures. Think not on the possibility of danger. That responsibility shall be my mantle, alone. I shall rout out any and all hazards and thwart peril before it afflicts or distresses my family. Think only of this grand adventure we encounter, united," Obadiah said.

They gazed at him with trusting eyes.

The Wright family walked on. Obadiah hoisted the girls back onto the bench, and Nellie and Obadiah walked side by side next to them.

"Who *was* that peculiar little man?" Nellie asked.

"I am ignorant of his name," said Obadiah. "Have no fear, I predict very little time will pass before we are spoon fed, in agonizing detail, not only his name but his whole life's history."

They laughed and continued their forward motion.

"Mercy!" Nellie exclaimed as she looked toward the horizon. "Our gaze encompasses the most splendid of scenery."

"Jumping Jehoshaphat! Cornelia Rose, your utterance is the highest form of praise—a statement against interest. 'Most splendid' is an unqualified superlative from one so enamored of her Hudson Valley," said Obadiah.

Nellie blushed. "I realize I have spent my life praising the beauty of the Hudson River and Highlands and its surrounding landscape. Its scenery is imprinted upon my heart. Howsoever, I do believe I have never trod upon such a picturesque expanse as this prairie," Nellie remarked. The sun warmed her back and the view that stretched out before her was beautiful in an exotic way, different from any other landscape she had known. "We walk over hill and dale, one more resplendent with wildflowers than the next."

"Mama, this looks like the biggest flower garden in the world!" shouted Emma.

"The biggest flower garden in the boundless sea of grass," Cornelia agreed. She helped the girls down from the wagon and they ran with glee through the fields of wildflowers, stopping to pick armfuls. Nellie marveled at the overabundance of the early spring flowers. "See Mama—thorny roses, sunflowers, and asters, just like at home," said Emma, holding up the different bunches.

Perhaps this passage from civilization through the wilderness shall *be a lark,* she thought, just as she spotted a crude wooden cross.

"Obadiah," she whispered, tugging on his sleeve. She looked at her daughters now riding on the lazy board Obadiah pulled out from under the wagon, arranging the wildflowers they had gathered. *I must not arrest their attention.* "Can that cross be naught but a grave marker?" she asked in a soft whisper. "Or that roughly scratched stone?" The words caught in her throat, for she knew the answer. As they plodded forward, she saw the trail was pockmarked with graves all along its way. She began to count.

"That's twenty, within about three hundred steps!" she exclaimed, still keeping her voice low, so her daughters would not overhear. Obadiah whispered back, "The talk in Council Bluffs was of the cholera that plagues the emigrants and follows them down the path, leaving grave markers in their wake."

Nellie shook her head. "This is grim news."

"Surely not news," replied Obadiah. "We have anticipated, and prepared for, this disease. You yourself have equipped us. Armed with your medical knowledge, we shall scrutinize all the water we consume, vigilantly boiling it, to ensure its purity, before ingesting."

"Aye, true. But still, the sight casts a rather melancholy pall over our journey," Nellie murmured.

"'Tis a grave sight," Obadiah deadpanned.

Nellie smiled at his play on words and sighed. "As in all life's journeys, I suppose we must simply trust in the Lord to keep us safe."

Obadiah smiled and squeezed her hand.

"'Tis a pall we shall bear, watching it wither in the full sun of our good health," Nellie offered, in a weak attempt to lighten their melancholy with her own pun.

Obadiah wagged his finger at her, "Pallbearer, grim shall be the fruits you reap from that pun."

She grinned.

Nellie watched the sun sink lower on the horizon. They walked on. They saw the lead wagon turning off the trail, as if to make camp. "I see no abrupt banks," Nellie said with a giggle.

With the site chosen, the men scurried about, settling the wagons, finding pasture for the cattle and picketing the horses and oxen. Nellie removed her engraved shovel from its place of honor, hung on a nail next to Obadiah's Winchester rifle, and dug her first small trench. *I suppose I must supply my own fanfare!* she thought with a grin. Rubbing the now aching small of her back, she sprinkled a confetti of kindling into the trench, smiled, and started a fire. Beans soon bubbled in a wrought-iron camp kettle, releasing a delicious aroma of molasses.

After cooking, and eating, supper, Nellie said, "Our first true night of encampment on the westward trail." The excitement in her voice caused her daughters to look up from their stick drawings on the ground and grin. Nellie plopped on top of the log in front of their fire and leaned on Obadiah. "Smell the lingering fire." Nellie inhaled a deep breath. "Feel the budding spring blossoms. Listen to the faint sound of the roaring Platte River far below these majestic river banks." She winked at Obadiah. "Find comfort in the slight bend of the river corralling our livestock. Mercy! The air is so fresh. Prithee, I do believe we shall be infinitely more comfortable sleeping here in our wagon than upon our shelf berths on the Erie Canal packet. Here we shall snuggle all together, so cozily." She turned around to smile at Obadiah. With a quick hug, she nestled into his arms. They gazed at the fire, and at their children, and Nellie counted her blessings.

The terrain changed again as they left the high plain for the low bottom of the Platte River. They walked through a flat basin and Nellie looked back at the high bluffs of the sandy plains on either side of the Platte River Valley. The well-worn trail unspooled through sandy dirt, covered only by a thin layer of new green grass. The only visible vegetation, clumps of cottonwood and thickets of willows, clustered long distances apart, dotting the shores along the Platte. Emma picked up a stick, and soon, Nellie and her girls retrieved every stray piece of firewood they spotted, collecting sufficient kindling for not only this night's camping, but for the unknown, woodless campgrounds they anticipated ahead.

"Emma put down the spyglass." Nellie turned from inspecting her churning butter to see Emma spying out the back of the wagon's cover. Emma jumped.

"Mercy, Mama. You needn't worry. I tender far more care in handling this valuable instrument than even Papa."

Nellie smiled. "I'll concede you do. However...."

Emma interrupted, "The tribe of Indians walking parallel to us along the higher ridge stopped!"

"Tarnation, you see Indians following us?" Nellie exclaimed, so startled she did not watch her tongue. "Why have the scouts not alerted us?"

Nellie grabbed the telescope and looked. But she did not see anyone on the ridge. She looked at Emma. "Are you quite certain?"

Emma looked offended. "Of course, Mama. I have been watching them all morning. Why would you doubt me?"

Nellie realized her oldest daughter, in spite of her tender age of four, was observant, and a reliable source of information. She searched the ridge again. Far in the distance behind them she saw barely discernible figures, clustered together. *So distant now it would serve no purpose to sound an alarm. I shall question Obadiah about the tribes residing in this area when we are alone tonight. I fear I only recall hearing of the presence of bellicose Pawnee in this region. I pray my recollection is faulty.*

As their path climbed back up the bluffs, Nellie's anxiety increased. *I fervently pray we do not disturb any tribes encamped atop these bluffs. Especially hostile ones!* she thought, as they walked along.

But the wagon train's turn in a southerly direction caused her to forget her unease. Nellie breathed a sigh of relief as she watched the wagons travel back down the sand bluffs toward the Platte River.

"What a blessing. All the sluices, streams, and crossings along this well-traveled part of the road have been bridged," Obadiah remarked to Nellie.

"After all, it is *anno Domini* 1857," Nellie said. "Emigrants have been traveling West since the '40s — the trails are now well marked, with forts, trading posts, and many additional signs of civilization along the way."

As they trudged across a bridge, Nellie took one look at the swift, rushing water and averted her gaze. She shuddered as visions of the roiling Hudson River during the *Henry Clay* disaster flashed before her eyes.

Obadiah said, "In crossing the Platte via bridge, why, we barely break our stride. Even in this remote territory, cultivation protects us from the full force and effect of nature."

"I pray all our river crossings pass as smoothly," Nellie replied, with another little shudder, eyes now fixated on the rapids in spite of herself. Obadiah let his raised eyebrows convey his skeptical opinion of Nellie's wishful thinking without uttering a word.

The trail along the south bank was much the same as the terrain on the north, and onward they marched.

'Tis quite the grand spectacle!

At the major fork in the road much publicized in guidebooks, she stood on the wagon tongue, rotating 360 degrees. The great visibility afforded by the emptiness of the plains allowed Nellie to view the junction of the two trails behind them. Packed end-to-end, wagons teeming with emigrants processed up the southerly trail, a path already conjoined from trails originating in St. Joseph and Independence Landing, Missouri. That merged trail met the long line of prairie schooners streaming along the westward emigration road beginning in Council Bluffs, Iowa. *Fleets of white-topped prairie schooners sailing through the plains like Mutter's painting of a convoy of British militia sailing up the Hudson,* she thought, blinking away a surge of tears at her own simile.

Shan't be helped. 'Tis incumbent I arm myself with positive thoughts, or my sorrow shall have no moderation. She inhaled deeply and gazed at the mass migration. She looked down at Obadiah, still walking alongside the oxen.

"From here I can see first-hand all manner of pioneers answering Horace Greeley's call to go West. The sheer volume staggers the imagination. They heed the expert advice and depart, *en mass*, in early spring to attain California or Oregon before the first snowfall." A thrill raced through her at the massive number of travelers thickly crowding the two roads. She turned to look ahead, seeing before her an unbroken line of wagons slowly winding their way westward across the waving grass of the broad plain. *Even attending parades in New York City, I have never seen such multitudes of people. Mercy! They trek in all manner of vehicles and conveyance. Could any of the population remain behind?*

CHAPTER 29
Southern Man

New Fort Kearney, Nebraska Territory, April 1857

"Behold the first dwellings we have seen since leaving the United States," said Nellie, shading her eyes to block the sun glare unimpeded by her bonnet and staring at the dark cluster on the road ahead.

The site of the fort does not disappoint, Nellie thought, as they entered the little civilization called New Fort Kearney. Sod walls, cut in adobe style blocks, formed a few large barrack buildings, and an earthen embankment. *Forsooth, this rather unremarkable group of buildings hardly deserves the hawkers' appellation 'impenetrable fortress'.* The sod embankment perimeter, formed around the low multipurpose buildings with grassy sod roofs, offered the sole protection against invasion. *Yet the formation shapes quite a pleasant place. I rather expected a stockade fence and a military aspect. Instead, here I discover one lone tower in the midst of the traditional stock depot, blacksmith, and trading post.* She looked to the left of the fort where a handful of colonial style houses branded the vast plain with cultivation. *The Platte River winds through a bountiful countryside supporting several neat gardens and ploughed fields. Genuine houses of wood construction! The world has turned too many times since we have last seen such a sign of society.*

The weary travelers drove the livestock past the sod embankments and circled their wagons around a parcel of land selected for its lush green grass. About a quarter of a mile outside the buildings of the fort, their livestock would feast on the excellent feed, in safety.

The girls flew out of the wagon, joyful at the opportunity to run. The men gathered to discuss the particulars of their stay. After digging the trench for their cooking fire and fetching water from the river, Nellie and her daughters scurried to the fort's buildings. Five unpainted wooden houses stood around a parade ground, where both traders and

Native Americans bustled about. Nellie glanced at some scruffy-looking trappers bartering pelts of fur in exchange for new traps. She tightened her grip on her daughter's hands.

At first, Nellie and her daughters clustered together in the square, watching the thriving community, overwhelmed by all the activity.

Gradually, they moved toward the post's store for a closer look at its wares. Soon, they wandered down the street off the square, from building to building, past the Officer's Quarters and the barracks.

The tempting aroma of fresh-baked bread wafted past Nellie's nose just as Elizabeth cried out. "Bread baking!"

Nellie smiled and the ladies followed their noses to the post's bakery. They walked inside, the little girls chattering with delight.

"Mama, fresh bread," Elizabeth said. "Want some?"

"Hush," Nellie whispered. "I believe these loaves are for the soldiers."

Embarrassed, Nellie looked up at the baker, dumping loaf after loaf out of their pans, on to wire cooling racks.

Red-faced and looking harried, the man did not even glance at them.

"Mercy, Mama, do not fret," Emma whispered in reply. "The scent is heavenly! 'Tis a treat just to smell it. We needn't taste it."

Sadness at the depravation their journey forced upon her children replaced Nellie's embarrassment. "Excuse me, Mister Baker," she said. "Might it be possible to purchase one of your temptingly aromatic loaves?"

"They look so lovely, crusty and brown," agreed Emma.

"And smell good," Elizabeth piped in.

The man looked up, a frown on his face. His eyes took in Nellie and then he leaned all the way over the counter to see her little girls. His features broke into a broad grin.

"What have we here? Two little ladies fresh in from the East Coast?" he asked.

"Yes, from Sing Sing New York," said Emma.

Before Nellie could extend some pleasantries of her own, Emma continued. "I am Emma, and this is my sister Elizabeth."

A hearty laugh escaped from the burly man. "I am Zebulon. From Nebraska Territory. Here, have a bit of dough."

The girls giggled and jumped up to grab the tiny fist-sized bit of dough the baker leaned far over the counter again to give them.

His face must have been red from the heat of the oven rather than ill-temper. One mustn't judge a book by its cover.

"Mama, can you bake this bread and make it smell as delicious as these loaves?" asked Emma.

"Elizabeth, take that out of your mouth!" exclaimed Nellie. "This is dough to knead, not to eat."

Elizabeth looked confused.

"But we do need the bread, Mama," said Emma, with a puzzled frown puckering her eyebrows. "We haven't had a single bite since we left Aunt Agnes, way back in Chicago."

The baker threw back his head and laughed. Emma looked startled and Elizabeth started crying at the loud, sudden, outburst.

The baker grabbed something from the shelf and ran around the counter. "This shall never do," he said with a stern expression on his face, towering over the girls. Elizabeth cried harder, and Nellie put her arms around both girls protectively.

The baker opened his hands, revealing a currant scone in each. The girls sorrow immediately changed to joy. Elizabeth took one and said 'thank you.' Emma looked at Nellie for approval, and when she smiled, Emma reached for one, curtsied and thanked the baker.

Through full mouths, her daughters murmured words of appreciation. Nellie again felt embarrassed. But the baker was smitten by the charms of the two girls.

"We can't be having girls, magically appearing in my bakery, disappear without sampling some of my first-rate crusty bread. You'll not taste bread this exceptional again until Californ-y, my little ladies."

"I fear we shall not taste any bread at all," Nellie said in agreement. "I imagine the closest thing I shall have the wear-with-all to cook on the trail may be some biscuits, boiling within a stew." Nellie offered some money but the baker waved it away. She took the bread with many expressions of thanks.

They lingered at the counter, the girls savoring their treats and peppering the baker with questions. A garrulous man, he talked as quickly as he worked. In just a few short minutes Nellie knew the history of the fort and the baker had another round of dough kneaded and in the oven.

Finally, full of sugar from the scones, the girls bounced outdoors and ran across the parade ground. Nellie scurried after them. They made a beeline to the fort's tower.

Her daughters clamored to climb to the top of the observation tower. Nellie hesitated. *I must remain vigilant, and assess the dangers that lay ahead* before *my daughters cause themselves injury.* But, curious herself to see the view, she nodded her consent. The girls skipped up the ladder, and Nellie tucked the prized loaf of bread under her arm and climbed after them.

"Cornelia Rose?" a male voice drawled.

Nellie's stomach did a strange flip-flop at the sound of her name carried by a familiar voice. She was unsure whether it was from joy or dread. She turned, one hand still on each of her daughters' shoulders, and looked around for the source.

"Cornelia Rose Entwhistle, I do declare. Is this some mirage my brain, addled from nigh a year's time in this wilderness, conjured to deceive me, or could I be blessed with a true visitation from my Rose?"

Nellie's mouth fell open in a positively unladylike gawk. There before her, tall and handsome as ever, was her rejected suitor, Lawrence Simmons Baker. *Mercy, curiosity again killed the cat! But for the fact that I permitted my daughters to climb this tower, I might have escaped this awkward encounter. Would it have been too much to grant, Oh Lord, for Baker to be occupied and away on assignment elsewhere? Must the arduousness of this journey be further augmented by ghosts from my past?*

Suddenly, she giggled. *Quite the handsomest ghost one could conjure, however. This fort holds many surprises — first manna from heaven, now a phantom of love forsaken.* Her mind flip-flopped to her next concern as rapidly as her heartbeat quickened. *I prithee Lord, detain Obadiah! Prevent his encounter with Baker. I have no desire to haunt him with yet another specter from my past.*

"Why Lieutenant Baker," Nellie said, extending her free hand. *Mercy, I hope my breathlessness is merely a product of mounting the tower ladder and not residual silly schoolgirl enchantment.*

"*Captain* Baker, at your service my little flower." Baker bowed over Nellie's hand. Suddenly he pulled her in close. "Have you come to find me? Have you reconsidered my offer of a lifetime of happiness?"

Nellie shook her head no with vehemence. She pulled back, squishing the bread tightly under her arm, and looked wildly around for her daughters.

A voice sounded behind her, interrupting the awkward scene. They turned and saw a large hat floating up the ladder through the opening to the tower platform. Nellie giggled. *How curious. A disembodied hat sent from heaven to alleviate this uncomfortable tête-à-tête and mercifully inject a humorous note.*

The hat caught on the ladder's top rung. There was a scuffling sound and a red-faced man jumped up to the platform, hat in hand. Nellie laughed.

"Allow me to formally introduce myself, Captain. I am Wilburforce Wells." The peculiar man from Nellie's wagon train rushed from the ladder to Baker and began pumping his hand. Baker looked both nonplused and confused. Wilburforce said, "I am the man who inquired down in the fort proper—how does one learn to be a tracker?"

"You little cotton-picker, I do recall. You have a most unexpected manner, my dear fellow," drawled Baker, smoothing his mustache, an attractive addition since Nellie had last seen him five years ago.

Nellie looked down to hide her smile and her emotions. *Baker even has charm when stating the obvious.*

Baker grabbed the man's arm and led him away from Nellie. "I do apologize. I've been busier than a moth in a mitten, and it plumb slipped my mind. Here, boy, you must dialogue with some of our Pawnee braves. There are many who live in the vicinity and trade at the fort. Bless your pea-picking heart, in point of fact, I do believe there are some braves loitering about the trading post, right this very minute." Baker pointed toward the trader's post and dismissed Wells with a curt nod.

Wilbur clambered back down the ladder. Nellie heard him miss the last two rungs, cuss under his breath and stumble to the ground. Baker stepped back toward her, again a little too close.

"Now, my sweetest little flower," he drawled, offering her his arm. "May I escort you to my officer's quarters?" he asked. Not expecting an answer, he took her hand and turned toward the ladder.

Nellie stood, feet planted. She pulled her hand back and adjusted her loaf of bread. "Not without my daughters," she replied, smiling sweetly into his eyes.

"My word you have been extremely busy," Baker said, as Nellie pulled her daughters from the wall where they stood on tiptoes peering over it. Nellie bent her head to hide her blush and assembled her girls in front of her like a shield. Her hands on her daughters' shoulders, her bread tucked under her arm, Nellie raised her eyes to meet those of the tall captain.

"As I am sure have you," said Nellie, deliberately ignoring the impertinence of his remark. "You have attained the rank captain! What, pray tell, do your duties entail?"

"Why, I command this fort. I survey the area, I negotiate with the railroad, I oversee the pioneers. My duties, you see, are quite extensive. Besides prospecting and arranging land leases with Grenville Dodge, the railroad surveyor, I supervise the distribution of supplies. The rest of my time, as you would expect, is spent on the obvious: I lead troops into battle, or dispatch them, as I see fit. We have some four hundred and fifty soldiers here at this present juncture." He pointed down into the square below them. "Observe, my little Rose, the execution of my orders as I speak — twenty-five government wagons begin their journey to Fort Laramie, loaded to the gills with provisions."

The Wright ladies looked appropriately impressed with this information. The reaction encouraged Baker to continue. "Yessir. *One hundred* and twenty-*five* yokes of oxen, hauling *six tons* of precious provisions to a wagon, from iron kettles to desiccated vegetables, constitute that train.

"Our timber for this fine village of houses was imported all the way from Missoura," Baker mispronounced in his pride-filled southern drawl, gesturing to the cluster of houses just below them.

"Captain Baker, *we* have been imported all the way from Sing Sing, New York," Emma said, with an earnest look at the formidable man.

He gave a hearty laugh. "I see you have inherited your mother's pluck and wit." Nellie smiled at her daughter and at the sideways compliment. *How lovely to be known and appreciated.*

"Your little one has a discerning eye. She knows I am not telling a thumper when I list my credentials." Baker winked at Emma, who blushed and stepped behind Nellie's skirt. "I welcome you little ladies. You now stand at the Gateway to the Great Plains.

"I insist that you spend your short stay here in my house," Baker drawled. He stepped a pointed toe forward, and executed a grand bow ending in a flourish of his hand. The little girls giggled and Nellie suppressed a grin. He again reached for Nellie's gloved hand. "If I do say so myself, the best one of the only *eight* wood frame houses is the place I call my home. Why should you spend your time here assembling your campsite only to dismantle your handy work upon departure in two days' time? My housekeeper will provide you access to our laundry kettles."

Baker stepped in again, just a little too close, lifted her hand and brought it to his lips, his eyes smiling at her. "Land sakes, I'm grinnin' like a possum eating a sweet tater. Does a man's heart glad to see your beautiful face again, my little Primrose. Allow me the small pleasure of saving these beautiful hands from a few menial tasks in your journey of grand deprivations and hardships."

I would never have thought my joy would peak upon hearing the words laundry kettles, Cornelia grinned to herself. She gave Baker a small curtsey and looked into his eyes with delight, then hurriedly cast them back down. *Mercy! I must ensure my joy at a laundry kettle and two nights of comfortable sleep does not convey an altogether different message to the ever-enchanting Captain Baker. I'll grant the man this—he certainly has not lost his Southern charm.*

"I must confer with my husband, of course," Nellie said. Baker's face fell. "Although, I am most certain he too shall be delighted at your hospitality."

Baker's eyes clouded with emotion as he said, "My joy knows no bounds at the sight of you. Whatever the circumstances, fate has seen fit to deliver you to me. I shall not vanquish my claim so easily this time."

Nellie frowned at the implications of his statement and pulled her daughters toward the ladder. They backed down, leaving Baker at the top.

"I suppose there *are* some benefits to encountering your beaus throughout this vast land," growled Obadiah when Nellie caught up with him at the trading post. He pulled the fresh loaf of bread from under Nellie's arm and broke an uneven chunk from the edge. He took a large bite, closed his eyes, and chewed with evident satisfaction. When he had swallowed, he smiled and said, "Fresh bread *and* some fresh straw tick on a tightly pulled rope bed! Now that's a fine treat, even for a jealous husband, after 150 hard miles walked, far away from civilization."

Desperate times call for desperate measures, thought Nellie with a giggle. *Or should I quote Shakespeare's line in The Tempest, 'misery acquaints a man with strange bedfellows'?*

CHAPTER 30
Escape

New Fort Kearney, Nebraska Territory, April 1857

If I had my druthers, I would choose dodging old beaus over walking the leather off my boots, any day. Moreover, the sport certainly accelerates time, making my days fly by. The duration of our respite at Fort Kearney seemed a mere heartbeat's length. Two nights on proper linen sheets constituted a luxury I feared I might never again experience. Now that we take our leave and I have skirted every opportunity for confrontation, I must confess, at least to myself, my delight at Baker's many attempts to charm me.

The wagon repacked, Nellie looked at the two-story box colonial house and sighed. *It seems I must repeatedly renounce civilization and the last vestiges of its amenities. The Lord teases me with little tastes of my former comfort only to force me to forsake them again.*

Nellie tugged the ox team into line behind the still overflowing wagon of the Wilton family. Unthinking, she bent and retrieved the youngest Wilton daughter's cornhusk doll, the latest casualty of the common happenstance of spillage. She handed the doll to Emma, seated on the wagon tongue, to hold, until one of them desired a walk ahead for a visit with the Wilton's wagon.

She turned at the sound of hoofbeats. Baker and his horse appeared at her elbow.

Captain Baker swept off his hat, its plume billowing grandly. "Come at once, Cornelia Rose Entwhistle Wright," he commanded.

Nellie squinted up at the commanding figure on the high horse. "I beg your pardon?"

"One of my soldier's wives has labored for over twelve hours now. Something is amiss. She needs immediate medical attention."

"Surely the post's surgeon," Nellie said, eyebrows frowning.

"Hell, Nellie, she's the wife of my sergeant major. That gentleman is the closest thing to kin I've had since I left my mama. The post's surgeon doesn't know a lick about birthing. I've oft heard him say 'just leave it to the womenfolk—they've been birthing babies out for centuries'. My man is distraught beyond imagination. You must save this poor woman."

Nellie hesitated. Her natural inclination was to drop everything to heed the call of her profession, but a tiny part of her was suspicious of Baker and the actual need for *her* aid in the emergency. All during their fairytale reprieve from the arduousness of travel, Nellie wondered whether Baker would make a last ditch effort to detain her. *Is this his scheme for melodrama, coming to fruition? Is this emergency merely a ruse?* She kept pace with the forward progress of the train as she contemplated her reply.

Nellie turned with relief at the sight of Obadiah running toward them.

"Trouble?" he called as he approached.

"I am faced with a dire need for a midwife," Baker answered. "We have a complicated birth that requires your wife's healing gifts."

"We cannot stop the train," replied Obadiah. "We cannot afford to dally here any longer. Delay would jeopardize the entire company's chances of timely, safe arrival in California."

"Jiminy cricket, not the train. I only need your wife," Baker said, staring down at Obadiah. *Mercy, that statement hardly addresses Mr. Wright's concerns.*

Obadiah tweaked his mustache and looked puzzled. "Surely you have a surgeon or someone at your establishment who usually attends these matters?"

"This situation is extraordinarily grave. The complications presented are far beyond anyone's capacity," replied Baker, trying to keep his horse in line with the wagon's slow moving pace.

"Not the priest's," countered Obadiah.

Nellie drew in her breath sharply.

"Surely, we cannot abandon someone to the jaws of death who may be still be salvaged from a terrible tragedy," Nellie cried. She looked at her husband in shock. "Death confronts us at every turn on this trail. Word came this morning that the thunderstorm yesterday smote two men and one child in a train ahead of us. I am armed with these skills and duty-bound to use them when called. Surely you understand?"

Obadiah caught her hand. "If you must," he said, but through gritted teeth. "But at what cost? Moreover, how in heaven's name will you rejoin us?"

Baker seized his advantage. "I shall send a military envoy with Mrs. Wright to return her to your wagon train, wherever its location."

Nellie shook her head. "Mr. Wright, I feel compelled to at least diagnose this medical emergency. If the circumstances are not as dire as Captain Baker foretells, I can prescribe care for the poor woman and rejoin the wagon before our noon repast. In this wilderness, both my training and my Christian obligation dictate my response."

"I cannot spare our horse," said Obadiah.

Nellie raised her eyebrows. *Is that truly the reason for his reluctance to agree to my decision?*

Baker quickly interjected, "I will transport your wife now and dispatch her the moment her skills are no longer required."

In an instant, Nellie climbed into the back of her wagon and retrieved her medical bag, along with a basket of herbs and potions commonly used in birthing. She kissed her daughters, wrapping them in tight hugs. She smiled at Obadiah, who held her eyes for a long moment. At last he helped her mount the back of Baker's horse. Sitting sidesaddle, she clung onto the leather of Baker's saddle to prevent herself from having to wrap her arms around him.

Baker wheeled the horse around and galloped to the sergeant major's quarters. It was quite the rough ride. *Is time truly of the essence, or does Baker simply ride as roughshod as possible to compel me to hold him, for fear I shall slide off?* Determined to keep her distance, Nellie hung on to the saddle with all her might. Baker looked down at her and with one strong arm pulled her up off the side of the horse and put her in front of him, all the while still galloping. Nellie breathed a sigh of relief. *'Twould have been a pity to die on my way to saving a life.* She relaxed, *just a smidge,* into the security of his arms.

Nellie rushed into the birthing room. With one look, her stomach dropped to her knees. *Baker's dire assessment of the progress of this birth was understated!* A cursory examination revealed the woman, almost comatose on the bed, slipping in and out of consciousness, her loss of blood significant.

Tarnation. Here we have maternal exhaustion, hemorrhaging, prolonged second stage delivery with little progress. Mercy! Nellie spoke gently to the woman, in spite of her apparent lack of consciousness. "I shall now perform a quick internal examination to determine our best course of action."

Nellie diagnosed the baby's distress. It was lodged in a sideways position that prevented it from entering the birth canal. *Would that it were an earlier point in the delivery, the mother could use our exercises to shift the position of the baby. Impossible now. Lord, help me. There is little time to rectify this matter. Forceps assistance offers the only possibility for saving either life.*

Without exchanging any introductions or pleasantries, Cornelia gave orders to the woman standing in the room to reheat the kettle, obtain more linens, and retrieve medicines and salves from her bag. Nellie sterilized the forceps and gently inserted one blade. She reached the baby and slowly tried to turn it. With her other hand, she massaged the mother's abdomen, trying to manipulate the baby's position from the outside while she continued to guide the forceps blade within.

Please Lord, guide me, and let me help preserve the lives of these two souls, Nellie prayed, as she carefully turned the baby's body. Soon she felt it line up, head first, with the birth canal. She slipped in the other blade of the forceps and gently guided the baby forward. Nellie was oblivious to all else around her, all thoughts of Baker, Obadiah, and her journey gone from her head as she concentrated on the task before her.

Carefully, carefully, she admonished herself. *Patience, patience,* she cautioned.

It seemed an eternity passed as Nellie, with an unfaltering hand, persevered in her ministrations.

"Here she is!" Nellie exclaimed. "Alleluia." The hands of the woman assisting her reached out and took the baby, as it gave a weak, but audible, cry. Nellie spun back to the mother, leaving the baby to the other woman's care. *This alarming loss of blood keeps this woman grappling with the grim reaper.*

"Where are the needles I requested sterilized?" she asked. The woman guided Nellie's hand to a linen, right at her elbow, where the needles lay, properly cleaned and threaded with her best silk thread. Nellie picked one up while her other hand remained pressed firmly on the largest rip in the tissue. *Mayhap some thread will close the tears and facilitate the repair.*

Her able assistant, the unknown woman from the fort, handed the baby to someone else and aided Nellie, applying more pressure to stem the bleeding while Nellie stitched.

Slumped over the table in the kitchen, uncharacteristically displaying bad posture, the trauma of the last several hours engulfed Nellie. Inert, she stared at her cup of tea, now lukewarm at best, not conscious of the passage of time.

A hand swam into her vision, interrupting her trance by placing a warm biscuit with melting butter atop it in front of her. *Manna from heaven or the equivalent, the post's bakery.*

Captain Baker sat down and pulled his chair close to hers. "My word, little Primrose, you are beyond doubt a miracle-worker," he drawled in his disarming southern accent.

Nellie shook her head and looked at him, blinking her dazed eyes. She caught a whiff of the enticing odor steaming from the baked good. Suddenly, she was ravenous. She smiled at Baker's thoughtfulness. Straightening into her usual good posture, she spread the butter towards the end of the biscuit and cut it into a bite-size piece. In a dainty motion, she picked up the fork and nibbled.

"I thought you might require a bit of nourishment after your many hours of grueling labor." Baker smiled at her, with adoration in his eyes.

Nellie smiled. *Mercifully, 'twas not my labor.*

"Just a little foretaste of tonight's elaborate feast, percolating and simmering now, at my behest, under the capable hands of my cook."

If he is anything like your baker, I am in for a treat!

Tarnation, she thought, reacting to Baker's implied dinner invitation. She shook her head in doubt and tried not to gobble the rest of the biscuit. *Anything cooked in a proper kitchen, augmented with bread from the bakery, would taste like a feast. But I shall not be seduced by a specially prepared meal. I must not allow my vulnerable state to cloud my judgment.*

"After our dinner, I have ordered a special activity, in honor of your extended stay. A miniature cotillion, military fort style. Between our bugler, and a fella that picks a mean fiddle, we have concocted a band to provide us with some fine dancing music."

A bugle band? Nellie shook her head again. *No matter, I shall not hear it, however worthy it may or may not be.* "I beg your pardon, I have forgotten myself. I must return to my emigration train. Please, Lawrence, you should be assembling my escorts at this very minute, not organizing a band."

"But my dear, sweet Rose. It is twilight. You toiled all last night and the better part of today. The night, the wolves, and the unpredictable savages are preparing to descend upon us again. No civilized person travels at this time of day."

Between her dismay at his use of the word 'savage' and her chagrin that the sun was indeed setting just outside the room's lone window, Nellie's spirits plummeted.

A plump, white-haired woman hurried into the room. "At last, I have located you."

Nellie leapt from her chair, ready to rush back into the birthing room.

The woman laughed, and laid her hand on Nellie's shoulder, returning her to her seat. "All is well! Regard, I have only come to report that all is well. The fever of the mother has receded and the baby now sleeps, having successfully nursed several times in lo these few hours since it arrived in this world. 'Tis the best medicine for a new mother, I always say."

"Truly this is good news indeed," said Nellie. A huge sense of relief flooded her entire body. *Mercy! Thank the Lord I am seated. I fear I have quite lost command of my limbs.* She smiled at the woman, mentally gathering herself. "Howsoever, I shall end my respite and ascertain the wellbeing and sustainability of the pair for myself."

"That would be right helpful of you." The woman smiled. "Nevertheless, you must rest assured, my credentials include facilitating quite a number of births. I am quite capable of assuming your responsibilities now, liberating you to return from whence you came."

Nellie looked at her sideways. *Have I usurped her authority? Have I inadvertently trespassed upon her territory?* "Mercy, I beg your pardon. In all of the trauma of the moment, in all the urgency of the situation, I failed to properly introduce myself."

The woman smiled. "As did I. You and I are kindred spirits. We both knew the formalities must wait whilst we attended to pressing business. I am Celinda Fisher. I hail from Boston, originally, and am no stranger to the healing arts. Yet I confess, I lack the depth of knowledge you command. I was quite at my wits end, despairing at the probability of the loss of yet another one of my sisters in childbirth, until you appeared, angel of mercy."

"You are kin to Greta?" asked Nellie.

"Not by blood," answered Celinda. "There are so few women in these parts we all become kin, from necessity."

Nellie smiled. "I am pleased to meet you, Celinda Fisher, and so very grateful you shouldered the burden of this task with me. Bereft of your skills, a successful outcome would have eluded us."

Celinda gave her a warm, motherly hug. "I echo your heartfelt sentiment. Your knowledge, skill, and equipment successfully increased this community by one person." Nellie returned the older woman's hug, thinking, *'tis a most bizarre utterance.*

Celinda said, "Mercy, what am I going on about? Our increase in the fold should be my last concern. You saved two souls, one from the certain eternal torture of limbo, for the baby surely would have died before we could baptize it."

Still a rather bizarre sentiment. Mayhap Baker can shed some light on this matron's reasoning. Mercy, Baker! Nellie twisted her head to look at him. He stood at courtly attention by the table, intent on their exchange, beaming at Nellie.

"Captain Baker, I shall monitor our patient, and then I fear I must either return to my family or retire to garner enough strength that I might rejoin my wagon train as soon after dawn tomorrow as possible."

Baker gently took her hand. "As I was saying, prudence prevents me from dispatching an envoy tonight. What I propose instead is long overdue; proper nourishment and *fêting* for our fort's angel of mercy. Tender handling shall place you in good stead, liberating your judgment, facilitating your assessment of your next steps."

Nellie frowned. Baker glanced at Celinda, who raised her eyebrows.

Baker cleared his throat and took a step back. "Mrs. Wright, my orderly shall show you to your quarters for the night. Prompt action affords you sufficient time for refreshing yourself before dining *and* visiting your patients' bedside, even though, as you have just learned, they are in quite capable hands.

"I expect you to report to dinner in the officer's quarters at eighteen hundred hours. You shall be our guest of honor."

Nellie looked at him, uncertain as to how to respond.

"You have been issued a direct order from New Fort Kearney's commander." His dazzling grin dominated his features, preventing her from noticing his love-filled eyes.

"I shall accompany you to see your namesake before you are shown to your quarters," said Celinda.

Nellie gave a squeal of delight. "Mercy, what an honor," she whispered.

Celinda smiled so hard her eyes crinkled. "Almost the exact words Greta used when she recuperated enough to be told the tale of her near demise, and salvation. It was an honor, she said, to be attended by a woman from New York, imbued with medical knowledge and expert skill. She hopes her daughter will follow in her namesake's footsteps." Tears sprang to Nellie's eyes as Celinda took Nellie's hand and squeezed it.

"Mercy, our patient still faces a precipitous uphill climb to reach a healthy state. We must conspire to ensure their return to hale and hearty health," said Nellie. Arm in arm, they walked across the fort's square to the recovery room.

Dinner took on the splendor of a grand ball in Nellie's tired eyes. The food was sumptuous. The table of officers and their wives erupted easily into laughter. Stimulating dialogue drew Nellie into engaging conversation. The husband of the new mother joined them and toasted Nellie, effusing heartfelt sentiment and lavishing extreme praise on her medical abilities.

Nellie blushed and smiled, enjoying the limelight.

The newly formed band struck up a Strauss waltz. *Mercy, Lawrence certainly remembers my weakness.* She listened to the first notes of music. *The bugle is a surprising asset to the fiddler and the Spanish guitar.* A second later Baker held out his hand and, in a voice infused with southern charm, asked, "May I have this dance?"

Nellie smiled, but thought, *the propriety of this entire situation is truly questionable.*

As if he read her mind Baker said, "Out here on the Great Plains, beyond all civilization, we must not eschew the small shards of cultured society we muster, but rather accept our duty to sustain these threads and weave them into a new fine art."

The officers at the table laughed and encouraged her to dance.

Nellie puzzled over his words. *'Tis the most convoluted, yet thoughtful sentence I do believe I have ever heard him utter.*

Three other officers, with their attendant wives, leapt to the floor attempting waltz steps too. "We don't oft have occasion to celebrate," one of the wives said, smiling as she waltzed past. "Our party shall end if you do not participate," said another, with a wink.

Heady from her triumph over death, and giddy from all the praise and attention, Nellie rose and took Baker's hand.

Lord have mercy on my soul. She melted into his arms. The music swelled around her, and she floated in the heaven of song and dance.

"Flitting back into my life like a dream come true. Butter my biscuits! Surely a sign from Divine Providence," Lawrence whispered into her ear as he twirled her around the real wood floor.

Mercy, the heady rapture of his exceptional dancing prowess quite overpowers my sensibilities. Baker swept her off her feet, quite literally, on a crescendo of music.

Nellie's head spun, not just from the dancing but from the dreamlike aspect of the evening. She felt as if she were plucked from her own life and inserted into someone else's. *How has Lawrence maintained his dancing proficiency here in the wilderness?* she wondered. *Mercy, I do believe his expertise has increased! How are his movements so lithe and dexterous?* She twirled around the floor, breathless, her whole body engaged in the joy of movement. *Ecstasy resides in this man's arms. I am in heaven.* She floated in his embrace, lost in the music, seduced by Baker's dancing charms.

The bugle player produced a flute and changed instruments. Another soldier jumped next to the new flautist and added his violin.

"The corporal plays the fiddle?" buzzed around the room

That upgrade ratcheted the music quality up several notches. Baker smiled and motioned to the newly augmented band to keep playing. The strains of Strauss's *Songs of Liberty* blended into his *Love Songs Waltz*. The titles of the dance music did not register with Nellie until the band began '*Man leibt nur einmal!*'. *How very appropriate,* she thought, somewhere in the back of her mind, '*Man Only Lives Once!' is an apt song for this evening.*

Nellie and Baker stopped, Nellie lingering in his embrace, as the music faded. A small squabble erupted as the band debated the next tune to play and the flautist demanded a mug of beer.

Baker pulled Nellie to an alcove. Catching her hands and pulling them to his chest, he reeled her back into his arms. "I hope to clip you, little Primrose, from your garden and place you in a vase of cherished honor, the solitary bee pollinating my own, fairest Rose." Nellie gasped as he bent down to kiss her. She pulled away.

"My every waking moment has contained thoughts of you," Baker whispered with passion.

"Lo these *five years?*" Nellie asked, incredulity raising her eyebrows up to her hairline.

"Lo these five years," Baker replied. "Whilst I enthusiastically joined the public tribute of my officer, to whom you have given new life, my heart harbors words for your ears only. Permit me this private declaration of my undying love, and my appreciation for your many charms. Not merely beautiful, not only the fairest Rose, but also the most brilliant, thrilling companion a man could ever want.

"I knew only you possessed the requisite expertise for saving that woman and child. Confident you employed far superior skills to any ordinary midwife, I knew I must engage you in this Herculean task. Please, my dearest Cornelia Rose, forsake me not! My need for the knowledge, care, and compassion only you possess grows ever stronger. Stay with me and make me the happiest of men for all my remaining born days."

Cornelia drew a deep breath. She shook her head; the reality of her situation crashing down all around her. *At first sight of Baker, after all these years, I surmised this speech was forthcoming.* She shook her head again and willed herself to overthrow his bewitching charm. She inhaled even more deeply. *Therefore,* she coached herself, *before I hyperventilate, I must summon the answer I previously prepared, locked and loaded, for just this situation.* Her deep inhale had not helped. She felt dizzy with emotion as the scent of Baker intoxicated her anew.

With effort she stepped back, pulling herself together. "Captain Baker, your words fill me with warm thoughts and quite truthfully, utter delight. Your dancing disarms me. Your compliments contain praise I forever thirst to hear."

Baker stepped in closer, reached his arms around her. Nellie stepped back again.

Yet another type of dance at which this gentleman excels.

Nellie cleared her throat. "Yet, while your words are pleasing to my ear, my heart knows I may not abandon nor forsake all those to whom I have already sworn allegiance."

Baker blinked. "But surely your words belie your heart and your true intent?" Nellie shook her head, and Baker's eyes hardened. "I would be remiss if I did not attempt one more persuasive declaration of true love. My Primrose, you must remain with me. Think of all you forsake when you rejoin that wagon train!"

Nellie fully regained her command of the present. "Lawrence, as I conveyed five years ago, I shall always treasure you in my heart. But mercy! Any ship we could command together sailed long ago. I have chosen Obadiah. Moreover, in spite of the many temptations with which you seduced me since my arrival, endeavoring to entice a reversal of my charted course, I remain steadfast in my decision."

Lawrence looked at her, his blue eyes willing her to make a different choice. He again reached for her hand and tried to pull her close.

Nellie stepped back again, but Baker did not release her hand. "Mercy, Lawrence, please. You must not press me any further, especially tonight in my weakened, post-duress state. A woman in my condition should not be so taxed."

Lawrence looked puzzled. "Condition...?" He frowned at her, then the light dawned and he swore. "Yet another burr in my saddle! As if those alluring, tender shoulders do not bear sufficient burden?"

Nellie smiled at him. "'Tis not a burden, but a joy, and I pray one day you will be so blessed."

Baker's face crumpled. He looked down at his hand, still clutching hers. "I concede defeat. I comprehend full well the consequences of contravening your diktat once you have determined your course."

He lifted his pleading eyes to hers, a tear glistening in one. "Please, reward me with a small talisman of good fortune. A piece of you I might treasure always."

Nellie pulled her lace handkerchief from her sleeve and presented it to him with a flourish, relieved that he did not press her further. "Here. My handkerchief. Recently crocheted with the finest of lace, and my own initials."

"My Primrose, I shall treasure it and the memory of you always. If ever you find yourself in a reversal of circumstances, advise me. I shall travel from the ends of the earth to be at your side."

CHAPTER 31
You're My Home

Plum Creek, Nebraska Territory, June 1857

Captain Lawrence Simmons Baker and Cornelia Rose Entwhistle Wright galloped twenty-something miles across the Great Plains in little more than a morning. *My feet were spared two solid days of walking!* Nellie thought, enjoying her ride on the fine army horse Baker loaned her.

As they neared the wagon train they both presumed was Nellie's, Baker slowed his horse and turned to her. "I shall yearn for you every remaining day I trod upon this earth. You are the fairest Rose; your thorns have irrevocably pierced my heart."

Nellie smiled and pointed to the wagon train.

Baker spurred his horse and galloped off at a pace even more frenzied than before. Nellie galloped after him.

I find consolation in the thought that I shan't be forced to take refuge in his arms for fear of falling to my death on this reckless ride. She grimly clutched her reins and dug her knees into her mare's sides. *Thank the Lord I wore my bifurcated skirt. If I were forced to ride sidesaddle, I never could have stayed astride at this pace.*

Their gallop lasted longer than Nellie anticipated, for upon closer inspection, nothing about the wagon train they first spotted looked familiar. *This train cannot be mine,* she thought as they galloped past. *Not only do I fail to recognize any of the emigrants, no wagon is filled to overcapacity like the Wilton's.*

She called to Baker, and they both pulled back on the reins. "Your train must be further ahead," he said gruffly and resumed his furious pace.

After another twenty minutes of rough riding, Nellie felt her fatigue, and began to worry that the excessive jostling would harm her unborn child. She dared not slow her pace however, for fear of losing sight of Baker.

Two minutes later she reined her horse into a canter. *I fear wandering alone in the wilderness far less than continuing this frenzied gallop, deleterious to my health. Let Baker arrive at my wagon train alone, and trigger an alarm dispatching the scout of the day in search of me. I can ride along the well-established trail and observe the parties that follow our train. What care I if Baker looks the fool?*

Mercy, 'tis a long journey. My company has made astonishing progress....

At that very moment Baker turned around. Apparently noticing she no longer rode beside him, he wheeled his horse and came galloping back. He pulled up at her side and doffed his hat. "A brilliant thought, my Primrose, dally, and delay this reunion with deprivation as long as possible.... Better still, extend our moments together indefinitely."

Nellie opened her mouth to argue, but a sudden thought gripped her. "This seems an expanse incredible to attain in little more than two days. By the distances calculated in the guidebooks, I surmise we should be nearing the Plum Creek crossing of the Platte. Lansford Hasting's guidebook lists the distance as twenty-six miles."

"Like everything that shameless promoter Hasting's guidebook articulates, we must take the distances he formulates with a grain of salt. His persuasive claptrap gave all citizens, disenchanted with failing banks and high taxes, a glamorized and idealized picture of the West." He shook his head. "Surely, I believe in Manifest Destiny—Jiminy Crickets! 'tis the very reason I aim to clear this land of savages. However...."

Nellie stood up in her saddle. "My word! That precise language is the very reason you shall return to your self-proclaimed mission alone."

Baker swiveled his head toward her, looked her in the eyes, made a fist and punched his saddle.

Nellie softened. "I beseech your pardon for my harsh words. Howsoever, your cruel words regarding fellow human beings and worthy souls rend my heart in two."

"Worthy souls? They are heathens," Baker declared and glared at her.

"How can we, mere mortals, unworthy souls ourselves, judge? Only God our Father can judge a soul's worthiness. I presume they are worthy—'tis the Christian way. These people are simply unschooled in our ways."

Baker shook his head. "Be that as it may, I shall remain true to the assignment for which I was trained. We both have chosen our paths. We shall never again debate this subject."

The handsome captain heaved a sigh of heart-wrenching melancholy. Nellie steeled herself for another confrontation. But he squinted off into the distance and shook his head. "Now. Reverting to our mission here, and that doggone jack-a-napes Hastings. His treatise certainly led the Donner Party astray. Therefore, I trust my military intelligence and my own recognizance on the particulars of this terrain. I think more likely the distance from New Fort Kearney to Plum Creek crossing is thirty-five some odd miles."

"All the more reason we surely should have crossed paths with my company," said Nellie. "Truly, the lion's share of this distance is too great to walk in less than two days. I believe we should reverse and reconnoiter campsites."

Baker stopped his horse, pushed up his hat and leaned on his saddle horn. He rubbed his kid-gloved hand over his mustache and looked at Nellie. "What strategy do you propose, that shall produce different intelligence from what we have already garnered? Every site in which a train could conceivably camp is visible for miles in this here Platte River Valley. We would have seen any wagon trail on this side of the Platte as we passed, regardless of their state of locomotion."

Nellie shaded her eyes and squinted south, examining every blade of prairie grass, and every clump of vegetation she could see. The grass waved and wind blew, and nothing was visible save the tail end of a wagon train Nellie knew for certain was not her own. *The prairie wind sounds suddenly lonely and desolate in my ears. I have lost my....*

Suddenly, she jerked her horse around and looked north, to the other side of the Platte. "You said 'on *this side of the Platte'*.... Often the route preferred by those seeking their fortune in California is the trail on the north side of the Platte, *n'est-ce pas?*"

Without waiting for a reply from Baker, she spurred her horse towards New Fort Kearney and shouted over her shoulder to him. "For foolish reasons unbeknownst to me, my company must have crossed back to the north side of the Platte. Giddy up!"

Baker was at her side in a heartbeat, reining in her horse. "Assuming your hypothesis is correct, we can cross these horses safely and handily at a juncture a little closer to my fort, and peruse the north trail emigrants from there. Due to the dip in terrain and the clumps of vegetation along this bank, it can be difficult to view the trail on the north side from here. Follow me."

This time Nellie galloped faster than Baker. After a few minutes, he pulled alongside and shouted, "Your excessive speed prevents you from searching the other bank for evidence of your train."

Nellie slowed to a trot. "You advised nothing on the other side would be visible."

"I humbly apologize if I misled you. From time to time along this path glimpses of trains on the north bank do appear. Vigilant watch might well be rewarded, as 'tis still an hour's ride back to the most efficacious fording site."

They cantered side by side, Nellie closest to the river, scouring the opposite bank.

Her heart leapt into her throat when she caught a glimpse of a train. But nothing about the travelers looked familiar.

They rode on.

Baker attempted conversation, but Nellie had no desire to turn her head away from her scrutiny of the north bank to listen. After a few more of his observations passed Nellie unheeded, they rode on in silence.

Suddenly, she gasped, "I believe I discern a recognizable figure." *Could that be the dour Mrs. Clayton?* She squinted, then rubbed her eyes, examining whatever bits of wagons she could see across the water, up the bank, and through the scruffy bushes and clumps of cottonwood.

"The overflowing Wilton Wagon!" she shouted, digging her heels into the side of her horse and pulling the reins toward the river.

Nellie let out a holler that sounded like a war cry, and spurred her horse so hard the mare nearly bucked. She charged into the water.

"No, not here. The riverbed is quicksand!" She heard Baker call to her back. But she galloped even faster, praying she would not get stuck. In three minutes, she was across and racing up the bank. Nellie jumped off her horse and threw the reins over its head. Seconds later, she pulled Emma and Elizabeth from the wagon bench into her arms, smothering them with kisses. The girls squealed with delight. They squirmed, hugged, and all tumbled to the ground in a bundle of love and emotion.

Obadiah ran around the oxen to her. Nellie smiled up at him.

"Such an extravagant display of emotions is best left to theatrical performances," Obadiah chided, roughly pulling her by her elbows to her feet.

Nellie held onto her daughters, walking to keep abreast of the wagons and looked at him, aghast. *My heart fair breaks with this terse greeting.* She hugged her babies and said, "I sorely missed my family."

Before Obadiah formulated a reply, her daughters peppered her with questions.

"Is the mother alright?" asked Emma.

Tears sprang to Nellie's eyes and choked her words, as memories of the traumas of the complicated birth rushed upon her. All she could do was nod.

She put the girls on the ground and they walked next to her.

"Where's baby?" asked Elizabeth.

Without thinking, Nellie's hand jerked to her own abdomen, as she looked at Obadiah. He stared at her, grim faced. But she saw his eyes startle at her gesture, and she knew he understood what it meant.

Nellie took a deep breath. "The little baby is well, thank the Lord. And her mother also returns to good health. Surely, in no time at all they will both be fit as fiddles."

"What is the baby's name?" asked Emma.

"Is she girl?" asked Elizabeth.

Nellie laughed. She grabbed her daughters' hands and squeezed them tight as she walked them back to their seat on the driving bench. "Wonder of wonders, they christened her Cornelia Rose. Does that name sound familiar?"

"Your name, Mama!" both girls chorused.

Baker materialized. He reined his horse at the side of the Wright's wagon and smiled at Nellie's daughters. "'Tis only fitting. Little ladies, you must be right proud of your mama, saving two lives with her medicinal know-how."

"Yes, yes," the girls chorused.

Obadiah walked silently next to Angel the ox.

Nellie looked at her husband. He still had not smiled at her. "How comes it our wagon train is on the north bank of the Platte?" she asked.

"That fool of a captain, Hines." Obadiah gave a terse reply. He turned to Baker. "I see you have kept your word and returned Mrs. Wright to me. I thank you for this service."

Baker looked down at Obadiah from his seat in the saddle. He shook his head in the negative and looked at Nellie with raised eyebrows.

Nellie blushed but shook her head no.

Baker broke the awkward silence with a touch of his hat, drawling, "You can always count on the word of a Southern Gentleman, my friend. Even when the promise inures to his own personal detriment." He looked at Nellie, touched his breast pocket where her lace handkerchief protruded, grabbed the reins of Nellie's mare, and wheeled off toward the river.

Nellie watched him slosh back across the river and gallop east toward his fort, with only a twinge of regret. *'Tis just a reaction to Obadiah's harsh words.* She shook herself.

"I beseech forgiveness for my unladylike deportment," said Nellie, reaching again to squeeze the hands of her daughters. "I confess a dearth of rational thinking, after the grueling events of these past two days. The great effort to endure the vicissitude of the medical emergency, followed closely on the heels by...." She swallowed, thinking of the soiree and Baker's pass at her. "...The foray to join our train.... The utter desolation of not knowing your whereabouts, fear I would never abridge the distance between us—it simply caused me to be in quite frangible sentiment." Nellie smiled at her daughters and looked at Obadiah as she walked next to him. "I shan't even add 'travel weary' to my list of travails."

"Thinkest thou *I* have had an easy time? Do you imagine my days have been a lark? Having to dig a trench for supper and warm up the meal you prepared for us?"

Nellie could not believe her ears. "But *I* prepared the meal, thus sparing you much effort. Moreover, you did no more than I do each night, in fact, *far less*."

"Are you forgetting these chores were heaped atop my own duties?" snarled Obadiah. "Moreover, to what end? While you traipse off, who knows where, abandoning us whilst you aid some stranger...."

Nellie blinked back tears. "Mercy, Obadiah, I never thought I'd hear such unchristian speech from your lips."

"That fool Hines," Obadiah muttered, looking chagrined. "What hubris! Taking us across the river, wasting our time, misguiding our steps. Does he hold the guidebook upside-down, thus intentionally leading us astray?"

Emma and Elizabeth giggled at the thought of the captain reading the book upside-down. Nellie realized no good would come of further harsh words.

"As little pitchers have big ears," she said, blinking back her tears. "I shall take my gear, properly stow it and then settle myself inside our wagon for a brief spell."

She held out her hand. Obadiah, still avoiding her gaze, unloaded her medical bags from his arm.

Her daughters safely perched on the driving seat and Obadiah walking stoically beside their oxen team, Nellie stole into the back of the wagon.

By the time Nellie replenished her supplies in her emergency medical kit and stowed her other gear, exhaustion overwhelmed her. She lay down upon her eiderdown comforter, thinking, *I'll only tarry a moment.* She closed her weary eyes as tears slid down her cheeks. *Do not dwell upon Lawrence Simmons Baker,* Nellie commanded herself. *Simply because your husband appears unconcerned as to your whereabouts and apathetic as to your return, is no reason to revisit emotions you have summarily dismissed, again, once and for all. Lord, I have already sought forgiveness for succumbing to his dancing charms. I thank you, Lord, that he did not tempt me with his passionate kisses. Mercy,* she chided herself again, *I mustn't let the thought of his kiss ever again enter my mind. I am a happily married woman who is simply fatigued. My husband is right and proper to conceal in public any emotion at my homecoming.*

Nellie laughed at herself. *Homecoming? Now I am referring to the trail in the middle of nowhere, far from civilization, as home?*

Nellie opened her eyes with a start, and saw Obadiah's head and shoulders sticking into the wagon bed from the canvas covering.

"I am sorry to abandon my post," said Cornelia, snapping to attention, shrugging off the comforter, and struggling to stand.

Obadiah tumbled into the wagon bed. "Tarry a moment."

"We mustn't leave our daughters unattended," Nellie protested.

"Did you call me, Mama?" asked Emma, sticking her head in the wagon cover from the front bench.

"Or me?" asked Elizabeth, her cherubic face joining her sister's.

Nellie giggled.

Obadiah said, "You may continue to drive the team. We are right here, available to be called upon at any moment." He waved them back. Their heads disappeared.

Obadiah scooted next to her and whispered in her ear, "Now then, a moment to settle this score."

Nellie turned, her face inches from his, her eyes looking into his. "You must whisper," she said. "I do not wish our daughters to overhear any discord."

They looked at each other for a long moment. Finally, Obadiah put his lips on her ear and whispered, "It is nigh impossible for me to *whisper* discordant words into your perfectly shaped ear."

Nellie pulled away and looked into his eyes. "I had hoped you would throw the gates of love open, wide open, with golden hinges moving, to paraphrase Milton, at my return."

A frown hopped from one of Obadiah's eyebrows to the other, but before it traveled to his lips, he pulled her close and whispered, "Then this little soiree...." Nellie's guilty conscience winced at the word, "...of yours has disappointed both our expectations."

Nellie pulled away and looked at him. *What expectations could he have...?*

"I fully expected you to return last night, immediately upon the conclusion of your labor," Obadiah whispered.

An absurd giggle rose in Nellie's throat at Obadiah's word choice. She ignored it and whispered, "I endeavored to do exactly that, but was unable to obtain a guide."

Obadiah made a fist and whispered in a terse voice, "Why that lying, boot licking scallywag! I have half a mind to...."

Nellie laid a hand on his arm. "Obadiah, we must let sleeping dogs lie. I am beside myself with exhaustion even after a night's repose; I fear I might just have fallen from the saddle, sound asleep, had I journeyed after sundown, upon completion of my task."

Obadiah took a deep breath. He let it out slowly, contemplatively, and whispered, "Truly, the main fact is the wilderness has returned you to my arms. *Ipso facto....*" *for this reason,* Nellie translated the Latin in her head. "...there can only be gratitude in my heart." He wrapped his arms more tightly around her, and she felt his warmth and his love.

She relaxed into his embrace. *After all my toil, at long last, heaven.*

After a moment, Obadiah whispered, "Now, since my lips are within whispering distance of this luscious ear, it seems the appropriate time to...." His lips kissed her ear, and her neck, and then returned to nibble on her ear again.

Delicious tingles ran up and down Nellie's spine. She turned her head slightly and landed a kiss... on his nose, for she caught him as he bent his head. Obadiah's gentle hand turned Nellie's head and he licked her neck. His tongue slid from ear to shoulder, lightly, delicately, flicking little shivers of electricity along its path.

His lips at her ear again, he whispered, "You rest. I will resume my post. We shall recommence this non-verbal dialogue later tonight."

Before Nellie could utter a word of protest, she saw him jump out the back of the wagon.

Nellie looked at the wagon cover ceiling for a second, stretching and smiling. Rejuvenated, she scrambled out the opening after him.

Obadiah turned in surprise and handed her down. Smiling in the bright sun of the Great Plains he said, "I thought you desired a respite after your trying several days."

"Your love strengthens and nourishes me with renewed vigor," replied Nellie.

Obadiah did not hesitate, or even look around to see if anyone was watching. He bent his head forward and gave Nellie a long, passionate kiss, as they both continued walking, keeping pace with their wagon.

After an elongated moment, she was dimly aware that her daughters were giggling at them. She smiled at her two adorable girls and stretched to grab a hand of each daughter. She felt Obadiah place his hand on the back of her neck.

Clinging to one another, they walked in happy silence. Nellie felt the sun warm her shoulders and heard the prairie breeze, now soft and comforting, whisper in her still tingling ears.

My walk across this vast land resumes, taking my home along with me. In my wake, beaus and hand-wrought lace handkerchiefs strewn across the wilderness.

Acknowledgements

Thank you to Kimberly Goebel, editor extraordinaire, for sharing my vision and believing in my characters. I could not have written this book without your support and guidance.

Thank you to my hardy band of travelers—Jess, Jocelyn, Alicia, Bennett, Abigail, Paul, and Lauren—for your continued love, support, and positive feedback.

About the Author

Jane Frances Collen has spent the last umpteen years practicing as a lawyer—but don't hold that against her! She has made a career of protecting Intellectual Property, but at heart always wanted to be writing novels instead of legal briefs. She has written award-winning children's books, "The Enjella® Adventure Series," using fantasy as a vehicle for discussing the real world problems of children. She has tried to use her talent for storytelling for good instead of evil.

But her real love is history. One of her many hobbies is traveling to historical sites around the world and reading the biographies of the people who affected these places. Her books depict modern dilemmas in historical settings, with a touch of humor. Since only one of her parents had a sense of humor, however, Jane feels she is only half as funny as she should be.

Much to her husband's dismay, they still live in New York.

For more, please visit J.F. Collen online at:
Website: www.JFCollen.com
Facebook: Jane.F.Collen

What's Next?

Watch for the third book in this "Journey of Cornelia Rose" series to release within a few months of this book:

PIONEER PASSAGE

Cornelia Rose thought leaving the comforts of home and her family would be the greatest challenge she would ever have to face.

Life on the Oregon Trail is full of more deprivations, difficulties, and challenges than Cornelia ever imagined, in spite of her research and preparations for the rough road ahead. She summons all her resourcefulness to combat the hardships leading them to her greatest unknown. What will be waiting for them in the Great Salt Lake City, and who is that silent brooding man who seems so familiar on the wagon train with them?

More from Evolved Publishing

We offer great books across multiple genres, featuring high-quality editing (which we believe is second-to-none) and fantastic covers.

As a hybrid small press, your support as loyal readers is so important to us, and we have strived, with tireless dedication and sheer determination, to deliver on the promise of our motto: **QUALITY IS PRIORITY #1!**

Please check out all of our great books,
which you can find at this link:
www.EvolvedPub.com/Catalog/

Thank you!

CPSIA information can be obtained
at www.ICGtesting.com
Printed in the USA
JSHW010310090920
7733JS00006B/6

9 781622 536375